The Woodcutter's Wife

David Johnson

David Johnson

ACKNOWLEDGEMENTS

To undertake writing a book of historical fiction required me to do extensive research. I'm immensely grateful to the following for sharing their insight and knowledge with me:

- The interpreters at the 1850s Homeplace in Land Between the Lakes, located in northwest Tennessee and western Kentucky and maintained by the US Department of Agriculture Forest Service, especially Cindy Earls
- Suzette Raney at the Chattanooga Public Library
- The rangers and staff of Chickamauga and Chattanooga National Military Park, especially historian Jim Ogden
- The civilwar.org websites, which give a wealth of information on all the major battles of that conflict
- Marc McCutcheon's book *Everyday Life in the 1800s*
- Donald L. Winters's book *Tennessee Farming, Tennessee Farmers*
- And a very special thanks goes to my friend, Katy Dycus, who did the most amazing job in helping me edit the manuscript.

The cost of war cannot be measured by counting the price of bullets and guns. It must be measured by the toll it takes on the human heart.

Chapter One

MARY

Struggling to catch her breath, her face glistening with sweat, Mary finally made it to the top of Bitter Hill, which formed one side of the hollow where her and William's cabin lay. The top of the hill was no peak; rather, it looked as if the top had been sliced off with a large knife, leaving a small, flat, half-acre area. In the valley to her right, she saw an autumn fog lying over the flowing waters of Chickamauga Creek as it wound its way toward Chattanooga and emptied into the Tennessee River. She watched in silence for a few minutes, then turned to face her final destination—a large, spreading American chestnut tree standing in the center of the clearing, with low-hanging limbs that seemed to bid her enter their embrace.

The leaves crunched underneath her knees as she knelt beneath the tree and stared at four small wooden boards sticking out of the ground. From a pocket on the front of her dress, she withdrew a small book: *In Memoriam, A.H.H.* by Alfred Tennyson. The book had become her constant companion ever since she purchased it a month ago. She'd never read anything that grasped the depth to which grief can take a person better than Tennyson did.

She flipped through pages until she found the passage she

was looking for and read it aloud:

Old Yew, which graspest at the stones
That name the under-lying dead,
Thy fibres net the dreamless head,
Thy roots are wrapt about the bones.

Returning the book to her pocket, she placed a goldenrod bloom at the base of each of the boards, then, slowly, read the engraving on each of them, starting with the one to her left:

Elizabeth Thomson
Born January 23, 1854
Died January 27, 1854

Alexander Thomson
Born April 30, 1857
Died April 30, 1857

Naomi Thomson
Born May 28, 1860
Died August 20, 1860

X Thomson
Born July 3, 1862
Died July 3, 1862

After reading the last one, she said, "You are the one I feel the most pity for because we didn't even give you a name. I should have insisted, but your father, William, had decided that maybe it was bad luck for us to name a child before it was born and that was why none of your siblings survived. But I know the truth. The truth is that I am cursed by God. For reasons that I don't understand, he has decided that grief will be my constant companion and that loss will follow me everywhere I go."

She lay down on her back so that some part of her body was on top of each of the tiny graves. Tucked inside her cap, her long, thick, flaxen hair provided a pillow for the back of her head and framed her smooth-skinned face. As she looked up through the branches of the chestnut tree, a single tear, a small reminder of the untold number of tears she had shed under this tree, slipped from one of her blue eyes.

At least I'll never suffer the pain of losing another child, if what the doctor said is true. And I'm glad of it! I'm soul-weary of getting my hopes up and having them repeatedly smashed.

She knew that her barrenness was a bitter disappointment to William, and while she appreciated his efforts to hide it, there were times when he said things that made it clear he still wished for children.

There was a time she had longed for the joy of seeing children grow and thrive and work alongside them on the farm, but when she learned that the opportunity for this had ended, she became determined to fill the void in her life and his by being the perfect helpmeet, working the farm side by side with him and having him teach her how to make the chairs, baskets, and tables that he sold during the winter months. She would be his partner in cutting and selling firewood to people who lived in the nearby city of Chattanooga.

After a few more minutes, she arose, said good-bye to her children, and headed back down the hill. Halfway down, she paused to catch her breath and sat down on a large limestone rock that jutted out from the hillside. From her vantage point, she could look down and see the cabin and barn. There was no sign of William, but she knew he was busy, probably still feeding the livestock or out hunting meat for their table. A thin trail of smoke from the chimney of their house snaked upward toward the top of the ridges on either side of their hollow. As she followed its journey, she took note of the rust-colored leaves of the sycamore trees, the hickory trees' deep gold color, the bright reds of the red maples (her favorite), the dashes of crimson from poison sumac, and the earth tones of the oaks.

Suddenly, she heard the sharp snap of a twig close by and jumped, every nerve alert and heart pounding. She turned her head this way and that until she spotted the intruder coming through the thick foliage. She frowned. "You startled me."

William strode toward her, his rifle hanging comfortably in one hand. The cheeks of his ruddy face glowed bright red. "You don't need to walk off by yourself without letting me know where you're going. You gave me a fright. I've told you that you need to be more careful. There is war all around us. What if I had been a Yankee soldier or a Rebel deserter? What would you have done?" With concern etched on his face, he sat down beside her.

It was a familiar chastisement, one that rankled her. "If you're really worried what might happen to me, then teach me to use a gun like you promised to!"

"Yes, yes, I know. I just never think of it at the right time." His dark eyes slipped from her gaze, and he looked up the hill. "Why do you go up there so often?" he asked. "It always makes you melancholy."

She pulled her knees to her chest. "I'm fully aware of my melancholia. I live with it every day and don't need you to remind me of it. I try hard to fight against it, and sometimes I win, but other times, it is too overpowering. What I don't understand is why you don't go up there at all."

"I just try to keep it pushed out of my mind and focus on what's going on today."

"I wish I could do that," she replied. "I can't help feeling like they are lonely. I don't know if they knew they were loved. So I go up there to tell them about you and about me and how much they meant to us." Suddenly, sadness, pity, regret, anger, and frustration all filled her chest, and she felt as if it were about to burst. *I thought I was past all this. Perhaps the grief of losing a child never completely leaves a mother's heart.*

William laid his hand against her cheek. "You know," he began, "the doctor could be wrong. Perhaps we can still have a child."

Mary slapped his hand away. "I'm still not enough for you, am I? Why must women always be measured by their ability to give birth, not just by men but by other women, too? It's always the initial question I'm asked when I meet women for the first time—'How many children do you have?' they ask. What I'd like to tell them is that I have four children, and then I'd like to take them up here on Bitter Hill and show them the markers and see what they have to say. And if they gave even a hint that my four babies don't count, or if they looked at me like they pitied me, I would"—her hands balled into fists—"I don't know what I would do, but they would surely never do it again."

She saw the hurt on William's face and knew she should apologize for speaking so harshly, but at the same time, she didn't mind that he felt some pain. She always loved him, but sometimes, like right now, she hated him—hated him for not feeling like she did, for being able to push the pain so far away from him that he seemed unaffected by it, and there were times she hated him for continuing to insist they try to have a child, even after they had lost the first two.

She took a deep breath and let it out, in an effort to let go of her hatred and to grab hold of love. Finally, she said, "I'm sorry for how I speak to you sometimes and how I treat you. In Tennyson's poem that I am always talking about, he says, 'I sometimes hold it half a sin to put in words the grief I feel; for words, like Nature, half reveal And half conceal the Soul within.' That is exactly how I feel. I don't even know how to talk about how I feel.

"But this I know, you will never know how sorry I am that I can't give you children. I know you wanted a son more than anything on—"

William reached over and covered her mouth with his hand.

"Shush, Mary Elizabeth. Don't say another word. I know you don't always mean what you say because I know you love me. Losing your babies has changed you, but I know that the woman I married is still in you and will live and breathe again someday. I should be apologizing to you. I shouldn't have said what I said to you. It was thoughtless of me. To be blessed to have a wife like you, the most beautiful woman in the land, is more than I could have ever dreamed of. If it is God's will that we have no more children, then it is my place to accept that and be content with it. And I promise you, I will."

It was hard for Mary to appreciate William's attempts at easing her burden because all that she could hear him say was that he *would* accept her barrenness, not that he *had* accepted it.

Chapter Two

MARY

The next morning, Mary woke before daylight and lay listening to William's steady breathing. She wanted to see if the melancholy from yesterday would still be draped over her like heavy linen. *Please, dear God, give me a reprieve. Let this day be a good day.*

She stared blankly into the inky dark and noticed there was no heaviness in her chest or sadness in her heart. Breathing a silent prayer of thanks, she slipped out from under the covers and lit the candle on the table beside her.

After dressing, she walked across the porch connecting the bedroom to the kitchen. She lit the wick of the Betty lamp, set the candle on a small table, and waited until the light slowly chased the dark into the corners of the room. In the dim light she located her apron, slipped it over her head, and tied it around her waist, then began preparing breakfast.

An hour later, the door of the kitchen opened, and William walked in carrying a wooden bucket. "How about some fresh milk?" he asked. "Those Ayrshire cows my father, God rest his soul, brought over from Scotland never fail to produce plenty of milk."

"I suppose we could drink some of it," Mary answered, "but we need to keep enough out that I can churn for butter because I'm almost out, and I know how much you like butter on your bread."

"Very true," William agreed, "but your bread is so sweet it practically melts in my mouth, even without any butter. One thing you Germans do well is make bread."

"My great-grandmother's recipe has certainly stood the test of time."

"God bless your great-grandmother!" William emphasized his blessing by giving Mary a kiss on the cheek and a swat on the backside. It made Mary jump just as she was cracking an egg into the spider skillet that sat on hot coals at the edge of the hearth. "Now look what you made me do! I broke the yolk on your egg."

He looked over her shoulder. "But how do you know that's my egg?"

"Because I'm the one cooking!" She playfully slammed her hip sideways into him, which made him stumble to his right. She laughed. "Don't mess with a broad-hipped German, you scrawny Scot!"

He walked around the kitchen with an exaggerated limp. "I'll keep that in mind. You seem to be in a good mood this morning."

"I'm sorry I was so out of sorts yesterday. I never know from one day to the next how I'm going to feel. Some mornings I wake up and feel like there's a buzzard on the bedpost waiting to devour what's left of my shredded heart."

"You don't have to apologize. It's okay."

"That's a kind and thoughtful thing to say, but it's a lie, and I know it is. I can't stand to be with myself some days, so I know it's difficult for you, too. Now, would you mind pouring us some apple cider? This bacon and these eggs are about done."

"I'd be happy to."

As they sat down across from each other, they bowed their heads. William said, "Our Father which art in heaven, we thank you for the blessed night's rest and for this food we are about to receive. Amen."

They eagerly began eating.

"What we have hanging there," Mary said as she pointed to the bacon over the chopping block, "is the last of our bacon."

William glanced up at the meat. "It won't be long before we slaughter our two hogs. Then we'll have meat aplenty. They really grew over the summer, more than usual. It must have been the heavy crop of hognuts and walnuts. At the next cold snap, we'll butcher them and start curing the meat."

"I'm also about out of wheat flour," she said. "Are you almost ready to go into Chattanooga with a load of firewood and some chairs? We could swing by Bird's Mill to get some flour on the way to town."

"I found a downed white oak tree yesterday while hunting.

If we get it cut up and split, that'll give us a nice load of firewood to sell."

"And the chairs?"

"I've got four more for you to put cane bottoms in. That'll give us ten chairs to sell."

"I think that will take me a couple of days to finish," Mary said. "I've got to go in the woods to cut some more strips. You hitch the mules to the dray after we finish breakfast, and I'll go with you to the woods."

Putting his hands on his hips, and with a twinkle in his eye, William said, "Is that an order or a suggestion?"

Mary put on an air of aloofness. "It's the decree of the queen. Obey, or I'll have your head."

*****

By the time Mary finished cleaning and straightening things in the kitchen and headed outside, William was driving the dray, pulled by their mules, Pat and Mike, up to the house. He stopped the large wagon and jumped down to help Mary up and onto the seat.

"I can do it myself," Mary said.

"I don't mind helping," William said as he put his hands on her hips.

She grabbed the side of the seat and pulled while William assisted with a push. She landed in the seat and said to him, "You just like the view from back there. That's why you like to help."

William climbed aboard and sat beside Mary as she scooted over to make room for him. "I'll not deny your assertion," he said, smiling. He grabbed the reins and slapped the mules on their rears. "Giddap, Pat and Mike! Haw!"

The tall, lanky mules threw themselves into their harness and pulled the dray at a steady pace while at the same time obeying William's order to turn to the left.

Mary glanced at the bed of the wagon and noticed the broad ax, one-man crosscut saw, bucksaw, iron wedge, wooden maul, small hatchet, and William's rifle lying in the bed of the dray. "Where is the tree that you want to cut up?" Mary asked.

"It's down by the creek on the other side of the field we planted in corn this year," William answered. "It will be easy to get to."

Light from the rising sun filtered through the remaining leaves on the trees lining the side of the lane the mules followed. Droplets of dew hung on to the ends of the leaves and glistened like shiny earrings. A pair of squirrels scurried up a tree and barked at the wagon and its company for intruding on their search for acorns. Suddenly, a covey of quail burst into the air beside Mike. The thundering beat of their wings startled both mules, who made as if to bolt into a run. The trace chains rattled, and the dray lurched.

But William's hand was quicker than the mules, and he pulled back hard on the reins before they could break into a run. "Whoa! Calm down. It's not the first time you've had that happen. Just take it easy."

The mules calmed down almost immediately in response to William's steady hand and even voice. Pat snorted loudly, and Mike stomped his front foot. Their long ears pointed straight up, alert to any other signs of danger.

Mary let go of her grip on the side of the wagon seat and said, "That was close. I thought we were about to be flying across the field up ahead and that everything in the dray, including us, would be bounced out."

"That's why I prefer mules to horses when doing work on the farm," William said. "They're more reasonable and even-tempered. If that had been our Percherons, they would still be running, and we would indeed be lying in the field somewhere." He steered the mules back onto the path.

Just before the tree-lined path opened up to the stump-littered field, William pulled back on the reins. "Whoa."

William and Mary looked off the left side of the wagon at two grave markers underneath a cedar tree.

She put her hand tenderly on his arm. "You still miss them, don't you?"

Nodding his head, he said, "My mother and father were some of the grandest people on earth. If they were still alive, they would love you as much as I do."

"It was always sad to me that they died before we married."

"They got sick and died so quickly," William said, shaking his head. "Just six weeks after I kissed you for the first time

13

at the shucking bee, dysentery and whooping cough took them both. I think that quack doctor from Chattanooga was to blame."

"Do you want to get down and walk over to the graves?"

"No, that's okay." William tipped his hat toward his parents' remains, then turned toward the mules and said, "Giddap."

After a few moments of silence, Mary said, "You know, I think the fact that your parents died hastened our decision to get married. I know everyone thought we were impulsive by getting married only six weeks after our first kiss, but I always knew you were the one I wanted to marry. When your parents died, there was no reason to wait until we could build our own cabin on the farm before we married. I couldn't stand the thought of you living alone in that house."

"And I still can't help but wonder if your marrying me had anything to do with your father selling their farm and moving to Germany."

This was a point they'd discussed many times through the years, and although Mary believed William was correct, she refused to admit it to him and add to any feelings of guilt he might have had for causing a rift between her and her parents. "I've told you—Father talked often of going to Germany. He never did adjust to the hot summers here."

Suddenly, William jerked back on the reins. "Whoa!"

Mary looked around but didn't see any signs of the tree

William told her they were going to cut up. "I don't see—"

"Shhh!" William cut her off. Whispering, he said, "Look at the far end of the field."

She looked where he indicated but saw nothing at first. Then she saw movement in the thick brush just beyond where the field had been cleared. "Can you tell what it is?" she whispered.

"Looks like a company of soldiers."

Chapter Three

MARY

"Are they Union or Southern?" Mary asked.

"Looks like Southern to me," William answered. "They must be crossing the Chickamauga at that shallow ford."

"What if they see us?"

"We've got nothing to hide. About the only thing they could question is why I've not joined the war."

Mary gripped his arm. "And how will you answer them?" She watched the muscles in his jaw flex as he chewed on her question.

Without looking at her, he said, "I'll tell them that I'll join when I'm ready to join."

"This is one of the reasons that I love you."

"What do you mean?"

"Most men pay no heed to their wives' wants when it comes to political requests. And I don't know any man who would set aside his own desires just to please his wife. But you have proved time after time that you will do anything that you believe will bring me happiness. I know that the real reason you haven't joined the war is because of me. The only thing that scares me is the new conscription law."

"Damn the conscription law!" William snapped. "It's trying

to turn all of us white men into slaves, too. There's more men than just me who have yet to yield to it."

They sat in silence until they could see no more movement at the end of the field.

William shook the reins at the mules, who awakened from their brief nap and began pulling the wagon. "You know, Mary," he said in a serious tone, "I can't avoid the fight forever. I'll be damned if I'm going to sit idly by and let the Yankees subjugate us. My family came to America in order to be free from tyranny. I don't want anyone telling me what to do and how to live my life, especially the federal government."

As Mary watched the color rising in his cheeks, fear seeped into her chest like a dense fog and made her heart beat faster. "But what if . . ." she began. She stopped, unable to bring herself to utter aloud the deepest dread she held in her heart. As much as she had tried to convince herself that she had divorced her heart from feelings in order to protect it from being hurt, it was impossible to deny how strongly she clung to William's presence in her life.

William turned to look at her. "Listen to me, Mary Elizabeth, I know what you're thinking. I want to tell you something that I don't want you to ever forget: If there is ever a time I must leave you, for whatever reason, there is no power on earth that will keep me from returning home. Do you hear me?"

The earnestness in William's voice caused tears to sting Mary's eyes. She whispered, "I had a dream last night. In the dream, I awakened in the morning and found that you were not in bed with me. I got up and called your name, but there was no answer. When I stepped out onto the dogtrot, there was a fierce wind blowing that ripped off my nightcap and made my hair swirl around my face. I yelled your name into the wind, but the sound got swallowed up. Suddenly, I saw the barn door fly open and three horses and riders walk out. You were in the middle on one of our Percheron horses, and there was a Yankee soldier and a Southern soldier on either side of you. Your hands were tied behind you, and you were blindfolded. I tried to run to you, but for some inexplicable reason, I couldn't move. I screamed, but you didn't hear me. The three of you turned and began trotting up the hill and into the woods. At the same time, the roof of the barn tore loose, filling the air with debris, and then the entire barn collapsed. And there the dream abruptly ended." Mary pulled up the folds of her dress and wiped her face. "I have a fear that more loss is coming to my life because of the curse that has been placed on me."

"Hush your silly talk. I've told you that there's no curse on you. And a dream is nothing more than that, just a dream."

Mary said, "I just don't want to ever lose you."

He reached over and put his hand on the outside of her thigh. Pulling her to him, he said, "Don't you worry about that." He smiled. "You couldn't get rid of me if you wanted to."

She rested her head on his shoulder and closed her eyes. *I pray that's true.*

Several minutes passed before she felt William pulling back on the reins and the wagon coming to a stop. When she opened her eyes, she saw the Chickamauga through the trees and spied a large tree lying on its side perpendicular to the creek. "Is that our prize?" she asked.

"That's the one," he answered. "There's lots of firewood in that tree. The positive thing about it is that it's a white oak and will split easily." Stepping out of the dray, he held up his hands to help Mary down.

She brushed his hands aside. "I can get down by myself." She put one foot on the wheel rim and, while holding the edge of the seat, lowered herself until her other foot rested on the hub of the wheel. Then, letting go of the seat, she dropped to the ground.

He stood back, looking at her. "How come you don't ever do that when we go to town or to church?"

She shook her dress, trying to get all her slips unbunched. She brushed back a wisp of hair and said, "Because I don't want to cause any old woman to have a fainting spell. They like to act so helpless, as if a woman can't take care of herself, which is absurd. And don't you say it because I know my mother would say it, too—it's just good manners to allow a man to help you. I say pishposh to that. I think if I worked at it I could do nearly anything a man can do."

"Now you've gone too far," William said as he lifted his tools out of the bed of the wagon and leaned them against its side.

Mary grabbed the hatchet and brandished it at him. "Don't

ever argue with an armed woman."

He laughed. "Good lord, Mary, there'll never be another woman like you." Picking up the broad ax, he made his way toward the tree.

Mary said, "After you cut the limbs off, I'll come help you saw up the trunk. I spotted a few small hickory trees a little ways back, and I'm going to strip some bark off them for the chair bottoms."

He stopped and turned around. "How far back?"

"Not far. Maybe fifty or sixty feet. Don't worry. I'll be fine."

"Don't get so busy that you don't keep your eyes peeled for danger. There's always the chance a straggling soldier could come by, and bears are looking for places to hibernate. Don't let one sneak up on you. They'd much rather bed down on a full stomach than an empty one."

"You're just saying that because you think I'm as sweet as honey." Mary turned and walked away.

"Quit your joking," William called after her. "I'm serious."

"You're always serious!" Mary yelled back.

Grasshoppers flew through the air as Mary waded into a patch of blooming tickweed, which she always thought of as autumn's answer to summer's black-eyed Susan. Inside the woods, sunlight flickered through the limbs and remaining autumn leaves. Walking up to a smooth-bark hickory tree, she struck it lightly with the hatchet. Twisting the hatchet until the edge of the bark separated from the tree, she gripped the bark with her fingers and pulled downward. In seconds, she was holding a strip nearly four feet long. The white phloem of the tree, which only moments ago was hidden underneath the bark, shone brightly in sharp contrast to the dark gray bark on both sides of it.

She continued harvesting the strips from several different trees, in order to avoid killing a tree by removing too much bark; at the edge of her hearing, she detected the sound of William's ax striking the tree in the distance.

After an hour or so, she had a stack of strips that would be a double armful. She paused and wiped the sweat from her brow with the back of her hand. Leaning against a tree, she closed her eyes and let herself feel the coolness of the breeze. She listened to the raspy complaint of a nearby blue jay.

Suddenly, she opened her eyes as she remembered that William had taught her to heed the warning sound of a blue jay because it only complained when there was something around that it wasn't used to seeing or if something was threatening its territory. She strained her eyes to see if there was something hidden by the camouflage of the trees and vines that had alarmed the bird. A movement at her periphery caught her attention, but when she looked in that direction, she saw nothing. She wanted to call out to William but was unsure if it was safe to because, as yet, she wasn't certain if there was any reason to be alarmed, and if there was, whether it was man or beast.

Just then she heard something behind her. When she wheeled around, there was a black bear fifteen feet away, staring at her.

Chapter Four

MARY

With her heart hammering against her chest like thundering hoof beats, Mary stood perfectly still as she watched the bear sniff the air and cast its head from side to side. She'd heard from others that bears have very poor eyesight, so she was uncertain if the bear had seen her. But it seemed pretty clear that it had caught her scent and had stalked her by circling around and coming up behind her. Her hope was that the ever-shifting breeze would keep the bear confused enough that it would walk past her.

The bear emitted a low growl and pawed the ground, flinging dead leaves and small sticks. It took three steps toward Mary, then it reared up on its back legs.

Certain now that the bear had seen her and was coming for her, Mary flung aside caution and screamed, "William!" She suddenly remembered the hatchet and realized she'd been holding it all along. She squeezed the handle tightly.

The bear gave a loud roar and began walking toward her on its hind legs. It held its front legs open like arms meant to hug and crush her.

A part of Mary told her to run for her life, but another part of her felt furious that, one more time, fate and nature seemed determined to join forces and bring harm to her. "You took my children when I couldn't fight back," she said through gritted teeth, "but I warn you, this time you will have a fight like you've never seen. So come on!"

She held the hatchet over her head as the bear closed the distance between them. She could see the froth around its mouth lined with sharp teeth, and she could smell its putrid breath. When the bear roared again, the sound was so loud it hurt her ears.

When the bear was less than two feet away, Mary swung the hatchet. "Take that, you beast!"

It struck the bear square in the face, splitting its nose in half.

A different roar came from the bear—one of surprise and pain. It grabbed its face with its front paws as blood covered its muzzle and ran down its neck and chest. As it shook its head in an effort to sling the hatchet from its face, blood spattered across the front of Mary's dress and struck the side of her face.

The bear staggered and swung wildly, striking Mary on the arm.

The force of the blow slammed her against a tree. Mary saw stars and fell to the ground. Desperation attempted to pull her to her feet, but everything was spinning, and she collapsed back onto the carpet of leaves.

She heard a loud explosion but couldn't figure out which direction it came from. She lay still and listened but heard no sounds of the crazed bear. The sound that finally did register was someone calling her name. It took her a second before she recognized William's voice. She tried opening her eyes again and discovered that the world was no longer spinning. The bear was lying on its side at her feet, the hatchet still buried in its face.

"Mary!" She heard William calling to her and crashing through the woods toward her. She looked in the direction of the sound and held her arms out toward him. "William."

With his rifle in one hand and his ax in the other, William paid her no attention; rather, he focused his full attention on the bear. He pushed on it with the end of the barrel of his rifle. When it didn't move, he dropped his weapons and fell on his knees beside Mary. "You're hurt! Lie still while I go get the wagon."

He started to get up and leave, but she grabbed his wrist. "I'm all right. I don't need the wagon."

"But you're bleeding." He pointed at her face and chest.

Mary looked down and saw the blood on her dress. She touched the side of her face and discovered blood on her fingertips. "I don't think it's mine. It must be the bear's."

He grabbed her and hugged her to his chest. "Oh my God, Mary, I thought . . ." His voice choked off.

She wrapped her arms around his neck and squeezed tightly. "I know, I know. I did, too. If you hadn't come when you did . . . Oh, William."

They held each other and rocked back and forth gently until the adrenalin drained from both of them. They unclenched their embrace and looked at the bear.

25

"Tell me what happened," William said.

As best she could, Mary related to him the details of what just happened. "How far away were you when you shot him?" Mary asked.

"Too far. But I had no choice. It was a lucky shot, perhaps eighty yards. Let's see where I hit it." He got up to inspect the bear more closely.

Mary joined him but had difficulty staring at the macabre scene of the hatchet buried in the bear's face. A shudder ran through her, as she could still see the angry mouth of the bear coming toward her. "I didn't know what else to do."

William got on his knees and began running his hands over the bear. Grunting, he rolled it on its other side and continued his exam. Finally, he looked up with wide eyes. "Mary, you killed this bear."

Mary frowned. "What do you mean? You shot it. You killed it."

"I shot at it, but I missed it. I can't find an entry wound anywhere on its body. You killed it with the hatchet. Mary, you single-handedly killed a bear."

She blinked at him, hardly able to comprehend what he was saying. Her knees began to tremble, and she eased herself to the ground.

He clapped his hands together and said excitedly, "You're going to be more famous than Daniel Boone or Davy Crockett! The woman who killed a bear with her bare hands! Somebody will write a song about you."

She looked up at him as he started dancing a jig around her and the bear. She started to chastise him but could see how excited and proud he was, so she let him and his male pride run amuck. She smiled at him and said, "And you'll be married to the woman bear killer."

He stopped dancing and stuck his thumbs under the front of his shirt, making it pooch out. "Men will say, 'My wife cooks a good ham,' or 'My wife can plow a garden,' or 'My wife makes excellent wine.' And then I'll step up and say, matter-of-factly, 'My wife killed a bear.'" William broke into a dance again. "I can see their faces now. No one will have anything to say that can top that!"

Mary had heard enough. She held her hand out toward him. "Hush your foolishness."

William grabbed her hand and pulled her to him.

They put their arms around each other and stared into each other's eyes.

Mary said, "I love you, William Thomson."

"And I love you, Mary Elizabeth Thomson."

"What are we going to do with it?" Mary asked, pointing to the bear.

"I'll skin it out and take the hide with us. I never heard anyone say bear meat was any good to eat. But let's go over to the creek now and get us a drink and wash you off."

Mary fell in step behind him, and soon they were on the bank of the creek. They knelt down and cupped water from the creek to their mouths. Mary felt relief from the cold water as some of it escaped her mouth and ran down her neck and in between her breasts. Once she'd slaked her thirst, she washed her face and the back of her neck. Only then did she begin feeling more like herself. She turned her head to see what William was doing and found him squatting beside her and staring.

"What are you looking at?" she asked.

"The most remarkable woman I've ever known," he replied.

Mary felt herself blushing at his praise. She tried to deflect the attention off herself by saying, "We'd better get busy cutting wood and make up for our lost time."

"Even if we return to the cabin with an empty dray," William said, "I will never forget this day, for it reminded me once again that I am truly the most blessed man in the territory."

She gave him a crooked smile. "Only the territory?"

A smile played across his face. "Well, until I'm able to sample women outside the territory, I can't make a fair judgment."

She stood up and began walking toward him. She gave him a playful yet menacing look. "Until you sample them? I'll make you think sample them!"

He covered his head with his arms. "Have mercy on me, Bear Slayer."

"I'll show you mercy," Mary said as she shoved him backward into the creek.

William landed with a splash and cried out, "She's going to kill me! The Bear Slayer is going to kill me!"

After Mary stopped laughing at the surprised look on William's face, she waded into the water midcalf deep and offered her hand to help him up.

Sitting in the stream, William grabbed her hand and clasped it tightly.

It was then that she realized she'd miscalculated how far William might go to get revenge.

He grinned and started pulling on her arm.

She tried to jerk free, but his hand held fast. "You better not," she said. "I'm warning you." As he started pulling her toward him, she felt herself losing her balance. "William Thomson, if you get me wet, I'll—" Her words changed into a scream as William jerked hard, and she fell face first into the creek and in between his legs.

He quickly let go of her hand and grabbed her shoulders, turning her over onto her back.

Mary spat water out of her mouth and gasped for air. When she sat up, facing William, and saw him laughing, she swung her fist at him.

He dodged her blow and caught her fist in his hand. "Easy there, Bear Slayer. You might hurt someone with that."

She pushed back a strand of hair that was hanging between her eyes and said calmly, "You know who cooks your meals, don't you? It would be a sad thing if you died mysteriously one day. I'll just let you think about that." Her efforts to keep a serious expression on her face failed, and she smiled broadly. "We are a pair," she said with a laugh.

William stood up and offered his hand to her. "Yes, we are."

Before Mary took his hand, she asked, "Are we through playing in the water?"

William chuckled. "Indeed."

She took his hand and tried to get up, but her dress and multiple layers of underthings had become waterlogged. She staggered and fell to her knees. "My clothes are so heavy I can't stand up."

"Then let me help you take some of them off." He knelt down in the water behind her and began unbuttoning the back of her dress and untying the sash from around her waist. As he did so, he kissed the back of her neck.

His warm lips caused a chill to run down her back. She pulled the top of her dress forward and slid her arms out of the wet sleeves, then let the top fall. Then she raised her hips off the bottom of the creek and pushed the dress down over her hips.

As she did so, William moved in front of her and pulled the dress off.

They stared into each other's eyes, but neither said a word.

Mary looked down and saw that her breasts, with their hard nipples, were staring at William through the now wet and transparent linen camisole meant to conceal them. She looked up at him and saw that he was taking off his shirt.

He stood and held his hands toward her. "Come make love with me," he said in a husky voice.

He led them out of the creek and along the bank until they found a bed of thick moss.

Mary lay down on the soft, green bed and let him watch her as she removed the rest of her clothes. She felt her cheeks burning and her breath becoming hot. She noticed the bulge in William's breeches and watched him finish undressing.

*****

Some time later, as she laid beside her snoozing husband, who was lying on his side, Mary thought about all the women she knew who complained about having sex with their husbands. She actually looked forward to being with William because it was only in the white-hot moments of lovemaking that she could be completely free of her melancholy and of memories of her babies. Her only wish was that she could make the moments last longer, for as sure as the passion subsided, there was a good chance that her dark mood would return.

She remained there, listening to the gurgling sound of the Chickamauga beside them until, shivering, she stood up and pulled on a minimum of her cold, damp clothes.

As she did so, William stirred and rolled onto his back.

Mary looked at him and smiled. "And so once again you've caused us to miss a day of work because of your fleshly lusts."

He sat up. "I thought you might go cut some wood while I was taking a nap."

"Well, you know what? You thought wrong. Get dressed and help me carry all these wet clothes to the dray. Then we can gather all the strips of bark I cut for the chair bottoms. At least we got that much done today."

"Don't forget about that bearskin," he said. "That's going to be awfully nice to crawl under this winter. They say there's nothing any warmer, unless it's a buffalo hide."

*****

It was dusky dark when they finally arrived back at their house.

"Drive on to the barn," Mary said. "I'll milk the cow while you tend to the mules, and don't forget to feed the pig. We want him as fat as he can get before we slaughter him."

Later, as they lay in bed, William said, "What a day, what a day this has been."

"Indeed it has been," Mary agreed as she let herself feel the heaviness of fatigue pressing her deeper into the bed.

"You know, I nearly lost you today. It scares me to think what would become of me if something like that ever happened."

Mary turned toward him. The moonlight shining through the window reflected off a silver tear running down the cheek of the man she loved. She leaned over and kissed the tear. "I'll always be here for you."

He sniffed loudly. "That's good because I don't think I'd ever be satisfied with another woman after I've slept with the Bear Slayer."

Immediately, he howled in pain as Mary grabbed his nose and twisted it.

Chapter Five

JOHN

As soon as John fell asleep, he tumbled into the recurring dream, assembled from fragments of memory that had plagued him for thirty years.

His hands were tied in front of him with a piece of leather, and there was a rope around his neck. "My name is Kwasi Poku!" he yelled at his captor, a vicious slave trader whose reputation was known up and down the Gold Coast of Africa.

The only response the man gave him was to jerk on the rope, causing John to lose his balance and fall to the floor of the Ghanaian jungle.

His captor wheeled around and yelled at him while also kicking him in the side.

The man's words meant nothing because his language was unknown to John.

Up ahead, the dim shadows of the jungle gave way to bright light. He smelled the ocean breeze. When he and his captor broke through the edge of the jungle and onto the beach, the sound of the ocean waves filled his ears. Squinting against the sunlight, he saw several lines of other Africans being led in the same direction while being struck on their backs with lengths of leather by their captors. He lifted his head to look for their final destination and saw the castle of Elmina perched on a cliff.

He had heard of this place while sitting around ceremonial fires and listening to the elders tell stories of the Ashanti's past. The castle had been built many generations ago by people called the Portuguese. It was a structure of such size as to be laughed at, for who would build a dwelling that couldn't be moved to follow the migration of the animals that fed him and his family?

As generations passed, other white men fought for control of the castle, especially as the slave trade became an important industry. "Many have been taken to Elmina," an old man told him one time, "but none have ever returned to tell what happens there."

Suddenly, John was struck across his face with the leather strap in his captor's hands. The man's face was red and angry as he jerked him forward, leading him toward the castle. The closer they got to it, the larger it appeared. John had never dreamed of such a large place.

They paused at the base of it as his captor and another man first exchange words, then gold coins. At that point, the end of the rope around John's neck was passed to another man, who led him up a long flight of steps until they came to an opening in the castle wall. From inside came the wails and cries of desperate men and women and even children. Just before he was shoved inside, his nostrils were hit with the strong odor of human excrement. He staggered in the darkness of the windowless room and fell face down on the wet and slimy floor.

John jerked awake from the nightmare of his past and stared wide-eyed at the barn loft he slept in last night on the outskirts of Washington. Even though the night had been cold, he wiped beads of sweat from his face. In spite of the fact that his time in Elmina castle was half his lifetime ago, he could not escape the memory of its horror.

He stood up and stomped his feet to get them warmed up. Leaning over, he rubbed his bad knee, which had become quite swollen from all the walking he had done over the past weeks. Looking out the window of the loft, he straightened the cap on his bald head and looked toward the sunrise. Then he reached inside his knapsack and pulled out a worn copy of *Incidents in the Life of a Slave Girl*. He thought, with gratitude, about the white family he was owned by for a while who made an effort to teach their slaves to read and write.

He fanned the pages of the book until they stopped at a marked place, and he pulled out a three-inch-square piece of tattered cloth. It was the last remnant of his family kente cloth he had brought with him on the slave ship that transported him from West Africa twenty-nine years ago. He said, "My name is Kwasi Poku. I am of the Ashanti tribe. My father was a prince, a direct descendant of Okomfo Anokye." It was a recitation he had uttered every morning since being captured by the slave traders.

A groan drew his attention to the stack of hay he slept on last night. Nunly, his companion, was waking up.

Nunly yawned. "Where are we going today, John?"

John had never liked Nunly. From the moment they had met as slaves on the ship, the USS *Planter*, Nunly had shown himself to be lazy. There were many times that John ended up doing both men's work in order to avoid the wrath of the captain and the sting of his whip.

The thrill that John had felt after helping commandeer the ship and turning it over to the Union six months ago had quickly faded when a few short days after that celebration, he and the other seven slaves were unceremoniously placed in a dinghy. "Yonder is the mouth of the Potomac," the captain had said, pointing toward the shore. "You are free now."

"Free to do what?" John had asked.

"Whatever you wish," had been the reply.

As the dinghy began drifting away from the ship, John had called out, "I wish to go home to Africa." Though his words had rung across the water, they had fallen unheard into the deep, as no one had remained standing on the edge of the deck to hear them.

John and the other slaves had turned and looked at Robert Smalls, their fellow slave who had led their escape and piloted the *Planter* out of Charleston Bay.

"Grab those oars and start paddling toward the shore, or the current will take us out to sea."

Used to being obedient, the slaves had quickly slipped the oars into oarlocks and begun rowing. When the bow of the boat had finally touched land, they scrambled ashore.

"What do we do now?" one of them had asked.

"We head north," Robert told them.

There was no discussion as everyone fell into step behind him.

John was easily the oldest man in the group, and it wasn't but a few hours into their journey that he finally stopped and sat down. Gasping for breath, he rubbed his right knee.

Robert had halted the others and said to John, "What's the matter with you? You have to keep up. We have to get as far away from the Southern army as we can."

John had waved his hand at him. "You all go on. I can't keep up. This old knee of mine hasn't been right since it got broke the first time I tried to escape from one of my masters."

The others looked at him then back at Robert. "We've got no choice," Robert said. "Good luck to you."

As they begin trotting off, John saw Nunly at the back of the pack slowing down, then stopping, and then walking back toward John.

"What are you doing?" John had asked him.

"I don't feel like running no more."

While John had initially been pleased to have someone stay with him, as time went by, he'd learned that Nunly's lazy behavior on the boat was not a result of his efforts to frustrate the whites; it was a result of his overall character.

Nunly never felt like doing anything that required effort. The only thing he was good at was waking up the instant John tried to slip away from him and go it on his own.

"I'm tired of wandering around the countryside, begging for and stealing food, and sleeping in barns," John said. "I been thinking about going and trying to see Mr. Lincoln. Maybe he can help us out."

Nunly rolled over, turning his back to John. "There ain't no way a nigger can show up and get in to see the president."

John considered trying to reason with Nunly, but he knew it was pointless. Besides, it would be fine with him if Nunly refused to go along.

He got up and walked over to a watering trough. Before he dipped his hands in it to wash his face, he saw reflected in the water the scar around his neck, peeking out from the collar of his shirt. He touched it and remembered the first time he had an iron collar fastened on him, in the bottom of the slave ship, and then the second time, when he was part of a coffle of nearly one hundred slaves taken on a forced march from Boston to Charleston. More than once during those experiences, he would wake and find that the person chained next to him had died during the night. The placid faces of those who died belied the torturous death they endured. But John wasn't sorrowful over their deaths, for death was oftentimes a blessing. Rather, he loathed the fact that they had to meet their ancestors without being robed in ceremonial gowns and with no gifts to offer them.

He washed his face, making as little noise as possible,

hoping Nunly would fall back asleep so that he could leave without being followed. Picking up his knapsack, he eased out the barn door into bright sunshine. He gazed at the western Maryland countryside. After looking up at the sun and fixing his bearings, he struck off in an easterly direction. "I'm going to see Mr. Lincoln."

John had walked for about thirty minutes when he heard horses coming up behind him. He stepped off the road and watched a company of cavalry pass, with six cannon in the rear being pulled by horses. John covered his mouth with the sleeve of his jacket until the cloud of dust had settled, and then he continued on his way.

Inside the city, the streets were choked with soldiers, horses, and wagons. Civilians, both black and white, were moving up and down the edges of the street.

Unsure which direction he should take, John grabbed the arm of a young black boy and said, "Where does Mr. Lincoln live?"

"He lives over yonder way," the boy replied, pointing in a general direction.

Trusting the boy to know what he was talking about, John headed in that direction. He passed by an open door, and the aroma of fried ham and sweet bread filled his nostrils, causing his stomach to growl. He reached inside his knapsack and took out a corn pone he had pilfered.

After eating it, he stopped at a horse trough for a drink. Water dripped off his chin as he straightened up and looked down one of the other streets. "Lawdy mercy, that must be it," he said to himself. At the far end of the street sat a house that was bigger than any of the big houses John's owners lived in. Buoyed with renewed energy from having found it, John headed that way, though now with a limp, as his bad knee could no longer ignore the long journey it had been on.

The closer he got to the house, the greater the feeling of awe and respect in his heart. *Who am I to think that Mr. Lincoln will even give me the time of day? Nunly was probably right.*

He walked onto the front lawn, where people were milling about; some, dressed in fine clothes, appeared to be engaged in serious conversation, while others, dressed more like John, were lying on the ground napping. Some had even spread a cloth on the ground and were eating a meal. John wondered how people could be so casual about being this close to Mr. Lincoln's home.

Just as he reached the front of the house, a large company of men poured through the front door, all talking at the same time. In the middle of the group, one man's head rose above all the others. His face was swarthy, and he had bushy black eyebrows.

Someone on the fringe of the group yelled, "Mr. Lincoln, a word with you, sir!"

The tall man stopped and turned toward the voice.

A chill ran through John. *That's him!*

He couldn't hear what the two men discussed, but presently

the group began moving again.

Without thinking, John called out, "Mr. Lincoln, a word with you, please, sir!"

Lincoln stopped, looked over at John, then stepped closer.

John hadn't expected Mr. Lincoln to be so tall that he could actually look him in the eye without bending or stooping.

"Yes, sir," Lincoln said. "What can I do for you?"

His voice was thin and twangy, not anything like John had imagined it sounding. John removed his hat and said, "Mr. Lincoln, I don't know what to do with myself."

"That's a quite troubling place to be, isn't it? Sort of reminds me of the first time I lost an election. I had to take stock and decide what to do next."

"Yes, sir, that's me."

Lincoln looked at John's neck. "I can see you've been a slave in the past. How long have you been free, or are you a runaway?"

"I suppose I'm a bit of both. I was a slave on more than one plantation, once as a field hand and once as a carpenter. But my last owner bought me to work on his ship, the *Plantar*."

"My God, man, you mean you were on the ship with Robert Smalls?"

Surprised Lincoln should know this, John answered, "Yes, sir, I was."

Lincoln turned to the men surrounding him. He clapped John on the shoulder and said, "This man was one of the ones who helped shanghai that Southern ship, the *Planter*." Lincoln grabbed John's hand and shook it. "My man, what you did changed my mind and the mind of many others about whether or not blacks should be allowed to fight in this war. You say you don't know what to do with yourself—why not fight to preserve the Union?"

John hesitated, feeling overwhelmed. He said, "Begging your pardon, Sir, I don't know much about this 'preserving the Union' as you say."

"Do you want to continue living as a free man?" Lincoln asked.

"Yes, sir, I do."

"Then the Union must win this war."

"Well, sir, what do I need to do to start fighting?"

"That's what I like—a man who, when things become clear to him, is ready to act. Too bad there aren't more men like him in Congress."

There was a ripple of laughter from the other men.

"You need to head to Massachusetts. Just this month, Governor John A. Andrew issued the war's first call for black soldiers. You go find him and tell him I sent you." Lincoln patted John on the back and continued walking while surrounded by the band of men.

John stared after Lincoln. A slow smile spread across his

features. He held up his right hand and, looking at it, said, "Mr. Lincoln shook that hand."

Chapter Six

MARY

Three days after the incident with the bear, Mary and William boarded their wagon with its bed loaded to the brim with firewood and several handmade chairs tied down on top of that.

William turned his attention to the pair of muscular Percheron horses hitched to the dray. "Giddap," he said as he slapped the reins against their rumps.

Moving as one, the horses threw themselves against their horse collars. At first nothing happened, and then the dray crept forward.

"Come on," he encouraged them. "You can do it. Pull hard!"

The iron shoes of the large-hoofed horses left deep u-shaped tracks in the dirt as, eventually, the wagon moved along at a walking pace.

Mary applauded. "You are amazing!" she called to them. "No other pair of horses in the state can outpull you!"

"They surely do eat a lot of food," William commented, "but when it comes to jobs like this, they're worth their weight in gold. Did you let Thomas know we're coming to the city?"

"I sent him a letter last week and told him it would be in the next ten days or so. He'll be ready for us. Besides, he's told us we don't have to let him know when we're coming. He said anytime we show up, we'll be welcome."

"I know what he said, and I know he means it, but I don't like to show up unannounced."

"That's because you're a planner. You want it all scheduled out. It wouldn't hurt you to be a little more spontaneous and just let things happen as they come. That's the way Thomas is. He just takes things one day at a time."

"I guess that's how he's kept his sanity after what he's been through. I know if it happened to me, I'd lose my mind."

"Death comes in many forms, William, and at any time. You know that as well as I do. The only thing that's promised us on earth is death."

"But at least Thomas had his daughters to live for after Anna died. If anything happened to you, I don't have that blessing."

Once again, William's blundering words bludgeoned the areas of Mary's heart that couldn't seem to heal—that she had left him childless and that she would never know the joy of raising a child. As tears stung her eyes, she gritted her teeth to keep from lashing out at him. But it didn't prevent the loosening of the door to her grief over losing her closest friend, Anna, as her mind was flooded with memories.

Oftentimes, her pregnancies and Anna's had dovetailed one after the other. Anna had consoled her like no one else when she lost her babies. And Anna had understood when there were times Mary could take joy in Anna's daughters and other times when it made her envious and sad, sometimes even angry.

The great shock had been when Anna died while giving birth to her last daughter. The doctor gave no explanation for it. He had simply shrugged his shoulders as if that was an excuse for his lack of knowledge.

William cut in on her thoughts. "Thomas is a strong man, maybe not physically strong like me, but he has a strength of character, a true man of his word no matter what may come."

"I'm glad you two are such good friends," Mary said. "I know it began with doing business with each other—you buying things from his general store and Thomas selling your chairs for you—but it grew through the years to true friendship."

"You're right. Thomas is the best friend I have in this world. I just wish there was something more I could do to help him overcome his sense of loss since Anna's death. Perhaps he just needs more time."

"Time doesn't heal all wounds, William. It only wraps another layer of burial cloth around the memory as the years pass." Mary felt the edges of her melancholia creeping closer to her like the hands of a murderer about to choke her. *Stay away! Leave me alone!*

She bit her bottom lip, a trick she'd stumbled upon that sometimes thwarted the efforts of melancholia to overwhelm her. The sharp pain seemed to somehow insulate her. Sometimes she bit so hard she tasted blood.

When William gave no response to her comment, she knew he was choosing to be silent rather than risk saying anything that would hurt her or lead them into an argument. It seemed to her that this had become their pattern more and more. Whereas in the early years of their marriage they could talk for hours about all sorts of serious topics, now it seemed like they tiptoed around them and chose silence over dialogue. This made her feel guilty because she believed she was the cause of it. *It's this cursed melancholia that taints how I hear things and tinges my tone of voice with a sharpness that cuts William to the quick.* So she chose to fall silent, letting the swaying and bumping of the wagon act like a sifter as she sorted through her thoughts and feelings.

The traffic on the road picked up as they approached the city. Mary noticed that instead of the usual casual greetings that passed between travelers, people were more likely to keep their heads down, or if they did look, it was with an expression of suspicion. "Have you noticed how no one wants to speak to us?" she asked William. "What is wrong with everyone?"

"I've noticed it, too. I'm not sure what it means. Maybe Thomas can shed some light on it for us."

At the edge of town, they stopped at a large barn with a corral full of horses. Someone had used a wide paintbrush to paint a sign across the side of the barn: "Barton's Livery and Blacksmith"—although the *e* in *Livery* hung slightly askew above the *v* and *r*, evidently after someone pointed out the spelling error. The bright, ringing tones of Robert Barton striking his anvil with his hammer came from the other side of the barn.

William pulled the horses to a stop. "I'll speak with Robert while you check with Gertrude to see if they need some firewood."

Mary walked to the house sitting beside the barn. From the looks of it, it was obvious that Robert Barton was more diligent about tending to the upkeep of animals than he was on the upkeep of his house. Several wooden shingles hung at a forty-five-degree angle, having loosened themselves from the nails holding one of their corners. A good gust of wind was all that was needed to free them from the other nail, and they would either come sliding onto the ground or end up flying through the air.

Mary deliberately stepped over one of the rotting steps leading up to the front porch. She knocked on the front door and waited.

In a moment, a tired-looking, thin wisp of a woman answered the door.

"Hello, Gertrude," Mary said cheerily.

Gertrude's expression did not change. "Hi, Mary." As if it took all her energy to greet Mary, she said nothing else, nor did she invite her in.

Gertrude's manner used to alarm Mary—she had thought something was seriously wrong with her—until she realized, over time, that this was always the way with Gertrude Refusing to let the sour atmosphere envelop her, Mary smiled and said, "William and I have come to town to sell firewood, and I thought I'd stop to see if you need any."

"I suppose so," Gertrude answered. "Just unload it down at the barn, and Robert can bring it up later."

Mary made a stab at engaging Gertrude in more than perfunctory conversation. "It seems like there's an awful lot of people traveling in and out of the city."

Gertrude's flat affect remained unchanged. "Really? I hadn't noticed." Without another word, she shut the door.

Mary shook her head in disbelief and headed back to the livery. She muttered to herself, "Some people."

When she stepped around the corner of the barn, she saw Robert running his hands down the neck of one of their Percherons, then down the side and over the rump, while William looked on. The top of Robert's bald head shone from sweat, and the bulging muscles in his forearms and biceps couldn't be missed since he had removed his shirt and hung it on a nail by the door of the barn.

As she got closer, she heard Robert say, "This is the finest set of Percherons around. I know a couple of farmers who would give a high dollar for them. Why don't you sell them to me, and then I'll split the profit with you?"

Mary started to utter a protest but knew that it would displease William for her to interrupt the proceedings. She was relieved to hear him say, "But how would I replace them? No sir. I know what a good thing I've got. They're not for sale."

Robert patted the horse's rear. "I don't blame you. But you better be careful, or the army will take them from you." He suddenly noticed Mary. "Good day to you, Miss Mary."

Mary smiled. "Hi, Robert. What's this about the army taking horses?"

"It's happening," Robert said. "I've heard of people having some of their livestock taken by soldiers who are following orders."

"Which army are we talking about?" William asked.

"It depends which one the wind brings in. Sometimes it's the Union Army, and sometimes the Southern. We're catching this war on both sides. It's a hell of a thing." To Mary, he said apologetically, "Excuse me for swearing."

William bristled. "It'll be over my dead body if anyone tries to take what's mine! I say, to hell with tyranny, wherever it comes from."

"Just be careful who you say that to," Robert said. "There's spies all around. You can't tell who you can trust anymore."

Mary saw that William was about to offer another retort, so she placed her hand on his arm. "Gertrude says she needs some firewood and that we're to leave it down here."

William looked at her blankly for a second, and then

understanding showed in his expression. "That we'll do. Show me where to stack it, Robert."

"Just stack it against the front of the barn," Robert directed.

Chapter Seven

MARY

Mary and William made a few more stops to sell some firewood before they pulled up to the front of Henry's General Store.

From a second-story open window of the building, twelve-year-old Florence Henry screamed in excitement, "It's Mary and William!"

Mary braced herself for what was to come—the onslaught of Thomas's daughters. They would make a fuss over her and William, but especially her—climbing onto her lap, touching her face and hair, begging for her attention. It had been that way ever since Anna had died, and although Mary understood the why of it, what she couldn't control were her own feelings about it. Part of her embraced the attention and knew it was good for the girls to have a surrogate mother figure, but another part of her wanted to push them away and tell them to leave her alone. Their attention and adoration caused feelings to push to the surface that she wanted to keep buried. *I'll never be a mother, and that's that! Deal with it and move on.*

Just as a man and woman exited the front door of the store, arms laden with staples, nine-year-old Emma Henry darted out, weaving in between the couple, and raced toward Mary and William's wagon. As she climbed up on the wagon, she said, "Father said you were coming. I've been waiting a long time to see you. What took you so long?"

Mary and William took turns hugging her, then she climbed onto Mary's lap.

By this time, Florence had made it down from the upstairs living quarters of the store and was walking across the front porch toward them. Holding the hand of four-year-old Mary Beth Henry, who was pulling backward, she spoke sharply to the youngest sister. "Come on! You know you want to see Mary and William. Remember? Mary is who you were named after."

Mary sat Emma aside and climbed down from the wagon to greet her namesake. It had been a tearful surprise when Thomas informed her, less than an hour after Anna had died, that he was naming the new baby after her. Mary's heart had still been reeling from the blow of watching her friend die, and Thomas's unexpected announcement left her with mixed emotions.

"It's what Anna would want," Thomas had told her, "because you were her best friend. I'm glad you were with her at the end. I'm certain it meant a lot to her."

Mary got down on her knees beside the wagon and smiled at Florence and Mary Beth. She and Florence exchanged an eager hug, and then she turned to little Mary Beth and opened her arms toward her. In a soft voice, she said, "I'm so happy to see you again, Mary Beth. Would you like a hug?"

The child's head was bowed as if she were praying, but she lifted it just enough to look at Mary from underneath her eyebrows. She scuffed at the ground with the toe of her shoe and twisted back and forth, which caused her dress to flare out around her, giving her the appearance of a hand bell.

Perhaps she's like me. Maybe part of her wants to love another motherlike person, but another part of her doesn't trust that this one won't leave her, too. To Mary Beth, she said gently, "Come see me."

Finally, whatever emotions were keeping Mary Beth anchored to her spot released their hold on her, and she practically ran into Mary's embrace.

William joined them, along with Emma, and put his arms around all of them. Then he gave Florence a hug.

"You three are the prettiest girls in the territory!" he exclaimed.

Mary winked at Florence, and in a voice tinged with mock hurt, she said to William, "And where does that leave me?"

Without hesitation, William replied, "Aye, but you're the handsomest *woman* in the territory."

The two oldest girls laughed at the adult repartee.

Mary said to the girls, "Let this be a warning to you. Never trust a red-headed Scotsman with a slick tongue because you can never be certain when he's telling the truth."

William laughed. "Clearly I am outnumbered here. I'm going inside the store to see if I can recruit some male assistance."

As he turned and headed toward the store, Mary and the girls followed.

When they stepped inside, Mary noticed several men standing around the potbelly stove in the center of the store. Thomas Henry, who was a head taller than those around him, appeared to be holding audience with the men. His thick brown hair was falling over his low forehead and into his dark eyes. He used his index finger like an exclamation point to emphasize each of his words.

"Patrick Henry was the greatest patriot of all time!" Thomas exclaimed loudly. "I challenge anyone to argue that with me!"

William looked at Mary with a wry expression and said, "It's the 'Patrick Henry speech' again. He never tires of dragging it out, does he?"

Mary smiled at William.

Speaking loudly, William headed toward the group of men. "The only reason Patrick Henry was such a great man was because his father was from Scotland!"

Everyone in the group turned to look at William.

When Thomas laid eyes on him, he broke into a broad grin. "William!" he exclaimed and strode over to embrace him.

"Don't let this braggart fill your ears with a bunch of balderdash," William said to the men. "He's been trying to ride on the coattails of his distant relative for years. I'm not for certain he didn't have his last name changed to Henry just to achieve popularity."

All the men broke into riotous laughter.

Thomas maintained his composure in spite of the rowdy laughter. "Laugh if you will. But I know the truth." Using his height advantage, he placed William in a headlock. "And whatever you do, don't listen to this redheaded blowhard. He's just jealous of me."

Mary forced herself in between William and Thomas, pushing them apart. "Will you two children please behave?" she exclaimed.

This brought another roar of laughter from the audience, and they began dispersing.

Thomas embraced Mary. "Mary, it's so good to see you." He released her and said, "It's good to see you both. We all so look forward to your visits, don't we, girls?"

Florence, Emma, and Mary Beth gave an enthusiastic chorus of affirmation.

"What a blessing you have," William said to Thomas, "to be surrounded with such a beautiful bouquet of daughters. A man with daughters will never have to worry about being taken care of in his old age."

Mary squeezed her eyes shut for a second as she felt irritation rising. When she opened them, she was about to take her anger out on William until she saw Thomas looking at her with a sympathetic expression. Just knowing someone understood how she felt and how hurtful

William's words were was enough to mollify her. She turned away from both men and said, "I want to see what new fabrics you have in so I can make myself a new dress. You girls come help me pick something out."

Like baby chicks scurrying around a mother hen, the three girls followed her to one side of the store. When they arrived at the bolts of cloth stacked beside each other like soldiers at attention, Florence and Emma put their hands on two different patterns and began telling Mary why she should select theirs.

"Both of those are really pretty," Mary said, looking thoughtful. "But I wonder which one you think would look best, Mary Beth."

The small child looked up at her and shrugged her shoulders.

Mary squatted in front of her. "No, no, I really want to hear what you think. Show me which one is your favorite."

Mary Beth stepped forward and touched a bolt of gingham with various shades of red stripes intersected by deep yellow stripes.

"Ooo, that is pretty," Mary said. "And no doubt William will like that it is plaid, provided it doesn't remind him of some distant family that the Thomson clan has feuded with in the past." She lifted the bolt and carried it to the front counter, then pulled out a piece of paper from inside the front of her dress. Opening it, she said, "I need some coffee, salt, and sugar." Though she was familiar enough with where everything was in the store so that she didn't need any help, she let Florence and Emma lead her around while she carried Mary Beth on her hip.

"Is Abigail still living with you all?" Mary asked.

"Yes, ma'am," Florence said.

"But Mary Beth doesn't nurse anymore," Emma added.

"Emma!" Florence said harshly.

"What?"

"You're not supposed to talk openly about those kinds of things," Florence instructed her younger sister.

"Well, it's the truth," Emma countered.

"I know it's the truth but—" Florence looked to Mary to help support her argument.

Mary said, "It's okay if it's just us women talking about it." She bounced Mary Beth in her arms. "So little Mary Beth isn't so little anymore, is she?" She looked at each girl and said, "Would you all like for me to fix your hair?" One thing she truly enjoyed was doing things with the girls' hair, as it reminded her of her mother doing the same with her when she was growing up.

All three girls gave an eager cheer of "Yes!"

"Then let's go upstairs."

In the girls' bedroom, Mary worked on brushing and arranging Florence's hair, then turned her toward the mirror and said, "How do you like that?"

Florence smiled and touched her hair. "It's beautiful. I love it. I wish I could learn how to make it look like that."

"You can," Mary said. "You just need to practice." She looked at the other two girls. "All of you need to make it a habit to brush your hair every night before you put on your nightcap and go to bed."

Emma said, "Will you take down your hair so we can see it?"

Mary had learned that this was a special treat for the girls. She removed her cap and began pulling out hair pins until she leaned her head back and shook it. Her long tresses cascaded down her back like Rapunzel's.

Mary Beth said, "Ooo, pretty."

Florence began untangling the hair with her fingers while Emma picked up the brush and began stroking it.

This was the self-indulgent moment that Mary allowed herself to have. She felt chills trot across her skin, and she closed her eyes. From a dark, windowless place in her mind, a recurring, tormenting thought escaped from behind a wall: *Wouldn't it be wonderful if I had daughters to do this with?*

She tried hard to shove the thought back to the closed-off place where she had kept it, as if she were trying to hold the door against an intruder. But it was too late. The question was the tip of a dagger that produced not blood from her heart but tears of sadness. She sniffed hard against her tears, but one escaped and began rolling down her cheek.

She felt one of the girls touching the trail of the tear and heard Mary Beth say, "You hurt?"

The unpretentious, innocent gesture almost succeeded in overwhelming Mary's resistance. She didn't say anything at first, fearing her voice would be trembling, but finally, she took a deep breath, opened her eyes, and said, "Do I smell Abigail's cooking? I'm getting hungry. Let's go eat!"

Chapter Eight

WILLIAM

While Mary was busy upstairs with the children, William and Thomas walked outside to the back of the store where wagon parts and farming equipment were kept.

Thomas pointed to a plow and said, "Look at the name stamped on there."

William bent down for a closer look. "The Tennessee Plow Factory."

"Yep," Thomas said. "Located in Nashville. I bought some of the first ones they produced. They're a lot cheaper since they don't have to be freighted here from so far away."

William said, "It's about time we started producing some of our own things down here and not depend on the factories up north. If war did break out, the northern factories might stop shipping things down here."

"What do you hear about the war out where you live?"

"Not much. I know the Calhouns' two boys left out to join the Confederate Army, and I heard that Ezra Lattimore joined the Union Army. But as far as what's really going on in the war itself, I couldn't say."

"It's all anyone talks about here in Chattanooga," Thomas said. "There's a fight nearly every day in the saloon between someone who supports the Union and someone who supports the Confederacy."

"If it comes down to it, which side will you fight for?" William asked.

"What if I turn the question to you? Which side will you fight for?"

William studied his friend before answering. "That is one question I have spent lots of time thinking about. I don't think it's right for the government to tell a man how he should live his life. My family came to this country to escape that kind of tyranny. I fear that if the Union wins the war, their next step will be to take our lands and businesses or at the very least tax us until we can't afford to keep them. While I hate to see this country split into two countries, if that's what it takes to be free, then I will fight for the Confederacy."

"But what about slavery?" Thomas asked. "What's your position on the question-- do you think a man should own the rights to another man's life? That's where everyone wants to draw lines."

"I say let each man's conscience direct him on that question. For me, I'll never be a party to buying and selling of slaves. But just because that's my feeling doesn't mean that it should be forced on anyone else."

"I can't believe you would say that—you, the man who believes in individual freedom as much as anyone I know. That you can abide any man owning another man is a surprise to me."

"What about your Abigail?" William countered. "Didn't you buy her so that you could have a wet nurse and help in raising your daughters after Anna died?"

"But I had no choice," Thomas answered defensively. "I had to have help, or little Mary Beth would have died. And there was no way for me to run my business and take care of three girls, too."

"I see. So it's okay for you to own a slave but not for anyone else. You're talking out both sides of your mouth, Thomas."

"Perhaps you're right. But which side I would fight for is a moot point anyway. I could never leave my three young children and go away to fight in a war. I've decided that I will plow the middle ground between the Union and the Confederacy."

William frowned. "What does that mean?"

"Whichever side controls Chattanooga, that's the side that I'll support. Otherwise I risk them taking everything from my store or perhaps burning it down. There are rumors that there's a Union general who employs that tactic—that is, he destroys everything behind him by setting it on fire. It's like the story in the Old Testament of Samson tying burning torches onto the tails of foxes and turning them loose in the fields of the Philistines."

"Then your conviction is nothing more than what's convenient for you."

"So you're telling me that you would leave Mary and your

farm and go fight, not knowing if either would be left by the time you returned?"

"I would have left already," William answered, "but Mary is loath for me to join the fight. That's the only thing holding me back. She has lost so much already, I would not want to burden her heart with worrying about me every day."

"And how is she doing these days?"

"For the most part, she seems quite fine. But there are days when she climbs the hill behind the house and spends time at the graves. On those days, she can be quite melancholy. And there are times that her tongue is as sharp as a man's razor."

Thomas nodded his head. "That I can understand. Even after four years, I have those days myself."

William noticed the lines of sadness growing deeper on the face of his friend. He regretted that their conversation had turned in this direction. He put his hand on the handle of the plow beside them and said, "I will buy one of these. And if it doesn't do as you claim, I'll come drag you out to my farm and make you pull it yourself."

Both men laughed, thankful for an excuse to turn away from looking at the darkness of grief.

Walking back to go inside the store, Thomas said, "You always talk about how fortunate I am to have my daughters, and you are correct. But you also need to recognize how fortunate you are to have a wife like Mary. My girls think she is an angel. They love it when you two come for a visit."

William stopped and looked at Thomas. "I thank God for her every day. She's the finest woman I know." Tears welled up in his eyes. "And that's why I want to ask you to do something for me."

Thomas frowned. "What?"

"If I do go fight in the war and don't make it back, I want you to take Mary to be your wife."

Thomas staggered back a step as if he'd been punched. "You're talking foolishness. You're not going to war, and you're not going to get killed. That's all there is to that."

William grabbed both of Thomas's arms. "Just promise me you'll do as I ask."

"Okay, I'll make you that promise, but it's a promise I'll never have to fulfill because nothing can kill a redheaded Scot."

When they reentered the store, another group of men had gathered around the stove. As William joined them, he saw Mary and the girls returning from upstairs. He pointed at her and said, "See that woman there? She's now known as the Bear Slayer!"

All the men turned to look at Mary, and though William saw her frowning at him, he had been busting to tell the story ever since they arrived in town. "Yes sir, that woman killed a bear with her bare hands." Stretching his arms over his head, he continued, "The bear was at least eight feet tall! It was the biggest bear I've ever seen. It was reared up on its hind legs and closing in on Mary. She stood there as calm as if she was looking at a field of flowers. 'Go away and leave me alone!' she warned it. But the bear gave her no mind. It gave a mighty roar, its four-inch fangs shining in its red mouth. It took one more step toward Mary, and she swung her hatchet and buried it right between that bear's eyes! For one second the bear looked surprised, then its eyes glazed over, and it fell like a giant oak tree. Even as far away as I was, I felt the earth tremble!"

An old man in the group said, "You expect us to believe that a woman killed a bear without using a gun?"

"Whether you believe the truth or not is up to you, my friend. But don't be trying to call me a liar."

William felt a twinge of nervousness and uncertainty as Mary waded through the group of men to stand beside him. *Lord, what is she going to say?*

All eyes were fastened on Mary. "My husband is not a liar. It happened just as he said it did. And this winter we will sleep under the warmth of a bearskin."

There were mutters of surprise and admiration from the group of men.

Relieved, William smiled broadly.

One man asked with a laugh, "Do you hire her out? I've seen a bear around my place."

Mary looked in the direction of the man's voice. With an icy tone, she said, "You couldn't afford me."

Everyone erupted in raucous laughter and applauded Mary's sharp and quick response.

"Folks," Thomas announced, "it's closing time. We're going to eat supper."

William, Mary, and the children waited until he rejoined them after escorting everyone out and locking up the store.

"Now, then," Thomas said as he approached them, "Let's go to the kitchen and eat. Maybe Abigail made us some dumplings!"

When they walked into the kitchen, they were greeting by the broad grin of Abigail. She was wearing a headscarf, and there was a sheen of sweat on her face. "Miss Mary and Mr. William, it is so good to see you again. Soon as I heard you all was here, I made up some more cornbread. If these young'uns will mind their manners, there should be enough for everybody."

William said, "You know how I love your cornbread. That extra pan might have to be all mine."

"Yes sir, I do remember," Abigail said with an even broader smile. She turned her attention to the girls. "Now you chilluns go wash up."

Emma headed to the back porch as Florence grabbed Mary Beth's hand and took her in tow.

Abigail pointed to the table and said to Thomas, William,

and Mary, "You folks go ahead and sit down. Everything's just about ready. Them's your chairs anyway, Mr. William."

"Best investment I ever made," Thomas said.

William hefted a chair off the floor and inspected it. "They've held up well, haven't they?"

"Don't no one make a better chair than you," Abigail said. "Everyone around knows that."

"Remember," Mary said, with a smile, "I'm the one who canes the bottoms of the chairs."

"And what's a chair good for without a bottom?" Abigail asked.

Just then, the girls filed back in and took their seats at the table.

Abigail set steaming pots of potatoes and beans on the table, then added a plate of ham and a skillet of cornbread.

"This looks delicious!" William said enthusiastically.

Mary Beth reached for the spoon in the beans, but Emma grabbed her hand, "Not yet. Papa says we have to have prayer before we eat."

"William," Thomas said, "will you do us the honor?"

"Certainly." As everyone bowed their heads, William said, "Thank you, Holy Father, for this food we are about to receive and the wonderful home in which it is served.

Amen."

As soon as the *amen* was said, Thomas asked, "So, Mary, did you really kill that bear like William claims?"

"Listen to my best friend," William said, "accusing me of lying. You tell him the story yourself, Mary."

With a twinkle in her eye, Mary said, "Nearly everything William said is true."

Thomas pointed his finger at William. "See? I knew you were spinning a yarn. Which parts weren't true?"

Mary said, "The bear wasn't eight feet tall. It was ten feet tall."

William almost spat out the mouthful of cider he'd just sipped. Pointing at Thomas, he laughed and said, "The look on your face is priceless!"

Mary smiled. "I was just kidding!"

"You two are a pair," Thomas said.

"So did or didn't you really kill a bear?" Florence asked.

"I hit it with a hatchet, more out of fear than anything, and it died. It was a lucky blow."

"Have mercy!" Abigail exclaimed from the stove.

Everyone looked to see Abigail fanning herself with the end of her apron. They all laughed.

"Don't faint, Abigail," Mary said.

"At least not until you bring me some more butter for my cornbread," William added.

Chapter Nine

WILLIAM

"Because I'm ready to go home!" Mary snapped.

William recognized the dark circles under her eyes as the warning sign that her melancholia had returned. It was at times like these, when he was caught between doing the right thing and doing the thing that she wanted him to do, that he didn't know what the best thing to do was. He decided to try reasoning with her. "But we've only been here two days. We always stay with Thomas longer than that."

"I'm sorry, but I just can't be here any longer. I'm feeling smothered by the girls—and I know how awful that sounds! It even sounds awful in my ears. I hate feeling this way, but I can't help it. If you don't take me home, I'm going to end up saying something hurtful to them or to Thomas. Or I'm going to barricade myself in this spare room and not come out, which will make me look like an insane person. And all of that is the last thing in the world I want to do. Just please take me home."

Recognizing his only option, William acquiesced to Mary. "Okay. I'll get the wagon hitched and make excuses for our early departure. You stay up here until I come and get you."

She grabbed his arm, and he winced in pain as her fingernails dug into him. "Don't make me sound like some kind of demented woman when you make your excuses to them—you hear me?"

He leaned in to kiss her on the forehead, intending to reassure her, but she shoved him back.

"Don't! That's not going to fix anything. Men always think that's the answer. Just do like I said, and hurry up about it."

William exited the room with his heart like a heavy stone in his chest. He heard Mary sobbing on the other side of the closed door. It took everything in him not to follow his instincts to go back in and try to comfort her, but he'd learned that there were times that Mary was inconsolable. And now seemed to be one of those times.

He found Thomas in the store and told him that they were going to have to cut their stay short.

Thomas looked at him with sympathy in his eyes. "Is it Mary?"

William, true to his word not to say anything that would paint her in a bad light, simply nodded his head.

Thomas placed his hand on his shoulder. "It's okay. I truly understand. Trust me, this won't last forever. One day, the Mary that you wed, the one I used to know, will show back up. Just give her time."

William swallowed the lump in his throat and left to go hitch the team to the wagon.

After he pulled the wagon around to the front of the store and retrieved Mary, they sat on the seat looking at Thomas, surrounded by the girls, standing on the porch of the store.

"When will we see you again?" Emma asked.

"It'll depend on farm work and when we can get another wagon load of firewood cut," William replied. "It's hard to keep enough firewood cut for ourselves and at the same time accumulate enough extra to sell. If we're lucky, we'll be back around Christmas. If not, we'll see you sometime in January."

Thomas put his arms around his daughters and said, "That sounds lovely. We love you." With a smile, he added, "Mary, keep your eye on that redheaded Scot you're married to. He's nothing but trouble."

William was encouraged to see that she managed a weak smile.

"I'll do my best," Mary replied.

They pulled away from the store, and William focused on navigating through and around the other horse and wagon traffic on the crowded street.

After traveling a few hundred yards, William pulled the horses to a stop because of another wagon that sat in the middle of the street.

The driver of the wagon was talking to someone on horseback who was stopped beside him.

"What are they doing?" Mary asked in an agitated tone.

"I don't know. Probably just visiting. They'll move along

in a minute."

"I don't want to wait!" Suddenly, she stood up and yelled, "Hey, get out of the way. Some of us have places to go!"

"Mary!" William said as he grabbed her arm. "Sit down!"

She jerked away from him. "I'll sit down when they move out of the way."

The two men turned to look at them. The man in the wagon had a gray beard and a patch over one eye, while the man on horseback was much younger and was wearing a leather vest with silver buttons on it. The white handle of a pistol was sticking out of a holster.

The man on horseback said angrily, "We'll move when we get ready."

In his peripheral vision, William could see people stopping to see what the commotion was about.

The man looked directly at William. "What kind of man are you who can't control his woman any better than that. If she was mine, I'd—"

In a flash, William jumped to his feet, his blood boiling. "Hold your tongue! I'll not have you talking about my wife! Just get out of the way, and we'll be on our way. I'm not looking for trouble."

The man kicked his horse in the ribs, causing it to spring forward toward Mary and William.

Just before the man made it to the side of the wagon,

William reached under the seat and took out the seldom-used horsewhip. He swung it in the air and made it crack right in the face of the horse.

The horse reared up and moved sideways at the same time, throwing itself off balance. One second it was reared on its hind legs, and the next it fell over and landed on its side with a loud thud. The rider yelled in agony as the horse landed on his leg. Unfortunately, the frightened horse, in an effort to get away, rolled across the body of the rider. Scrambling to its feet, the horse left the rider motionless on the ground. A trickle of blood could be seen coming from his mouth and running down the side of his face.

William stared in shock as the crowd closed in. "Oh my God," he said under his breath. He looked at Mary and saw astonishment on her face.

"Hurry, let's leave," she said.

"We can't do that," he replied, surprised by her suggestion. "I've got to see how he is."

Walking over to the body, William heard someone say, "I think he's dead."

"What happened?" someone else asked.

"His horse fell on him and crushed him."

"He and that man there were arguing," someone said and pointed at the approaching William.

William saw the bearded man from the other wagon approaching with the aid of a cane.

He and William arrived at the body at the same time. There was no doubt in William's mind that the young man was dead.

The bearded man knelt down and placed his hand on the man's chest. After a few seconds, he stood up and faced William. "You killed him!" In a surprisingly quick move, he struck William on the neck with his cane.

Just as the old man was about to strike William again, a hand reached through the crowd and caught the cane in midswing.

"What's going on here?" the man who caught the cane said.

Everyone turned to see the sheriff, a red-faced man with a potbelly and a handlebar moustache.

The old man pointed at William and said, "He killed my grandson!"

Feeling sick about what had transpired, William said to the man, "I'm so very, very sorry that this happened. I had no intention of harming anyone. It was just an accident."

The sheriff turned William so that they were face-to-face. "I know you, don't I? Aren't you the Woodcutter?"

"That's what some people call me," William answered. "My name is William Thomson. Honestly, Sheriff, I never laid a hand on his grandson. He was trying to start trouble with me and my wife. When he charged my wagon on his horse, I snapped my horsewhip in front of his horse just to make it stop. The horse reared and fell on him. That's what happened. I truly am sorry.

The sheriff looked at the crowd, "Did any of you see what happened?"

"It's just as the Woodcutter said," someone answered. Others offered agreement to the assertion.

"Okay," the sheriff said, "let's break it up. Everybody go on about your business. Somebody go tell the undertaker we've got a warm one for him."

Slowly, the crowd dispersed. Once they departed, the bearded man said to the sheriff, "What are you going to do about this?"

"Not a thing, Amos. I hate it for you, but you know good and well that your grandson was destined for a short life. He was reckless and arrogant and always itching for a fight. What happened today was going to happen sooner or later. It just so happened that today turned out to be sooner." He looked at William. "You and your wife can be on your way. If the judge decides to do anything about it, I'll let you know."

"There's other ways to get satisfaction!" the old man said angrily. Shaking his cane at William, he said, "I'll find you, and when I do, I won't come alone. You're going to pay for this."

"Amos," the Sheriff said, "I know this is an awful thing that just happened, but you need to shut up, or I'll throw you in jail. And if I find out about anything happening to the Woodcutter here, I'll personally slip the noose around your neck at your hanging." He motioned with his head at William.

William took the cue and walked back to the wagon to join Mary.

As they drove through the street, people peered out of store windows and pointed at them.

Once they were out of town, William said, "Mary, what I'm about to say to you may make you mad, but I have to say it. You know I've never told you what to do or say because I've always wanted you to be your own person, but you could have gotten yourself killed back there. It was a rash and foolish thing that you did."

"I wish he had killed me," Mary replied calmly. "Then you would be free from the curse of me. You deserve better than me. Sometimes I don't recognize who I have become, and I fear I will never be who I was. I'm sorry for that, sorry that you have to put up with me. You would be much happier without me."

William pulled the horses to a halt and turned to face her. Laying the reins in his lap, he took her hands in his. In a voice choked with emotion, he said, "Mary Elizabeth, you are the reason I get up every morning, the reason I work our farm, and the reason I pillow my head at night in peace. I love you more than the air that I breathe or the water I drink. I love you more than the ground I plow. If I was to ever lose you, my life would have no purpose. Yes, you are not the person I married, but the person I married is still inside you somewhere—I believe that with all my heart.

And if it's possible for love to bring that person back from the darkness of melancholia, then I promise you that it will happen one day because no one has ever had the amount of love for another person that I have for you."

By the time he finished speaking, tears were streaming from Mary's red-rimmed blue eyes. "I don't know why God blessed me with a man like you," she said. She opened her mouth to say something else but closed it and laid her head on his shoulder.

Chapter Ten

JOHN

On the outskirts of Boston, John laid on his back, looking up at the blanket of stars made brighter by the moonless night, and thought about how these were the same stars his people in Africa looked at. *The same stars but worlds apart.* He wondered if there were any of his people left, or if they had all been taken into slavery by now. It was a thought that used to disturb him, but like a rough rock in a riverbed that has had its sharp edges smoothed over time, he now thought about it wistfully.

Around him, he heard the soft footfalls and low voices of soldiers moving in and settling around his campfire. His fire had become one of the more popular ones as a gathering place, especially for the young soldiers, not because of the warmth it gave but because they wanted to hear John, the oldest black man they knew, tell stories of life in Africa and of his journey to America. John enjoyed regaling them with stories of his royal heritage and the customs of the Asante people, often letting them hold the ragged piece of his kente cloth.

He rose from his blanket and pitched a few more sticks onto his campfire. A flurry of bright orange sparks flew into the night sky, perhaps wishing they could join their cousins, the stars. Instead, like shooting stars, they burned themselves out quickly or fell back to earth, only to be stamped out by a soldier's boot.

He returned to his blanket and sat down cross-legged. The light from the campfire danced in the eyes of the young men gathered around and made their skin shine.

Sixteen-year-old Thaddeus, who was John's tentmate and one of the youngest soldiers in the camp, spoke up. "You've told us about being captured and taken to Elmina castle. What was it like there?"

Reluctantly, John closed his eyes and allowed his memory to travel to the scariest place he'd ever been to, up to that point in his life, not realizing there would be scarier to come. After a few moments, he opened his eyes and said, "They shoved us men into this room. There was so many of us that we couldn't lie down, so we slept standing up. The only light in the room was from small holes at either end of the ceiling or when they opened up the doorways. Everyone did they business right there on the floor, so that we stood in it and stepped in it, like we was animals or something. Sometimes they'd give us water but never anything to eat.

"The women was put in a different room. It wasn't until I ended up on the slave ship that I learned that the white men would take the women out of their room and rape them.

"And anyone who tried to lead a revolt was taken away and never seen again.

"Sometimes we could hear the white people singing in the castle in a room above us. Someone told me they was singing the songs white people sing when they worship their God." Shaking his head, he added, "I just never understood what kind of God it was that made them feel that treating us the way they did was the right thing to do.

"On the side of the castle that faced the ocean was the thing we dreaded the most. It was the door of no return. For once you passed through that door and were lowered into the boats that took you to the big slave ship, you would never set foot in your homeland again."

When John fell silent, no one said a word. The only sound was the crackling, hissing fire and an occasional whippoorwill in the distance.

Finally someone asked, "How long have you been in America?"

"I suspect I been here right at thirty years."

"How old are you?" another one asked.

"I think I'm around sixty years old, give or take a year or two."

A murmur moved through the men.

"You boys think that's old, don't you?" John asked. "I suppose in some ways it is. Time's a funny thing, though. Sometimes it moves as slow as molasses and other times as fast as water pouring over a waterfall. There's been times I wished time would stop and let me take a deeper drink of a moment, but there's been other times that I wished it would hurry and get over with."

"Tell them why you joined the army," Thaddeus prompted him.

John smiled and looked around the circle. "Some of you think an old man like me's got no business fighting in this here war. You don't have to say so. I can tell. I am a free man, though I was a slave. I was given my freedom because of happenstance. I was a slave on a small Confederate ship, with no hope of being free. But one night the crew of the ship went ashore without realizing they left one of the other slaves, Robert Small, unshackled. He released the rest of us, and we sailed the ship out of Charleston harbor and turned it over to the Union. They told us we were brave and granted us our freedom. But I wasn't brave. I was afraid. And I'm still afraid—afraid that if the Union don't win this war, all black people will be slaves. I met Mr. Lincoln a few months ago—"

An audible gasp from his audience caused John to pause.

"You met Lincoln?" someone asked.

"Ain't no way you ever met him," another commented.

"Yes, it's true," John affirmed. "I met him outside his house in Washington. He shook my hand and talked to me like I was someone who had some sense about me, not like I was some kind of ignorant nigger. I told him I didn't know what to do with myself. He explained that preserving this here Union was the only way to guarantee that all slaves could be free. He convinced me that the thing I needed to do was try to protect the freedom of my people by joining this Fifty-Fourth Massachusetts Infantry and fighting in the war."

Someone said, "But will they let us fight? All we do is drill,

drill, drill. Back and forth, back and forth. Load, aim, shoot. I'm getting bored."

"What you say is true," John said. "But maybe that's because they want us to be the best unit in the army. We're the only black unit in the entire army. We have to prove to folks that we know how to fight, that we will fight, and that we can win in battle. I've heard some of the officers say we be leaving out tomorrow and heading south. What awaits us at the end of that journey, none of us knows. But if drilling can get a person ready for battle, then we will sure enough be the most prepared of anyone."

Another soldier spoke up, "Then maybe the army will pay us thirteen dollars a week like the white soldiers, instead of just ten dollars like they offered us. I still don't know why everyone told us we had to refuse to take the ten."

"Because," John said, "accepting less than the white men would mean they could keep treating us like slaves, even though we be free. We have to be free in more than just name. We have to be treated like free men. And look at what our commander, Colonel Shaw, and the other white officers did. They refused to take their wages, too. That is a leader worth fighting for."

There was a brief silence as everyone took in the import of John's words.

Thaddeus said, "I'm ready to get out of this camp before I die from dysentery or chicken pox like many have."

Many voiced their agreement.

"And I'm ready for some fresh food," John added. "This hardtack and salted pork they've been giving us, while it's better than nothing, does get tiresome after a while."

A subdued cheer erupted from the soldiers.

John yawned. "Tomorrow will be a big day for us. We will do something never heard of in America." The volume of his voice increased as he spoke. "Over one thousand black men will march to war, united in our hearts, and though my heart may be filled with fear, I will fight fearlessly, like the Asante warrior that I was born to be!"

An uninhibited cheer exploded from the tense soldiers. They rose and began dispersing to their tents.

John stood up to retrieve his bedroll and headed toward his tent. Just as he got there, Colonel Shaw stepped out of the shadows.

Though surprised, John snapped to attention and gave a reflexive salute.

"At ease, John," Shaw said. "That was an inspiring speech you just gave, perhaps one of the more inspiring ones I've ever heard."

"Thank you, sir. I was just telling the boys what I thought."

"You are highly respected among all the troops, John. You've played a very significant role in shaping this unit by the example you've set for everyone, including some of my officers. I hold you in my debt."

John felt as if the buttons on his shirt would pop off his

chest, he was so filled with pride. "Thank you, sir. May I speak honestly, sir?"

"Certainly."

"You are the finest white man I have ever met. It's an honor to follow you."

John was surprised to see the colonel's eyes fill with tears.

"And you, John," Shaw said, "are one of the finest men I've ever met—black or white." As if the colonel was shutting a door, his emotions shut down, and his demeanor completely changed. "Now, you better turn in for the night. We will have a long day tomorrow."

John watched the colonel disappear into the shadows, then unrolled his bedroll by the fire. The last thought he had before falling asleep was Colonel Shaw's words, "one of the finest men I've ever met—black or white."

*****

The next morning, John and Thaddeus made ready to join the rest of the troops who were marshaling in Boston Common.

Thaddeus said, "I heard there has been an announcement by the Confederate Congress that every captured black soldier will be sold into slavery, and every white officer in command of black troops will be executed if caught."

John slipped his arm through his rifle's shoulder strap. "That won't never happen to me because I won't be captured. I'll die fighting first."

At nine o'clock, the Fifty-Fourth's 1,007 black soldiers and 37 white officers gathered in the Boston Common, prepared to head to the battlefields of the South. Cheering well-wishers, including the antislavery advocates William Lloyd Garrison, Wendell Phillips, and Frederick Douglass, lined Boston's streets.

At the close of the parade, John Andrew, governor of Massachusetts, spoke. "I know not where in all human history to any given thousand men in arms there has been committed a work at once so proud, so precious, so full of hope and glory as the work committed to you."

Colonel Shaw, mounted on his horse, led his men on a march that ended at the docks.

John looked around in confusion, having anticipated a long overland march.

Soon the word spread through the unit that they would be boarding a transport ship bound for Charleston.

And so, I came from Africa and landed in Boston, only to return there to become a soldier. In Boston, I was sold to a slave trader who delivered me to Charleston, and now I head back to Charleston. I wonder where my journey will one day end.

Chapter Eleven

MARY

On Christmas Eve, Mary brushed her hair one more time, excited that the barn dance at Jacob and Nancy Colmers' gave her an excuse to leave her ever-present cap off. While William had always loved her dimples, she had always thought her best feature was her hair. She knew many women were envious of it, which gave her a little guilty pleasure. And while she certainly didn't want to flaunt it, she did enjoy showing it off on occasion.

She was especially happy that her melancholia had stayed away for the past few days, allowing her to breathe easier and feel more like herself.

William came through the door to their bedroom accompanied by a swirl of snow.

"Oh, it's snowing!" Mary said excitedly.

"It's trying to," William answered as he brushed off his coat. "I've got the horses hitched to the wagon if you're—" He finally looked up at her.

Mary felt a surge of emotion as she saw his eyes light up.

"Oh, Mary, you look beautiful. You still take my breath away sometimes. I could just sit and look at you all day and never grow weary of it."

Mary felt her face blushing. She walked deliberately

toward him and said, "And you, you redheaded Scotsman, still make my heart skip a beat." She put her hands on the side of his face, pulled him close, and kissed him. Her mind flashed through scenes of their lovemaking through the years, and she felt like there was a hot coal in her belly. *If it could just be like this all the time.*

Reluctantly, she pulled her mouth away from his. She saw the color in his cheeks and desire in his eyes.

He said, "Mary Elizabeth Thomson, one more kiss like that and we won't be making it to the barn dance. Which would be fine with me, but I know you've been looking forward to it. And to showing off your hair."

"We'll finish this when we get home," she said in a sultry voice. "But you're right—I don't want to miss a chance to show off a little. Let me get my coat, and I'll be ready to leave."

When they headed toward the Colmerses', Mary wrapped a scarf around her face to protect it against the cold wind and stinging snow. The bearskin that William had thrown across their laps helped hold their body heat in.

The quarter moon shed enough light that there was no need to hang a lantern on the wagon. As they got close to their destination, Mary could see several wagons in front of them and others approaching from the opposite direction.

Once they arrived, they could see lighted torches that lit the way to the barn. The other women had their faces wrapped in a manner similar to Mary's, so it would have been impossible to recognize any of them if their husbands hadn't been walking with them. As it was, Mary greeted several of them with a muffled "Hello" and a nod, while William called several of the men by name and tipped his hat to the women accompanying them.

Walking through the doorway of the barn, Mary was reminded of the fairy tales written by Hans Christian Andersen she used to read as a child. The lanterns that were hanging everywhere had chased away the darkness of night. Music and laughter filled the air like fall leaves swept up in dust devils. Everyone who only moments before had been semi-mummified, had now thrown off their heavy coats and scarves, revealing smiling faces and rosy cheeks. Two large stoves at either end of the barn were doing their best to keep the chill at bay.

"Oh, William!" Mary exclaimed, listening carefully. "It's the Virginia reel."

Without another word, they took their place with the other couples. William's dancing skills had been a pleasant surprise to Mary when they were first getting to know each other. She had never seen a man who was so light on his feet. And when he performed one of his native Scottish dances, his feet would move so fast they were a blur. So now, during every barn dance they attended, there was always a call for him to showcase his skills. Mary had seen the looks of envy on the other women's faces because their husbands were best known for stepping on their partners' feet when they danced.

When the song ended to joyous applause, Mary made her way to a clutch of women, while William moved to another corner to join a group of men.

"Mary," one of the women said excitedly, "you are going to do a reading for us, aren't you?"

Mary smiled. She couldn't remember exactly when this tradition began, and even though she wasn't always comfortable with all the attention it brought her, she was proud of the talent she had for reading in public. Anytime there was an event like this Christmas party, another barn dance, or shucking bee, the women expected her to read for them.

Reaching inside a pocket of her dress, she withdrew the Tennyson book and said, "I've lately been captivated by this poem by Tennyson. I certainly won't read it all, but I marked this passage to read for you tonight." She opened the book, found the passage she was looking for, and began reading:

My love has talk'd with rocks and trees;
He finds on misty mountain-ground
His own vast shadow glory-crown'd;
He sees himself in all he sees.

Two partners of a married life—
I look'd on these and thought of thee
In vastness and in mystery,
And of my spirit as of a wife.

These two—they dwelt with eye on eye,
Their hearts of old have beat in tune,
Their meetings made December June

Their every parting was to die.

Their love has never past away;
The days she never can forget
Are earnest that he loves her yet,
Whate'er the faithless people say.

Her life is lone, he sits apart,
He loves her yet, she will not weep,
Tho' rapt in matters dark and deep
He seems to slight her simple heart.

He thrids the labyrinth of the mind,
He reads the secret of the star,
He seems so near and yet so far,
He looks so cold: she thinks him kind.

She keeps the gift of years before
A wither'd violet is her bliss
She knows not what his greatness is,
For that, for all, she loves him more.

For him she plays, to him she sings
Of early faith and plighted vows;
She knows but matters of the house,
And he, he knows a thousand things.

Her faith is fixt and cannot move,
She darkly feels him great and wise,
She dwells on him with faithful eyes,
'I cannot understand: I love.'

When she finished, and before anyone could react, a gunshot rang out inside the barn. Mary jumped, and several of the women screamed.

A man's voice yelled out, "I'm looking for the Woodcutter!"

There were frightened shouts, intermingled with the women's cries, as people began running in random directions until only one person was left standing in the middle of the barn floor. An old man with a gray beard leaned heavily on his cane. In his other hand, held aloft over his head, was a Colt revolver. A wisp of smoke lingered around the end of the barrel like low-hanging clouds on a mountain peak.

"I'm looking for the Woodcutter!" the old man repeated his demand. "He killed my grandson, and I'm going to kill him!" He turned in a circle while brandishing the Colt.

Peering back at him, frightened faces were made ghoulish by the lantern light that found them partially hidden in the shadows. An eerie silence fell, broken only by the crackling fires in the stoves.

Mary recognized the man and turned her head to try to spy William.

Just then, Jacob stepped out of the shadows and took a step toward the intruder. "We have all gathered here as friends on this Christmas Eve. Why would you burst in here and spoil this peaceful moment? Come join me, and we'll have a drink together. I'm sure there's—"

"Stop right there, or I'll shoot!" the man cried as he leveled his pistol at Jacob.

More screams of alarm erupted from the crowd that was held hostage.

"I've got no quarrel with any man, save one," the man said. "And that's the Woodcutter. I'll not leave here until I get satisfaction."

There was movement in the crowd, and William stepped forward.

Mary clapped her hand over her mouth to keep from screaming. A ribbon of fear ran down her neck and back like a squirrel in a tree.

"I am the one known as the Woodcutter," William said. "My name is William Thomson. I am very sorry about what happened to your grandson, but I stand here with a clear conscience with regard to what happened. It was he who was the provocateur. I was only protecting what was mine when he died. The sheriff himself told you that your grandson was destined for a bitter end."

The old man pointed his pistol at William, but the weight of the Colt began taking a toll, causing the end of the barrel to waver. "You're a bald-faced liar! My grandson was a good boy."

It was then that Mary saw the weight of grief on the old man's heart as his eyes grew red and full of tears.

His voice broke as he said, "He was all I had left in the

world. And you took him from me." He let loose his hold
on his cane, and it clattered to the barn floor. Using both
hands, he gripped the pistol and pulled the hammer back.
"You have to pay for what you've done."

Suddenly, Mary rushed forward and placed herself between
the man and William. With a heart full of sympathy, she
said to the man, "I know how it feels to lose what you love,
and so does my husband. There is a hill behind our house,
on top of which are buried four tiny infants. None of whom
saw their first birthday." Her vision blurred as tears poured
down her cheeks. "I would do anything in the world to
bring them back, but nothing will accomplish that. And
there is nothing that will bring your grandson back, even
killing my husband."

The top of the old man's gray beard was dark from the stain
of his bitter tears. He motioned with the gun for Mary to
get out of the way. "Move out of the way. My quarrel's not
with you. 'An eye for an eye,' the Good Book says."

Mary swiped at her tears with her hand. She walked
quickly toward the man, stopping when the end of the gun
barrel touched her chest. "If you must kill my husband,
then you must do me the favor of killing me, too, for if I
lose one more thing in my life, especially the one most dear
to me, I could not bear to live. So go ahead and do what
you came to do. I'm prepared to leave this life along with
my husband and see my sweet babies in heaven."

The icy resolve that had brought the old man all the way
from Chattanooga was no match for the heat of Mary's
fervor. He slowly lowered the pistol and let it drop to the

floor. Several men rushed forward and grabbed him. When they started to drag him out of the barn, Mary said, "Stop!" She reached her hand toward William, who stepped up and took hold of it. "It's Christmas Eve," Mary said. "It's a night to be grateful and forgiving."

"I agree," William said. "How heartless it would be of us if we sent this poor man out into the cold and dark of night. For whatever brought him here is of no consequence now. He is someone who is in need of the love and fellowship of his fellow man."

Mary's heart swelled with emotion at William's eloquent words. She stuck her hand out toward the man. "My name is Mary."

With a trembling hand, he grasped Mary's. He tried to speak but had to clear his throat in order to get anything out of it. "My name is Amos."

"Come," Mary said, "let's get you something to eat and drink." She and William took each of Amos's elbows and guided him toward the food and drink.

There was a smattering of applause from those in the barn at the charitable gesture of Mary and William.

"Musicians!" Jacob said loudly. "Play us a tune! Let's dance and be joyful!"

Later that night, as the midnight hour approached, Jacob announced, "It is our tradition to end this evening with everyone joining in and singing Christmas carols."

The crowd all pulled together in a tight circle and began singing as Jacob led them.

Silent night. Holy night.

All is calm. All is bright.

Round yon virgin mother and child

Holy infant so tender and mild

Sleep in heavenly peace

Sleep in heavenly peace.

Afterward, Mary and William bid everyone a fond adieu and headed home.

"This was a night to remember," Mary said.

"Aye, that is was," William agreed.

"I'm so glad we have such good neighbors. We all look out for each other."

"It was a brave and foolish thing you did with that man, Mary. You could have easily been killed. Then what would have become of me?"

"You would be married again within a month," Mary said with a laugh.

"Hush! Don't talk such foolishness. I'm serious. You're all I have in the world."

Mary scooted closer to him. "And you're all I have, too."

After a bit of silence, she said, "What was all the gossip among the men tonight?" Mary asked.

William paused a bit before answering. "There was lots of talk of the war."

"Blast the war! I'm tired of hearing of it and ready for it to be over."

"Mary," William said somberly, "like it or not, one day this war will come to our house, and difficult choices will have to be made."

Chapter Twelve

MARY

A week later, on New Year's Eve, Mary and William gathered around the dining table at Thomas's, along with his daughters. Soft amber light from lamps and the crackling fireplace caused everything in the room to glow. The aroma of cooked ham, fresh bread, and sweet pies filled the air.

"What a marvelous week it has been," Thomas said. "Hasn't it, girls?"

"Oh, yes!" Florence said.

"It's been wonderful!" Emma agreed.

"I've had fun," Mary Beth said.

"It's been perfect for me and Mary, too," William said, his face beaming.

Mary said, "I'm so glad you all have enjoyed your Christmas presents."

Florence stood up and turned around slowly, holding her dark blue gingham dress out on both sides. "I love my dress. It's beautiful, and it fits perfectly."

"I can tell you love it," Thomas said, smiling. "You've worn it every day since Christmas."

Everyone laughed.

"Laugh if you want to," Florence said, "I don't care. I may never wear anything else."

Emma stroked the two carved wooden statues standing beside her plate. "And I love the two horses you carved for me, Mr. Thomson."

"I admire those, too," Thomas added. "I could probably sell some of those in the store if you wanted to make some more."

William smiled. "Making something like that is pretty time-consuming. I think I'll stick to making chairs."

"And what about you?" Mary said to Mary Beth.

Mary Beth raised her two hands that had been hidden under the table. In each one was a corn-shuck doll. "I call this one William and this one Mary. I let them sleep with me."

"Then that's the best thank-you of all," Mary said as she kissed her on the cheek.

Just then, Abigail set a big platter of ham in front of Thomas. "And I am much obliged for the new shoes you gave me."

"You're welcome, Abigail," Mary said.

Abigail returned to the stove and retrieved a pot with sweet potatoes in it, a skillet of cornbread, and a pot of crowder peas.

Thomas stood up and said, "There is a saying that whatever you are doing on New Year's Eve you will be doing all through the year. If true, that is certainly my wish, that is, that we would share meals with you two throughout the next year. Your friendship means more to us as each year passes. Thank you for spending Christmas and this week with us." He picked up his glass of wine. "A toast to Mary and William."

All three girls lifted their glasses of milk to their mouths. Mary Beth left a white moustache on her upper lip as proof that she did indeed drink her milk.

When Thomas sat down, Mary nudged William with her knee.

He looked at her, then abruptly stood. "And our visits with you are like nectar to a bee. Listening to a house filled with the sound of children playing is something we—" He stopped in midsentence and looked at Thomas, then at Mary.

Mary saw his look of dismay that, once again, he'd fumbled himself into a way of reminding her that they'd never have children of their own. On the one hand, it greatly irritated her, and perhaps in a different setting she would have let him know that, but on the other hand, she appreciated the fact that he stopped himself when he realized where his words were taking him.

Thomas jumped in. "Well, let's be clear that sometimes the sound around here is yelling, fighting, and arguing. Living in a household full of women is nothing to be envied. As a matter of fact, some prayers on my behalf would be appreciated."

Thankful for their friend's rescue from an awkward moment, Mary and William laughed.

*****

Sometime after midnight that night, Mary, unable to sleep, slipped out of bed, wrapped a heavy shawl around her shoulders, and headed to the kitchen. Just as she walked through the doorway, she stopped short at the sight of Thomas sitting in a chair to one side of the fireplace.

Thomas turned at the sound of footsteps. "Mary?"

"I'm sorry," she said. "I didn't mean to disturb you. I just couldn't sleep and thought I'd come sit by the fire for a while."

Thomas stood. "You're not disturbing me at all. You're not the only one having difficulty sleeping. Come join me." He retrieved a chair and sat it across from his.

Mary felt a bit uncomfortable about being seen in her gown and nightcap by a man other than William, but she also felt a little excitement about doing something a bit risqué. She'd always thought Thomas to be a handsome man with a gentle heart, and there had been times she was envious of Anna. She loosened her grip on her shawl, letting it drop just past the edges of her shoulders, and sat down in the offered chair. "So what's keeping you awake tonight?" she asked.

"Probably eating too much of Abigail's cooking," he answered while patting his stomach with both hands.

"Then that must be what's keeping me awake, too. It was a delicious meal."

"I just hope she doesn't run off."

"Run off?"

"Yes, like a runaway. Lots of coloreds are doing it."

Mary let his comment settle in. "Would you buy another one if she did?"

"I don't think I would have a choice."

"There's always a choice, Thomas. You could hire someone to help. I know it's a heated topic to bring up, but it has never seemed right to me for one person to own another." She watched him raise one eyebrow.

"Does that mean you're a Northern sympathizer?" he asked.

Trying not to feel defensive, she replied, "William says we're not, even though he agrees with me about owning slaves. But he's most opposed to the federal government trying to dictate to people how they should live their lives. His family lived in oppression under kings for generations. They migrated to America to live free lives, he always says. Have you ever thought about giving Abigail her freedom if she would promise to stay for a wage?"

"Give her her freedom? She would leave before nightfall if I did that."

"I don't know," Mary said. "She loves your daughters and

would do anything for them. I don't think she would run out on them."

Thomas gave no reply but stared into the fire.

Mary watched the flickering firelight highlight first one aspect of his facial features, then another—his full lips, the strong jawline, his low forehead, and his dark eyes. *Yes, he is a handsome man.* She decided to release her conscience's hold on her thoughts and wondered what it would be like to lie in bed with him. Would he be as good a lover as William? Perhaps better? When she imagined being with him, she crossed first one leg, then the other. *Silly woman, you would never do such a thing.* But it was fun to fantasize about it. In an effort to put her mind somewhere else, she said, "I find fire to be quite hypnotic. It always makes me sleepy. The multicolored flames rising and falling over the red coals seem to be caressing the wood instead of devouring it."

Thomas said, "Anna used to love looking at the fire."

And that was all it took to completely wash aside any untoward thoughts Mary was having about him—the memory of her friend, Anna.

He continued, "There were many nights I would find her sitting in that very chair you're sitting in. You know what she would say when I asked her why she couldn't sleep?"

"No, what?"

"She would say she couldn't believe how lucky she was. She always thought she was the luckiest woman in the world and that she didn't deserve all the good that was in her life." Thomas inhaled slowly and exhaled loudly. "I guess even the luckiest people run out of luck. Funny thing is, I used to think I was the luckiest person in the world. To have Anna and Florence and Emma made for a perfect life. I know most men would say they wanted sons, and I guess I did a little during the first pregnancy, but I wouldn't trade any one of my daughters for ten sons. Where would I be now if I didn't have these amazing girls? I would be totally lost."

Mary had held her breath through Thomas's musings, for she had never heard him speak so openly about the pain of loss. She noticed a touch of gray hair at his temples, a follicle betrayal of the strain of his life. It made her wonder which of her features other people had noticed had changed because of her own grief.

He said, "Can I ask you something?"

A flutter of concern touched the back of her mind at not just his question but at his earnest demeanor when asking it. "Certainly you can."

He stared at her for a moment, then leaned forward and rested his arms on his knees.

Mary felt her heart begin to start racing.

Thomas said, "I have no right to ask you this, but I'm going to ask it anyway. If anything ever happens to me, will you and William take my daughters to raise as your own?"

So shocked was she by his question, Mary let go of her

shawl without realizing it, letting it cascade off her shoulders and onto the arms of her chair. Her head felt like it was exploding with hundreds of thoughts from every direction, so much so that she found it impossible to find an answer to give him.

"Did you hear what I said?" Thomas asked.

She swallowed hard. "Oh, Thomas, I'm sorry. Yes, yes, I did. I'm just shocked by your question. Why would you ask such a thing? Are you ill?"

"It's nothing like that," he assured her. "But you and I both know these are perilous times we are living in, where anything is possible. Answer me—will you take my daughters?"

All of the protests that sat upon the tip of her tongue were no match for her overall feeling that she needed to help her friend feel at ease, so she said, "You have nothing to worry about. Thomas and I will take care of them."

He sat back in his chair and gave her a smile of relief. "Then I can return to my bed and rest easy."

And I will pray earnestly every night that nothing ever happens to you.

Chapter Thirteen

MARY

Even though she had woolen mittens on her hands, Mary held her hands to her mouth and blew her warm breath through the fibers, trying to thaw her numb fingertips as wind slipped between the boards of the woodworking shed. After clapping her hands together a couple of times, she picked up the wooden maul and hammered together the stiles and rails of a chair. Outside the shed, she heard the echo of William's hammer blows as he used a froe and maul, riving boards to make shingles for the house, barn, and shed.

She looked at the four other chairs she'd put together, all looking brand new with the light-blond color of unaged hickory. Scattered around them on the floor were curly wood shavings and sawdust, a testament to the labor-intensive job of creating a chair from a block of wood.

Realizing that her hands were too cold and the strips of bark too stiff for her to weave a chair bottom, she decided to step outside and check on William. When she opened the door, a gust of wind nearly jerked it out of her hand.

William paused his work when he saw her walking toward him. He said, "And I thought the weather might warm a bit once February got here."

"It is bitter cold," Mary said. "Why don't I get us some hot coffee?"

"You go ahead. I'll be fine. I'm working up a pretty good steam here with this maul. How are the chairs looking?"

"Four are finished, except for caning the bottoms."

"Four? You're going to get better at making them than me." He leaned in closer while keeping his eyes on her face. "You're freezing, aren't you? It's too cold for you to be out here. Maybe we should look into one of those wood-burning stoves to put in the shed. You go on inside the house and warm up."

At the hint in William's tone of feeling sorry for her, Mary stood up straighter. "I'll be fine." She moved to the shingles scattered on the ground and bent over. "I'll stack these. Moving around will warm me up."

"Dear Lord in heaven, I hope you'll be prepared for this hardheaded woman when she arrives there. No doubt she will test your patience, for she always insists on doing things her way."

Mary swatted him on the backside with one of the shingles.

He howled.

"And Lord," she said, "this one will be trying to tell you how to run heaven, if you let him, for he always thinks his way is the best way."

The sound of hurried hoofbeats drew their attention to the lane leading from their house to the main road. Six soldiers in gray uniforms turned into the lane and raced toward the house. "Back there," one of them said loudly as he pointed at Mary and William.

One of the horses reared and pawed the air as the soldiers jerked hard on their reins and turned toward the back of the house. They came to a stop ten feet from the couple, with their horses' nostrils flared and sides heaving from an apparently strenuous run. In spite of the cold temperature, there was a line of frothy sweat across the horses' chests.

"Are you the Woodcutter?" one of the soldiers asked.

"I am William Thomson. Some call me the Woodcutter."

"My name is Sergeant Terrance. We've been told you have two Percheron horses. Where are they?"

William took a step toward the speaker. "What business is it of yours?"

"We need horses to haul our cannon. The horses we had pulling the cannon have died. We're in a hurry. We're supposed to be in North Carolina in two days." The sergeant spoke to his men. "You two go look in the barn."

The two obeyed immediately and spurred their horses toward the barn.

William jumped in front of the horses and grabbed their bits. "Hold on here! What are you doing?"

"We're taking your horses for the army," the sergeant answered.

Without thinking, Mary stepped forward and said, "You can't do that!"

"We can, and we will. What's the matter with you two?" Looking at William, he asked, "Why aren't you fighting for our glorious cause? Are you Quakers?"

William thrust his chin forward. "No, we're not Quakers; I've just had no reason to join the war. I live a peaceable life and mind my own business. You have no right to take our horses. We depend on them to make our livelihood."

"And we need them to help us defend ourselves against the Northern aggression. If we don't, we'll have the boot of Washington on our necks forever. I don't have time to argue with you. Under the articles of war, I have the right to requisition your horses or anything else I might need."

"I wouldn't mind requisitioning her," suggested one of the men; he had a black powder burn on the side of his face.

Mary felt her blood run cold.

Two of the other men laughed at their comrade's comment.

William let go of the horses' bits and walked toward the leering man. To the sergeant, he said, "Is this the kind of talk you allow from your men? Somebody needs to teach them some manners."

The man interested in Mary pulled his pistol out of its holster, aimed it at William, and cocked the hammer.

Mary screamed.

"Wainwright!" the sergeant barked. "Put your gun away. We don't have time for that." To the two who had started for the barn, he said, "Check the barn like I told you, and be quick about it."

William looked at the one called Wainwright, then at the men headed for the barn. He took a step in one direction, then the other.

"I see you have some chickens," the sergeant commented. "We need some of those, too. My men haven't eaten in three days. I'll let you choose some for us that aren't laying eggs. And give us one of your hams from the smokehouse."

Mary started toward the chicken coop, eager to give the desperate men what they wanted and have them gone.

"Mary, stop!" William said harshly. He stepped up to the horse of the sergeant. "This is America, the land of the free, where no government is to treat its citizens with such disregard for their rights. This is my land, my horses, my chickens, and my meat. If you'd come here as a stranger asking for help, I would have gladly given you what you needed. But to come in here like some agent of the king and take what's rightfully mine—I'll not have it. No sir, I won't have—"

Before William could finish his sentence, the sergeant whipped out his pistol and struck William on the side of the head.

William crumpled to the ground as Mary screamed his name and rushed to his side. By the time she reached him, blood was oozing from the side of his head. "What have you done?" she yelled at the sergeant.

Ignoring her, the sergeant said to his men, "We've already

spent more time here than we should have. Hurry up with those Percherons. Find us a ham, and catch some chickens."

Mary was barely aware of the swirl of activity around her as she cradled William's head in her lap. She kissed his forehead and his closed eyes. "Speak to me, William," she whispered. "You can't be dead. You can't."

Suddenly, she was aware of footsteps coming toward her.

"I am to have me some of this before we leave." It was the voice of the lecher, Wainwright.

Mary looked furtively around her and spied the froe lying on the ground within arm's reach.

Just as the man grabbed her left arm, she seized the froe with her right hand. As he jerked her up off the ground, she swung the froe at his head. Caught off guard, the man only had time to lean his head to one side in an attempt to avoid being struck. The move prevented Mary from striking a mortal blow to his head but didn't keep the froe from striking his ear and slicing it off.

The man howled in pain as he let go of Mary and clutched the side of his head. Blood leaked between his fingers and ran down his hand. "I'll kill you!" he yelled at Mary. He lunged for her just as a lasso dropped over his head and around his chest. Suddenly, he was jerked onto his back.

"You had your chance," the sergeant said, "and you were bettered by a woman. Now get on your horse. We're ready to leave."

The man struggled to his feet and gave Mary a malevolent stare. "You've not seen the last of me."

She watched in shocked horror as the company of men headed out their lane with her and William's beloved Percherons in tow.

Turning her attention to William, she put her hand on his chest and felt relief at finding his heart was still beating. *Yes!* She kissed him on the lips and said, "You are not going to die on me, you hear? You're not going to leave me."

William's eyes remained closed, and he gave no indication he heard her.

She moved his arms above his head, and, grabbing his wrists, began dragging him toward the house. By the time she made it into their bedroom, she was panting heavily, and her red face was covered in sweat. But she hadn't thought about the difficulty of lifting up and onto their bed.

"I'll make you a bed on the floor until you wake up and can get in bed by yourself," she said to her inert husband. She laid a quilt on the floor, rolled him onto it, and then covered him with another one.

She then turned her attention to his wound. She rotated his head toward the lamp and pulled back some of his hair. She winced at the sight of the deep, red gash staring back at her. Though it was still oozing blood, she could tell that it had started to clot.

She raced to the kitchen and returned with a basin of water, soap, a clean cloth, and a small tin containing dried leaves from a shepherd's purse plant and sheep sorrel leaves. After she set her items on the floor beside William, she took the lamp off the fireplace mantel and set it by his head. With a gentle hand, she cleaned his wound and hair, all the while talking in low tones to him.

Opening the tin, she sprinkled some of the leaves on the wound. "This will stop the bleeding and help with infection," she explained to him. "But I'm going to have to sew it shut. It's too deep and wide to leave open like it is."

She found her sewing basket and pulled out a needle with a trail of bright blue thread hanging from its eye. Kneeling beside William, she said, "I hope blue is okay with you. And even if it's not, I don't care, for blue it's going to be."

She tied a knot in the end of the thread and leaned in closer. *Lord, Jesus, guide my hands.* She pinched the wound closed, pushed the needle through, and pulled the thread tight. All along the length of the wound, she made tight stitches as she would if she had been sewing a dress.

When she finished, all the feelings and tension she had ignored while taking care of William suddenly fell on her shoulders with a force that drove her flat on the floor beside him. Laying her arm across his chest, she fell asleep.

Chapter Fourteen

MARY

It was on a warm day in May that Mary used a tapered, narrow hoe to loosen the soil around a stump she and William had yet to clear from the field beside the Chickamauga. Off to her left, she heard the familiar sound of the chuck-a-luck as William used it to plant corn seed around another stump she'd finished with. Even though it had been months since his near-mortal blow from the soldier, she still thanked God daily for not taking him from her and for helping him survive without any lingering effects.

She was about to stop hoeing and ask William him if he wanted some water when a movement on the backside of the stump she was working around caught her eye. She stood perfectly still as the red, forked tongue of a snake tested the air, and then its broad, diamond-shaped head eased into view.

Though her feet told her to run, Mary stood her ground and slowly raised her hoe above her head. The snake slowly slithered into the open, keeping its copper-and-black patterned body wrapped around the base of the stump. *My God, it's as thick as my forearm!* She waited for the snake to separate itself from the stump so that she could have an unobstructed chance at chopping its head off.

Just then, William tapped her on the back of her shoulder. "Are you thirsty?"

Mary jumped and screamed.

William flinched and hollered, "What? What's wrong?"

Mary saw the snake quickly retreating, then she turned on William. "What do you think you're doing, sneaking up on someone like that? You scared me to death!"

"I wasn't sneaking up. I even spoke your name before I came up on you. Look at you—you're as white as a sheet."

Though her heart was still galloping like a runaway horse, Mary began to see what had happened. She shaved off the edge from her tone of voice and said, "What you didn't know is that at the very moment you touched my shoulder, I was about to swing my hoe and chop off the head of copperhead." As she explained things, she saw the humor in the scene and chuckled. "I guess I scared you pretty badly, too."

"Scared me? You nearly made my heart stop beating. Lay your hoe down, and let's go down to the creek and get a drink of water."

"That sounds like a good idea." She propped the handle of her hoe against the stump so that she could find it among the other stumps when she returned.

William grabbed his rifle as they headed to the creek. Mary had noticed that ever since the Percherons were stolen, he rarely went anywhere without it being close by his side. It was just another telling sign of the increased level of tension felt by everyone they knew. As more and more reports came in of battles where tens of thousands of men

were killed, there was a sense among the people in and
around Chattanooga that a noose was slowly tightening
around their necks. Mary still shuddered when she thought
about the battle fought at the western end of Tennessee,
where twenty-three thousand men lost their lives at a place
called Shiloh.

When she and William reached the banks of the
Chickamauga, she knelt down and cupped water to her
mouth. The cool water felt good on her hands, which were
hot from the hoeing she'd been doing. She glanced at
William and saw that he was still standing, looking up and
down the creek and scanning the dense undergrowth lining
its banks. He held the barrel of the rifle in his left hand
while his right hand gripped the stock just behind the
trigger guard, giving the appearance that he was ready to
aim and fire at the first sign of danger.

Mary stood up and held out her hand. "Let me hold that
while you get a drink."

Without a word, William handed her the rifle and knelt
down to slake his thirst.

This was another change in him since losing the
Percherons. As soon as he had been able to, William started
teaching her to use the rifle. To both her and his surprise,
she proved to be quite a good shot, so good that now he
trusted her to do as good a job of keeping guard on things
as if he were doing it.

She listened to William slurping water but kept her eyes
peeled just as he had done. As she looked upstream, she

noticed that the normally clear water was turning brown. Pointing in that direction, she said, "Look."

William stood up beside her. "Somebody's crossed upstream from us," he said. "Let's see how long it takes the water to clear."

After fifteen minutes, he said in a low tone, "That must be a full company of soldiers. Maybe even with artillery. See? The water hasn't cleared up yet."

"Whose army is it?" Mary whispered.

"No way of knowing. We need to get back to the farm because no matter whose it is, they'll take what they want if we're not there to prevent them."

As he took a step toward home, Mary, remembering their last such encounter, put her hand on his arm to stop him.

William stopped and looked back at her. "What?"

In his face she saw the fierce, unflinching bravery that she'd always loved him for. She swallowed her apprehension and said, "I'm right behind you."

As they drew close to their house, Mary conjured up dozens of frightening scenarios they could find when they got there. But when the house came in sight, some of her scenarios evaporated, for she could see no signs of men or horses or wagons present.

It is not until they walked to the area between the barn and the house that fear and reality met. She and William stopped and stared in disbelief.

To their left, the door of the smokehouse hung open on one hinge, like someone giving a sideways yawn. The door to the barn also stood ajar.

Mary and William walked in silence, like disembodied spirits, William toward the smokehouse and Mary toward the barn, to see what had become of their life-sustaining possessions.

The first thing that Mary noticed was that there was none of the constant clucking the chickens made as they scratched for food in and around the stalls. The milk cow was gone. The two young pigs they were going to turn loose and let fatten up over the course of the summer were gone, too.

William came inside and said in a flat tone of voice, "The smokehouse is completely empty—nothing left at all."

Mary held all this at arm's length, not willing to contemplate how they would survive. She walked back out into the sunshine, but felt no warmth from it; rather, she felt like it was mocking her misfortune.

She suddenly remembered her garden plot and hurried to the south side of the house, only to have her feet turn to lead when she arrived—the garden had been decimated. Anger boiled up inside her as she walked onto the soft ground where boot and horse prints were scattered about. In her mind's eye, she saw the soldiers ripping and uprooting everything. It was as if her garden had been raped.

Finally, overwhelmed with feelings, she felt her knees buckle, and she fell on her face. She pounded the dirt with her fists. Gripping two handfuls of dirt, she rolled onto her back and cried out, "How many times, O Lord, will you take from me? Is there no end to my curse?"

*****

Later, after William said he was going to go into the woods to see if perhaps some of the animals escaped, Mary climbed the Bitter Hill. Never before had she felt so much melancholy as she did at that moment. The recent raid on their farm had left her feeling the same as when the soldier tried to rape her—powerless and violated. *There is nothing that can't be taken from you. So what are William and I working for? Certainly not for our children. What's the point in what we're doing? It's all senseless.*

As she reached the crest of the hill, the wind suddenly picked up, and dark clouds boiled overhead. She looked down at the pistol that hung heavily in her dirt-covered hand and remembered how she'd initially protested William's insistence that she learn to use it and always have it with her.

Stroking the dark metal barrel, she spoke aloud, "Guns can prevent things from happening, but they can also put an end to things."

She walked forward and went to her knees in front of the grave markers. "My dear babies, hope is gone. All that's left is for me to join you."

She laid down across the graves, pulled the hammer back on the pistol, and put the end of the barrel to the side of her head. She looked up at the massive chestnut tree as it swayed in the strong wind. Some of the leaves were stripped from the branches and twigs and flew through the air like sparrows. "What would you say to me?" she said aloud to the towering tree. "You're much older than I and have seen much more than I have. What's the sense in life?"

The tree shook its limbs and leaned to one side, then straightened itself. Rolling thunder from another hollow approached Mary until it burst above the chestnut tree. From the opposite direction, a brilliant bolt of lightning struck the side of the tree. A severed limb hit the ground twenty feet from Mary, the cauterized end sending up a trail of smoke. She winced as a deafening crash of thunder reverberated across the hilltop.

Anger suddenly surged through her. She stood up, pointed the pistol toward the sky, and with her other hand struck her chest. "If you want me dead, strike me, not this tree!" Dropping the pistol to the ground, she grabbed the front of her dress with both hands and ripped it open. "Please, I'm begging you, strike me! Take me away from this sorrow-filled world!"

As if in reply to her request, the wind increased and tore at her dress. The chestnut tree bent so low that its leaves fluttered against Mary's face. She heard its limbs cracking and expected to see them ripped from the trunk and scattered across the hillside, but suddenly, the wind stopped, and the tree righted itself. Like a pregnant pause before an orator delivers his final point, an eerie silence filled the air. Without warning, Mother Nature ripped open the sky and hurled hailstones at Mary.

Crying out in pain from the icy shards that struck her, Mary looked around for a place of cover. Finally, she stepped to the trunk of the chestnut and hugged it, pressing the side of her face against it. Even though she could hear the hailstones shredding the leaves, the thick foliage prevented most of them from striking her. The hailstorm lasted for only a few minutes and stopped as suddenly as it started. In its place, the sun broke through the clouds, sending streaking beams through the damaged foliage of the tree.

Mary released her hold on the tree and squinted up at the sun shimmering off the leaves. She felt as if something fundamental had shifted inside her. *You great big, beautiful tree!*

A noise from below the hill caught her attention, and she recognized that heavy footsteps were growing closer.

"Mary!" she heard William call out. "Are you there?"

"Yes, William, I'm here," she called back. "And I'm all right."

William appeared, riding bareback on one of their mules. He jumped off and ran to her. "Are you sure you're all right? I saw the lightning strike your tree. And then the hailstorm . . . I was afraid . . . I wasn't sure . . ."

Mary put her arms around his neck. "I'm fine. As a matter of fact, I'm better than ever."

"But after all that we lost today, how can you say that?"

She grabbed his hands. "The most amazing thing has

happened, William. When I came up here today, I was at the end of my rope. I felt there was no reason to keep living."

"Mary Elizabeth, don't talk like that. There's always—"

Mary put her finger on his lips. "Just listen to me. I want you to look up at this big old chestnut tree. How old do you think it is?"

Looking up, he said, "Probably at least one hundred years."

"I agree. Which means it was here during the Revolution and when the Indians were driven from here. Think of all the pain and suffering it has witnessed, enough for two or three lifetimes. And how many storms has it endured? Today, this tree talked to me. I know you're thinking I've lost my mind, but I haven't. It showed me how it has survived through all the tragedies."

"How so, Mary?"

"You bend, but don't break. That wind a moment ago was strong enough to uproot this tree, but it didn't because the tree allowed itself to give in a bit, to bend, and let the wind pass over it. Then, after the storm passed, it sprang right back—straight and tall. It also showed me that it understands its reason for living is not for itself but so it can help others. This tree saved my life. It let the lightning hit it instead of me, and it let the hail shred its leaves rather than letting it beat on me." She searched William's face. "Do you understand what I'm saying?"

"I'm trying to."

"I came up here today because I felt sorry for myself for all has happened to me, as if my life was about nothing more than me. What I forgot about was all the people who love me and need me." Unexpected tears sprang up in her eyes as warmth filled her chest and spread into every part of her. In a choked voice, she continued, "Thomas and his precious daughters need me—and you, my dearest William, especially you need me. And I need you."

Tears ran down William's red cheeks. "My sweet Mary, don't ever believe that you don't matter to other people or that you don't matter to me. I live for you, Mary. You're my reason."

"And I live for you. Forgive me for being weak and selfish. What happened to our farm today is bad, but it's not the end. We will bend, but we won't break. We'll find a way to survive because you and I are survivors, aren't we?"

"Indeed we are." William kissed her and wrapped his arms around her.

A gentle breeze moved through the tree, and it showered them with pieces of leaves, like flowers thrown at a wedding.

Mary pulled away from William and opened her arms wide. Looking up, she smiled and turned in a slow circle as the leaves fell on her face and in her hair. "Thank you, my great big, wonderful tree." She stopped and looked at William, who was smiling at her. "So what should we do next?"

"I've been thinking about that," he replied. "Thankfully, I

found both our mules in the woods, so let's go to the city and see Thomas. We'll get enough supplies from him to replace what we lost. And I'll kill more game than usual for our meat."

"And I'll plant a late garden," Mary said. "We might not have as many vegetables this winter, but we'll still get apples, peaches, and pears from our trees this fall."

"And we'll pick berries this summer for our wine and brandy," he adds. "You see? Things are not as bleak as they seemed."

Smiling, Mary said, "That is so true."

Chapter Fifteen

JOHN

From the moment John set foot on the ship with the other soldiers, old memories of his time on the slave ship filled his dreams, so much so that he preferred not to succumb to sleep at all. It had been so dark in the belly of the slave ship that no one could tell when it was night or day. Over three hundred slaves were crammed into shelves that were only eighteen inches apart, making it impossible for someone with John's broad shoulders to turn on his side. Iron rings had been fastened around the slaves' necks and ankles, then bolted to the shelf. And there they had lain, naked as the day they were born, through smooth weather and rough storms, writhing in their own feces and urine mixed with the excrement from the slaves on the shelves above them and from those lying beside them. The lack of fresh air in the slave hold, coupled with the humid ocean air and the odor of body waste, made it nearly impossible to get a deep breath.

Every moment of every day, the sound of moaning and wailing had filled John's ears. Some slaves begged the companion beside them to end their misery by choking them to death—and some obliged the request.

Every few days, some sailors would come below, remove the dead bodies, and unceremoniously throw them overboard. Twice during the voyage, all the slaves had been brought onto the deck, where they had to watch helplessly as the white men raped the women and girls.

To John, the saddest sight had been the emaciated, starving children, who stared with expressionless, dead eyes. One could easily do a visual count of each of their ribs resting above their distended bellies. Their subdued movements on deck had been waiflike, as if they knew death was only steps away.

Remembering those days from long ago, John was grateful that the troop ship was at sea only five days after leaving Boston harbor. As he and his fellow soldiers disembarked, he heard someone say they were on Hilton Head Island. He was surprised to see how many other battalions were already bivouacked there.

His excitement, and that of his comrades, about an impending battle erased the fatigue that his body felt.

However, the excitement quickly waned in coming days as their lives returned to the monotony of daily drills. The only difference was that this time, they drilled in concert with other battalions.

It was perhaps a week later that Colonel Shaw came riding through his company and told the men to be ready for an expedition in thirty minutes. It was exactly the word they had been waiting for. Suddenly, the unit was a whir of activity, with men checking and rechecking their rifles, squaring away their uniforms, and packing away their camping equipment.

"Is this going to be it?" Thaddeus asked John.

"Could be, son, could be. I just know we need to be ready because when that moment gets here, we don't want to be unprepared."

When night fell, they boarded steamboats that took them into the mouth of a river. All through the dark night, they inched their way upstream. Anxiety, fear, and excitement held their tongues, as hardly anyone said a word.

At the gray light of dawn, John suddenly recognized where he was. He said to those around him, "This is the Altamaha River. I've been here before. Up ahead is the town of Darien."

All the soldiers had their thumbs on the hammers of their rifles and peered intently in the dim light for any signs of the Confederate Army.

Suddenly, cannon fire erupted from one of the other steamboats. Houses along the bank exploded, and women and children, backlit by fire, could be seen running into the early morning. Their screams skittered across the surface of the river and struck John's ears in such a way that made him feel sorry for the people. As the cannon fire continued, house after house along the river bank was destroyed.

"What are they shooting at?" Thaddeus asked. "I haven't seen a single Johnny Reb yet, only women and children. And nobody's fired at us."

Confused himself, John had no answers.

The steamboat approached the riverbank and came to a stop.

Colonel Shaw's voice rose above the sound of the cannons and ordered everyone to shore. When they assembled there, Shaw addressed them. "Men, we've been ordered by my commanding officer, Colonel Montgomery, to go into the city and loot all the homes and businesses and bring all movable objects back here to the boats."

The soldiers looked at each other in bewilderment.

"But, sir—" John began.

"There will be no 'But, sirs'!" Colonel Shaw barked. "We've been given orders, and we will obey them. It's what good soldiers do. Do you understand?"

With one voice, the men replied, "Yes sir!"

Even though John had heard his commanding officer's words, he had been close enough to read the colonel's face and could see how distasteful his own words were to him. He'd never seen the colonel so angry.

As wrong as John felt the orders to be, it was because of his deep respect for Colonel Shaw that he set about doing as he was told. At the first house he came to, he knocked politely on the door, only to be shoved to one side by a young, wide-eyed soldier who kicked the door open and charged inside. John heard the screams of children within and hurried inside. He got about halfway through the house when he was met by the same young soldier coming toward him, dragging two screaming children by their hair.

John stepped directly into the path of the soldier, who came to an abrupt halt. "What are you doing?" John asked. "Our orders were to loot the city. That does not include harming the people."

The soldier looked down at the children, who had fallen silent as they watched the confrontation. He looked back at John with an expression of uncertainty.

John said, "Let go of them children and start hauling stuff out of the house, starting with that big mirror on the wall."

The soldier couldn't have responded any more quickly if John had been Colonel Shaw himself. He relinquished his hold on the children, who fell to the floor and grabbed for each other.

John got down on one knee and said to them, "Where's your mother?"

"She's hiding in a closet upstairs," one of them said.

"You two run up there and hide with her, and don't come out until you don't hear no more soldiers in your house, you hear?"

They both nodded and scampered up the stairs.

John stood up and saw soldiers coming into the house empty-handed, while others exited with their hands and arms full of loot.

The scene was repeated over and over throughout the day: defenseless women and children huddled in fear outside their houses as they watched all their worldly possessions being taken away.

As the hours passed, John could not believe the huge pile of plunder that was being amassed on the shoreline of the river.

The sun was setting as John happened to pass by close enough to Colonel Montgomery and Colonel Shaw to overhear them in a heated argument.

"You *will* burn the town to the ground," Montgomery said.

"What barbarous sort of warfare are we engaged in?" Shaw replied.

"Southerners must be swept away by the hand of God, like the Jews of old."

"I object and won't be held responsible for this!" Shaw said, his voice rising.

"Your objection is noted. I accept full responsibility," Montgomery said. Turning to the gathering crowd of soldiers, he yelled, "Put the torch to the town! Leave nothing standing!"

A few hours later, John and the rest of the Fifty-Fourth assembled to hear Colonel Shaw address them. The orange glow of the burning town behind the soldiers reflected off their commander's face and gave his visage a sharp edge. He began, "Men, you behaved well today in that you obeyed orders to do a distasteful deed. I, for one, am furious about what has happened. We have not trained in the art of warfare for months to be sent to destroy an undefended town. Well, never again! First thing tomorrow morning, I am sending a dispatch to General George Strong asking if he will allow the Fifty-Fourth to lead the next Union charge on a true battlefield."

A relieved and jubilant roar erupted from the men.

John held his rifle over his head and yelled his approval of Shaw's words.

Had he known what was to happen next, his reaction might have been quite different.

Chapter Sixteen

MARY

Trying to keep the hot August sun off her face, Mary tugged at her bonnet as she picked up the potatoes she'd dug earlier that morning and dropped them into a bushel basket. Once the basket was full, she lifted it to her shoulder with a grunt and headed to the three-foot-deep storage pit William had dug the day before. She had made him dig it eight inches deeper than last year's pit because the winter freeze had ruined many of their potatoes. "We're not about to work this hard growing and harvesting these potatoes," she'd told him, "just to lose them because we got tired and didn't want to dig deeper."

Kneeling down by the side of the pit, she poured the potatoes in and arranged them evenly across the bottom. Then she returned to fill her basket.

As she did so, William walked out of the barn carrying a double armload of straw and laid it beside the pit.

In practiced moves that needed no commentary, the two of them alternated a layer of potatoes and a layer of straw until all the potatoes had been gathered. William then shoveled soil on top and packed it down. When finished, he said, "We need to cut hay today. The morning dew is probably dried off by now."

"I put on some sassafras tea this morning," she replied. "Let's drink a cup of it before we go."

After their tea, they walked through the barn on the way to the hayfield and picked up a pair of scythes. William carried a scythe in one hand and his rifle in the other.

Cicadas sang high in the trees as the couple walked down the path to the field, and an occasional grasshopper glided through the air in front of them. There was the distant sound of a woodpecker looking for a meal.

As they cut through the cornfield, Mary said, "The cornstalks always look so naked after we've cut off the leaves and tops to save for fodder."

"They do, don't they?" William agreed. "Using every part of everything we grow, that's our motto, right?"

"It certainly is."

They waded into the waist-high field of grass and, in perfect rhythm, begin slicing down the grass.

As Mary's blade swept through the grass, the grass remained erect for a second, seemingly unaware it had been severed from its roots, before falling gently to the ground.

When she and William had cut half the field, they heard a rumbling sound approaching in the distance.

"What is that?" Mary asked.

Dropping his scythe, William said, "Let's move back to the edge of the woods and watch." As they reached the edge of the field and stepped into the shadow of the trees, he retrieved his rifle that he'd left propped against a tree.

The volume of the rumbling continued to grow, but nothing came into view.

Mary pointed in the distance to a spot above some trees. "Look at that cloud of dust. It's huge."

They both stared in silence.

An ominous feeling began to build in Mary's chest, and she wanted to shut her eyes to keep from seeing what was coming. She knew in her heart that, in some form or another, the war was coming to their door again.

Several more minutes passed before they saw Yankee soldiers on horses, riding four abreast. Row after row rode along the lane that passed the far end of the field they were working in. After innumerable soldiers passed by, more cannons than Mary ever dreamed possible passed by in single file, pulled by horses. Scores of wagons followed them.

She glanced at William and saw his jaw set hard and his eyes squinting. *Dear Lord, protect us from being drawn into this war. Keep William with me. Help him control his temper.*

As two soldiers headed toward them, riding fast, William started to raise his rifle.

Mary put her hand on his shoulder and said quietly, "Don't. There are too many of them."

William slowly lowered his rifle until the stock rested on the ground.

The two soldiers stopped their horses just before running into Mary and William. The horses pawed at the ground, and their nostrils flared.

"Lay your weapon down," one of the soldiers said to William.

"You have no right to tell me what to do," William replied.

The soldier drew his pistol and pointed it at William. "This says I do. Now lay it down."

The other soldier asked, "Are you a deserter? If so, from which army?"

William took a step toward the horses before Mary grabbed his arm. "I'm a Scotsman and have never deserted any worthwhile cause!"

"So whose side are you on?"

"I'm on the side of freedom."

"So you're too chicken to join the war?"

William jerked free from Mary's grasp. "Step off that horse, and I'll show you if I'm afraid to fight or not!"

The first soldier said, "We're wasting time here. Let's take them to General Rosecrans and let him decide what to do with them." To Mary and William, he said, "Follow me." To his fellow soldier, he said, "You bring up the rear. If either of them tries to run, shoot and kill them both."

An hour later, with faces covered in dirt streaked by sweat,

Mary and William found themselves standing in front of a large tent perched on top of a high hill. Soldiers moved in every direction as cannon were being arranged in a line. In the valley below, Mary could see Chattanooga.

The two soldiers who brought them there dismounted and disappeared inside the tent. They came back out quickly and stepped to one side.

The next man out of the tent had a sword at his side and gold epaulets on his shoulders. He stepped up to Mary and William. "I'm General William Rosecrans. And who are you?"

William spoke, "I'm William Thomson, and this is my wife, Mary."

Rosecrans eyed them carefully. "My men say you were spying on us. Is this true?"

"We have no reason to spy, sir," Mary said.

"We were cutting hay in our field when we heard you coming," William explained. "We stepped back in the shade only to see who it was, not to spy."

"Hmmm, I see. And what is a young man like you still doing farming? Why haven't you joined this war? Are you Quakers?"

"We are not Quakers, sir," Mary answered.

Looking directly at William, Rosecrans repeated his question. "Why haven't you joined this war?"

William didn't answer immediately, and Mary knew why. She took a small step forward. "It's because of me, sir."

Rosecrans looked surprised and turned his attention to Mary. "What do you mean?"

"It's because I don't think I can bear to lose one more thing. On a hill behind our house are buried our four children that never lived to six months of age. And I will never bear children again. To live alone would bring me to an end. So I've pressed my husband time and again not to leave me. And thus far, he's granted me my wish."

Tears pooled in the general's eyes. "My condolences, madam. My Anna and I have been blessed with eight healthy children. I cannot imagine the heartache of losing one, save four children." He turned to the two soldiers who had brought Mary and William to the camp. "Set these two on horses and return them to where you found them." To Mary and William, he said, "Stay on your farm, and don't go into Chattanooga, for I plan to shell the city into submission and occupy it. Once my forces are in place in the city, you will be safe to go there. May God bless you both, and may God bless the Union."

Though she was relieved to be sent away with Rosecrans's good wishes, panic seized Mary as she thought about Thomas and the girls lying in the crosshairs of the storm that was about to rain on them.

*****

By the time Mary and William finally arrived home, the setting sun had filled the sky with bright orange, yellow, and red. Standing together on the porch, Mary said, "What are we going to do?"

"I must ride into the city and warn Thomas," William answered. "He and the girls need to come stay with us."

"You can't do that. You could be caught in the middle of the shelling and get killed. Besides, I don't think Thomas will abandon his store when there's a chance people could loot it. And if the townspeople panic, the soldiers will most certainly loot everything in sight. Do you think the Union could actually take the city?"

"I'm not a soldier and know nothing about the art of war, but if they array all those cannons on the high ground around the city, I don't think there's a defense against that. Thomas has written us that the Confederate general Braxton Bragg and his army have been in firm control of the city. It seems to me Bragg would have been smart to have had some of his men deployed on the high points to, if nothing else, give him warning if the Union tries to take them. You need to write Thomas and tell him to get prepared."

"And how does one prepare for such a thing?"

There was a long pause before William answered, "Tell him to pray, Mary. Tell him to pray."

*****

That night, before retiring to bed, Mary sat at a small table. A candle, sitting on one corner, spilled yellow light across a sheet of paper. She picked up her quill, dipped it in an inkwell, and wrote:

August 19, 1863

My dearest Thomas,

It is with a heavy heart, full of dread and concern for you, Florence, Emma, and Mary Beth, that I write this letter. Just this day, William and I have learned that Chattanooga, and thus you, are in imminent danger. As we were cutting hay, we saw a massive Union Army move into position on the high ground around the city. Thinking we were spies, they captured us and took us before the commanding officer, General Rosecrans. Before you fear the worst, let me say that no harm befell either of us. As a matter of fact, the general was very gracious.

But he informed us that he intends to shell the city and occupy it. And William says he has the cannon power to do it. (I pray that no Union soldier intercepts this letter, for we would then most certainly be viewed as spies for the Confederacy.)

William wants you to bring your girls and stay with us until this campaign is resolved. I would wish it, too, but I told William I doubted you would leave your store during such a crisis.

Mary paused as a new idea came to her. Refilling her quill, she wrote:

However, the thought did occur to me that perhaps you would let Abigail bring the girls to us. I believe they would be much safer here than in the city, unless the overflow of the fighting spilled out this far.

I confess to you that my greatest fear is that all of this is bringing William one step closer to joining the war. I saw it in his eyes today when we were accosted by the Union soldiers. He's fiercely independent and does not tolerate well being told what to do by anyone. When I think about the possibility of him leaving, I find it difficult to breathe, and my heart races away with me.

Please seriously consider the different options I have presented to you.

Tell the girls that we love them.

We will pray fervently for your deliverance.

Affectionately,

Mary Thomson

Blowing out the candle, Mary stood and made her way to the bed. She crawled in and lay as close as she could to William, who was softly snoring.

He stirred and put his arm around her shoulders.

She kissed him lightly on the lips.

His eyes flickered open. "Did you write Thomas?"

"Yes, I did."

"Hopefully he'll receive it in time."

"What are we going to do in the meantime? I feel like I'm

already holding my breath, waiting for the sounds of cannon fire."

He hugged her. "As best we can, we are going to continue our daily lives as we always have. Tomorrow we'll return to the field and finish cutting our hay."

William's simple answer made sense to her. She lifted her gown, took his hand, and placed it between her thighs. "Come lie with me."

*****

Morning's gray-streaked dawn found Mary sitting in a chair, looking out an open window. In her hand, she held the envelope containing the letter to Thomas, but she was thinking instead about her time with William last night. Although their lovemaking had always been something she looked forward to and enjoyed, the passion of last night had a desperate urgency to it that she'd never felt. It was as if they both wanted it to last forever and were reluctant to release each other. *It was like I would wish it to be if I knew it was the last time we would be together.* At this thought, a chill ran through her.

She shook herself to throw off the feeling, in the same way she would throw off a shawl, and headed to the kitchen to prepare breakfast.

A bit later, William walked in, rubbing the sleep out of his eyes. "You're up early this morning."

"I couldn't sleep, and I didn't want to miss the chance to give Thomas's letter to the postman."

William kissed her on the back of the neck. "Everything's going to be all right, Mary. You'll see."

"How do you know that?"

"Because whatever happens, we will cope with it. We have made our way through the most difficult waters anyone can pass through, in the loss of our four children."

Mary turned to face him, surprised to hear him speak so openly on a topic he rarely broached.

"We've taken the worst that life can throw at us," he continued. "Thomas told me once that he believed our loss made us stronger while his loss made him weaker. I don't know if I'm stronger or weaker. But I know that it showed me I can tread deep water. There's truly only one thing I'm afraid of now, and you know what it is. And we'll not speak of it. You and I are here today, together, and that's good enough for me."

Mary fought back tears. "Those are the most tender and touching words you've spoken to me in a long time. I don't know what to say back to you."

Giving her a teasing smile, he said, "It would be nice if you could say breakfast will be ready soon."

Before she could make a move to swat at him, he backed up and danced a jig around the table. "You're getting slow in your old age," he said with a laugh.

Mary raised one eyebrow and said, "The art of killing a rabbit is not running it down. It's waiting until it's still and then knocking it in the head. You just remember that."

*****

That afternoon they arrived at the field to cut hay, William with his rifle and Mary with her pistol.

"What's natural now seems unnatural," William said.

"How so?"

"This calmness and quietness is how it's supposed to be out here, but we both know that a mile away, there is a flurry of activity, with soldiers and cannons making ready for war."

"When do you think they'll start?"

Laying his rifle down and picking up both scythes, William said, "There is no way to know for certain, but I don't expect it will be too long from now."

She took the scythe as William handed it to her and said, "Tomorrow is the day that President Jefferson Davis has designated as a day of fasting and prayer. Let's make certain we go to church. Perhaps someone will be there who has heard more details about the Union's plans."

He nodded. "That sounds good."

He turned and, taking the lead, began the slow, swinging waltz through the tall grass. The severed stalks bowed and fell as the couple passed.

Chapter Seventeen

MARY

Three weeks later, a postman dropped off a letter addressed to Mary and William. Mary immediately recognized Thomas's handwriting and ran to find William.

"Quick, open and read it," he said. "It's been three weeks since we sent him our letter."

Mary tore open the envelope and read aloud:

September 13, 1863

My dearest friends,

It has happened—Chattanooga has fallen into the hands of the Union. For two solid weeks, Rosecrans bombarded our fair city, then Braxton Bragg's army deserted us in our time of need, and for that, I shall never forgive him.

I did receive your letter, but it was the very day that the bombardment began, and up until now, it has been impossible to get a letter out of the city. I am sorry for the worry that must have caused you.

When the incessant shelling of the city ceased, people ventured out of their houses like corpses from their caskets, looking as if they didn't know where they were. And indeed there was reason to feel that way because much of the city has changed. Houses and buildings were smashed to splinters. Some even lay still smoldering. It is nothing short of a miracle that my store and house escaped unscathed.

All of us, myself, Abigail, and the girls, are unharmed in body, but Mary Beth seems to have become like a little child again, wetting her bed and sucking her thumb. She even asked Abigail if she could nurse on her. I don't know what to make of it. Florence and Emma fuss at her about it and sometimes make fun of her. I scold them both for doing so because I know of no benefit such behavior could have for Mary Beth. My hope is that when our lives return to normal, she will become as she was before all of this.

But will our lives ever return to normal? William, I know I told you that I was not going to choose sides in this war but work to get along with whichever army controlled the city. I can no longer say this. Since these Yankee soldiers have inundated the city, I have witnessed such boorish and obscene behavior that should shame any man. It is not safe for any female, young or old, to be out on the street.

And they come into my store and take what they wish, without paying for it. Apparently, their general, Rosecrans, is a base man who does not exercise discipline over his troops.

If I didn't have my daughters to be concerned over, I would be dead by now because I would have shot several soldiers for their behavior.

There are whispers that Bragg is going to launch an offensive to retake the city. I would gladly join that effort, but, alas, family obligations prevent me from doing so.

I now understand the Apostle Paul's admonition that being

single is preferred over being married. Married life and family tie a man's hands and keep him tethered to his commitment to them. Not that I regret being married or having children, it's just that if I weren't, things would be much different.

Mary's heart hammered against her chest as she read Thomas's words that no doubt echoed William's feelings. She blinked away tears and continued:

What is happening to our world where brother is fighting against brother, where lives by the tens of thousands are lost in a single day? What is to be the end of us?

But I have made this letter all about me. How is it with you two? Have the ravages of war bypassed your lovely farm and home? Is William as stubborn as ever, and is Mary as fair as a rose?

They both smiled and laughed.

One last thing—I know this is asking too much, but it would be ever so meaningful to us all if you could come visit us. There seem to be no present hostilities in or around the city, with the rebel forces having withdrawn, so I think you could travel safely in the open.

With abiding love for you both, I remain affectionately yours,

Thomas Henry

"There are some postscripts," Mary said.

P.S. I miss you very much and very much want to see you.

Emma

P.S. I, too, miss you but am trying to be strong for Father. I hope we will see each other soon. Florence

P.S. This is Florence, too. Mary Beth asked me to tell you she misses you, too.

William took a deep breath and blew it out slowly between his pursed lips. "That poor man."

"And those poor girls," Mary added as she folded the letter and returned it to its envelope. "My heart aches for them. Do you think we dare chance going to see them?"

"Yes. We should go in our wagon and carry a few chairs, so if we're stopped, we can say we are going there on business. But I think we need to only stay overnight, then return home and bring the girls with us. It might lighten Thomas's load if we let them stay with us for a while."

"That's what I was hoping you would say! I'll get some chairs out of the shed while you hitch up the mules to the wagon."

*****

William steered the mules and wagon through the cratered streets of Chattanooga, past destroyed houses and businesses. The sound of hammers rang out from every direction as men worked to repair damaged porches, board up windows, or replace clapboard siding that unexploded cannonballs had torn through. The only business that appeared to be thriving was the saloon, as the sound of an out-of-tune piano and boisterous laughter drifted out its swinging doors.

"I hardly recognize this place," Mary said in a low tone.

"I know," William replied out the side of his mouth. "War looks different when it's up close and personal rather than something you read about that has happened way off somewhere."

When they arrived and walked into the store, Thomas was the only person in sight. His elbows appeared to be nailed to the counter and his face glued to his hands.

"Thomas?" William said.

Slowly, Thomas pulled himself out of whatever place his mind was in and stood erect.

Mary was shocked at his appearance. He didn't look as if he had changed his clothes in quite some time, and there were black smudge marks on the shoulder, arm, and front of his tan coat. His hair hadn't been combed in days, nor had a razor touched his face in the same amount of time. The dark circles under his eyes and the deep lines on his face made him look like he had aged ten years.

Thomas stared at them as if they were part of a dream, but when recognition finally registered on his face, his knees buckled, and he nearly fell to the floor.

Mary and William rushed to his side, and each grabbed an arm.

"Thomas, are you all right?" Mary asked. As Thomas

looked from one of them to the other, Mary noticed the red lines etched across the whites of his eyes.

In a trembling voice, Thomas asked, "Is it really you?" And he began to cry. Turning toward William, he put his head on William's shoulder. "Forgive me for crying."

William embraced him.

"Oh, dear Thomas," Mary said as she laid her face on his back and patted his shoulder, "cry if you need to."

"It's okay, my friend," William said in a voice choked with emotion. "We're here now. It's going to be okay."

"Mary, is that you?" a child's voice drifted across the store.

Mary stood and looked in the direction of the living quarters of the building. "Emma! Come here and see me!"

"Oh, Mary!" Emma squealed and ran toward her.

As she entered Mary's embrace, another voice said, "What's going on?"

Mary spotted Florence. Hugging Emma with one arm, she held her other arm open and said, "Florence!"

Florence walked calmly to her and kissed her on the cheek. In a voice devoid of emotion, she said, "Hi, Mary. Hi, William. Things have been very bad here, but we are doing nicely. How are you?"

Mary found Florence's demeanor odd and disconcerting.

"Florence has been a real trooper through all this," Thomas

said. "I don't know what I would have done without her."

"You girls give me a hug, too," William said. Emma eagerly obliged, whereas Florence gave him a perfunctory hug.

"What's all the commotion?" came the sound of Abigail's voice.

Mary looked as Abigail walked into the room and saw that Mary Beth was in her arms, sucking her thumb.

"Well, Lord have mercy!" Abigail said. "If it ain't Mr. William and Miss Mary! It is so good to see you." Mary Beth buried her face in Abigail's neck and refused to look at anyone.

"Hi, Mary Beth," Mary said. Holding her hands out to her, she asked, "Will you come see me?"

The child grunted and squeezed Abigail's neck even tighter.

Abigail shook her head. "I don't know what we're going to do with this one."

"She's being a big baby," Florence said. "She needs thrashing."

Mary frowned and looked at William, who returned her look of concern.

"Don't be so harsh, Florence," Thomas said. "We must give Mary Beth time."

The scowl on Florence's face showed she did not share her father's opinion.

Emma interjected, "Florence thinks she knows everything." Making a face at her sister, she said, "You're too bossy."

Florence lunged for her sister, grabbed a handful of hair, and jerked. "I am not!"

Emma screamed in pain and slapped at Florence.

Mary looked in shock at the melee, expecting Thomas to firmly restore order.

But it was Abigail who, with her free hand, grabbed Florence and pulled her back. "You girls stop that! You're acting like you ain't got no raising. And right here in front of Miss Mary and Mr. William. You ought to be ashamed! Y'all come with me upstairs."

After Abigail and the girls had left the store area, Thomas turned to Mary and William. "That's how it's been for a while now. They fight all the time. And Mary Beth . . . I don't know what to say about her. I'm tired of dealing with them and calling them down all day long."

Mary laid her hand on his arm. "Then let us help you."

He looked at her quizzically.

"William and I want to take the girls home with us for a few days, just so you can have some time to rest and gather yourself."

Thomas replied, "But what kind of father can't take care of

his own daughters?"

"Nobody's saying you can't take care of them," William explained. "We're just giving them and you a holiday, a break from the tensions of the past few weeks."

"Perhaps it would be good for them," Thomas said. "And maybe it will help Mary Beth overcome whatever is troubling her."

"Then we're agreed?" Mary asked.

"Yes, and I can never thank you enough."

The three of them shared an embrace.

*****

When Mary and William and the girls arrived back on the farm, William stopped the wagon beside the house.

Mary stepped down and helped the girls out of the wagon. To William, she said, "You go unhitch the team, and I'll rustle us up something to eat."

"That sounds good."

In the kitchen, Mary put on her apron and said, "Maybe I could fix us up a big pot of vegetable soup and some cornbread. How does that sound?"

Florence's stoic stance finally broke. "Oh, that would taste wonderful! We've had no vegetables in such a long time."

"Then you stir the fire and put another stick or two on it, while Emma and Mary Beth help me get all the ingredients together."

Twenty minutes later, Mary carried the heavy pot of vegetables to the fireplace and hung it on an S-hook over the fire. It was then that it dawned on her that although he'd had plenty of time to unhitch the horses, William hadn't yet returned to the house. She looked out the window and saw that dusk was settling in. Frowning to herself, she said, "You girls stay here and watch things while I go see what's taking William so long."

"Yes, ma'am," Emma said.

Mary wiped her hands on her apron and headed to the barn. The closer she got, the faster she walked. Everything seemed uncharacteristically quiet—there were no sounds from inside the barn of trace chains clinking together or the mules stomping impatiently.

Walking through the open barn door, she found the wagon with the mules still hitched to it, as if William had driven them inside only seconds before. She held her breath, listening for any kinds of sounds, then turned in a circle looking for signs of William.

It felt as if the barn had joined her in holding its breath.

In a loud whisper, she called for him, "William?" The silent barn soaked up her question.

Next, she ran to each stall to see if perhaps he had fallen and been knocked unconscious. It was when she found the last stall empty that fear and panic, the twin horses of a runaway imagination, seized her. She ran out of the barn and, cupping her hands to the sides of her mouth, yelled, "William!" The only reply she received was her own voice thrown mockingly back at her by the tall hills bordering her hollow.

With wide eyes, she looked in every direction. When she didn't know what else to do, she fell to her knees and screamed, "William!"

Chapter Eighteen

MARY

Mary watched as the girls came running out of the house toward her. They fluttered around her like butterflies and peppered her with questions:

"What's the matter?"

"What happened?"

"Why did you scream?"

"Are you okay?"

Mary finally interjected, "It's William. He's disappeared."

Florence frowned at her. "What do you mean? He came out here to unhitch—"

"I know what he was supposed to be doing!" Mary snapped angrily. "But he never unhitched the team, and he's nowhere to be found." What she wanted to do was to shoo away the girls so that she could focus her full attention on finding William. She shouted his name again. "William!"

Florence and Emma imitated her and began calling for William.

Without intending to, they all three stopped at the same time and listened. Silence fell on them like a heavy blanket of snow.

"Let's go look for him," Emma said. "He has to be around here somewhere."

Mary realized that she needed to calm down, if for no other reason than to keep the girls from being so frightened. "It's going to be dark very soon, and it won't be safe for us to be wandering through the woods. Let's just go inside and eat. Perhaps William will come through the door while we're eating and give us a very sensible reason for his disappearance." *I don't believe that for a minute. William has never gone off without first letting me know where he's going and when he'll be back.*

They headed toward the house when Mary suddenly remembered the wagon and team. "I forgot that I need to unhitch the team. You all come inside the barn with me."

Inside the barn, Mary lit a lantern, but instead of it giving everyone a sense of security, the soft yellow light created frightening shadows. Dark, ominous corners held a portent of danger, and though the evening was warm, Mary felt a chill tiptoe across her shoulders.

The sisters practically clung to Mary's dress as she unhitched the team, returned the tack to the tack room, and fed and watered the mules.

Though Mary was going through the motions of paying attention to the chores, her mind sifted through possible reasons for William's disappearance. *Maybe he saw something unexpected and went to investigate it.* But when she looked underneath the wagon seat to see if his rifle was still there, a drumbeat of dread slammed against her chest.

The rifle laid there, along with its powder horn and lead pouch, staring back at Mary. She knew William well enough to know that he would never step out of the barn willingly without his rifle.

The sound of one of the girls' stomach growling pulled Mary out of the fearful land of supposition and conjecture and into the land of what must be done. While love for William was pulling at her to keep searching, responsibility for the girls pulled her in the opposite direction. "I'm finished here," she said to them. "Let's go to the house."

Inside the kitchen, Florence gathered some bowls without being asked to. She said to Emma, "Get us some spoons."

The normally obstinate Emma complied without a word.

One by one the girls walked up to Mary and let her put a dipper of soup in their bowl before taking their seats at the table.

When Mary joined them, they looked at her expectantly. Unsure of what they wanted, she said, "Is there something wrong?"

"Don't you think we should pray for our food?" Emma asked.

"And for Mr. William?" Mary Beth added.

Emma and Florence stared at their sister.

Florence whispered to Mary, "It's the first time she's spoken in days."

Mary thought how ironic it was that the tragedy of William's disappearance had unloosed the small child's tongue. She said, "Yes, let's pray. Holy and Reverent Father, we thank you for this offering of food before us, the direct result of your bountiful hand. And we beseech you, Lord, please . . ." She thought she would be able to hold her emotions away from her long enough to say the prayer, but they pushed up and choked off her voice. She knew if she tried to say another word, she would burst out crying, so she squeezed her fists and bit her lip, waiting for the rush of emotions to subside.

Into the silent space that followed, Florence spoke. "We beseech you, Lord, please find it in your mercies to return William here unharmed. Amen."

Mary unclenched her fists and blinked to clear away her tears. Clearing her throat, she said, "Let's dig in." She caught Florence's attention and mouthed "thank you" to her.

*****

After everyone finished eating, Mary said, "It's a warm night; why don't we sleep outside on the porch?"

The sisters were quick to agree to the idea and helped her gather quilts and pillows and spread them on the porch.

When Mary lay down, she looked into the moonless, star-filled sky. *Dear God in heaven, wherever my William is, help him follow these stars back home to me.*

*****

A violent wind woke Mary during the night. When she stood up, the wind tore at her dress and whipped her hair around her face. Out of the corner of her eye, she spotted the barn door opening as three horses with riders walked out. It was at that moment that she realized she was once again caught up in this repetitive nightmare.

Unable to stop the dream, she watched as one of the soldiers, a Yankee, checked the leather thongs that bound William's hands behind him, while the other soldier, a Confederate, placed a blindfold on him. Just before the blindfold completely covered his eyes, William turned and looked directly at her. He called out, "I promise I'll be back."

This new twist to the old nightmare jerked Mary out of her sleep, and she sat up. Rather than the sound of wind or William's voice, all she heard were crickets and frogs singing their nighttime courting song.

Mary Beth sat up and rubbed her eyes. Looking up at Mary, she said, "I heard Mr. William."

Though she knew it was impossible, Mary couldn't help but look toward the barn, but the barn stood alone and silent. She held out her arms to Mary Beth. "Come here."

Mary Beth got up slowly and stumbled into Mary's arms.

Mary held her to her chest, began rocking back and forth, in the same way her mother used to rock her when she awoke from a dream, and said, "I think you must have been dreaming. I've been awake and haven't heard a thing. Just go back to sleep."

With her voice muffled by Mary's breasts and the folds of her dress, Mary Beth said, "But he told me to tell you not to worry."

Halted by the small child's words, Mary could find no reply to the illogical message, until she said, "Maybe it was an angel whispering to you in a dream."

*****

It was the sun shining on her face that awakened Mary the next morning. She was immediately in a cross and ill mood. *I should have been searching for William at dawn! And these girls! I can't do anything with them here. They're simply in the way.*

As she thought about taking them back to Thomas, she realized she would lose a whole day of searching for William to do it—plus, they were supposed to be staying with her in order to give Thomas a break. At that moment, despair slipped in and pushed aside hope, like someone rearranging furniture in a house. *Who am I kidding? William is gone, long gone, from here. There's no point in looking for him.*

So for the next five days, she engaged the girls in helping her do the chores on the farm: pressing more apples, gathering nuts, splitting and hauling firewood, stuffing the mattress with fresh straw, cooking, and cleaning. Because those were things they never did in the city, the girls attacked each activity with enthusiasm. Florence was even proud of a blister she got splitting wood.

One day, as they paused to eat lunch, Mary Beth asked,

"Did Mr. William die?"

The question drew sharp looks from Florence and Emma, but neither of them scolded her.

Mary was surprised, as she had often been by the girls as they'd grown up, by the honesty of youth and its willingness to ask the questions that no adult will ask aloud. She hung her answer on a hook of hope. "I do not believe he is, or I think we would have found him. I can't for certain say what has happened, but I know he'll come back."

"But why would he disappear like this?" Florence asked.

"I've decided he must have been kidnapped by one of the armies, and they have pressed him into fighting this war. He's been telling me for some time that the war would come to our door eventually. Well, I guess it has arrived."

*****

When she finally took the girls back to Thomas and explained to him what had happened, it threw him into a fit of anger.

"This damn war! I'm sick of it!" He slammed his fist on the counter, causing the lid on the empty candy jar to rattle. Looking at Mary, he said, "You're going to have to stay with us. You can use Abigail's room, and she can sleep on the floor in the kitchen."

His proposal surprised Mary. "I can't do that. I have to keep the farm going. There are things that have to be done every day."

"And what will you do to protect yourself if trouble comes?"

"I know how to use both the rifle and the pistol. I can take care of myself. The thing I most want is when William comes back to me, I want him to find the farm just as he left it, with everything in perfect order."

"But, Mary," Thomas said in protest, then stopped. "Of course that is what you will do. And no woman is better suited to the task than you. Perhaps even now William has escaped and is waiting for you to return home."

Though she appreciated the hopeful words and tone of her friend, Mary could tell by the furrow between his eyebrows and the downward slant of his eyes that he didn't believe it to be true.

She gave him a quick hug and kiss on the cheek. "I have to be going."

*****

When Mary reached home, she unhitched the mules and bedded them down. By the time she left the barn carrying William's rifle, dusk had fallen. In the distance, she heard the dull thud of heavy cannon fire. She paused and frowned but calculated that the fighting was miles away from her, and so she moved on to the house.

Darkness shrouded the house, both outside and inside, as if it were sitting inside a dark cave. She stood wavering in front of the door, not wanting to step into the emptiness inside, because although it wouldn't be the first time she would have been there without William, it would be the first time that she had no idea where he was or when and if he would return.

"You can't stand out here forever," she said to herself. "Best get inside and be about your business." Spurred by her father's oft-stated philosophy, she entered and lit a lamp, but instead of the lamp making the room feel warm and welcoming, everything the light touched reminded her of William.

She walked over to the fireplace and stirred the coals, then put a few sticks of wood on them. Next, she found a block of homemade cheese wrapped in cloth and sliced off a thick piece. She dipped a cup in the bucket of milk and let it fill. Sitting in a chair facing the fireplace, she let out an exhausted sigh.

*****

The next morning, Mary lay in bed listening to the steady sound of cannon fire to the south and wondered if it was the rumored counteroffensive by Braxton Bragg. Each thud felt like a hammer blow that nailed her to her bed, making just the thought of getting up too big a task to accomplish.

She rolled over and looked at the empty space beside her, then closed her eyes so that she could see William lying there. Reaching under her pillow, she brought out her copy of the Tennyson poem and flipped through pages until her eyes fell on these lines:

Tears of the widower, when he sees
A late-lost form that sleep reveals,
And moves his doubtful arms, and feels
Her place is empty, fall like these;

Which weep a loss for ever new,
A void where heart on heart reposed;
And, where warm hands have prest and closed,
Silence, till I be silent too.

A tear slipped from her eye, rolled down the edge of her nose, and dropped onto the page, giving it a mark of punctuation no pressman could have made.

"Will you lie here in this bed until death finds you," she asked herself, "or will you fight against the thought of giving up?"

It was thoughts of what William would want her to do that finally gave her the will to rise. *One thing at a time, that's all I can do. I'll do one thing at a time and do the best I can.*

She decided that the first thing she would do would be to cut firewood from the tree William had chopped down a week earlier.

Soon she found herself riding through the woods in the wagon, trying to find the tree. For the most part, she let the mules have their head, trusting that they would know where she wanted to go and would take the same path they had with William driving. More than once, as she moved through the shady timber, she had to lie down in the seat to avoid being knocked off by a low-hanging limb. "Pat and Mike!" she yelled at the mules, "I know how cantankerous you can be. You're just doing that on purpose!" The only obvious response Mary got was the long ears of the mules flopping back and forth, but it wouldn't have surprised her to learn that they smiled at each other and winked.

A half hour later, the mules slowed to a stop where weeds and small saplings had been trampled flat. Mary looked to her right and spied the felled tree fifty feet down a hill. "It would have to be at the bottom of a hill," she sighed.

After an hour of working, both the back and the front of her dress were dark with sweat, and she sat down to catch her breath. After a few seconds, she realized the cannon fire had ceased and wondered if it was a good sign or a bad one and if William was anywhere close to the fighting.

She worked a few more hours before she was satisfied she had a decent-size load of wood on the wagon, more than enough to keep her busy for some time with the bucksaw at the house.

She climbed back onto the seat of the wagon and was about to head to the house when she heard a commotion farther up the hillside beside her. Her heart jumped in her throat as she saw scores of Rebel soldiers running through the woods, yelling excitedly. Then, suddenly, she saw soldiers on horseback charging toward her; it was impossible to make out if they were Union or Southern. She pulled her rifle out from under the wagon seat, made sure it was loaded, and stood up, facing the oncoming soldiers. A ferocity boiled up in her as she took aim. *If this is the way it will end for me, do not expect me to go easily or quietly!*

She saw a sudden a look of surprise come over the riders when they spotted her, and she realized they weren't coming for her. Several of them rode past her in a gallop, whooping and hollering as they went. She held up her hand to try to stop one of them, but to no avail.

Finally, a boy, who looked to be no more than fourteen, pulled his horse to a stop beside her. His face was flushed with excitement.

"What's happening?" Mary asked.

"We've whipped Rosecrans and got him on the run!"

"Rosecrans? But I thought he was in Chattanooga."

"It was a trap that General Bragg laid for him. Rosecrans thought he could pursue us into Georgia. But we outfought his army at Chickamauga Creek, and he had to hightail it back to Chattanooga. We've got him on the run!" With that explanation, the grinning adolescent soldier slapped the rump of his horse with his hat and raced to catch up with his Rebel comrades.

Chapter Nineteen

JOHN

John and Thaddeus sat beside their small fire, drinking coffee and listening to the soft murmur created by low, idle conversation around other campfires scattered across the field. The bright, full moon reflected off the canvas tents, making them appear to be glowing from light within.

Thaddeus said, "I'm tired of just sitting around doing nothing. When are they going to let us do some real fighting?"

Steam from John's cup rose and encircled his face as he took a sip of the hot brew. "I can remember the time I would have give anything to do nothing. When you is bone-weary from working in the field from sunup to dark with shackles and chains around your ankles, and all you've had to eat the whole day is a cold biscuit, all you want to do at night is lie down and sleep, but when you do, it seems you have just closed your eyes when the overseer is waking you up to start the next day. That's when I would have give anything to do nothing. I always thought to myself back then, 'One of these days, John, you are not going to work unless you want to, and you'll sleep as late as you want to.'"

"Then how come you joined the war?"

John paused before answering. "I used to know why, but lately it's hard to remember them reasons. I think it was because I hadn't never done nothing before, so I didn't know how to do it when I was give my freedom. Then when I met Mr. Lincoln and he told me that this war was about freeing slaves, I sort of felt like I ought to do my part."

"So you want to kill some Johnny Rebs, don't you?"

"Not unless I got to. What I want is for every man to be free, that's all. I wish all them states that have seceded would give up their fight and that this war would end without more killing."

Thaddeus set his cup down beside the fire. In a timid voice, he asked, "You ever kill a man, John?"

John considered his answer, then said, "Yes, I have." He watched the eyes of his young friend grow wide.

Thaddeus asked, "Really? What happened?"

"I killed a man in Africa who was from another tribe because he killed my wife."

"We've been together all this time, and you ain't never told me you used to be married. How come?"

"I've never told anyone I was married because it was too painful to speak of. When sadness slips out of your heart and turns into words that come out of your mouth, it pains your ears to hear it, which just multiplies the sadness in your heart. It's a vicious cycle. That's why I just kept it to myself."

"Why did the man kill your wife?"

"It was because of me. Our tribes were friendly with each other. He and I were friends and would sometimes hunt together. The problem was, we both wanted to marry the same girl. He told me he would never let her marry anyone but him. I just didn't know how strongly he meant that. So when she chose to marry me over him, he killed her."

Thaddeus sat quietly with this new revelation.

After a few moments, John interrupted whatever musings Thaddeus might have had by sharing another bombshell. "That's not the only man I've killed."

Thaddeus stared in disbelief.

"I worked at a plantation one time that had a slave who treated the slave women as bad as or worse than the white owner and the white overseer. He would brag to the rest of us men about how he would sneak over to the women's quarters and do all sorts of animal-like things to them and make them do things to him. It made my blood boil, and I decided that kind of man didn't deserve to live. So one night I snuck up on him and killed him, then buried the body. Nobody never said nothing about it, other than the overseer saying he figured he'd run away."

John fixed Thaddeus with a stare. "Listen to me, killing a man with a rifle like we've been trained to do is one thing, cause that man's so far away you can't really see his face that good. But killing a man with your bare hands, when you can see the color of his eyes and smell his breath—that's another thing."

Just then the voice of Sergeant Smith rang out. "Assemble

the men! Colonel Shaw will address the men!"

Swiftly, all the men of the Fifty-Fourth Regiment gathered in parade formation. Bright torches blazed at each corner of the assembly.

Colonel Shaw sat astride his horse in front of the men as the light from two torches on either side of him made his features glow. "Men, Brigadier General Quincy Gillmore has been assigned to lead a campaign against the city of Charleston. Tomorrow we will join other regiments and begin the push toward the city. We will begin by taking Morris Island. Fight bravely, men!"

His few sentences were like a short fuse in a powder keg, and a rousing cheer erupted from the men. Shaw saluted them, turned his horse, and trotted away.

The next morning, John, Thaddeus, and the rest of the Union soldiers landed at the southern end of Morris Island and quickly pushed back the meager Confederate forces holding that part of the island. A feeling of victory surged through the men until they moved farther across the island and came within sight of the Southern Fort Wagner. A stronghold created out of sand, earth, and palmetto logs, it bristled with fourteen heavy guns, mortars, short-barreled carronades, and fieldpieces.

John spoke in solemn tones to Thaddeus. "That right there is going to be a problem."

The following morning, Brigadier General George Strong sent out the Seventh Connecticut, the Seventy-Sixth Pennsylvania, and the Ninth Maine in an attack on Fort

Wagner. But as evening fell, the fight died down, and barely a third of those forces returned.

That night there was a heavier throng than usual around John's campfire. He saw that the brash bravery of the morning had now turned into fear and uncertainty. "Being afraid ain't nothing," he said to them. "I been afraid lots of times, but I always come through those times. Let's wait and see what our Colonel Shaw decides to do. He'll come up with a plan."

True to John's prediction, the next morning, Shaw gathered six hundred of his men, including John and Thaddeus, on a narrow strip of sand just outside Wagner's fortified walls. "Here is the plan, men," Shaw began. "Throughout today, there will be a heavy land and sea bombardment of Fort Wagner. Then, when night falls, we will lead an assault on the fort by traveling up the beach."

*****

An unnatural silence fell over the battlefield just as the sun was setting.

Lying on the sandy beach with the rest of Shaw's men, Thaddeus whispered to John. "This is it, isn't it?"

John heard the fear in the boy's voice. He spat sand out of his mouth and whispered, "Yes, it is, but we've been trained real good how to fight. This is our chance to show the nation that black men are just as good at fighting as white men are. Don't be afraid." He saw Shaw approaching. "Here comes the colonel."

Keeping low to the ground, Shaw said, "I want you to prove yourselves. The eyes of thousands will look on what you do tonight." Positioning himself at the front of the charge instead of the rear, Shaw looked over his shoulder at his men and yelled, "Charge!"

With a chorus of victory in their throats, the six hundred men charged the fort. Rebel artillery rounds exploded amid their ranks, and musket fire shredded them.

On all sides of him, John saw men falling to the ground and body parts flying through the air. "Stay with me!" he yelled at Thaddeus.

In spite of tremendously heavy losses, the remaining members of the assault group reached Fort Wagner and began scaling its earthen walls.

At the crest of the walls, Colonel Shaw shouted, "Onward, boys! Onward, boys!" As he did so, his body was riddled with Confederate bullets, and he died in front of his men.

Both angered by his commander's death and inspired by his words, John fought his way to the top of the wall as the buzz and zing of bullets whistled past his ears. The noise of cannons and rifle fire was so deafening that he was unable to hear the shrieks and cries of the men. He tumbled over the wall and into the fort. As he got to his feet, he saw a Rebel soldier drive his bayonet through the throat of Thaddeus. Unable to load and fire in such tight quarters, John swung his rifle like a club and burst open the side of the Rebel soldier's head.

For the next hour, using his knife as his only weapon, John

engaged in hand-to-hand combat, stepping on the bodies of fallen comrades and slipping in the grisly viscera on the ground. But neither he nor any of his fellow soldiers were able to make headway deeper into the fort; rather, they were pushed back, one step at a time, until they were repelled back over the wall. As John and the approximately three hundred other survivors ran toward the beach, victory cries and Rebel yells rang out from the walls of Fort Wagner.

Once he knew he was safely out of rifle range, John collapsed on the beach, gasping for air. His throat burned, both from thirst and from inhaling so much gun smoke. He reached to wipe the sweat off his face with his hand and felt something wet. Holding up his hand, he saw that the end of his ring finger and pinky finger had been severed just above the second knuckle. Fatigue prevented him from being shocked, and he looked at his hand out of curiosity. *When did that happen?*

He tried to remember details of the battle, but everything seemed a blur. Suddenly, he both remembered the pain of being stabbed in the shoulder by a bayonet and felt the pain from it. Reflexively, he reached for the wound and decided that he must have grabbed at the bayonet when it went in, and when the Rebel pulled it out, it sliced off the ends of his two fingers. Taking off his kerchief, he wrapped it around his two bloody stumps.

Sitting up, he unbuttoned his uniform to see if there were other wounds he was unaware of. He gingerly touched the stab wound in his shoulder and was thankful that there appeared to be nothing broken. He discovered a bullet hole in his uniform where a bullet passed underneath his armpit. Looking at his belt buckle, he saw a bullet buried in it and realized that his stomach was sore from the impact.

And then he saw that he was barefoot. *What happened to my boots?* Uncertain as to when they came off, he guessed it was either in the wet sand of the beach or in the bloody mire inside the fort.

He looked back at the fort and the trail of dead bodies and holes caused by exploding cannon shells that lined the path to it. *Where is the sense of it? What was the point? What did we prove? That a black man can die as easily as a white man?*

He watched as the remnants of his company limped back to the rest of the soldiers. As he did so, he came to a decision. Standing up, he took off his shirt and threw it on the ground. He gripped the stripes sewn on the sides of his pants and ripped them off. Then, barefoot and clothed only in a pair of pants, he walked away from the war with no other purpose in mind than to head west.

Chapter Twenty

MARY

October 19, 1863

My dear friend Thomas,

It has now been a month since I returned your daughters to you and a week longer than that since William disappeared. I tried to go to Chattanooga to make sure you and the girls were okay, but I was turned back by Rebel soldiers and warned not to try again. That was when I learned that Bragg had laid siege to the city.

Now I am left with my wonderings. Are you safe? Are the girls safe? Do you have food to eat (for I was told by the Rebel soldiers that people in the city will soon have to resort to eating their horses)? My mind is filled with all sorts of frightening scenes that could be happening to you. I try to brush them aside and not worry, but they are as difficult to be rid of as a case of chiggers. I go to bed with my worries and wake up with them, or should I say they are there in the morning because most oftentimes, sleep eludes me. No matter how fatigued the body may be, nothing prevents sleep more than a worrisome mind.

As for things out here, I have started gathering corn, later in the year than William would have done it, but it's as soon as I could get to it. The crop was not a very good one, much of it having been trampled down or stolen by soldiers from both armies. But I don't have the numbers of animals we normally fed over the winter, so what I have should be enough. The next problem involves shucking it. There aren't enough people left living around here to hold a shucking bee, so that means I will have to shuck it myself.

Yesterday, while cutting wood, I stumbled upon a beehive full of honey inside a hollow beech tree. I was quite excited and went back during the night to harvest the honey and ended up with three quarts. William would love it! He has always loved sweets.

I think of him constantly and pray for his safety every night. I ache to see his bright red hair and to be held in his arms.

I feel so isolated and lonely out here by myself. I do the best I can to keep busy on the farm, but even working in the field or woods can be a lonely proposition when you are doing it by yourself. And God forbid that I should come down with some sort of illness, for then what would happen to things around here?

Please pray for me, as I pray for you and your family. And I offer a special prayer that this letter will find you and that I'll hear from you soon.

Affectionately,

Mary

Chapter Twenty-One

MARY

[Unbeknownst to Mary, her letter never reached Chattanooga. Braxton Bragg's forces tightened the noose around the city, choking off all commerce. But in late October, General Ulysses S. Grant arrived in the city to assume command of the Union forces and replaced Rosecrans with General George Thomas. Under cover of darkness, the Union floated down the Tennessee River, past Confederates on Lookout Mountain, which led to the opening of a new supply route, the Cracker Line.

Grant also brought General William T. Sherman's army to the city. Thus buoyed by rations and forces, the Union launched an attack against the Confederate forces, and two days later, the Confederate forces retreated south into Georgia, leaving the Union firmly in control of Chattanooga.]

Mary sat in the woodshed as she finished caning the bottom of a chair. Eyeing the finished product, she felt somewhat proud of her efforts but knew the chair wasn't as solid as William would have built. *That's the best I can do right now, but I'll get better.*

She stood up and arched her back to get the stiffness out of it, then stepped out of the shed. When she did, she found herself face to face with a Confederate soldier who had a bloody bandage over his right eye. Startled, a small cry escaped her, and she backed up against the closed door of the shed.

The soldier gave her a gap-toothed grin, and she noticed what she suspected were powder burns on his cheek. His long, stringy hair hung to his shoulders. His coat had holes in it, and his pants were tattered. Looking at his feet, she noticed he was barefoot. Thankfully, she saw no sign of a weapon. "Can I help you?" she asked.

"Well, if it's not the Woodcutter's wife," the man said with a sneer.

There was something familiar in the man's tone of voice and demeanor; she couldn't figure out what. "Do I know you?" she asked.

"Oh, we've never been formally introduced, but we've certainly met before." With a sinister edge in his voice, he added, "I told you then that I'd be back."

Though she tried, Mary could find no recollection of who this man could be. "I'm sorry, but I don't remember—"

He interrupted her. "Maybe this will help." He lifted his hair on one side of his head.

Fear stabbed Mary in the chest with the force of a hunting knife as she saw the intruder was missing an ear. Her eyes grew wide.

"That's right," he said with a smirk. "It's me. The one whose ear you sliced off. I told you I wasn't finished with you. Now I've come back to take what I want."

As he took a step toward her, Mary kept her voice even and

said, "My husband will be here any minute. You best leave before he does, or he will most certainly kill you."

He backed up a step and laughed. "That's not likely to happen. I saw your husband running for his life with the rest of the army, heading to Georgia."

Fear moved over and made room for excitement and confusion in Mary's heart. "How can you be certain it was him?"

"'Cause I've been with him ever since we kidnapped him."

"You kidnapped him?"

"The general made us come get him because we were told that no one knows the woods around here better than your husband. He wanted him to show us all the high points around the city so that we'd have an advantage on those Yankees. Your husband threw a fit about it and tried to refuse to help, talking about him being a free man and all. But he had a change of heart when Bragg told him he'd put him in shackles around a tree and leave him there. After a while, he saw there wasn't any way to escape, so he asked for a uniform and weapon so he could fight with us." He snorted, "A uniform! We haven't had new uniforms since the war started."

At first, Mary thought he might be bluffing about knowing where William was, but the details of his story convinced her he was telling the truth. Relief swept through her heart momentarily, knowing that, at the least, William was still alive. But the realization that she was in a vulnerable and perilous position, with nothing to use as a weapon, caused fear to quickly regain control of her.

"There's no use looking around," the soldier said. "No one's coming to save you, and you don't have no weapons on you. At least none that I can see." He moved closer to her and grabbed the front of her dress. "But I aim to find out what all you do have underneath that dress."

He stood so close to her that the smell of his putrid breath caused a wave of nausea to pass through her.

Suddenly, he jerked and ripped open her dress.

Mary screamed and knocked his hand away. She took off running to the house to try to fetch her pistol, but she barely covered ten feet before the man tackled her to the ground. Her face slammed against the hard-packed earth, causing her to see stars.

He grabbed a handful of her hair and yanked back on it. He growled in her ear, "Not so sure of yourself now, are you?"

Anger suddenly surged through Mary, and she rolled onto her back, pushing him away from her. Scrambling to her feet, she looked for anything she could use as a weapon, but everything was too far away to grab quickly. She squared herself to face her attacker, fists clenched.

He stood up, looked at her, and smiled. "You're a real wildcat aren't you? I've tamed worse than you." He feinted with his right hand as if he were going to hit her in the face. When she threw up her arms to block him, he punched her hard in the stomach.

Mary's breath whooshed out of her, and she doubled over in pain. She tried to straighten up but couldn't. His next blow struck her in the kidneys and knocked her to her knees.

As if she were a tree whose trunk had been sawed through and was teetering on the verge of falling, he gave her shoulder a nudge, and she fell face first to the ground. Rolling her onto her back, he sat on top of her. He grabbed the front of what was left of her clothes and tore them away, exposing her breasts.

In a last desperate attempt at thwarting his intentions, she reached up and dragged her fingernails across the side of his face. Red streaks appeared, and blood trickled from a few of them.

The man howled in pain and backhanded her.

Everything went dim for a moment as she almost lost consciousness. When her senses returned to her, she felt him pulling up her dress. She tried to buck him off but to no avail. Finally, she decided to become calm, close her eyes, and accept whatever was about to happen as inevitable. She prayed a silent prayer. Suddenly, thoughts of William came to her. She opened her eyes and said, "Please kill me. I'd rather be dead."

The soldier stopped and looked at her. "I may kill you, but not before I get what I came for." He began unfastening his pants.

Just before she closed her eyes again, she saw a blank stare come across her assailant's face. His eyes lost focus, and blood appeared at the corner of his mouth. Like a ship taking on water, he began listing slowly to one side until he toppled off her.

In his absence, Mary's field of vision was filled by a black man holding a bloody knife.

She stared in shock and disbelief at the rangy-looking black man.

He wiped the bloody knife on his pants and stuck it in a scabbard on his belt. He said, "My name is Kwasi Poku, but people call me John."

Mary looked over at the limp form of the soldier beside her.

"Don't you worry, ma'am," John said. "He won't bother you no more. He's dead."

Mary suddenly remembered her torn dress and exposed breasts. She sat up and gathered the tatters of cloth to her chest.

John removed his too-small coat and handed it to her. "You can use this."

Mary noticed the scars around his neck and wrists. Her head was full of questions, but she couldn't get her mouth to utter anything more than "Thank you." Standing up, she turned her back to John and slipped on his jacket. She held the front of it together with one hand and turned back around.

She had decided this man meant her no harm, or he would have already done it. She said, "I don't know what to say.

Clearly you saved me, but I don't know why. Where are you from? How did you show up just now? Why are you here?" Pointing at the dead man, she said, "Did you know him?"

John rubbed his hand over his chin. "That's a mouthful of questions. I don't mean to scare you none, and I'm not going to hurt you. I've been sort of hanging around your place for the last week or so."

Mary's jaw dropped. "You've been hanging around here? I haven't seen you."

"That's because I didn't intend for you to see me. I just stumbled upon your place after I left Camp Contraband over there in Chattanooga."

Mary frowned. "What's Camp Contraband?"

"It's a place where all the escaped slaves have started gathering. I didn't go there on purpose myself; I just heard about it and wanted to check it out. But it's no place for a man to stay. There's not enough food and no clean, dry places to sleep. So I decided I'd leave and continue heading west."

Mary found herself mesmerized by John's easy nature and his deep, sonorous voice. She felt her heart and breathing returning to normal. "Are you hungry?" she suddenly asked.

"Well, I do pretty well eating rabbits and nuts, but I haven't had potatoes in so long I can't remember. A potato would sure taste good."

Mary smiled. "I don't have much around here myself, but one thing I do have is potatoes. Give me a minute to go inside and change clothes, then we'll dig up some potatoes, and I'll cook them for you."

John closed his eyes. "Ma'am, that sounds like music to an old man's ears." When he opened his eyes, he looked down at the dead man and said, "But first I need to get rid of this body."

Mary looked at the corpse, and a wave of nausea hit her as she thought about how close she came to being raped. "What are you going to do with him?"

"If I bury him in your barn, your mules will pack the ground down good and hard, and there'll be less of a chance of the body being found. If we throw him in the creek or bury him out in a field or the woods, somebody might find him and start asking questions."

"I'll help you after I change clothes."

"No need for that. I'll take care of it." He reached down, grabbed the man's feet, and dragged him toward the barn.

Inside the house, Mary changed clothes while she talked aloud to herself. "You must have lost your mind. You've only known this man a matter of minutes, and now you're going to feed him? And he is a runaway slave. What would William say? William would say he's a man just like him and deserving of a warm meal, that's what he'd say. And he'd thank him for saving my life. What mother would say if she could see me now is a completely different matter."

She headed out to the barn and found that John had already got a good-size hole started. She grabbed another shovel and started digging with him.

"Ma'am, what are you doing?"

"I'm helping you get rid of this piece of white trash."

"But this here is a man's work."

At this Mary stopped and held her shovel in front of her. "You say you've been watching my place for a while now. Have you seen a man anywhere around here helping me do the work?"

"I can't say as I have."

"No, you haven't. And have you seen me taking care of every chore, even those a man usually does?"

A hint of a smile flickered at one corner of John's mouth. "Ma'am, seems like ol' John doesn't always know when to keep his mouth shut. Let's get this hole dug before you change your mind about feeding me those potatoes."

Shovelful by shovelful, Mary matched John's pace as they dug. Mary had come to believe she was as strong as many men and was surprised at how well John kept pace with her because she guessed him to be twice her age.

She found herself amazed that she was working side by side with a black man—a black man she didn't even know—with so little trepidation. *War places people alongside others who would never otherwise be so. But necessity demands they both put aside any differences they might have in order to survive.*

Eventually, John said, "I believe that's deep enough."

Mary gladly stopped and propped the handle of her shovel against the barn wall.

John rolled the man to the edge of the hole and shoved him in; he landed with a dull thump.

Mary looked in. He was facedown, and his legs and arms lay at odd angles.

"Did you know him?" John asked.

"Several months ago, he and some others raided our farm. They pistol-whipped my husband; then this one tried to rape me like he did today."

"What stopped him?"

"I cut his ear off with a froe."

John stared at her wide-eyed. "With a froe?"

Mary realized how absurd her story must sound. She shrugged. "It was the only thing lying close by that I could get my hands on."

John shook his head. "My Lord, my Lord, you're not like any white woman I've ever known."

"You simply do what you have to do to survive," she replied.

"You have spoken a truth right there, ma'am," he said

solemnly.

Chapter Twenty-Two

MARY

After Mary cut up some potatoes into a pot and added some rosemary and thyme, she hung the pot over the fire, then looked out the window toward the barn. John was heading toward the house, but first, he stopped at the well and washed off his face, arms, and hands. It suddenly dawned on her that she hadn't considered where John would eat. To allow him into her kitchen would be one thing, but to sit at a table with him would cross cultural barriers she'd lived her whole life.

She thought about how Abigail had cooked for Thomas and the girls all these years, seeing to their every need but never being allowed to join them in a meal. She'd seen it and thought about the unfairness of it, but she never spoke about it. Now, though, that it was about to enter her own life, she found herself looking in a moral mirror, seeing the reflection of her heart, and not liking what she saw. *Am I really prejudiced? Do I think I'm better than other people simply because our color is different? Why should I care what other people think if they hear about me sharing a meal with John? I now live in a changed world, and I will craft it to look the way I want.*

She watched John step up on the porch and went to the door to meet him. "Come on in. The potatoes will have to cook a bit before they're ready."

John looked down at his feet, then up at Mary. "I don't

think I should, ma'am. It wouldn't be proper."

Mary realized she wasn't the only one who was about to cross cultural boundaries. "It's okay," she said. "It's my house, and I decide what's proper in it."

"But ma'am, you're . . . you're a white woman, and I'm a—"

"You're a Negro, and I'm white," Mary cut in. "You're stating the obvious."

"And you're a married woman, and your man is not here."

Mary folded her arms across her chest. "John, I'm well aware of what it means for you to come into my house and share a meal with me, or at least what others would say about it. But for me, this is just two people who are trying to survive a war. It seems a very small thing for me to repay you for saving my life by giving you something to eat. I'm certain if my husband were here, he would insist you eat with us."

John still hesitated. "If a white man caught me with you in your house, he would beat me and hang me. I'm an old man. Hanging would be a relief because I could finally go home to be with Jesus. But the beating . . ." He closed his eyes and shook his head. "I've had too many of them and don't think I could bear another."

This stopped Mary. To have someone talk so calmly and openly about being treated like an animal peeled away the veneer that many slave owners she'd known used to cover their harsh treatment of their slaves. A fierceness rose up in her chest. She wanted to grab John and pull him inside her house and tell him to damn what others might say or do. But she realized it wasn't her place to force him to do anything, for that would just be more of the same that he'd been subjected to. She softened her tone and said, "I understand. I don't like it, and I don't agree with it, but I understand. Do you want to wait here until it's done? Or would you rather wait in the barn and I'll bring it to you?"

"If it's okay with you, ma'am, I'll just sit here on the porch and lean my back against the wall. That late afternoon sun feels mighty good."

Mary smiled. "Help yourself. And you don't have to keep calling me ma'am. My name is Mary."

Like an old hunting dog, John folded his lanky limbs and lowered himself onto the porch. Leaning back against the house, he sighed and said, "Now that feels right nice."

Mary went back inside and opened some apple cider. She poured some for John and took it out to him. "Take a drink of this, and tell me what you think."

John squinted into the sun as he took the mug from her. He sniffed it first, then smiled and drank a swallow. "Mmmm, mmmm. That is some fine apple cider. That's as good as I ever drank. Where did you get it?"

"I made it."

After taking another drink, he said, "You did?" He pointed toward the orchard and asked, "From them apple trees out there?"

"My husband's parents planted them years ago. William and I started making cider out of them when we took over the farm."

"William, is that your husband's name?"

"Yes."

"Can I ask where he is?"

"Yes, you can. But I have no answer. He disappeared one day when the Confederate Army kidnapped him, something I didn't know for weeks until that man you killed showed up here and told me."

"And you haven't heard from your husband and don't know where he is now?"

"Not a word."

John shook his head. "The unknown is what's hard to bear. If you know a thing, then you can decide how you're going to deal with it. But until you know, all you can do is chase your worries. And trying to sleep with worries is like trying to sleep on a bed of pinecones."

Mary felt her throat choking with emotion and walked back inside to check on the potatoes. She swiped at a tear and stirred the pot, then made up some cornbread and poured it into the spider skillet. It sizzled as it hit the hot cast iron.

Several minutes later, she carried a bowl of potatoes with a piece of cornbread sticking out of it to John.

He stood up and took the bowl. His eyes grew wide, and he

held Mary with his gaze. "Miss Mary, this is the first home-cooked meal I've had in . . . in a long time." Tears filled his eyes.

Mary was touched by his emotional transparency. She went back into the kitchen and returned with her own bowl of potatoes.

The sun was saying good night to the hollow as it kissed the top of the western hill on its descent for the night.

Mary settled into a chair and faced John. "Will you tell me your story?"

He swallowed a mouthful of potatoes and said, "I'll talk as long as you want me to, just so you bring me more of these potatoes."

They laughed together. His laugh reminded her of an over-the-shoulder tuba she heard in a band concert when she was a little girl.

He began his story in Ghana, Africa, and showed her the piece of kente cloth. By the time he finished, the dark of night had wrapped itself around them, much like the shawl Mary had around her shoulders. Silence filled the distance between them. Their bowls and mugs, which a few hours ago had been warm and held such interest, now sat beside them, empty and cold.

A barred owl interjected its haunting call from the top of Bitter Hill. Instead of taking it as a cue to comment on John's story, Mary felt prompted to tell him her and William's story—all of it.

It was the first time Mary had told the entire story at one time, and even she was struck by the amount of loss she had experienced in her short life.

When she concluded her story, the Seth Thomas clock in the house could be heard striking twelve.

"Miss Mary," John said, "that's as sad a tale as I've heard. You are one strong woman to endure such and to keep carrying on. How do you keep doing it?"

"Because I've learned how to bend but not break and because I know that William is going to return to me."

*****

JOHN

Even at 4:00 a.m., John was still lying awake in the barn where he had told Mary he would spend the night. Trying to sort out his thoughts and feelings about the events from yesterday had kept sleep at bay. Never had a white woman talked to him like she did, as if he and she were equals. As hard as Commander Shaw had tried to talk to the troops like they were equals, he never quite accomplished it, though John admired him for trying. With Mary, however, there was no pretense. Her attitude was genuine and sincere, of that he was certain.

Then there was her story, told with such bare-bones honesty that John winced at parts of it. Since he had come to America, many had been the times that he learned of Negro women who were separated from their children, sold, and carried away to different states. But those women had always held on to the hope that one day they would somehow find their children and be reunited. Mary, though, had no such hope as an anchor.

He thought about how a woman in Mary's situation would have fared back in Africa. He remembered the proverb his mother often stated: "A barren wife never gives thanks." Time and again it was made clear, though never stated aloud, that among the Ashanti, motherhood was a woman's fulfillment. A woman who could not bear children faced an uncertain future, with no one responsible for seeing to her needs, because her husband would send her away and take on another wife.

Another proverb came to him: "A woman is a flower in a garden; her husband is the fence around it." Mary's story made it clear that her husband, William, had built a fierce fence around her, but now that he was gone, there was no one to tend to that fence. Perhaps she was one woman who would not need a man to do that for her, for anyone who would fight a man and cut off his ear with a froe was a woman to be reckoned with.

What confused John was a feeling that he needed to protect Mary, to somehow take the place of her husband, not really like a husband but like a caretaker. *Why should I care about her? What is she to me? What do I owe any white person? I need to keep traveling west and leave her to herself.*

He sat up and held his hands to his mouth to warm them with his breath. "She could let me live out here in the barn and help her with her farm. The Union is in control of this area, and it looks like the Rebels is like a coon up a tree surrounded by hunting dogs—everybody knows what's going to happen. I could stay here and be safe, at least until her husband comes home—if he comes home."

He puzzled over how he could present his idea to her without making her feel like he thought she needed help. "She's a proud woman and would bristle up like a porcupine if she thought I felt sorry for her."

Suddenly, an idea struck him, and he smiled.

He walked out the barn door and nearly ran into Mary.

Mary blinked her puffy eyes. "I came to check on you. Did you stay warm enough last night?"

"I was fine. I just burrowed down in the hay there and slept like a baby," John lied.

"I'm glad you did because I didn't sleep hardly a wink. I was up and down and dreaming. I'd have been better off doing some work in the woodshop."

John wished he hadn't lied about his own lack of sleep, so before the opportunity passed to fix things, he said, "Well, truth be known, I didn't sleep either. I just told you I did because I wanted to let you know how grateful I was for having a place to sleep."

"And why couldn't you sleep?"

John thought about his idea from earlier and said, "I was trying to figure out how I could ask you to let me stay on for a few days. I've got this bad sore on the bottom of my foot where I stepped on a stob. It makes it awful painful to walk. I was going to head out west and see where my travels might take me, but then I did this." He reached down and rubbed the bottom of his foot. Out of the corner of his eye, he watched Mary.

"Well, that's interesting," she replied, "because I was trying to figure out how I could ask you to stay on and help me shuck my corn. There's not enough neighbors to have a shucking bee like we always used to have. I can't do it all by myself and still take care of everything else that needs done."

He straightened up. "It seems our minds was traveling on separate trails but trying to arrive at the same place."

Mary shifted her weight. "You have to understand that I can't pay you anything. I don't have any money. But I can give you some food to take with you when you leave out."

It dawned on John that he hadn't even thought about getting paid for helping her. Getting paid for work was something he'd never experienced until he joined the army. He was moved by Mary's generous spirit. "I'm sure we can figure something out when my foot heals enough for me to leave."

Mary seemed like she wanted to say something else. After a second, she stuck her hand out toward him. "Then let's shake on that."

John looked at her white hand and hesitated. Then he wrapped his black hand around hers and shook it.

Chapter Twenty-Three

MARY

Mary led the way to the house, relieved that, at least for a number of days, she would have help doing the chores. When she opened the door and walked into the kitchen, she felt John come to an abrupt halt behind her. Turning to face him, they looked at each other from opposite sides of the threshold—not just the threshold William made, but a threshold built by generations before them. "John?"

"Yes, ma'am?"

"I am going to insist that part of our arrangement will be that you come and go in this kitchen as you please, whether I'm in here or not. I'm neither your owner nor your master. What we are is two humans who need each other's help, and that makes us equals. If somebody shows up and tries to make trouble about it, I'll"—she paused and smiled— "I'll cut their ear off with a froe."

John smiled and rubbed his chin. "You have a way of putting things that makes it hard to argue against you."

"Then come inside."

Once he passed through the doorway, Mary shut the door and started making breakfast.

"How did you come by that?" John asked.

Mary turned and saw him pointing at the bearskin in the

corner.

"William and I were in the woods working, and I killed it."

"You must be some kind of a good shot."

"Actually, I killed it with my hatchet."

John clapped his hands together. "So you're the one!"

"The one what?"

"I was standing outside the general store in town one day, listening to this man telling tales to some of the officers. He told about this woman he call the Woodcutter's Wife and how she killed a bear with her bare hands. When he said that, I turned and walked away because I knowed nothing like that could be true. But he was talking about you, wasn't he? Are you called the Woodcutter's Wife?"

Mary blushed. "William was known as the Woodcutter. So, yes, some people call me that."

"My Lord a'mighty!" he exclaimed. "If you lived in Africa, you would be a princess or queen."

Smiling, she pointed toward a chair and said, "Have a seat."

When John sat down, he said, "Whoever built this chair knew what they were doing. Its joints is solid, and the seat is sturdy."

Smiling even more broadly, Mary said, "Thank you. William and I make chairs, or we used to make chairs. It's what we do with our time in the winter as a way to bring in money."

"Well ain't that a coincidence. One plantation I worked on they made me a carpenter, and one of the things I learned to do was make chairs."

Mary latched on to that piece of information and turned it over in her mind. "What do you think about this idea? I know you don't intend to stay here very long, but while you are here, we could make chairs together and split the money we make on them. That's the only way I'll be able to pay you anything for helping out around here."

Without hesitation, John replied, "Miss Mary, that's the best offer I've had since I sat foot in this country thirty years ago. It would please me to do that."

*****

The week before Christmas, Mary and John worked to get the chairs into the wagon. As they panted, tiny white clouds revealed how cold the morning air was.

John said, "Are you for certain you want me to go to the city with you?"

Mary replied, "We've been over this several times. Yes, I want you to go with me. The farm will be fine for a few days without anyone being here. Things have definitely been lots quieter since the Union took over Chattanooga. I haven't heard any fighting or seen any soldiers in nearly a month, so I don't think anyone's going to be raiding the farm." She gave a wry laugh. "Besides, there's not much to raid."

"But your friend, Thomas Henry, what's he going to say about you having a Negro along with you? You going to tell him I'm your slave?"

"Of course not. Besides, he wouldn't believe me if I did. I'll tell him the truth: that you saved my life and that you've been working for me since then. I do wish I'd taken the time to write him and let him know what's been happening, but we've been so busy making the chairs that I've been too tired at night to write. It's a bit unusual, though, that I haven't received a letter from him. We had been writing regularly for a while. I just hope everything is well with him and the girls, which is another reason to go to the city. We're going to check on him and his family, sell our chairs, and buy some supplies. Now climb on board, and let's go." Without waiting for a reply, she pulled herself up and onto the seat.

John climbed up the other side and stood in the bed of the wagon.

Mary turned around to look at him. "What are you doing?"

"I'm ready to go."

"You planning on riding to town back there?"

"Yes, ma'am."

"Don't be silly. Get up here and sit in the seat with me."

"Now, Miss Mary, you need to listen to me on this one. For a Negro to ride in the same seat with a white woman won't do nothing but stir up trouble. There's no sense in challenging people's way of seeing things by pushing their face into it. It'll just make them mad. We don't need to bring no grief on ourselves if we can help it."

Mary's first impulse was to fire back and argue, but the logical part of her knew John was right. "Okay. I'll agree for you to ride back there this time, but one of these days you'll ride up here with me—just not today."

"Now that's being sensible," John said. "Tell them mules to get to pulling and take us to Chattanooga."

*****

As they entered the city and passed the livery stable, Mary sensed a different mood in the air than when she last visited. There were several horses in the corral, and the ringing tones of Robert Barton's hammer on the anvil echoed from inside the barn. She spied two steamers tied off at the river landing, being unloaded.

Rolling past a parked wagon carrying ducks and chickens in cages, John said, "It sure would be nice to have fresh eggs for breakfast."

Mary followed his line of sight and pulled back on the reins. "Whoa!" As Pat and Mike came to a stop, she said to John, "Maybe he'll trade some for a chair. I've just got to find the owner." She stepped off her wagon and walked around the parked wagon, examining the birds.

From underneath the wagon came the sound of a man coughing.

Mary bent down and saw a man dressed in grease-stained buckskin lying on the ground.

Although he was lying on his back, his large stomach still provided an arching profile. He coughed again and sat up but banged his head on the bottom of the wagon. Swearing, and with an ample amount of grunting, he managed to roll over and crawled out on his hands and knees. Grabbing the spokes of the wagon wheel, he pulled himself to a standing position and donned a leather hat with a floppy brim. His gray beard stuck out in every direction, and his eyes were bleary. When he let go of the wagon, he staggered to his left and grabbed the side of the wagon to steady himself. In a voice that sounded like he had gravel in his throat, he said to Mary, "Good day to you, ma'am. Might you be in the market for some ducks or chickens?"

"Actually, I am," Mary replied. "But these are some of the scrawniest I believe I've ever seen. They'll never lay eggs."

The man blinked slowly for a second or two. "Madam, you have cut me to the quick. I've raised these fowl since the day they were hatched. They've been fed daily and just yesterday produced a dozen eggs."

"I find that hard to believe. Half of them are molting, and everyone knows they don't lay when they're molting."

As if this were news to him, the man's eyes grew wide, and he looked at the chickens as if this were the first time he'd seen them. "Perhaps they just started molting today."

Mary laughed derisively. "You might find a customer for them, but it's not going to be me." She started back for her wagon.

"Perhaps you could at least make me an offer," the man said.

"I'll tell you what I'll do," she said, "and the only reason I'm doing it is because I feel sorry for the ducks and chickens. I'll give you one of my handmade chairs for the whole lot of them. You'll come nearer selling the chair than you will those fowl."

Right on cue, John lifted a chair out of the wagon and handed it down to her.

Mary held it out to the inebriated man. "It's stout enough it'll even hold you up."

He took the chair, ran his hands over it, then looked from Mary to the chickens and ducks, then back at the chair, and then at Mary. "Well, go ahead and take them, then. I'm tired of hauling them around all over town."

John stepped out of the wagon and transferred the fowl to Mary's wagon with her help.

When they finished, she looked for the poultry man and spotted him a hundred yards down the street, carrying the chair with him.

John said, "That man's going to wake up tomorrow and wonder what in the world happened to his ducks and chickens and will have no idea where he got that new chair."

Grinning, Mary climbed back onto her wagon and

commanded the mules, "Giddap!"

From the bed of the wagon, John said, "Lord help the man that tries to trade with you. He'd better have his money in his boot, or he'll find himself going home a poorer man. You and I both know fowl don't molt in the winter. If they did, they'd freeze to death."

Mary smiled. "I almost felt guilty about taking advantage of a drunk man. I said *almost*—but not quite."

John laughed heartily.

A few minutes later, Mary drove the wagon up to the front of Thomas's store, joining several other wagons that were parked there.

Exiting the store was a woman carrying several bundles, followed by a man who appeared to be her husband, carrying additional heavier packages. The woman instructed the man exactly where she wanted the bundles placed in their wagon, then turned her attention to Mary. "You buying or selling?" she asked.

Still holding the reins in her hands, Mary said, "I'm selling." As the woman approached, Mary climbed down from her wagon.

The woman spoke to her in a quiet voice, "You shouldn't climb out of a wagon by yourself. Your ankles were showing."

Mary put her hands on her hips. "So you think I should just sit there until a stranger comes by and I ask him to help me down? Having a stranger stand below me with my hips in his face and letting him put his hands around my waist is not something I care to do. Nor do I intend to let a stranger help me down while I'm facing him so that my breasts are in his face. I prefer to do things myself without having to depend on a man, especially a strange man. Now, are you interested in buying some of the finest-made chairs in the state?"

The woman tilted her nose up and said, "Well, I never!"

"Suit yourself. I'll just sell them to someone else."

Covering his mouth to conceal a smile, the husband stepped up. "We need some chairs. Let me see one of them."

John, making no effort to conceal his smile, handed down one of the chairs.

The husband inspected all the joints, then sat down in it and wiggled. Standing back up, he said, "You're right. That's a mighty well-built chair. I'll take four of them."

As the husband and wife drove off, Mary started toward the store.

John said, "I'll wait here by the wagon while you go inside. I'm not going to let anyone steal any of our chickens or chairs."

"Okay, for the time being," Mary agreed. "But we'll find a safe place to put the wagon, and then you can come in."

The first thing Mary noticed when she entered the store was that the shelves were brimming with goods. The second thing was the number of people who were there buying things. She had expected to find Thomas in similar dire straits as herself.

She walked to where she could get a view of the store stove, hoping to see a crowd being entertained by Thomas's stories. Instead, all she was an old man smoking a pipe; to one side of him was a younger man leaning on a crutch, and on the other side was a man with a folded white cloth wrapped around his head and covering his eyes. The old man took hold of one of the blind man's hands and placed the bowl of his pipe in it. The blind man then took two long puffs before holding the pipe out for the old man to take back.

Disheartened by the sight, Mary turned her attention away from the ravages of war and saw Florence across the room helping a woman. But there were changes in Florence since the last time she'd seen her—her figure was rounder, as womanhood appeared to be blooming in her. Mary stood still, watching and waiting for Florence to look in her direction.

After a few moments, Florence looked up and saw Mary. Immediately, her expression changed, and the composed, adult face that showed while she waited on a customer fell away, leaving a delighted little girl's face in its place. "Mary!" She left her customer open-mouthed and ran toward her Mary.

Mary opened her arms as Florence leaped into them. She hugged her tight and lifted her off the floor. "Florence, it's so good to see you!"

"It's been forever! Father says he hasn't heard anything from you. We were worried. Is William home? Is he with you?"

"No, William has not come home yet."

Florence's happy face broke into pieces like a window pane struck by a rock. "Where is he? What's happened to him?"

From across the store, Thomas's voice boomed, "Mary Elizabeth Thomson! Can it be?"

Mary turned and saw Thomas covering the distance between them in quick, long strides. Gone were the dark circles that had been around his eyes the last time she saw him. It was as if he had turned the hands of Father Time backward, looking younger than before the war.

The two friends embraced. Mary felt his strong arms around her, hugging her. A feeling of safety and security filled her, a feeling she hadn't felt since William disappeared. There was a part of her that wished he would never let her go.

They kissed each other on the cheek and finally broke their embrace. As they faced each other, Thomas took her hands in his and said, "I haven't heard from you in so long. I've been quite worried. Is William home? Is he with you?"

"No. I've heard nothing from him since the day he disappeared. Although I did learn for certain that he was kidnapped by Bragg's army and must have gone with them to Georgia after the Union took Chattanooga."

"That saddens me greatly," he said as he squeezed her hands. "So you've been out there all by yourself all this time? How have you fared? Other than looking a bit tired, you're as beautiful as ever."

"We can talk about all that later. You look better than I can remember. And look at your store." She waved her hands at the shelves and counters. "It's stocked completely full. How has all this happened?"

"It's the most remarkable thing. Ever since the Union was able to control the river and the trains coming in and out of Chattanooga, supplies have poured into the city. And people have started moving back, though not everyone. Even some new people have moved in and bought stores and land. It's like Chattanooga is booming. My business has never been better."

"I'm thrilled for you," she said, though a tinge of jealousy touched her heart when she thought about how desperate things had been for her.

All of a sudden, there was a commotion at the door as it was flung open. John came flying through the opening and landed heavily on his side on the floor. A man wearing a badge, whom Mary had never seen before, stepped through the door and looked around. In a loud voice, he asked, "Whose wagon is that outside with the chairs and chickens in it?"

Mary faced him. "That would be my wagon."

Pointing at John, he said, "I caught that nigger skulking around your wagon like he was going to steal something.

He claims he works for you. I told him we'd see about that. Give me the word, and I'll throw him in jail."

As silence filled the room, Mary walked over to John and helped him to his feet. Turning to the sheriff, she said, "This *man* and I work together on my farm. He was keeping an eye on the wagon to prevent anyone from stealing anything. I didn't realize there was a new sheriff in the city who pays such close attention to things." Her last sentence dripped with deliberate sarcasm, and she stared at the lawman.

The sheriff pulled up on his sagging gun belt and said, "There's no call to get smart with me. I'm just doing my job. There's lots of shifty characters on the streets these days."

Mary took a step toward him and said, "Yeah? And maybe you're one of—"

"Everybody calm down." Thomas cut Mary off and stepped between the combatants. "Jake's the new sheriff and doing everything he can to keep things under control." He took hold of the sheriff's bicep and tugged on him. "Come on over here to the counter and get some of that horehound candy you like so much."

As they walked off, Mary asked John, "Are you hurt?"

"No, ma'am. I've been laid down to sleep harder than that."

"Who is this?" Florence asked, looking at John.

"This is John," Mary said.

"Is he your slave?"

"No. John's a free man. John, this is Florence, the oldest of Thomas's three daughters."

"Nice to meet you, miss," he said.

Ignoring him, she said to Mary, "And he's helping you on the farm?"

"Yes, he is."

"Where did he come from?"

"That's a story worth hearing, but we'll need more time to do it. We've got lots of catching up to do. First of all, though, I need to see Emma and Mary Beth."

*****

A couple of hours later, after visiting with Emma and Mary Beth, Mary came back downstairs and made her way into the store, where she found Thomas.

He smiled at her. "I'm so glad to see you, and I know the girls feel the same way."

"I'll admit it feels good to be here and to get so many hugs. I saw Abigail, and she told me you gave her her freedom. I'm really proud of you for doing that."

Thomas replied, "It just seemed like the right thing to do. No one has ever been more loyal and giving than she has. I thought she deserved to go live her life however she wanted to. She surprised me when she accepted her freedom but chose to stay with us." His eyes reddened. "It was one of the most magnanimous gestures I've ever witnessed."

She laid her hand on his arm. "And she's tickled to death to be saving up the money you're paying her."

Laughing, he said, "She's going to wear it out because I see her counting it all the time."

"I need to ask you about something else. It's one of the main reasons we came to town." She walked out to her wagon, with Thomas following. "John here has been helping me make chairs, and I need to know if you'd be interested in buying some of them or at least trading for them."

Thomas clapped his hands together. "I'll buy every one of them and any more you can bring, as soon as you can bring them. People come in the store nearly every day asking for chairs."

Mary closed her eyes as a wave of relief swept through her. Coming here today, she'd expected to find Thomas in as bad a shape as she was and unable to buy or even trade for her chairs. His offer to buy them all was music to her ears. When she opened her eyes, she found him looking intently at her.

"You're having a hard time of it, aren't you?" he asked.

She threw on a protective smile. "We're making do, but you buying all these chairs will help immensely."

His expression of concern remained unchanged. "This is

Thomas you're talking to, not some stranger. I can tell you've had some hard times."

In spite of her best efforts to maintain her composure, a tear leaked from the corner of one eye. "We've all had some hard times, Thomas. But we keep pressing forward, right? That's what we do."

His face softened. "Yes, Mary, that's what we do. Tell me, how many days are you all staying with us?"

"We can't stay. We have to get back and take care of things on the farm."

"Excuse me for interrupting, Miss Mary," John said, "but I could go on back and take care of things while you stay here for a few days. I'm thinking it would be good for you."

"I can't let you do that," she protested. "We'll both head back."

"We have a saying in my country," John said. "'When a woman is hungry, she says, "Roast something for the children that they might eat."' You are that kind of woman, always thinking of other folks. Maybe it's time you let someone do for you."

John's words of ancient wisdom completely disarmed her, and she could find no way around them. She looked at Thomas.

Thomas said, "Stay with us until Christmas Day. It would make the girls so happy."

Memories of the sights and sounds of the girls on
Christmas morning through the years danced like fairies
through Mary's mind. But seeing William in each of those
memories and not knowing if she would ever have another
Christmas with him diminished the joy of the memories.
However, she decided she wasn't going to disappoint the
girls and said, "All right, then, you two win. I'll stay."

Chapter Twenty-Four

MARY

Several weeks later, Mary awakened with tear-dampened cheeks. Elements of the dream she just had lingered on: the smell of William, the touch of his hand, and the warmth of his kiss. She desperately tried to hold on to those feelings, but like trying to trap fog in a jar, it was impossible. The dream flew away like dried leaves scattered by the wind.

"William, come back to me," she whispered. "Wherever you are, please know that I love you and that I'm waiting for you."

She knew it was time to get up and start her day, but Melancholy, her dark and silent tormentor, had slipped into her bed overnight and filled her bones with lead, making the effort to rise from bed seem insurmountable. Guilt and regret ran through her veins as she thought about all the times she spoke harshly to William or was ill and cross with him.

She rolled onto her side and said softly, "My dearest William, I'm so sorry for the way I was, for the person I had become. If you will return to me, I promise I will be a changed woman. I will be kind and loving to you every second of every day."

Reaching over to the table beside her bed, she struck a match and lit a candle. When she saw her book of Tennyson's poem, she opened it and read one of the passages she'd marked:

And was the day of my delight
As pure and perfect as I say?
The very source and fount of Day
Is dash'd with wandering isles of night.

If all was good and fair we met,
This earth had been the Paradise
It never look'd to human eyes
Since our first Sun arose and set.

And is it that the haze of grief
Makes former gladness loom so great?
The lowness of the present state,
That sets the past in this relief?

Or that the past will always win
A glory from its being far;
And orb into the perfect star
We saw not, when we moved therein?

She sat up. "No that's not true—I don't feel that way about it just because of my grief. Our love was beautiful and our life together magical." She stood up and waved her arms and hands as if shooing away flies. "Get away from me, Melancholy. Do your tormenting of someone else today."

The physical effort got her blood flowing, and she felt somewhat better. She dressed herself and went to the kitchen to fix breakfast.

After she cooked some ham and made some coffee, she put

on her coat and gloves, wrapped the bearskin around her, and headed out to the woodshed. A sharp wind tried to knife its way through any tiny opening it could find in her outerwear, so she walked quickly to the shed and knocked on the door.

A second later John opened the door. "Come in, Miss Mary. It's a bitter-cold day today." He finished rolling up the blankets on his cot.

As soon as she stepped in, Mary began unwrapping herself. Pointing to the woodstove in the corner, she said, "That thing really works well, doesn't it?"

"It's worth its weight in silver to me," John replied. "I had heard of them but never seen one up close to see how well it works. It makes this a right nice room for me to stay in."

"Well, I wasn't about to leave you out in the open barn all winter and let you freeze to death. Installing the stove was Thomas's idea."

"Mr. Thomas was awfully kind to let us buy it on credit. He's a real nice man."

Mary noticed John's reference to "us" buying the stove. She was happy he felt a sense of partnership and ownership of how they made things run on the farm. "Thomas is a good man," she agreed. "William always said he was glad I met him before I met Thomas, or I might have married Thomas." She laughed. "I came out here to let you know breakfast will be ready soon. Come whenever you want."

Thirty minutes later, John came through the kitchen door.

"I had always heard old folks say that winter hurt their bones, but I thought they was just putting on. Now I know it's the truth. I feel that wind out there in my bones."

Mary sat a cup of steaming coffee on the table. "Drink some of that. It'll warm you up." She watched him as he cradled it in his hands and let the steam rise and bathe his face.

He said, "This coffee feels good twice, once when you hold it and smell it and the other when you drink it."

Mary smiles. "How many eggs do you want?"

"Just one this morning, ma'am."

Frowning, she asked, "Just one? What's wrong?"

"I'm just not feeling hungry this morning. Not sure why. Nothing to worry about."

"Okay, then."

As she turned to crack his egg in the skillet, John said, "You know one thing I still can't get used to?"

"No, what's that, John?"

"A white woman cooking for me. That's something I never dreamed about happening or even wished would happen. But here we are, me, an old black man, and you, a white woman fixing me breakfast. I still wish you'd let me cook sometimes. I know it wouldn't be as good, but I know a thing or two about cooking."

Mary carried the skillet to the table and slid his egg out onto his plate. "My mother always said there wasn't room for two cooks in the same kitchen, especially when there were sharp knives lying close by."

John laughed out loud. "I suspect your mother had some wisdom in those words."

In a few minutes, she joined him at the table with her plate of three eggs. "I've been thinking," she said. "If this wind will die down today, I may hitch the buckboard up and drive around to see what neighbors I still have. I really haven't been out to see what's changed since the battles around Chickamauga and Chattanooga. Maybe I'll luck out and see a stray cow. I surely do miss having milk and butter."

John said, "I don't like the sound of you riding around the countryside by yourself. There's still desperate men roaming these parts. Maybe I should go with you."

"Listen here," she said, with an edge in her voice. "I'm not going to live in fear and stay cooped up all the time or wait until I can have someone escort me around. If someone tries to make trouble, I'll give them all the trouble they'll know what to do with. I'll take the rifle with me and carry a knife, too."

"Can I ask you what your husband would say about it?"

Before she could think, she slapped him. "It's not your place to bring him up!" If she lived a hundred years, she would never forget the look of hurt in John's eyes. She threw her arms around him, "Oh, John, please forgive me. I didn't mean to do that." She pulled back away from him, hoping to find forgiveness in his expression. Guilt and regret reappeared and fell on her like the heavy bearskin she'd used earlier.

"I apologize," John said quietly. "That wasn't my place to bring him up."

His apology came so quickly and easily that it made her mad. "Don't apologize to me. You didn't do anything wrong. I'm the one apologizing to you. I need forgiveness, not you." Grabbing her cup off the table, she threw it across the kitchen. The tin cup clanked against the rocks of the hearth and bounced onto the floor. She stared at it until it stopped spinning. Speaking to no one in particular, she said, "Now that was a foolish thing to do." She looked at John. "I had a dream about him last night."

John nodded. "I see."

"It was so real. It felt like he had never left. But partway through it, I knew it was a dream. I didn't want to wake up, ever. I just wanted to hold on to the feeling. Holding someone in your dreams is better than not holding them at all."

Silence stepped between them and took hold of their hands as they stared off into their separate memories.

Several moments passed before John said, "I used to dream about Africa. But it's been so long now, I sometimes can't find the memories."

His comment pulled Mary out of her own grief, and she

tried to imagine what it would be like to have been taken to a foreign country against your will and sold like an animal. "I don't know how you've done it," she said.

"Done what?"

"Lived the life you've lived without becoming filled with bitterness and hatred."

"I remember a medicine man saying one time, 'There is no medicine to cure hatred.' And my grandmother used to tell me, 'If you offend, ask for pardon; if offended, forgive.' I have found it is much less work to forgive than it is to carry a grudge."

Mary looked at the scars just underneath John's sleeve cuffs and then looked at his face. "I know what you say is true, but I'm afraid I don't have as good a heart as yours. I don't know how to forgive when everything that matters the most to me has been taken from me."

He replied, "Then I suppose you must have felt like you deserved all those good things in life you had—good parents, plenty of food and clothing, a husband who loved you, a farm of your own—and that you didn't deserve to suffer any loss. The way I see it, it's the two sides of the same coin. In America, I seen men flipping a coin in order to make a decision or to win a wager. They call one side heads and the other tails. Then I seen a man who won his wagers every time, until someone discovered his coin had heads on both sides. That day he lost both his wager and his life. But isn't that the way folks want to play life? Have everything work out good for them and never have nothing bad happen?"

For not the first time since she had met John, his view of life forced her to look more closely at her own and to question whether or not she should change some things. One thing she had learned in her dealings with him was that she should always spend time thinking before she answered. She replied to him, "While I'm riding through the countryside today, I will think about what you have said."

*****

A couple of hours later, Mary drove the buckboard down the lane that connected her farm to the main road. The wind had calmed, like she had hoped it would, and a bright sun shone down from a cloudless sky.

She had decided she would first drop by Jacob and Nancy Colmers' farm to see if Jacob might have been able to save one of his heifers from marauding soldiers. When she pulled up to the front of the house, she saw no signs of life. Some of the windows of the large house had been broken out, and shutters hung at odd angles. And in spite of the cold temperature, the front door stood ajar.

Grabbing the revolver she had learned to always take with her on her outings, she walked toward the house.

Through the opening in the front door, she called out Nancy's name. When there was no answer, she called Jacob's, but again, the only answer was the echo of her own voice. Laying her hand against the half-open door, she pushed it wide open. Sunlight streamed through the opening and cast a rectangular, yellow light across the floor. Where the sunbeam ended, Mary saw the legs and feet of a man sitting in a chair.

She took a furtive step into the house. "Jacob? Is that you?"

A voice like the sound of a large, rusty hinge being opened said, "I'm home, Nancy."

Mary walked slowly toward the voice. "Jacob? It's Mary Thomson. I've come to see you." As her eyes became adjusted to the dimness of the room, she recognized Jacob, though it was obvious he hadn't shaved in days nor combed his hair. Every other button of his shirt was unbuttoned, his pants were only pulled up to his thighs, and his shoes were on the wrong feet.

Jacob stared past Mary toward the open door. "I'm home, Nancy."

Mary knelt down beside the chair and placed her hand on his forearm. "Jacob, look at me. It's Mary Thomson, the woodcutter's wife. Where is Nancy?"

Like the minute hand on a clock, Jacob's head turned slowly until he faced her. "Where is Nancy?"

"What's the matter, Jacob? What has happened?"

Staring at her with unfocused eyes, he repeated, "What's the matter? What's happened?"

Mary shook his arm. "Look at me! This is Mary. Where is Nancy?"

He fell silent and turned his head to stare at the front door.

Confused, Mary stood and went into the kitchen, where she found half-eaten food sitting on plates on the table. She headed up the stairs to their bedroom.

When she found the bedroom door shut, she called out, "Nancy!" She gripped the doorknob but found it was locked. "Nancy!" she called again. "This is Mary Thomson. Let me in." She jerked back and forth on the doorknob, causing the door to rattle against the jamb.

She hurried back downstairs to Jacob. "Where's the key to the bedroom, Jacob?" When he didn't reply, she grabbed the front of his shirt and shook him. "Where's the key?"

Suddenly, a key fell from his hand and clinked against the wooden floor.

Mary grabbed the key and raced back upstairs. When she finally got into the bedroom, a still form in the bed was spotlighted by sunlight coming through an open shutter.

"Nancy?" Mary said, in a quiet voice. She approached the side of the bed and recognized the sunken, ashen-gray face of Nancy. In a large circle underneath her head, the white sheets were the reddish-brown color of bricks, and in the center of her forehead, there was a small black hole.

Mary closed her eyes to block out the horrific sight. "Oh, Nancy, what has happened?" With leaden feet, she made her way slowly back downstairs. Halfway down the steps, the sound of a gunshot reverberated through the house. "Jacob!" Mary screamed and ran to the front room.

Before she reached his chair, she spied blood and gray matter glistening on the floor. On the other side of the chair, a smoking revolver laid on the floor.

Suddenly, rage surged through her. "What's the matter with you?" she yelled at Jacob's dead body. "What kind of coward are you? Is this the best you could do? Kill your wife and then kill yourself?" She kicked over the chair and stormed out of the house, leaving his crumbled body on the floor.

Still shaking with rage, she sat down on the porch. *What's the matter with people? You can't just give up. I'll never give up.* But then she stopped, as she remembered those moments when Melancholy had taken away her own desire to live.

She returned to the buckboard and was about to head home when she thought of Daniel and Lavina Embree. *I'm only a half mile from their farm. I think I'll swing by there and check on them.*

When she arrived, she helped herself to a drink at the well before knocking on the closed front door. When no one responded, she called out, "Lavina! Daniel! It's Mary Thomson." Again she waited, but again, no one came to the door.

When she tested the doorknob and found it was unlocked, she opened the door and stepped inside. Holding her breath, she listened for any sounds of life. A second later she thought she heard someone's voice. "Lavina?" she called.

This time she was certain she heard someone's voice,

though it was quite faint. She took a couple of steps in the direction she thought the voice was coming from. "Lavina? Where are you?"

At the sound of breaking glass, Mary's head jerked in the direction of the kitchen. Pulling the hammer back on the revolver, she walked stealthily toward the kitchen, silently cursing the creaking boards under her feet.

At the edge of the door to the kitchen, she took a deep breath, stepped in the doorway, and swung the revolver up in front of her. Immediately she saw Lavina sprawled on the floor. "Lavina!" she cried.

She rushed to her side. "Lavina, are you okay?" Thankful to see that her friend was not dead, she put her ear close to Lavina's mouth to hear her weakened voice.

"It's Daniel," Lavina whispered. "He's very sick."

Mary touched the back of her hand to Lavina's flushed face. "Goodness, Lavina, you have a fever yourself. Why are you in here on the floor?"

"I came to get some water for Daniel and passed out. But I don't know how long I've been lying here. Please, go see about Daniel."

"I'm going to run outside to the well and get some water. You just lie still. I'll be right back." As quickly as she could, Mary returned and found a cloth to bathe Lavina's feverish face.

Lavina grasped Mary's wrist. "See about Daniel."

"Okay, okay, I will." In their bedroom, she found Daniel lying in bed. "Daniel, it's Mary Thom—" She cut her words off when she saw his frozen features staring at the ceiling. "Oh, Daniel," she said in despair, "what has happened?" Seeing no signs of violence, she headed back to Lavina.

Squatting beside her friend, she slid her arms under her shoulders and legs and picked her up. "I'm going to carry you to the spare bedroom."

"How is Daniel?" Lavina whispered.

"Let's get you taken care of first. You're burning up with fever." Once Lavina was settled, Mary asked, "How long have you two been sick?"

"Daniel came down with a fever ten days or so ago. I've been by his side ever since. But he just didn't seem to be getting any better. I was afraid to leave him and go to the city for the doctor. How is Daniel?"

Mary's heart grieved for her friend. Taking Lavina's hand in her own, Mary said, haltingly, "There's no easy way to say this: Daniel is dead."

Lavina said, "I thought he was. I just couldn't say it to myself. Will you put me in bed beside him and leave me to die?"

Recoiling, Mary declared, "Absolutely not. You are not going to lie down and die. I'm not going to let you give up. I'm going to be right here with you until you get better."

"But I don't want to get better. I want to be with Daniel."

"Well, you know what?" Mary said, with an edge in her voice. "You don't get to make that choice. So until God's ready to take you, you're going to stay here with me. I'm going to go put some water on to heat up and make some broth of some kind for you." She laid a damp cloth across Lavina's forehead and left.

For the rest of the day and into the early evening, Mary kept wiping Lavina down with a cool, damp cloth. As she did so, she saw red splotches on Lavina's skin that let her know that this must be typhoid fever.

By the time Mary lit a lamp in the bedroom, Lavina's breath had become more and more shallow, and she had stopped responding when Mary spoke to her. "Please don't die, Lavina. You're my closest friend out here. What will I do without you and Daniel if William doesn't return?" She closed her eyes and silently prayed.

When she looked again, she saw that Lavina was no longer breathing. Mary stared at the now useless damp cloth in her lap.

Some time later, Mary stood up and walked out of the house, leaving the door wide open. As she climbed onto the buckboard, the revolver landed with a heavy thud as she pitched it to the floor. Exhausted, she decided to give the mule its head, rather than using the reins, and let it find its way back home in the dark.

It was well into the night when she was awakened by the sound of John's voice.

"Miss Mary!" With a lantern in his hand, he ran toward the buckboard as it rested outside the barn. "Where have you been? I've been worried sick, imagining all sorts of terrible things."

She let him help her down and guide her into the kitchen.

He sat her in a chair and handed her some cider to drink. "Tell me what happened."

In a monotone, Mary described the details of her day.

The only passionate tone in the telling came when John occasionally interjected a low, "My Lord," or "Have mercy," or "God rest their souls."

Chapter Twenty-Five

JOHN

Five days later, John had finished all his before-breakfast chores and looked toward the house. It puzzled him to see all the windows in the house still dark. *Hmmm, that's not like Miss Mary.*

He quietly entered the kitchen, walked to the fireplace, and held his hand out toward it. *There's been no fire in there since last night.* Frowning, he stirred the coals left from last night's fire and added some kindling. As it began blazing, he added a few pieces of firewood, then lit the lamp on the table and sat down to wait for Mary.

When an hour and a half passed without any sign of her, he opened the door of the kitchen and looked across the dogtrot to see if there was any light coming from underneath her door. The sun had already risen so high that in the bright light, it was impossible to tell.

He sat back down beside the fire. *Something's not right. I can feel it. It's not just her sleeping late because she's tired—she never does that. But maybe today is different. Maybe she decided she wants to be lazy today. A body's got a right to be lazy every once in a while if they want to. Nothing wrong with that. I believe I'll just fix me some breakfast and put on some more coffee for Miss Mary. She'll be rising soon.*

Another hour and a half later, John, filled with concern and anxiety, stood outside her bedroom door. He tapped lightly on the door and said, "Miss Mary? You all right?" He thought he heard a moan from inside the room. "Miss Mary. This is John. Are you all right?"

The faint sound of Mary's voice answered, "William, is that you? Help me, William."

Alarm knocked down the wall of reticence John had about entering Mary's room. Inside, he discovered her lying in bed, her face red and the edges of her hair wet with sweat. "Oh my Lord, Miss Mary, you got the fever!"

She looked at him with feverish eyes and reached her hand toward him. "William, you came back."

He took her hand, laid it back down on the covers, and noticed rose-colored spots on her arm. "No, Miss Mary, this here is John. You've done come down with the fever and are talking out of your head. You lie right here while I go get some water and a cloth."

When he returned, he found her sitting up in bed, holding her arms out in front of her. She said, "I see my babies. Come to Mama."

"Oh, Miss Mary, your babies are with Jesus." He laid his hand on her shoulder and pushed her toward the mattress. "Lie back down here and let me try to cool you down."

She didn't resist his efforts, but nothing about her expression indicated she'd heard him or understood him. Her head kept turning as she looked around the room, apparently at more apparitions.

He sat on the edge of the bed and dipped the cloth into the bucket of cool water. He squeezed the cloth, then laid it across her forehead. "This here is going to help. You'll see. You'll be better in no time."

She moaned, "I'm coming, Mama. I'll be there soon."

"Hush that kind of talk," John said. "You're not going anywhere. What am I going to do if you leave? What about when your William comes home? You want him to come home to an empty house and find you dead and buried? No sir. You're staying right here, and I'm staying right here beside you." He dipped another cloth in the water and rubbed it slowly over her arms.

The rest of the day, he sat by her, occasionally exchanging the water in the bucket for cooler water and trying to keep her head and arms cool. There were times when Mary fell into a restful sleep, but those didn't last long until she began talking out of her head and trying to sit up.

As daylight faded, John said, "Miss Mary, what are we going to do? Your fever hasn't gone down one bit that I can tell, and we both know that it's going to get worse when nighttime comes. That's what fever does. During the day, it makes you think it might be leaving, but when the sun goes down, it rears up like a wild horse and makes a body miserable again."

He lit a lamp and looked at her still form under the covers. He felt his stomach twisting as he thought about what to do. "Miss Mary, what I need to do is pull your covers down, so it'll help you cool off. But that's something that only a woman's husband or another woman ought to do. It's not fit nor proper for me to do it."

She turned her head and looked at him with unseeing eyes. "I need help."

Twin tears ran down both sides of his face, leaving silver tracks behind them. "I know you do. And I'm trying to help the best way I know how. Maybe you need to be drinking more water. Maybe that'll cool you down from the inside."

He hurried back outside and refilled the bucket, then gently lifted her head with one hand as he held a cup of water to her lips.

As Mary sipped, some of the water escaped and ran down her chin and neck and pooled in the small depression at the bottom of her neck.

When the cup was empty, John eased her head back down and wiped her chin and neck. "Do you want some more?"

"Yes," came her whispered answer.

John became excited at this seemingly coherent reply to his question. "Yes, ma'am! I'll bring you all the water you can drink."

After she drank a second cup, she lay back down and appeared to go to sleep.

A few hours later, John was startled out of his own sleep by Mary's screams.

"Get away from me!" she screamed toward the wall.

Swinging wildly, she said, "Stop! Don't!"

John tried to catch the wrists of her flailing arms but only managed to grab one, while her other fist caught him on the corner of his mouth. His head snapped back, and he immediately tasted blood in his mouth. "Lord have mercy, Miss Mary. I've not been hit that hard in a long time. Now you got to calm down."

She looked at him and said, "Thomas? Where have you been? Have you come to help me?"

John saw her skin glistening with sweat. "Your fever's gone up again, just like I figured. Now lie back down." He rushed out to refill the water bucket.

When he returned, he said, "Miss Mary, I've decided I've got to do what I've got to do. I apologize for it. But I promise you nobody except you and me will ever know about it."

She said, "Do what you must, John. It'll be all right."

He stared at her in disbelief. "Excuse me?"

But the window of lucidity that opened for a moment was quickly slammed shut as she said, "Where are my babies? Does anyone know where my babies are? Take me to Bitter Hill."

Lord Jesus, forgive me for what I'm about to do. Standing up, he pulled down the bedcovers to the foot of the bed.

Mary's thin cotton gown stuck to her damp skin in places and allowed the rosy glow of her feverish skin to show through from underneath.

John felt embarrassment and quickly averted his eyes. Instead, he focused on bathing her arms and face in cool water and letting her get a drink.

As an idea suddenly struck him, he propped open the bedroom door, then opened the window. Immediately a cool breeze wafted across the room. *Why didn't I think of that before now?*

He looked at her arm and saw goose bumps appear. He took that as a good sign and bathed her again in the cool water. Looking at her feet at the end of the bed, he decided to bathe them, too. "We going to get you cooled down one way or the other," he said. "I'm here, and I'm not leaving."

*****

MARY

When Mary opened her eyes, her head filled with nonsensical pieces of information: there was a Negro sleeping in a chair by her bed; it was broad daylight outside; her mouth felt dry and sticky. It took a second for her mind to put things into place and remember who John was. She stirred and tried to sit up but found herself too weak to do so.

John awoke and looked at her through bloodshot eyes. He managed a weak smile. "Good day, Miss Mary."

She tried to speak, but her mouth and throat were so dry she only made a raspy sound.

John quickly dipped a cup into a bucket of water beside the bed and held it to her mouth, while helping support her head. "Take a good drink of this."

Mary eagerly drained the cup and said in a clearer voice, "More."

"Yes, ma'am. That's a good sign. I believe the fever has finally left you."

She emptied the next cup before replying. "I feel as weak as a newborn. Will you help me sit up?" She held the edge of her covers up to her neck to protect her modesty as John assisted her.

"What are you doing in here?" she asked.

"You been mighty, mighty sick, Miss Mary. I been doing all I knew to do to help you."

A feeling of umbrage rose in her. "You mean you've been staying in my bedroom with me?"

John looked down at the floor and said quietly, "Yes, ma'am. I didn't know what else to do."

"Just because I was feeling bad last night is no defense for doing that, John."

He lifted his head and looked at her with an expression of surprise. "You done lost track of time, Miss Mary."

"What do you mean?"

"You been in this bed for the past eight days."

Mary felt shocked. "Eight days? I've been lying here for eight days?"

"Yes, ma'am. I thought a time or two that you were going to die on me. But you are a fighter."

"What did you do for me?"

"All I knew to do was keep wiping your face and arms with a cool, wet cloth. There was a time or two when your fever got real bad that I—" He hesitated.

"You what?"

He looked down at his hands. "I pulled your covers down and opened the window and door to let the cold air in. Miss Mary, I'm so sorry. I didn't know what else to do. I wasn't going to just sit here and let you die."

Mary's emotions ranged from shock to embarrassment to indignation when she pictured John seeing her in her nightgown. She started to upbraid him but stopped when she saw tears dropping onto his folded hands and realized there couldn't have been anything untoward in his actions. She then thought about what would have happened to her if he hadn't been here. She said, "I can't imagine what a difficult time you've had, John. It appears I owe you my life for the second time."

He looked at her and said, "You're welcome. I'm just glad you finally pulled through. But I expect you're going to be as weak as a baby for a little while, until we get you built back up. Water and a few sips of broth is all you've had for eight days. But I got some soup on in the kitchen."

"Soup sounds good." As John headed to the kitchen, she closed her eyes and thought about what he had told her. It seemed incomprehensible to her that a former slave would go to such lengths for a white person. Then her mind drifted back to when William had lain unconscious for days from the blow to his head. From there, she traveled further back to their first kiss at the corn-shucking bee. His dancing eyes and bright red hair burned brightly in her memory. But the memory dissolved into a blur, then evaporated.

She heard John reenter the room but kept her eyes closed, hoping for just another glimpse of William.

"Miss Mary, you been crying. Are you okay?"

She opened her eyes and looked at him through the prism of tears that clung to her eyelashes. His face appeared to be set in a field of stars. She said, "I was thinking about William."

"And I bet wherever he is, he's thinking about you, too. Now let's try sitting up and eating some soup."

Mary let him help her to a sitting position and opened her mouth as he offered her a spoonful of soup. Every taste bud in her mouth erupted into applause at finally being touched by something flavorful. "Oh, John, that may be the best-tasting thing I've ever put in my mouth. It is wonderful." Her stomach growled its own approval.

"Now that's sure enough a good sign," John said. "Your body's going to start waking up and looking to eat. I best make you some bread you can have sitting around here, so you'll have something to eat anytime you want it."

"You know how to make bread?"

"I can't make the kind of bread you make with yeast, but I can make cornbread and hoecake. Eating that with honey on it will give you back some energy. And some blackberry wine will be good for your blood."

"How's everything with the farm?"

"I really ain't been tending much to the farm, but now that you're better, I'll get back to taking care of things around here. It's February now, and as soon as it's dry enough, I'll hitch the mule to the plow and start breaking ground for spring planting."

Mary ate a few more bites then said, "I believe that's all I can eat. My stomach must have shrunk."

"No doubt that's true," John replied. "You just lie back and rest. Things will get back to normal soon."

As he started to get up, she took hold of his hand.

He looked at her with surprise.

She said, "I want to tell you again how thankful I am for all that you've done."

"You're welcome, Miss Mary." Just before he walked out the door, he turned and said, "You know, I asked myself a time or two why I was taking care of you and why I didn't just leave. The answer I kept coming up with was because you a good woman who has lost much, and maybe God sent me here to show you some mercy."

Before she could react, he closed the door behind him.

Chapter Twenty-Six

MARY

February 14, 1864

My dear Thomas,

On this day set aside for lovers, I write to you, my companion in lost love, to bring you up to date on the happenings in my life.

As you can tell by the tone of my first sentence, there has been no sign of William. But you probably already knew that because if he had returned, you would have heard my cries of joy all the way in Chattanooga. I cling to hope as a new calf does to its mother's life-giving teat, for hope is all that is keeping me alive. For the life of me, I do not understand why I haven't heard a word from William. My postman has told me that letters regularly travel between soldiers and their families back home, even sometimes between prisoners and their families. So why hasn't William written me? I refuse to consider the fact that the worst has happened—I refuse!

I now understand, in a way I never could before, the loneliness you felt when Anna died. I apologize for being selfish about my own loss of a friend and not being as sensitive as I should have been to your plight. I can only say that you appeared to have shouldered your loss much better than I am mine. Even though I believe William will return to me one day, that does not change the fact that he has not been here since the day he disappeared.

But just as you are not completely alone, with your daughters and Abigail, I am not completely alone either ever since John came to stay here. And for his coming, I am eternally grateful and must consider him as a gift from above, as I will soon explain.

A few weeks ago, I drove myself to a couple of the farms of neighbors to see how they were doing. I will not describe to you what I saw or what happened there, for to put it down on paper would bring the nightmare back afresh. But, simply put, it was horrific; the worst part being that I was exposed to what I believe to have been typhoid fever. I came home and was fine for a few days, but ultimately was stricken by the fever, and stricken would be the proper word, for it felled me like a tree before an ax.

For eight days, I knew neither whether I was alive or dead and have no memory of those days even today. I lay in my bed all day and night. The only thing that saved me was the watchful eye and care of John. He sat by my bedside both day and night, trying to cool the fever. You may react to that news as I did when John first told me and feel aghast and angered that he would cross all bounds of propriety. If you do feel so, perhaps two things will temper your feelings.

One is that I most certainly would have succumbed to the fever if John had not cared for me.

And number two is if you could have seen his demeanor when explaining to me what happened while I was out of my mind with fever, you would know that it was very difficult for him to do what he felt to be wrong in order to save my life. There was nothing untoward in any of his attitude nor, I'm confident, in his actions. If it can be said that a Negro is a gentleman, then John is certainly that.

The fever sucked nearly every ounce of life from me and left me as weak as a baby. Only now am I beginning to be strong enough to be outside working, and that not for very long at a time.

John has been plowing with the new plow William bought from you. He says it slices through the ground like a knife through butter. I have not asked him when he is leaving, for fear he will set a date. Neither has he approached me about our financial arrangement, so I must assume he's content for the time being with the agreement we came to regarding the chairs we make. But that doesn't seem fair to me since little time is now spent making chairs. I would value your input into these matters and solicit your advice.

Please write me soon and let me know how things are with you and the girls. Tell them all that I love them. I look forward to seeing all of you again, though I am not sure when I will be feeling up to making the trip, for as I mentioned, I fatigue so easily. I wish it was not so hard for you to get away from your store because then all of you could come for a visit, even if just for a day.

I close by sending you my heartfelt best wishes, my dear friend, in hopes I will see you soon.

Affectionately,

Mary

Chapter Twenty-Seven

THOMAS

February 16, 1864

My dear, dear Mary,

I was excited when I saw your name on the envelope of the letter I received, and yet I immediately felt guilty because I have been lax in writing to you. But when I opened your letter and began reading, my excitement turned to horror over the ghastly events that have transpired since last I saw you. To read that you nearly lost your life to typhoid fever made my heart stop, for now that William is gone, you are my dearest friend.

I will admit that when you began telling of John's role in helping you recover, I was indignant, as you so rightly guessed I would be. For a Negro slave, even a former slave like John, to sit at the bedside of a white woman and care for her night and day while she is sick would be unthinkable to everyone we know and would set idle tongues to wagging. However, the tender picture you painted of how he cared for you, both his attitude and demeanor, melted my indignation and turned it into admiration and thanksgiving. I close my eyes when I think of what would have happened if he hadn't been there for you.

You refer to John in your letter as a "gentleman." I would proffer this assessment of him—he is a noble man, and as such, he is set apart from most men. I will do this when next I see him: I will offer him my hand and thank him heartily! I might be so overwhelmed with appreciation that I hug the man!

You mention that he has started preparing ground for spring planting. I'm pleased that the plow works so well! As you begin thinking about the crops you will plant, let me offer a suggestion. The army that has occupied the city this winter shows no sign of leaving but rather is going to stay here to protect both the city and the railroad and waterways. Because of this, they are in chronic short supply of fresh vegetables. As a result, I have learned that the US Sanitary Commission has purchased one hundred and fifty acres of land at the edge of the city for the soldiers to grow vegetables on. This may seem like a vast amount of land for such a purpose, but there are tens of thousands of soldiers who have to be sustained. So my suggestion to you is to consider planting large amounts of vegetables for a cash crop and raise only what grain you will need for whatever livestock you might still have. I can assure you that there will be no shortage of market for the vegetables because there are even new civilians who enter the city almost daily, and they will need food, as well. This might prove even more profitable to you than your chair making.

And now I turn my attention to your loneliness of heart. The heart is not one vessel that contains a concoction of feelings; it is a large vessel containing many small vessels, each filled with its own powerful potion. There is a vessel that contains the love you have for a friend, another with the love you have for your children, another that contains hatred, another with bitterness, another with how you feel about God. And then there's the vessel that contains what for you and me is the most intense of all, your feelings for your spouse. And once that vessel gets knocked over so that all the feelings spill out, it can never get filled again, at least not with the warm feelings of love.

What happened with me when Anna died is that mine refilled with pain, the kind of pain that makes your chest feel like it may cave in. It makes sleep impossible to achieve, and food holds no interest for you. Eventually, my pain drained away, and anger took its place. I was mad at everyone and everything, especially God. But that didn't last forever either. It went away and was replaced by loneliness, the kind of loneliness that makes your body ache, ache to be touched and held by someone you have shared your bed with. (I hope you don't mind me speaking so plainly.) It sits on your shoulders during the day and on your chest at night. It makes you think you cannot go on living. This is the loneliness you are feeling, Mary. There is no simple cure for it, and it lasts longer than the pain and anger, which is why you probably feel like giving up at times.

I can tell you, though, that the intensity of the loneliness lessens, at least I think it does. Perhaps I've just grown accustomed to it, and it has changed the shape of me, like honeysuckle vines do when they grow and wrap themselves around the trunk of a young tree, squeezing, bending, and shaping it. I still miss Anna, sometimes to the point of tears, but not every day. That may sound strange and like I never loved her that much, but that is not true. It's just that time has a way of lessening the pain of a wound.

I wish I could come take your pain away and carry it for you, for I would readily do so. But no one can do it for you. Just know that you are not walking it alone. Though we don't see each other every day, I think of you and William every day and pray for you both. Florence, Emma, and Mary Beth mention you every night in their prayers. They could not love anyone more than they do you. In fact, I often think they love you more than me, which only makes me smile, for they couldn't love anyone better than you.

I have spoken to the girls about us coming to see you, and they are thrilled. So we are making plans to come on Sunday, February 2. We will rise early that day and get there as quickly as we can so that we can have as much of the day to visit as possible, and then we will return home that evening. I think a brief visit is best until you gain back more of your strength. I hope you will find these plans satisfactory.

I sign this letter as:

Your dearest friend,

Thomas

Chapter Twenty-Eight

JOHN

At midday, on April 19, John took a break from splitting rails out of a chestnut log that would be used to repair the fence beside the barn. From his position in the woods, he looked across the clearing that contained the house and barn and spotted Mary walking up the steep hill behind the house. When he noticed that she was carrying neither the pistol nor the rifle, he frowned. *Miss Mary knows better than that.*

He continued watching as she sat down on a rock halfway up the hill and seemed to be looking in his direction. He started to wave before he figured that she probably couldn't see him anyway through all the foliage. When she resumed climbing up the hill, he puzzled over where she must be going because although they didn't always tell each other what they would be doing on the farm each day, they generally had a good idea, and she didn't mention anything this morning about going off into the woods. It was when she disappeared over the summit of the hill that he decided to see for himself and make sure she was all right.

Ever since Mr. Thomas and his family came for that visit back in February, he'd been concerned about her. She had seemed more uneven, some days being quiet like she wanted to be left alone and other days seeming to be extremely happy.

More than once, he'd turned over in his mind watching

how Mary and Thomas greeted each other. The way they had hugged each other seemed to be more than just two friends saying hello. It looked like neither of them wanted to let go of the other. But what did it mean? That's what he kept puzzling over.

He had also caught Thomas looking at Mary in a way that seemed like he loved her—and not just as a friend. *I can understand why Mr. Thomas would feel that way about her, his wife being dead now for several years; his heart has healed and is looking for love again. He sure couldn't find no better woman than Miss Mary.*

But John knew Mary was still in love with William. She refused to believe he wouldn't be coming back home any day now. *I just don't want Mr. Thomas to create any confusion in her heart or to cause her to do something she might regret.*

John supposed that if he had ever had children, he would have felt toward them much the same way he did toward Mary, which is why he hadn't made any effort to leave the farm nor had any thoughts about doing so.

When he saw the crest of the hill just ahead, he slowed his pace and listened carefully for any sounds up ahead. All he heard was the sounds of the cardinals, blue jays, and crows.

As he arrived at the plateau, the first thing he noticed was the giant, spreading chestnut tree; then he saw Mary kneeling underneath it.

He was uncertain what to do next. Clearly, she had gone there for a specific purpose and didn't appear to have any intention of going farther. As he looked more closely, he noticed there was something on the ground in front of her, but he was too far away to be certain what it was.

He took a few steps in her direction, then said, in a voice just loud enough that Mary could hear him, "Miss Mary?"

Mary jumped to her feet and whirled around.

Keeping still, he said, "Do you mind me being here?"

She rubbed her cheeks with her hands and motioned for him to come. "No, John, it's fine. Come here, and I'll show you something."

When he got closer, he saw red, streaked cheeks. "Miss Mary, you been crying. Are you all right?"

She turned her back to him when he reached her and waved her hands toward the objects on the ground.

It was then that he recognized that they were grave markers. Silently, he read the names and dates. *My Lord, this is her babies.*

She said, "Today would have been Alexander's birthday, April thirtieth."

"Yes, ma'am," he said reverently. "I see that."

She brushed aside some leaves from the base of Alexander's marker. "This hill is my hill. I call it Bitter Hill, after the story in the Old Testament of Ruth's mother-in-law, Naomi, when she returned to her home country after losing her husband and both her sons. She told

everyone to no longer call her Naomi but to call her Mara."
She paused before adding, "Mara means 'bitter.'"

John held his tongue to see if she wanted to say more.

"You would think," Mary continued, "that after you've lost
one child, it would get easier when you lost more, but the
opposite was true for me. Each one cut me deeper than the
one before because the hope kept getting larger each time I
got pregnant. William and I would say to each other, 'This
time it's going to work.' When the doctor told me after my
last one that I couldn't get pregnant anymore, William was
devastated, but I was relieved because I just didn't think I
could go through it all again—all that hope followed by the
disappointment."

John felt her looking at him and so turned to face her.

Mary said, "Do you think that's why William hasn't come
home?"

"What do you mean?"

"Did he find another woman, a woman who could give him
children? And now he's started the life he always wanted
but could never have with me?"

John felt the weight of her question pushing down on his
shoulders. Before he could reply, Mary continued.

"I wouldn't blame him if he did. Every man wants to have
a son. I couldn't produce a son or a daughter for him." She
turned away from him and looked back at the markers.

John slowly lowered himself onto his knees and looked

from one marker to another while searching his heart for the right words to say to her. "Miss Mary, I don't know your William except at how I've come to know him through your eyes and Mr. Thomas's and his girls' eyes. Everything I've learned about him says he would come crawling back here on his hands and knees if he could. He would have to be a fool to walk away from you. You're just thinking crazy stuff because don't you, nor anybody else, know why you ain't heard nothing from him."

Mary joined him on the ground. "You really think so?"

"For certain, I do."

They remained quiet for a bit. Then Mary said, "I named this place Bitter Hill because of how bitter I was about all that I had lost. I held on to and nurtured my bitterness. But as time has gone on, that bitter feeling has faded. When I came up here today, I didn't feel any bitterness and not even as much sadness as I used to feel when I came up here."

"Seems to me that's a good thing. A heart don't need to hold on to all that misery."

Mary nodded. "I suppose it is, but it also scares me."

"Why's that?"

"I'm not sure what to put in its place. Ever since William disappeared, I've been holding as tightly as I can to hope, letting that be my anchor."

John noticed as her chin began to waver.

She said, "But lately I've found my grip on hope slipping." She turned and looked at him. "If I have let go of my bitterness, and now I let go of hope, there won't be anything left in me." Tears began rolling down her cheeks, and she struck her chest with her palm. "My heart will turn black, it will turn to stone, and I'll stop caring about anyone or anything. There won't be any purpose in living. All of this," she waved her hand toward the farm, "it won't mean anything."

A daring idea occurred to John, and he hesitated about acting on it but decided it might work. "If that's how you feel," he said, "you wait here, and I'll be right back." He started to stand up.

"Where are you going?" she asked.

"I'm going to go get the pistol."

"The pistol? Why?"

"I'm going to bring it back up here and kill you, and then I'm going to kill myself." Her face registered the surprise, shock, and horror he hoped it would.

"What are you talking about?" she asked.

"You said all this don't mean nothing and that you didn't have no reason to keep living. If that's so, then let's both be done with this world because I sure don't mean to stick around here if you're dead. I ain't told you this, but I've already decided I'm too old to move on to anywhere else. I've made up my mind that I'm going to die on this farm. I just sort of figured it'd be when I got a little older. But dead is dead no matter when it happens. So let me go get the pistol, and we'll both be done with this life right here, right now."

In the midst of her confusion, Mary's face softened. "But what about Thomas and the girls? How would it affect them?"

"They don't mean nothing to you because you've done said that you don't care about nobody or nothing."

"But that's not really true. I love those girls just as if they—"

When she didn't finish her sentence, John said, "Just as if they were your children."

Tears reappeared in her eyes. "Don't say that out loud. I can't love them like that. They're not mine. Besides, I am cursed, and if I let myself feel that way for them, something terrible will happen to them, just like it has happened to everyone I have loved."

"What do you mean, cursed? You mean like a witch or somebody done put a curse on you?"

"No, God has. I don't know why, and I can't explain it, but it's the only reason I can think of as to why death and sadness follow me everywhere I go."

"If you've been cursed, Miss Mary, then I have been in a double measure." He turned around and lifted his shirt so that she could see the scars on his back.

She gasped, "Oh, John."

He turned back around and pulled the collar of his shirt down. "I know you've seen this." He lifted his pants leg and lifted up his foot so that the scars on his ankles showed. "And you've seen this. And all of that don't even touch the amount of trouble that's been heaped on me in my life. Are you telling me all this happened to me because I'm cursed?"

Mary opened her mouth but then closed it. She shook her head. "I don't know what to say."

"That's 'cause you can't explain it, and neither can I. What I try to pay attention to is things that I do know, not things that I don't. So here's what I know about you and Mr. Thomas and his girls—them girls love you just like you is their mother. I know that because I see it in their eyes when they're with you. Even if Mr. William don't come back home, your job here ain't done. You've got three girls who are depending on you to show them how to be a woman."

"And Thomas?" she said, tentatively.

"Mr. Thomas, he loves you, too. I'm not sure how he loves you, but he does. And since I don't know how it is, I don't worry about it. All will be revealed when it's time."

She gave him a weak smile. "So what *I* know about what you're telling me is that sometimes I think selfishly, thinking only about my pain and my sorry and troubles. You're correct. That's something I need to remember more often."

"I suspect we all ought to remember things like that."

Chapter Twenty-Nine

MARY

Mary eagerly opened the envelope addressed in Thomas's handwriting and took out the letter. She began reading:

June 25, 1864

My dear Mary,

It is with great fear and trepidation that I pen this letter to you, for I fear it could change things between us forever. I have battled back and forth with myself for days as to whether it is wise to share my thoughts with you, but ultimately, I decided I must be honest with you. Without honesty between friends, there can be no true friendship. So I begin by asking for your forgiveness for all that I am about to say, but I have to pour my heart out to you lest it burst.

If there is one man on earth I would give my life for, it is William. I have loved him like a brother, actually more than a brother, almost from the time we met. Our friendship often reminded me of that of David and Jonathan in the Old Testament, whose hearts were knit together. William's disappearance and subsequent silence have grieved me to no end. And now it has been nine months, and no one knows anything more now than when he disappeared that first day.

I, for one, do not understand it. Every day I see or hear of men who have deserted and returned home to their land and families, or there have been prisoner swaps between the Union and the South that allowed soldiers to return to their ranks and at least have the opportunity to send a letter to let loved ones know how they are doing and where they are. I ask myself, "Where is William in all this?" The answer was obvious early on, but I refused to let myself consider it. I wanted to believe with all my heart that any day would find him home again. But now, I must be honest with myself.

Mary slung the letter out of her hand like it was a poisonous spider. She ran out of the kitchen and into the yard, held her hands over her ears, and screamed William's name at the top of her lungs. The sound was so forceful it felt like it tore a hole in her throat, and she bent double, coughing.

When she caught her breath and was able to speak, she said aloud, "No, no, no. It's not so. It can't be. He will come home. He'll come back to me. I know he will. He has to." She staggered to the well and tried to drown the burning truth by guzzling some cold water.

After a few minutes, her breathing and heart rate slowed, and she looked toward the house like she would toward a cave that had a roaring mountain lion in it. She didn't want to go back inside, but yet she knew she needed to hear the rest of what Thomas had to say. So she walked slowly back into the cabin and picked up the scattered pages of Thomas's letter off the floor. She scanned down the page to the place where she had left off reading:

Dare I write these next five words? (Please do not hate me.) I believe William is dead. Even as I am writing, the words blur before my eyes because of my tears.

And what must this be doing to you to hear such painful words from your husband's best friend? I fear what you must think of me for saying them, but there is a future-looking reason why I speak so honestly with you.

Mary, I have loved you for many years and for many reasons. You were my wife's best friend, and you were the wife of my best friend. You have always been there for me, in sunshine and in shadow. After my wife, you are the most beautiful woman I know, and yet your outward beauty pales in comparison to your inside beauty. You have a strength about you that I envy. You are hardworking and unafraid. You and I, Mary, we could be good together.

Mary folded the letter shut and closed her eyes. In each sentence of this last paragraph, she could feel the cadence of her heart increasing. Feeling certain of where Thomas was heading with his thoughts, she was both excited but yet filled with dread. "My dear Thomas," she whispered, "you are asking me to close the door on my life with William. I don't think I can do that—not yet."

Opening her eyes, she continued reading.

I would like to ask your permission to call on you, not as a friend but as someone who wants to win your heart and your affection. I do not ask this lightly or boldly but, as it were, on a bended knee and with a bowed head of humility because what I ask, I don't deserve.

Please do not be hasty in your reply to me, but rather, give it your honest consideration. If you decline my request, our friendship, at least from my end, will remain as strong as ever, for I could never turn away from you.

I shall not breathe a word of this to the girls, or they would all three beat a hasty trail to your house to try and persuade you on my behalf.

I am your loving and devoted servant,

Thomas

*****

An hour later, Mary was still sitting in her chair by the fireplace in the kitchen when John walked in.

He said, "I went over to look at the hayfield today, and I believe it's about ready to cut. I haven't seen any signs of rain coming in the next few days, so maybe we should start working there in the morning. What do you think?"

Without looking at John, Mary held up Thomas's letter. "I got a letter from Thomas today."

"I can tell something's wrong, so the letter must have had some bad news in it."

Motioning to a chair on the other side of the fireplace, she said, "Come sit with me."

He immediately complied.

She looked at him and said, "I'm not sure how I would

characterize the letter as to whether it's good news or bad, but it for certain has left me particularly unsettled."

John sat quietly with his hands folded in his lap.

Mary continued, "He said some things I didn't want to hear but maybe I needed to hear, and he said some things that made me happy but frightened me, too."

"Hmm, that sounds like some kind of letter. I know Mr. Thomas has a way with words, so he must have said what he meant to say."

"Yes, he does, and I agree that there's no mistaking that he said what he meant to say. I just don't know what I should do about it." She hesitated, then said, "I would like for you to read the letter and tell me what I should do."

John held up both hands. "But, Miss Mary, that's something he meant for only your eyes to see. I would feel like I was peeking in the window of somebody's house. It wouldn't feel right."

"I understand, John. But who else am I going to go to for advice? We've worked side by side on this farm for the past nine months. I've come to trust you and have found you to be a man of wisdom. Isn't it fair that I ask you for help when I need it?"

He shifted uncomfortably in his chair. "It appears Mr. Thomas is not the only one who has a way with words." He reached toward her. "I'll read the letter like you've asked me to."

Mary handed the letter to him and watched his face as he read it.

He read for a bit, then looked up at her. "Miss Mary, are you sure you want me to read all of it?"

Mary nodded.

After he read for a while more, he folded it up and looked at her. "We had a saying in Africa, 'Only when you have crossed the river can you say the crocodile has a lump on his snout.' Now that I done read the letter, I understand why it left your heart all jumbled up. He said some awfully hard things, hard to accept, but probably hard for him to say, too. But he surely spoke some wonderful truths about you, truths that no man can deny."

Mary asked, "Do you believe William is dead?"

"Miss Mary, don't make me answer that."

She felt her heart sinking but pressed him. "I want to know what you think."

"You know, just because a man thinks a thing don't make it so."

"I don't care. I just want to hear you say it."

John looked down at his hands and laced his fingers together before looking back up. "If I have to say what I believe, then I believe he must be dead."

It was what she expected him to say, so she felt no shock at hearing it. As a matter of fact, she was surprised at what little emotion she felt. "What does it mean that hearing you say that produces not one tear in me? Have I been fooling myself into thinking I still love him and miss him? Has the harshness of life scarred me so that I can't feel anymore? When I first read Thomas's letter, it ripped my heart out, but maybe it was just the truth's way of finally being released. A person can know the truth but keep it buried and pretend they don't know. Then they end up walking around like an actor in a play and believe their own lie."

John said, "When I came here nine months ago, the first thing I learned was how much you loved Mr. William. I never saw anyone love another more. I think you still love him and always will, but your hope has finally run out. Can't nobody fault you for that. No fire can keep burning if you don't add wood to it. There just haven't been any signs that you could point to and place on the fire of your hope to keep it burning. All that's left now is the ashes. I've been noticing the signs of it for some time, but it wasn't my place to say anything about it. I knew you'd figure it out on your own. I suppose Mr. Thomas's letter acted like a small knife you'd lance a boil with—it let all your feelings out."

Mary took a deep breath and released it slowly. "You're right. I have known the truth. I just didn't want to face it. But all of this is only the first half of Thomas's letter. What about the other half? What am I supposed to do about that?"

"When it comes to matters of the heart, Miss Mary, I can't tell you what to do. You have to find your own way."

Chapter Thirty

MARY

John and Mary stood at the foot of Bitter Hill, looking at a wide, thick, reddish-brown chestnut board lying on the ground.

"Are you sure you want to do this?" John asked.

Mary waited for a moment, then answered, "Yes. July Fourth seems like the right time. It was a date marking momentous change in this country in 1776, and today will mark the beginning of momentous change for me. It's time to start looking forward and not backward."

John squatted down, tied one end of a rope around the board, and threw the other end over his shoulder. "Then let's start climbing."

Mary started up the hill ahead of him while he followed.

After several minutes, she said, "Let me know when it's my turn. We agreed to share getting it up the hill."

"It's surely going to get heavier the farther up the hill we get. But we'll get it there. I'm okay right now, but I'll let you know when I need to stop."

Mary thought about the first time she had climbed the hill, after the death of her and William's first child. They had both been in shock, having never even considered the thought that they could lose their baby. Neither of them had said a word while William dug the grave, placed the remains in the ground, recited the Twenty-Third Psalm, and offered a brief prayer. It hadn't been until the thud of the first shovel full of dirt landed that Mary felt something inside of her break. It hadn't been an audible sound, like the crack of the trunk of a falling tree, but the feeling was similar—the feeling of being broken in half. It was a brokenness she hadn't thought she would ever recover from. But time and William's love helped.

She heard John grunt and stumble behind her. When she turned around, he was on his knees. "John?" She stepped carefully toward him.

"I'm all right. It got caught on a rock without me knowing. Caught me off guard. Just give me a chance to catch my breath, and we'll keep going."

Mary lifted the board over the hidden rock and scooted it a little ways up the hill. Then she took the rope out of John's hand. "It's my turn to pull."

He gave her a weak smile. "I'll not argue with you."

As she headed up the hill, pulling the board behind her, John asked, "Can I ask you a question?"

"Of course you can."

"Well, here's the thing. It's been over a week since Mr. Thomas done asked you if he could call on you. I was wondering if you've decided what you're going to do about that."

"Do you think right now's the best time to ask me about that?" she barked at him.

"I suppose you'd know the answer to that. I apologize for asking."

Her foot slipped, and she reached out and grabbed hold of a maple sapling just in time to prevent her from falling. Swapping the rope to her other shoulder, she continued walking. "I'm sorry, John. I didn't mean to be so harsh. There's no reason for you not to ask me that question. I guess it irritated me because I can't make up my mind what to do, and that's not like me. I can't stand a person who won't make a decision, and yet that's exactly the place I find myself in. There's still so much uncertainty in the air, especially about the war. Who knows how it will finally end and how long it will take."

"I don't believe it's going to last much longer," John replied. "I know lots of folks been saying that for a while, but more and more Confederate soldiers are losing heart and deserting, and I think some of the people are getting tired of it, too. Last time we were in the city, I heard the Yankee soldiers talking about a man named Newt Jones who lives over in Mississippi. He declared loyalty to the Union and led a rebellion against the Southern army. He actually overthrew the officials in the county he lived in and raised the US flag over the courthouse. That tells you something about how not everybody in the South agrees with this war."

Mary stopped, sat down on a rock outcrop, and wiped sweat from her face. "That's unbelievable! I know that before the war started, there were lots of differing opinions around here about who was in the right, but no one ever talked about doing anything that dramatic."

There were a couple of beats of silence before John asked, "If the war ended today, what would you do about Mr. Thomas?"

"To even consider seeing another man feels like a betrayal of William. I don't know if my heart will let me. Thomas is a wonderful man, and I've loved him as a friend for years. To take that love and try to turn it into something else might ruin everything." She stood up and started walking up the hill again. "Indecision is like being tied to a tree. No one's going to move and nothing's going to change until the bonds are cut."

When they reached the top of the hill, Mary bent over and, with a grunt, lifted the board into her arms.

As they walked toward the massive chestnut tree and the row of tiny grave markers underneath it, a breeze rustled the leaves.

Mary knelt down at the end of the row of little grave markers and lowered the board to the ground. She and John stood it upright and braced it by putting rocks around the base of it. "You did a nice job of carving the words into it," she said. She read them aloud: "William Thomson, born 1830, died 1863. He was loved."

"I think it looks real nice," John said. "And that chestnut board will last a long, long time."

They both look at the marker for several moments before Mary said, "Will you sing a song?"

"Course I will. You got any particular song in mind?"

"No. I'll let you choose."

After a moment, John began singing soft and low:

Swing low, sweet chariot, coming for to carry me home.

Swing low, sweet chariot, coming for to carry me home.

I looked over Jordan and what did I see?

Coming for to carry me home.

A band of angels coming after me.

Coming for to carry me home.

Swing low, sweet chariot, coming for to carry me home.

Swing low, sweet chariot, coming for to carry me home.

Sometimes I'm up, sometimes I'm down.

Coming for to carry me home.

But still my soul feels heaven bound.

Coming for to carry me home.

Swing low, sweet chariot, coming for to carry me home.

Swing low, sweet chariot, coming for to carry me home.

If you get there before I do

Coming for to carry me home.

Tell all my friends I'm coming too.

Coming for to carry me home.

Swing low, sweet chariot, coming for to carry me home.

Swing low, sweet chariot, coming for to carry me home.

When he finished, a single tear clutched the bottom of Mary's jaw, quivering, not certain whether to let go and take the plunge into oblivion or hold on until Mary could touch it and absorb it back through her skin. Mary reached toward it with the back of her hand, but the teardrop let go and landed on her hand before it was touched.

"That was beautiful," she said to John. "Thank you."

"It was my honor to do it."

She kissed her fingertips, then touched the grave marker. "Someday I will join all of you. Then, finally, we will have our family." Standing up, she said, "I guess we're finished here."

Just then, she heard something that sounded like someone sneezing. She looked at John, who was looking back at her with a questioning look. "Did you hear that?" she asked.

"Yes, I did. Was it a sneeze?"

Their heads turned in every direction, looking for the source of the sound. When they looked back at each other,

Mary put her finger to her closed lips and pointed toward the back of the tree. She motioned for John to go one direction while she would go in the opposite.

Moving silently, they eventually met at the back of the tree, neither of them having seen anything.

There was another sneeze, this time giving a clearer sense of direction.

They slowly looked up.

Sitting among the branches were two small children, one black and one white.

"Sweet Jesus," John said, "what in the world is this?"

Mary stood with her hand over her mouth.

The children suddenly started trying to climb higher, but the white child lost his grip on a limb and tumbled downward through the branches.

Mary screamed and dove toward the spot where she believed he would land. Twisting her body in midair, she caught him just as they both landed.

The boy tried to scramble away from her, but she managed to grab his ankle.

John hollered up into the tree at the other boy. "You come on down here right this minute. I mean it. You come down, or I'm coming up there after you."

Slowly, the black boy reappeared out of the canopy of

leaves and began climbing down.

When he made it to the bottom limb, John reached up and took hold of his leg. "Jump on down here."

When he jumped down, John grasped his wrist.

Mary stared from one boy to the other. They were barefooted, and their clothes were ill-fitting and threadbare. The white boy's hair was matted and tangled. Their eyes look tired, not the kind of tired that's the result of playing or working hard, but the kind that happens when someone's soul is weary, an expression that is out of place on boys so young. "Where do you boys live?" she asked.

Pointing deeper into the woods, the black boy said, "We come from back yonder way."

Mary said, "That's just wilderness. Nobody lives in there."

"We does," the boy reiterated.

"What's your name?" John asked.

"My name's Pete. His is Frank."

"What are you all doing over here?" Mary asked.

"We got hungry," Frank finally spoke.

"Hungry? That doesn't make any sense," she said. "Where are your parents, Frank?"

"They gone," Pete answered.

"Gone where?" John asked.

"We don't know. We got up one morning, and they wasn't there."

Mary shook her head, perplexed by it all. "None of this makes any sense. How old are you, and when's the last time you ate?"

"I'm eleven," Pete replied.

"And I'm ten," Frank added.

"Last time we ate anything was yesterday morning. We found some berries." As if to emphasize the truth of his statement, Pete's stomach growled.

Mary and John exchanged a look.

John asked, "What are we going to do?"

"We're going to take them to the house and feed them. Then they're going to show us where they live."

*****

Two hours later, Mary and John were following the boys through the woods. The tree canopy was so thick that little sunlight filtered through. Thick, bright green moss surrounded the base of the tree trunks, and the air smelled musty and damp.

Mary said to John, "Do you think the boys know the way to where they were living?"

"I hope so. If not, then we've walked a long way for nothing. We need to keep a watch on the sun so that we get back home before dark."

"I've thought about that, too."

Suddenly, they entered a small clearing with a tiny, fragile-looking cabin sitting in the middle. Pointing at it, Pete said, "That's where we live."

Mary felt her heart sink. "That's barely more than a shed," she said in low tones to John.

"It's a pitiful sight," John agreed.

When she reached it, Mary stuck her head in the doorway of the windowless cabin and waited for her eyes to adjust to the dim light before she went in. It was a one-room structure, about twelve feet square, with a dirt floor. The only furniture in it was a table and two chairs. As John stepped in, she asked, "Why are these walls so black?"

John wiped his finger across one of the logs and smelled it. "Soot. That fireplace don't draw. Most of the smoke pours out into the room." With disgust in his tone, he added, "This ain't nothing but poor white trash that come here and built this. It's disgraceful!"

They stepped back out and faced the boys.

Mary asked, "How long ago did your parents leave?"

Pete and Frank looked at each other and shrugged.

Pete said, "I'm guessing ten or twelve days."

"What have you been eating?" John asked.

Pete answered, "We caught a couple of rabbits. I know how to make a rabbit trap."

Frank chimed in, "And we been eating berries and some nuts we found on the ground."

Mary said, "Tell me the whole story of how you all ended up here, and how you ended up with them, Pete."

With Pete doing most of the story, with occasional comments from Frank, the boys told how they came from Kentucky, where Frank's father was the overseer on a farm. When it became clear that the Yankees were going to control the state, Frank's father bought Pete from the owner of the farm, and they all headed south, full of talk about buying a big farm and slaves and making a lot of money.

The best Mary was able to determine, they had moved there last fall and endured a winter and spring, with the parents blaming each other for their dream not materializing. Apparently, they were quick to take out their anger and frustration on the boys by beating them, making them go without food for days, or forcing them to sleep outside on the ground.

As she listened to their story, she felt her heart swing from sadness and pity to a violent rage and urge to put her hands on the parents and dispense justice to them.

When they finished their pathetic story, Mary lowered herself until she was eye level with them. "Well, I can promise you this: You have gone hungry for the last time, and there'll be no more sleeping outside on the ground. You're going to stay with us until we can find someone you can live with."

The boys looked from one adult to the other.

Frank said, "But how will my parents find me?"

"I don't like telling you this," Mary answered him, "but your parents aren't coming back. And I'll add that they better not show up on my farm, or I'm liable to shoot them both for what they did to you boys."

Pete looked at John. "Are you her slave?"

"No, boy. I'm a free man."

Frank asked Mary, "What will your husband say? He might not want us there."

Mary replied, "My husband's dead."

Chapter Thirty-One

MARY

"Miss Mary, I feel like I need to mention to you that Frank and Pete have been with us nigh onto a month, and you still haven't gone to town to try and find somebody they can live with. The longer they stay here with us, the harder it's going to be for them to leave and go to somebody else."

"I know, I know," Mary said to John as she nodded slowly. "I think about it every day, and I need to get it done this week. When we brought them here to begin with, I thought they'd be here a couple of days, and I'd be ready to send them on. I didn't expect to be so captivated by them. To see them make such dramatic changes in just this short amount of time is amazing."

"You're right about that," John agreed. "I think they've both grown."

"And they smile now."

"Yes, ma'am, and ain't that a pretty sight?

"It sure is. But here's the problem with them staying here: feeding them a meal and putting clothes on them is one thing, but taking them to raise is another. I don't know a thing in the world about boys. It hasn't happened yet, but someday they'll start asking questions that I won't know the answers to. Then what will I do?"

"Begging your pardon, Miss Mary, but you talk like you're

going to be doing all this by yourself. I plan on being around to help, and I know a thing or two about boys since I used to be one." He delivered the last words with a sly smile.

Feeling a bit foolish, Mary said, "I don't know why I do that sometimes, think only in terms of me. You are very much my partner in running this farm, but sometimes I get to chasing rabbits in my head and forget about how good you are to help in everything. You're right, you would know more about raising boys than me." She started to share a hidden thought but decided to hold it close.

John said, "But maybe there's another reason you're reluctant to raise the boys."

Mary suddenly felt as if a big gust of wind had lifted her dress and exposed her in front of a street full of people. It was as if John knew what her secret thought was. "I honestly don't know what you mean," she said, trying to cover herself.

John's eyes held hers. "Honestly?"

She didn't like being caught in a lie but saw no way out other than coming clean. "You're right—there is another reason, but I'm scared to say it out loud because it will feel more real and more terrifying." She fell silent, not knowing what to say next but also fearful that her tongue would betray her.

After a few moments, John said, "Can I ask you how you feel about Pete and Frank?"

Mary felt as if John's simple question was one of her sharp paring knives that she used to peel apples with, and in his hand, it had sliced away her fear and reluctance, leaving behind the raw truth of her heart. She replied in an angry tone, "I don't want to care about them! I want them to leave, right now, this very moment!" She paced back and forth on the porch, biting her lip and hoping that the tightness in her throat would subside. When she looked at John sitting there quietly with no expression, she felt like slapping him. She stopped and faced him with her hands on her hips. "What are you looking at?"

"You're afraid, aren't you?"

"You don't understand, John. I've lost too much. I can't stand to think about taking the chance on losing again. How do I dare risk taking down the thorny, protective fence I've placed around my heart and risk loving and losing again?"

"Do you have that poem book on you that you're always reading from?"

Surprised, Mary felt the pocket on her dress and pulled out the Tennyson poem. "Yes, but how do you know about it?"

"I see you reading it. One day it was lying on the table, and I read some in it. I hope that was all right."

"Well, sure, I don't mind."

He reached out his hand, and she passed the book to him.

John turned through the pages until he came to a stop. He turned the book toward her and had his thumb pointing toward a stanza. "Could you read that to me?"

Like an obedient schoolchild, Mary took the book and read:

I hold it true, whate'er befall;
I feel it, when I sorrow most;
'Tis better to have loved and lost

Her voice caught, and the words on the page blurred as her eyes filled with tears. She blinked, and shards of tears cascaded. She bit her lip and tasted the blood, but she knew she had to finish the stanza. With much effort, she read:

Than never to have loved at all.

She looked at John through the prism of her tears.

He said, "I couldn't understand a lot of the words in that there poem, but I understood those, and I believe they are true, do you?"

Before she could answer, the postman came riding up to the porch and handed her a letter. She immediately recognized Thomas's familiar handwriting on the envelope and felt a twinge of guilt that she'd not yet replied to his last letter. "It's from Thomas," she said.

John rose and said, "The boys and I will see to some chores." He walked toward the barn.

Mary reflected on the things she and he had spoken about, and her thoughts turned to the changes she had been noticing in herself since the boys had come. She'd begun to look forward to the coming day, rather than looking at it as just another day to labor on the farm. She felt great pleasure in nurturing Pete and Frank, coaxing them out of their shyness and uncertainty, and in watching how heartily they ate her cooking. She'd forgotten how much she used to enjoy watching William eat. *Maybe what I feel is a sense of purpose. Is this what it's like to have children?*

She walked off the porch and into the shade of the oak tree, then opened Thomas's letter.

August 1, 1865

My dearest Mary,

It is not my desire or intent to rush you or to appear impatient (though that I am) in my writing you this letter, but I find it impossible to remain silent.

It has now been over a month since I asked your permission to call on you, and I've neither seen nor heard from you. As a result, my imagination has been running wild, looking for explanations. Unfortunately for me, all those imaginations are dark ones and fill me with despair.

Besides my own feelings, Florence, Emma, and Mary Beth are eager to visit with you. It seems the older they get, the more intense are their feelings toward you. Not a day goes by without one of them referencing your name. In my opinion, it takes a very special woman to generate those kinds of feelings in children she hasn't given birth to.

My dearest Mary, all I'm asking for is a chance to prove myself worthy of you. Yet even as I write those words, I know I can never do such a thing because I am not worthy of you. I don't believe there is a man on earth who is worthy of you. Only William was, and I'm not sure he knew fully what a blessed man he was to have you as his wife.

So here is my dilemma and the source of my sleepless nights: How shall I live the rest of my life without having the one thing that I desire the most?

I pray you will send me even the briefest of notes, letting me know which way your heart is leaning. That way I can at least settle my unanswered questions and begin focusing on accepting your answer.

I remain your devoted admirer,

Thomas

Mary folded the letter and stuck it inside the front of her dress. *You can't keep ignoring him. Make up your mind, and let him know your wishes.*

With that, she walked into her bedroom and, sitting down at a table, took out paper, quill, and ink.

August 3, 1864

My dear Thomas,

I feel like such a horrible person for not having answered you by now, but there have been some dramatic changes here that I must tell you about.

A month ago, John and I discovered two abandoned boys named Pete and Frank. One is white, and the other is a

Negro. Apparently, the white boy's parents are what we refer to as poor white trash and are nowhere to be found, neither is there any family in the area, for they are from Kentucky. Therefore I brought them here to feed and clothe them until I could figure out what to do with them. As decisions often do, this one took me to places I never expected. In this short time, I've grown very fond of them, and I believe they are fond of me as well.

She paused and said aloud, "You can't even write the word *love*. You've got a long way to go, Mary Thomson." She continued writing:

I do not know how long this arrangement will last, but for my part, I have decided it will last as long as they want to live here.

As a result, I have just now decided that John and the boys will add a room to the house for the boys. John and I both agree that he should remain living in the woodshed to avoid the appearance of any impropriety, though I'm less concerned what others think than he is. I cared little what other people said about me before William disappeared, and I care less now. Tongues will always wag, so let them wag away.

Since the boys have been here, I have felt a change coming over me. The future looks less bleak and purposeless. I find myself enjoying life more. Is this what having children does to a person? If so, I love it!

In spite of this dramatic turn of events in my life, I have not forgotten about your request. Truthfully, rarely has a day passed that I haven't tossed it about in my heart. If in your question you are asking if I can come to love you as a husband, then I will answer that I do not know.

So do I want to take the risk to find out? That is what the question has become for me. Somedays the answer is an adventurous "yes," and other days it is a fearful "no."

I pause now for you to catch your breath and present a different question to you, a question whose answer will weigh heavily in my considering what to do about us. I have already stated that I will not abandon Pete and Frank. They do not deserve to have that done to them again. That means that for the foreseeable future, they are in every sense my children. So here's my question to you: Does this in any way change how you feel about pursuing a relationship with me?

As you have given me time to contemplate your question to me, I will reciprocate. Take as much time as you need before you reply. I will wait patiently for your answer.

With affection,

Mary

*****

As the foursome finished supper that night, Mary said, "I've made a decision."

All three of them looked at her expectantly.

"I've decided we need to build a room onto the house for you two boys to sleep in and call your own. I'm not going to find someone else for you to live with. You will live here, with me and John, as long as you choose to."

Pete and Frank stared at her with their mouths open, while John smiled broadly.

Suddenly, the boys jumped up and yelled, "Yippee! We've got a new home!" They rushed around the table and hugged Mary so tightly that she almost choked.

"Easy boys," John said. "Don't choke her to death."

"I've never had my own room," Frank said.

"Me neither," Pete added.

Mary stole a look at John and saw that tears had pooled in his eyes. "Okay," she said, "let's get the table cleared, and I'll take you to your beds in the barn. But it won't be long before you'll say good-bye to that barn."

Like whirling dervishes, Frank and Pete cleared the table before Mary and John could rise from their chairs.

Laughing, John said, "So now we know how fast these two can work when they really want to."

John headed toward the door. "Good night everyone. You boys sleep well."

"Good night," the boys replied.

Carrying a lantern, Mary led the way out of the kitchen and

to the barn.

The boys jumped onto their straw-stuffed mattress and beamed smiles back at her that were a hundred times brighter than the lantern she carried.

She knelt down beside them. "Good night boys."

Pete said, "Good night, Mary. This is the most special night I've ever had."

Frank fixed her with a silent stare. "Can I ask you something?" he finally asked.

"Sure you can."

"Do you care if I call you Mother?"

Like a needle and thread in the hands of a skilled seamstress, Mary felt as though Frank's words had formed the first stitches in her torn and damaged heart and gave her hope that eventually, it might be whole again.

Chapter Thirty-Two

MARY

Four days later, Mary, John, and the boys headed from the field to the barn with a wagonload of hay. Red-faced and sweating, Mary led the mule at the front of the wagon while John and the boys followed at the rear. Working in hay, she concluded, is the hottest, itchiest, scratchiest job on the farm. It is invariably done in the hottest part of summer, and tiny pieces of grass and seeds seemed to find their way underneath one's most private clothing, no matter how tightly they fastened their collar and long sleeves. What she desired to do more than anything at that moment was to strip naked and jump into the cool waters of Chickamauga Creek; that way, she could be freed from the three-headed demon that was torturing her.

When she walked around the final bend in the lane leading to the barn and saw its yawning door up ahead, Mary heard a girl's voice cry out, "There they are! Here they come!"

Mary squinted against the bright sun to try to see who it was.

As John and the boys came up beside her, Pete asked, "Who is it?"

"I'm not sure," Mary replied.

Suddenly, from out of the darkness of the barn, three girls burst into the sunlight, holding hands and running toward the wagon.

"It's Florence, Emma, and Mary Beth!" Mary exclaimed. *What in the world are they doing here?* She ran to meet them, and they melted into a pile of arms, hugs, and kisses.

"We've missed you!" Florence squealed.

"And I've missed you all, too! Stand back and let me look at you. Florence, you are quickly becoming a young woman. Emma, it seems like you grow six inches every time I see you. And Mary Beth, you don't look like the baby of the family anymore. You're really growing up, too."

The girls beamed.

"But what are you doing here? Where's your father?"

"We all came," Emma answered. "Father and Abigail are at your house unloading food."

Mary thought how awful she would look to Thomas, like a real farmhand—sweaty, grimy, and her hair a mess. Reflexively, she pushed a loose strand of hair behind her ear. "I didn't know you were coming."

"Father says it's a surprise," Mary Beth said.

"He told us about your last letter," Florence further explained. "We're all excited about everything!" Pointing toward the approaching wagon, she asked, "Are those the boys who are living with you?"

Mary pulled her mind away from thinking how she could

possibly make herself look more presentable to Thomas. "Yes, that's them. Come with me, and I'll introduce them to you."

As they approached the wagon, Frank hid behind John, and Pete sidled up close beside him.

Mary puzzled over the boys' actions but decided it was because they had never been around people that much, more especially, young white girls. She held out her hand toward them and said, "Frank, Pete, come here. I want you to meet some very special friends of mine."

When neither of the boys moved, John said, "You heard what Miss Mary said. You boys step up and greet our guests. These are as fine a set of girls as you'll ever meet."

With their heads down and dragging their bare feet through the dusty trail, Frank and Pete eased toward Mary.

Pointing at them in turn, Mary said, "This is Frank, and this is Pete."

Pointing at Pete, Mary Beth said, "He's a Negro."

Florence gave her a scowl. "Yes, Father told us one of them was a Negro. Don't you remember?"

"There's nothing wrong with that," Emma added.

Mary looked at Pete to see if he was bothered by the comment and attention, but if he was, it didn't show. "Let's all head to the house," she said.

When they reached the barn, Mary said to John, "We'll

unload the hay later." As she passed by the well, she stopped to slake her thirst and wash her face, then she spotted Thomas and Abigail unloading things from their wagon and carrying them to the shade of the large oak tree beside the house.

Just before she headed on to the house, she heard Abigail exclaim, "Miss Mary!"

Abigail rushed toward them as she said, "It's so good to see you and John and these two fine boys!" She greeted them all with an uninhibited hug, despite the boys' obvious discomfort at being hugged by someone they didn't know.

"This one is Frank," Florence said.

"And this one is Pete, he's a Negro," Mary Beth said.

"Oh my lord!" Emma said as she rolled her eyes.

"How handsome they are!" Abigail said.

"Mary Elizabeth!" Thomas's voice boomed as he walked briskly toward her.

Mary was struck by his handsome features and clean-cut appearance, which made her all the more aware of how bedraggled she must look. Knowing there was no way to do anything about it, she forced a smile on her face and stepped to greet him.

He took her hand and kissed it. "It is so good to see you."

"I don't know how you can say that. I'm a mess."

"I could gaze upon you all day long, no matter your condition."

She brushed aside the compliment and asked, "What are you doing here?"

"As soon as I read your last letter, I told Abigail to get busy cooking—that we were going to come here and surprise everyone with a meal. I didn't want to wait until you and I swapped more letters. I wanted to come and tell you to your face the answer to your question."

Mary felt irritation climbing up her spine like hackles. She held up her hand. "Wait. You haven't even met the boys yet or gotten to know them." She didn't like Thomas's willingness to jump into something without really assessing all the factors involved. And she didn't like the feeling that he was pressuring her.

"Anything that suits you will suit me, Mary," he said. "I'm sure I'll be as taken with the boys as you are."

"No, you won't," she said bluntly, as she pulled her hand out of his grip. It was then she noticed that the girls were standing close by, watching and listening. All three of them looked as if someone had taken their favorite toy from them. She called to Pete and Frank, "Come here, boys. There's someone else I want you to meet."

When she introduced the boys, Frank said, "I don't like him."

"Frank!" she said sharply. "That's bad manners. Apologize."

"Apologize?"

"Tell him you're sorry."

"But I'm not. I don't like him."

Mary didn't like being caught in a public tug of war with Frank, but this was her first time to deal with this kind of situation, and she was uncertain what to do. She looked helplessly at John.

He stepped in and said, "Come with me, boys. We need to wash ourselves up."

As they walked off, she looked at Thomas. "I'm sorry. I don't think they've been around people that much."

"Don't worry about it," he said with a smile. "There have been times my own daughters didn't like me. In time, he'll warm up to me."

Mary turned her attention to the spread of food Abigail was arranging on a quilt on the ground. "Oh, my goodness— that all looks delicious! You must have been cooking day and night."

"When Mr. Thomas told me why we were coming, I told him I was going to fix an extra-special meal with everything I know you like."

Mary's eyes brightened. "You didn't, did you?"

Smiling, Abigail said, "Sure did. I baked you a ham with my special honey glaze on top."

Mary closed her eyes. "I can taste it now."

John and the boys rejoined the group, and Mary said, "Let's all sit down and enjoy this feast Abigail has cooked us."

All nine of them situated themselves around the edge of the large quilt.

Mary looked at John. "Would you offer thanks?"

"Gladly." He bowed his head and began, "O great God in heaven, what a glorious day you have given us this day. Wonderful weather to gather in our hay. Healthy bodies to gather the hay. And a fine barn to put in. Then you bring to us these fine folks from the city who want to share with us from the bounty you have given them, too. Thank you, Lord. And bless us all. Amen."

For the next few minutes, the only sounds heard were of spoons and forks scraping bowls and plates. Those sounds were soon followed by scores of compliments to Abigail.

"I'm telling you right now," John said solemnly, "if you laid a piece of this ham on my forehead, my tongue would beat my brains out training to get to it."

Everyone stared at him for a second, then burst into laughter. The boys rolled on their backs laughing, and Thomas got choked, he laughed so hard.

After everyone regained their composure, Abigail said, "I don't suppose we'll ever know the truth of that because I'm not sure you've got a brain."

This triggered another round of lively laughter, and no one

laughed harder than John.

Later, when everyone had finished eating, Florence said, "Can we go wading in the creek?"

"Yes, yes," Emma and Mary Beth chimed in.

Thomas looked at Mary. "What do you think?"

"You all don't have to come with us," Florence said. "I'm old enough to keep an eye on everybody."

Mary looked at Frank and Pete. "Do you boys want to go, too?"

The boys first looked at each other, then nodded their heads at Mary.

John said, "Maybe I should go along, too."

Looking offended, Florence said, "We'll be fine."

Mary looked at Thomas. "I suppose it'll be all right."

"Okay, then," he said. "Just be careful."

As the kids jumped up, Mary said to Pete, "Go to that straight stretch of the creek, right before the bend. You know where I'm talking about?"

"Yes, ma'am."

Squeals and peals of laughter accompanied the children as they ran toward their grand adventure.

Thomas said, "Oh, to have the carefree life and energy of

youth again.""

Mary said, "I'm glad to see Pete and Frank acting that way. When they first came here, there was none of that. I don't think their lives were ever carefree."

Thomas turned toward her. "And they were just abandoned in the middle of nowhere? What kind of person would do such a thing?"

"The kind of language I would use to describe them would not be considered ladylike. Just let me say that I better never run into them, or I won't be responsible for what happens." Through clenched teeth, she said, "It still makes me furious. You never saw a more pitiful sight than when John and I went with them to the cabin they had been living in."

Abigail chimed in, "Some peoples don't deserve to have kids."

"The cruel trick," John added, "is that those who don't deserve them, have them, and those who do deserve them, sometimes don't."

Mary knew his comment was meant for her, and she appreciated his sentiment. She said, "But life has lots of mysterious turns in it. I had four children taken from me. And where did I find two children who were gifts for me but on top of Bitter Hill, among the graves of my lost ones."

After a moment of thoughtful silence, the four adults rose from the ground, and John said, "I'll help Abigail get this food put away."

"Thank you, John," Mary said. As she strolled toward the barn, Thomas fell into step with her.

She was nervous and uncertain about what to do or say or what he expected of her. She tried to steal looks at him to see if she could read him, but she finally gave up. As they moved out of the bright sunlight into the dark interior of the barn, she pointed to the wagonload of hay. "That's what we gathered this morning. It's a really good crop this year. All the spring rains helped. This, plus what we've already gathered in, will be plenty to see us through the winter. Don't you love the way it smells?"

"It does have a nice sweet, earthy sort of smell," he replied. "You really love this farm, don't you?"

"Don't get me wrong, it's a lot of work and worry, but yes, I do love it. I don't think I'd ever be happy living anywhere else."

They turned and faced each other.

Thomas asked, "Is that one of the things you're worried about when it comes to you and me?"

Mary looked into his eyes, trying to gauge how honest she dared be with him. *If I can't be honest, there's no need in going any further.* She said, "Yes, it is. I could never be happy living in the city, and I'll never leave my farm. Perhaps you and I need to find a path through this issue before we invest lots of time and energy for naught."

He cleared his throat. "You know that I know nothing of farming and would be useless to you. My father was a shopkeeper, so it's the only world I know. And I, like you, enjoy what I do, so I would never sell my store. But here's the difference in our stations—I would enjoy closing my store at night and coming home to be with you here at this place. I'm sure the girls would love living out here. Your farm has always held a special place in my heart, with untold wonderful memories. When I come here, it's like my soul exhales and relaxes. It's like a tonic. There's no other place like it."

As he spoke so openly and eloquently, Mary felt her heart opening up toward him just the tiniest bit, like a child walking out on the small end of a tree limb, hoping it won't break. She reached carefully for his hand and smiled. "That makes me very happy and takes some worry off my mind, but you will still have to give me some time to consider the idea of marrying you. You've been single for a long time, while I've only been single for a matter of months. Though he is dead, William still owns my heart. I don't know if I can give it to someone else, even someone as deserving as you."

He placed his other hand on top of hers and eased closer to her.

Mary felt her heart jump.

"Mary, I would never want to pressure you into doing anything you weren't certain of, even though I would marry you right now. Pete and Frank have had quite a lot of change to get used to without asking them to adjust to even more dramatic changes. You're wise in saying we all need to get to know each other and get used to each other. And so that's what we'll do."

Suddenly, an unexpected cold chill ran across the back of Mary's shoulders. She shuddered.

"Are you okay?" Thomas asked.

"The children," she said in a hoarse whisper. "Something's happened."

"What do you mean, something's happened? How do you know?"

"I just know." She turned and ran out the other end of the barn. "Hurry!" she yelled over her shoulder. "We've got to find them!" She stopped and faced the house, yelling, "John! The children! Help!" Then she turned and continued running.

Chapter Thirty-Three

MARY

With panic-fueled energy, Mary ran as quickly as she could toward Chickamauga Creek and the spot where the children had been told they could play.

Thomas quickly caught up with her. "What do you think has happened?"

Between her rapid breaths, Mary answered, "I don't know. I don't know. But something hit me like a hammer when we were talking. It was like the tolling of a bell."

"How much farther to where they're supposed to be?"

"Not far. Maybe half a mile."

Eventually, he began falling behind.

She looked over her shoulder. "Are you all right?"

Red-faced and gasping, he waved at her to go ahead. "You keep going. I'll catch up."

Mary's steady strides stretched the distance between them. She breathed a silent prayer: *Please, God, let me be wrong. Don't let anything have happened to them.*

Up ahead, at the spot where she had intended to cut into the woods, Pete suddenly came running out.

He looked in her direction and yelled, "Help! Come quick!"

The sight and cry of Pete were like a whip smacked against the flank of a horse. Mary practically leaped off the ground as she raced toward him.

When she reached him, Pete could only spit out solitary, disconnected words, "Creek . . . Yelled . . . Don't . . . Emma . . . Splashing . . . Snake . . ."

Trying without success to grasp his meaning, it was his last word that gave a form to Mary's terror. She grabbed Pete's shoulders and stared into his frightened eyes. "Show me where."

He immediately darted into the woods.

Mary followed but had to duck and weave around trees and under limbs that he scooted easily past. At one spot, she was jerked to a stop when her hair got caught in a Hawthorne tree. She swore as she pulled her hair free while unsuccessfully trying to avoid pricking her fingers on the thorns. Ignoring the blood on her thumb and finger, she worked to catch up with Pete, while behind her she heard what she assumed was the crashing sound of Thomas coming toward her.

When Pete suddenly dropped out of sight, she knew he had jumped off the high bank of the creek to get to the edge of the water below.

When she reached the bank, she took in the scene below her. Emma, thoroughly soaked, sat on a sand bank just out of the water, crying. Florence was holding one of Emma's arms, and crying, too. Frank and Mary Beth were standing silently to the side, holding each other's hand, their eyes wide with terror.

Mary sat down and slid down the six-foot muddy bank.

Just as she reached the bottom, Thomas cried out in surprise and toppled down the bank, landing beside her.

She helped him to his feet and took his face in her hands so that he was looking directly at her. In a voice only he could hear, she said, "I think Emma's been bit by a snake. We have to keep calm and not scare her worse than she's already scared." She saw the panic in his eyes and that he was about to cry out. She clapped her hand over his mouth. "We have to act calm, okay?"

He swallowed and nodded.

Holding his hand, Mary turned and walked quickly to the children.

"Daddy!" Emma cried.

"I'm sorry!" Florence said as Thomas moved beside Emma. "It's my fault. I said I would watch them." She burst into tears.

Mary calmly said, "Someone needs to tell us exactly what happened."

When Florence was unable to regain her composure, Mary gave Pete a questioning look.

He responded, "We were wading in the creek, just like we said we would. There wasn't no problems. We were having fun. Then I seen a snake floating down the creek. I hollered at everybody to look out. We started making our way toward the bank just as it was getting close, but Emma slipped and fell. The snake floated right on top of her and wrapped around her neck. Then she screamed and jumped up. The snake fell off her and floated away. I think it bit her."

Mary looked at Emma being held in Thomas's arms and saw that her lips were turning blue, whether from the cold of the stream or from poison from the snake, she couldn't be certain. "Did it bite you, Emma?"

Her voice trembling, Emma replied, "My shoulder hurts."

Thomas pulled down the edge of her dress to reveal two dark holes on the side of her shoulder.

"Anywhere else?" Mary asked.

"I don't think so. Am I going to die?"

Mary gave Thomas the briefest of looks and could tell he was doing all he could not to burst into tears. "No, you're not going to die," she told Emma.

"She's not?" Florence suddenly said. "How do you know?"

"Just because I do. Right now, we've got to get her to the cabin, but she doesn't need to walk."

"I'll carry her," Thomas said, rising from the water's edge, with Emma in his arms.

"We'll have to walk upstream a ways where the bank isn't so high because you'll never carry her up that bank we just came down."

"Then let's get going," he said.

"I'll lead the way. Thomas, you follow me, and Florence, you and Pete make sure Frank and Mary Beth keep up."

Mary didn't have to go far before she found a place and led them out of the creek and through the woods.

As they approached the lane that followed the edge of the woods, she heard thundering hoof beats and the clatter of what she hoped was the buckboard being driven by John. Relief flooded her when she broke out of the woods into the bright sunlight and saw John standing in the bouncing buckboard as he applied the whip to the sprinting mule. Abigail was in the seat, holding on for dear life.

When John saw Mary, he hollered "Whoa!" and although he pulled back on the reins for all he was worth, the momentum of the mule and buckboard carried them forty feet past where Mary was standing. He quickly maneuvered the mule to circle back around and stopped directly in front of her.

"Lord, child, what's happened?" Abigail exclaimed.

"Emma got bit by a snake," Mary said. "We've got to get her to the house."

Just then Thomas appeared, carrying Emma. Her lips were decidedly purple, and she hung listlessly in his arms, eyes closed. One by one, the rest of the children appeared.

Abigail crawled out of the seat and onto the bed of the

buckboard. "Hand the child up here to me, Mr. Thomas, and then you can get in here with her."

John stepped down from the wagon and said to Mary. "You drive the wagon. I'll stay here with the other children and make sure they all get to the house safely."

Somber expressions sat on every face, like mourners at a funeral, as they silently followed instructions.

Mary grabbed the reins of the mule as she sat down. Everything in her wanted to lay into the lathered-up mule and have him return to the cabin even faster than he came to pick them up. Since she knew that would result in a violent ride for Emma, she made a clicking sound in her cheek, and the mule began walking.

After what seemed like an interminably long time to Mary, she finally pulled to a stop beside the cabin.

The three wagon riders moved into Mary's bedroom, where Thomas laid Emma on her bed.

The child's face was colorless, except for her lips.

"What do we do?" Thomas whispered.

"I've got a piece of lunar caustic that William bought one time specifically for snakebites. I'll go get it," Mary said.

"And I'll make a poultice," Abigail said as she followed Mary out of the room.

Once Mary found the lunar caustic in the kitchen and headed back to the bedroom, she found John and the children standing on the porch. "You all just need to wait out here," she said gently. "We're doing everything we know to do."

When she entered the bedroom, Thomas was kneeling beside the bed, holding Emma's hand. His forehead rested against the side of the bed, and his lips were moving.

While Mary didn't want to interrupt what she believed was his silent prayer, she also didn't want to wait another instant to treat the snakebite, so she moved quietly to the other side of the bed. She gripped the neck of Emma's dress in two hands, and with a quick jerk, she tore it open over her shoulder. The area around the dark puncture wounds had turned a deep crimson.

Thomas looked up at her with red and swollen eyes.

In them, she saw the eternal hope that every parent has for a child who is dying. She mouthed the words, "Keep praying."

Taking the silver lunar caustic out of the leather pouch, she broke it in two and sharpened both pieces with a knife she'd brought with her. Then she pushed them into the holes left by the snake's fangs.

In a moment, Abigail came in, holding a cloth. "This here poultice will help draw the poison out," she explained.

"What's in it?" Thomas asked.

"A spoonful of gunpowder, a spoonful of salt, and an egg yolk. What's that you've done there, Miss Mary?"

"It's lunar caustic."

"I've heard tell of that. Hopefully, two cures will be twice as good as one." She spread the cloth over the wound and pressed down on it.

"Now what do we do?" Thomas asked.

"We sit and wait and pray," Mary answered.

"Lord Jesus, yes, we pray," Abigail agreed.

Stepping out onto the porch in order to explain things to the children, Mary's heart had not been prepared for the palpable collective sadness coming from them as they fixed their eyes on her. "The first thing you need to know is that Emma is okay for now. We've put some medicine on the snakebite, and now we're just waiting to see if it works. But the second thing I'm going to tell you is just as important. What happened to Emma is nobody's fault, nobody's. You can't keep a snake out of the creek, and you can't keep a snake from biting somebody. Sometimes bad things just happen."

Frank asked, "Is she going to die?"

"Don't nobody know the answer to that," John answered. "That's in the hands of the good Lord. What we need to do is to ask him to let her stay with us and not take her to be with him in heaven just yet."

"But my mother and father said there isn't no God. They said if there was one that he would have taken care of us, and things wouldn't have been so hard."

The boy's innocent words, spoken in complete candor, took Mary's breath away, mainly because she had thought the very same thing in the past. She was at a loss what to say.

Abigail stepped forward and knelt down in front of Frank. "That's because your folks had the wrong idea about God. God's job isn't to make things easy for us. His job is to help us get through the hard stuff."

*****

In the darkness outside Mary's window, lightning bugs took turns blinking a silent vigil, while inside the bedroom, a solitary candle gave witness to the still form of Emma. Thomas and Mary sat on opposite sides of the bed, each holding one of the stricken child's hands. Somewhere close by, an owl intoned its haunting song.

Mary looked at the dark lines of concern etched across Thomas's face, made to appear deeper by the shadows cast by the candle. She wondered if the pain of losing a child you had raised for years felt any different from the pain she felt when she lost each of her tiny children.

Thomas interrupted her musings when he said in a low voice, "I don't know what I'll do if she doesn't make it. I know I have two other children, but that doesn't matter. She's what matters. And having other children will never fill the void of the one you lose." He looked up at Mary. "What will I do?"

Mary wanted to tell him that he would never be the same, that he was correct when he said a living child could never take the place of a dead one, that the grief of losing a child was like no other grief, that time wouldn't heal the wound but only make the pain less intense. But instead, she said, "That's not a question you're going to have to answer because she's going to be fine. She's just resting while the poison gets drawn out of her. Any minute now, her eyes are going to blink open, and she's going to ask for you."

"Do you really believe that?"

"Absolutely," Mary lied.

"I'm glad you're here." He reached his hand toward her.

Mary took it and held it tightly. "I'm glad I'm here, too." This was her second lie in a matter of seconds. The truth was that she would rather be anywhere in the world than sitting beside a dying child. She didn't want to see Thomas dissolve in front of her when Emma died. She could already hear the sound of him wailing. What she wanted to do was run away—run away from being the one whom everyone depended on, run away from her responsibilities, and find a place where she could live the life of a hermit.

Being there with Thomas in that most intimate experience, she felt herself being drawn to him. She'd seen up close the balance in him of both tenderness and strength, traits that were not often found in equal parts in a man. She said to him, "Why don't you go out and sit for a while with Florence and Mary? I'll stay here with Emma and won't hesitate to come get you if there's any change."

"But what if she wakes, and I'm not here? Or if she—" He didn't finish his thought.

"When she wakes up, I'll immediately call for you, and you can be here before she is completely alert. Now go on; those girls need to see you."

He released his hold on Mary's hand, then on Emma's. Rising from his chair, he walked to Mary's side of the bed, bent down, and kissed her on the forehead. "I just had to do that." Then he left the room.

Mary could still feel the warmth from the touch of his soft lips. His move had surprised her, yet pleased her, too. She looked at Emma. *What is this, God? Your way of making me and Thomas closer? Is that what you want?* She shook her head at the riddle of it all.

*****

Mary jerked awake, not realizing she had fallen asleep. The candle had long since melted away, and the soft, gray light of dawn was filtering through her window. It took her a second or two to get oriented and to look at Emma. She blinked and leaned over her to get a closer look. A thrill of excitement swept over her as she confirmed that Emma's lips had been restored to their rosy hue. She lifted the poultice and found that the wound had lost its angry-looking complexion. "Thomas!" she cried. "Come quick!"

Her call had barely left her lips when he thundered into the bedroom. "What is it?"

Pointing at Emma, Mary said, "Look."

Just as she did so, Emma's eyes opened slowly. "Father?"

"Oh, Emma," Thomas said as she rushed to her side. He placed his hands on both sides of her face and put his face close to hers. "You're alive."

"What happened?" she asked weakly.

"You were bitten by a snake while playing in the creek yesterday. We brought you to the house in the buckboard."

"I remember now. Is everyone else okay?"

"Baby, we're all just fine." Abigail's voice came from the doorway.

Mary turned to look and saw everyone craning to see what had happened. She stepped back and said, "Y'all come in and welcome Emma back."

Chapter Thirty-Four

MARY

Mary stood in front of the mirror in the girls' bedroom, sifting through the whirlwind of events of the past two weeks. When it had become certain that Emma was going to be all right, Thomas had returned to Chattanooga to tend his store, while the girls stayed with her on the farm as Emma regained her strength. It was during the recovery time that she had received a letter from Thomas asking if she would consider spending a few days in Chattanooga when she brought the girls home, so she and Thomas could have some time together. Every excuse she had given herself not to do so, she came to realize, was all about being afraid. So, in spite of her fear, she agreed.

Now, after having been there for three days, she and Thomas were going out alone for the first time, to attend Bishop's Variety and Cumberland Minstrels Show. He had bought her a new outfit for the occasion, which the girls had just finished helping her put on. She had never had such an elegant dress. The color was exactly the same shade of blue as her eyes, which she was certain was but a reflection of Thomas's sharp eye for detail.

The corset he'd bought her was different than ones she was used to. When Florence and Emma helped cinched it tight on her, she discovered it flared out at the top, so much so that she feared one of her breasts might pop out at any moment.

The one thing she had never worn was a hoop skirt. While she had seen other women wearing them, she thought them to be quite ostentatious, but because Thomas had bought it, she allowed the girls to help her into it. The skirt, with its gathers and knife pleats, had enough cloth in it to make two regular dresses.

The piece she liked the most was the hip-length jacket with its basque waist. It had a crisp flare over her hips and flaring sleeves, with a wide collar, covered in lace that fell across her shoulders.

What amazed her the most about the entire outfit was how perfectly everything fit. It gave her a bit of a thrill to realize Thomas had paid such close attention to her figure.

As she gazed at herself in the mirror, she felt like a princess, with her braided tresses forming a perfect crown.

She tried to think about what she and Thomas would talk about during the evening without having the girls or Abigail around to serve as buffers or topics to discuss. She and William had practically been able to read each other's mind, so much so that they no longer had long conversations like they did in the first years of their marriage. They had developed a knowing of each other and knew when it was time to talk and when it was time to let the other have quiet time. *Will I ever be able to achieve that with Thomas?* That was the question that always stopped her.

She remembered the time John had said, "Knowledge is like a garden: if it is not cultivated, it cannot be harvested."

There was only one way to discover if she and Thomas could achieve the kind of love they were seeking, and that was to get to know each other by spending time with each other. *Quit worrying and fretting about it, and just see what happens.*

When she reached the bottom of the stairs, Thomas appeared, dressed in a white shirt with a black silk tie tied into a half bow. On top of that was a double-breasted, black-and-white-checked vest. His pants were red-and-blue checked. On top of it all, he was wearing a wide-lapel, charcoal-colored jacket that reached to his knees. In his hand, he held a white top hat. Mary was stunned by how handsome he looked.

While William had been the most handsome man around, as far as she was concerned, his short, wiry stature was not the sort that most women were attracted to. And though she had always acknowledged to herself that Thomas was a handsome man, it had only been a passing acknowledgment. Looking at him now, though, she felt as if she had taken a polished gem that she'd always enjoyed looking at, held it up to a light, and turned it slightly, suddenly revealing facets of great beauty she had been missing. She smiled at him as he approached her. *Should I hug him? Should I offer him my hand instead? What about exchanging a friendly kiss on the cheek like we have done this week? Will a hug and a kiss mean something different to him tonight? Would they mean something different to me?*

"Mary," he said as he took her hands in his, "you look

stunning. You are such a beautiful woman, but as beautiful as you are, it is the person you are that makes you so attractive to me."

She felt herself blushing. That he was attracted to who she was and not just what she looked like was especially important to her because she knew that, given the life she had chosen for herself, that of working a farm, she would age more quickly than a woman who lived a life of leisure in the city. She took a breath and said, "I want to say something to you, Thomas. I do love you, maybe not in the way you want just yet, but you are a dear, dear friend, and I at least want the chance to get to know you better and decide if I want to spend the rest of my life with you."

She continued, "And here's another thing—you will learn things about me that you may not have known. There will be things you don't like about me, things that may make you decide you don't want to be with me and vice versa. I didn't like everything about William, and I'm not going to like everything about you, but that won't bring an end to things." She smiled. "I'll just have to decide if there's enough that I do like about you that will make me tolerate the things I don't like about you."

Thomas squeezed his eyes shut, then reopened them. Broken tears like shiny stars hung on his eyelashes. "Mary Elizabeth," he said in a husky voice, "I've never met anyone like you. You're the most fearless person I've ever met—man or woman. It's a trait that I'm lacking in. I sometimes make fearful decisions rather than fearless ones. Perhaps the losses I've had in my life have made me weaker, while your losses seem to have made you stronger. If nothing else happens between us, I need to learn that lesson from you and let you teach me how you've done it."

She stepped closer and moved his hands toward the back of her waist, then slipped her arms around his waist. She liked how she had to look slightly up at him. For a few moments, they simply stared at each other. She made note of the tiny things about his face that could only be seen when standing that close—a small scar on the edge of his bottom lip; the color of his eyes, which was the darkest brown she'd ever seen, making them look black sometimes; another scar, which started at the edge of his hairline on his left temple, then disappeared into his thick hair. She reached up and touched this last scar. She wondered if he could feel her heart slamming against her chest.

He whispered, "I'm afraid to say anything for fear I will awaken from this dream of a moment."

She stepped back, as much to try to find a breath of air as anything. "But you promised to take me to the minstrel show tonight. Shall we go?"

*****

At the conclusion of the show, they left the large tent arm in arm and got into Thomas's buggy. Mary leaned her head against his shoulder and squeezed his arm. "That was so much fun!"

"There were a lot of talented performers, weren't there?"

"Indeed."

Mary noticed he was driving them out of the city and heading, she hoped, to the grove of maple trees they'd been to earlier in the week. But that had been in the daytime, and now they were going there under the cloak of night.

Thomas eased the buggy off the road and pulled to a stop underneath the maple trees.

She said, "I think this is one of my favorite places that you've brought me this week. It's so still and quiet and peaceful. It's too busy in the city to suit me. I like quiet. Sitting on my porch and listening to the sounds of nature, that's where I love to be."

"You want to walk a bit?"

"Sure."

Thomas got out, and Mary forced herself to wait on him to help her. They had argued about it earlier during her visit, and she had decided it really wasn't worth fighting about. If it was something he enjoyed doing, why should she insist on having her way?

As they began walking, he took her hand. "May I?"

"Yes." Even though his soft hands were an indication that he had rarely done hard labor, she enjoyed how his enveloped hers. It was those kinds of little discoveries that she had taken pleasure in while being with him. Observing him as he ran his store, she had learned what a kind man he was, always willing to go out of his way to help a customer. "It's just good business," he had told her, but she believed it to be more a reflection of his character than a ploy to make money.

One thing she was anxious about was the fact that they'd not yet kissed each other, other than a polite peck on the cheek. She knew she was ready—more than ready. She just wasn't sure about him. *I just don't want to go home without knowing what it's like to kiss him.*

Their joined hands swung easily as they walked underneath the trees, to the accompaniment of tree frogs above them, a bullfrog in the distance, and an owl close by.

After a minute, Thomas said, "You know one of the things I enjoy about being with you?"

She stopped walking and leaned back against a tree. "No, what?"

"The quietness. We can be quiet together without feeling uncomfortable. I don't feel like I have to make something up to be talking about all the time. It's funny how close it makes me feel to you when we're quiet."

Mary looked at his eyes and then at his lips. Her heart quickened. *This is it.* As she felt blood rushing to her head, she pulled him to her and touched her lips to his. A surge of excitement ran through her as he put his arms around her and returned her kiss. She felt as if her neck and face were on fire.

Just when she didn't think she could go another second without taking a breath, he pulled back his head.

She gasped for air.

"Oh, Mary," he said and kissed her again, harder this time.

She hugged him and let him pin her against the tree trunk. Her head emptied itself of every care and rational thought it had ever contained. The desire for release, to become lost in passion, coursed through her veins. She put her hands on Thomas's face, then ran her fingers through his hair.

Again and again, they kissed.

His kisses moved from her lips to her cheeks, then down her neck, giving her chills and making her feel light-headed. "Oh, William," she whispered.

He stopped abruptly and pushed her back a bit. "What did you say?"

Her head was still foggy with passion, and his question confused her. "What do you mean?"

"What did you just call me?"

Suddenly, she heard herself saying William's name. "Oh, Thomas, I'm sorry. I didn't mean that. I wasn't even thinking of him. I was only thinking of you." She reached for him, but he blocked her hands, and she saw the hurt on his face.

"It's different for me than it is for you, Mary. It's been years since Anna has gone, but not so with William. Maybe it's too soon for you to do this if you can't help thinking about him when you're with me."

Mary suddenly started crying. She gripped his arms. "Please don't feel that way, Thomas. I don't know why I said his name. I promise I wasn't thinking about him. Maybe there was something about the moment that touched a part of me that had never been touched by anyone else but William. And if that's true, then there are going to be other moments in our relationship that are going to jog a memory, even if we're not aware of it."

"I don't know, Mary. I understand what you're saying. I just don't know if I can stand being compared to someone else."

She let go of him and wiped the tears from her cheeks. Her mind raced to find a way to explain herself so that he would understand. Suddenly, she said, "Growing up, who fixed the meals in your home?"

"Huh?"

"When you were a kid growing up, who cooked all the meals?"

"My mother did."

"So are you going to tell me that when you married Anna, you didn't compare her cooking to your mother's, even if you never said so out loud?"

"Anna was a wonderful cook."

"I know she was, but you didn't answer my question. How could you not compare her cooking to the only cooking you ever knew?"

"I suppose I did, but I never told her so."

"Of course not, because you would never want to hurt her feelings or make her feel like she had to measure up to someone else. Before tonight, there's only been one man in my life whom I have kissed, besides my father, and that was William. I don't know how many other women you've kissed, but tonight is the first time you've kissed me, and somewhere in you, you had to have compared me to someone else, even if you didn't say so or know so."

"I'll never measure up to William," Thomas said. "He was a much better man than I'll ever be."

"But you are not in competition with William, and I'm not in competition with someone else. You will take me and accept me as I am, for that's all I have to offer. And I will accept you on those same terms. You are not William and will never be. I am not Anna and will never be." She touched his face with her hand and in a gentle whisper said, "This is about you and me, Thomas—just us. Let's not make it more complicated than that. Try not to be angry with me for uttering the name of the only man I have ever loved, and I'll try not to be angry if you at some time mention Anna's name. If I didn't want to be here with you at this moment, I wouldn't be. And if I had not wanted to kiss you, it wouldn't have happened."

He gazed into her eyes, and his features softened. Smiling, he said, "For someone who says she doesn't have a way with words, you could probably deliver a speech that would make Southerners vote for Lincoln. I'm sorry for being small and childish and insecure. To be truthful, I've been fearful all along of the shadow of William and felt like I had to be him for you to love me. I now see, as you put it, that this is about you and me, no one else." He cradled her face in his hands. "What a woman you are, Mary Elizabeth."

Chapter Thirty-Five

MARY

As she walked to the barn carrying a large basket, Mary noticed steam rising from the roof of the barn as the sun melted the mid-November frost. Close by in an oak tree, two blue jays squawked at each other, arguing over who would get the acorn they'd both discovered hanging on a twig. The hog she had bought in September grunted a welcome as she passed by its pen. "You wouldn't be so friendly with me if you knew you'll be hanging in the smokehouse before too long," she said with a smile.

Passing through the dark hallway of the barn, she looked through the open door on the other side of the barn and saw that the mules were hitched to the wagon. John was sitting in the seat, and Pete and Frank were standing in the bed of the wagon.

"Come on, let's go!" Frank called to her as she walked into the sunshine. "We've got work to do."

Pete said, "The early bird catches the worm, while the late bird goes hungry."

Recognizing two of her favorite and oft-used phrases, Mary smiled back at the boys.

When she reached the side of the wagon, she shielded her eyes against the bright sun as she looked up at the boys. "At least I know you've been paying attention to what I've been telling you." She peered over the side of the wagon and saw various saws and axes lying in the bed. "Looks like somebody's planning on working today. Wonder what they're going to do when they get hungry?"

John winked at her tease.

"You can't fool us," Frank said. "You've got food in that basket."

"John, do you think I should let the boys hold the basket?"

"No, ma'am, Miss Mary. That would be like asking the fox to watch the henhouse. By the time we got to where we're going, that basket wouldn't have anything in it except crumbs. You best put it up here under the seat where you and I can keep a close eye on it."

Mary handed the basket up to him. "I think you're right."

Both boys made like they were reaching to grab something out of the basket as it passed hands.

John slapped at them playfully. "Lord, have mercy! You're worse than a swarm of bees."

They all laughed as Mary settled onto the seat next to John.

John spoke to the mules.

As the wagon pulled forward, Mary said, "You boys better rest while you can because at the end of the day, I want this wagon loaded with so much firewood that even those mules will grunt when they pull it. I want to see wood chips flying like a colony of beavers attacking a new woods."

Pete said, "Don't you worry about me and Frank. We'll work circles around that old man sitting beside you."

He and Frank howled with laughter.

John slapped the mules with the end of the reins, causing them to lurch forward.

The sudden movement threw the boys off balance, and they tumbled across the bed of the wagon, yelling in surprise and pain.

Turning his head halfway around toward them, John said, "I may be old, but at least I know how to ride in a wagon without falling down." This time he and Mary laughed.

John maneuvered the mules and wagon between trees as they headed into the woods. Up ahead was a medium-size white oak tree that he and Mary had felled back in August so that it could cure for a few months before they cut it up into firewood. He pulled back on the reins and hollered, "Whoa."

Pete jumped out of the wagon, and Frank started handing him the saws and axes one at a time.

Soon the singsong, buzzing sound of the boys with their bucksaws and Mary and John with the crosscut saw echoed through the woods, and plumes of sawdust drifted to the ground. Everyone worked in silence for a bit, until John broke into one of his call-and-response slave songs. While he had never done that with Mary, he began doing it with the boys soon after they had arrived and started working with him on the farm. Pete and Frank joined in heartily with the song, giving Mary reason to smile.

After a couple of hours, Mary said, "Frank, you and Pete come start splitting these blocks John and I have sawed off the trunk."

The boys left off trimming limbs out of the upper part of the tree and picked up the splitting wedges and wooden mauls. The sharp *thock* of the maul striking the wedge and then the scratchy sound of the wood splitting apart were added to the music made by Mary and John as they continued working on the trunk with their saw.

Keeping one eye on what she was doing and another eye on the boys, Mary marveled at how strong they had become and how much they had grown. Each of them had gained forty pounds and grown several inches. After they finished splitting a section of the trunk, they helped each other in throwing the firewood into the wagon and stacking it.

As the morning wore on, all four of them shed some of the clothes they had put on that morning to ward off the chilly temperatures. By noon, when they stopped to rest and eat, the wagon was chock-full of firewood.

Mary retrieved the basket of food and set it on a stump while the other three gathered around.

As she passed out biscuits and ham, John said, "I can remember when it took you and me two days of work to fill that wagon with firewood. These two boys have become mighty fine workers."

"I agree," Mary replied. "I was thinking today about how

much they've grown and how strong they've become."

Pete and Frank smiled at each other as they basked in the praise.

Frank asked, "Are we still going to Chattanooga today?"

Pete added, "And are we going to stay with Mr. Thomas for a few days?"

"You boys know we've talked about that," John answered them. "Mr. Thomas asked that the next time Miss Mary went to visit him, she bring you boys with her. I'll stay here and tend to things till y'all get back."

Frank studied his ham and biscuit as if he'd never seen them before.

"Frank," Mary said, "is there a problem with the plan?"

"No, ma'am," he mumbled.

"Is there something you want to say about it?"

He looked up at her. "Me and Pete was talking last night." He paused, then said, "You're not going to leave us, are you?"

Mary was shocked by his question. "Goodness, no! I have no intentions of doing that whatsoever. Both of you look at me."

Pete lifted his head, and the boys looked at her with sad eyes.

"I want you to listen very carefully to what I'm saying.

When you boys came to live with me, I had no idea that we would become family to each other, but that's what has happened, and nothing is going to change that."

Pete said, "But if you and Mr. Henry get married . . ." His voice trailed off.

"Thomas and I are very good friends," Mary explained, "and we enjoy spending time with each other. He has neither asked me to marry him nor have I told him I was going to. But," she added with emphasis, "if something like that were to happen, that would not change anything about my relationship with you boys. All it would mean is that Thomas and I would have five children: you two and Florence, Emma, and Mary Beth."

John chimed in, "And I can tell you boys this: Miss Mary is a woman of her word. If she says a thing is going to be a certain way, then that's the way it's going to be. You can count on that."

A look of relief came over the boys' faces, and their shoulders relaxed.

Standing up, Mary said, "Now let's head back to the house, and we'll gather up some clothes to take with us before we head into town."

John and the boys responded by gathering up all the tools while Mary returned the basket to the wagon and picked up everyone's coats. Then Pete and Frank climbed on top of the load of wood, and John and Mary took their places on the wagon seat.

After a while, when the house came into view, Mary saw a man and woman standing in the yard between the house and barn. "I wonder who that is."

"I can't tell," John said.

Frank and Pete leaned in between them to have a look.

Pete swore under his breath.

Mary's head snapped in his direction, and she was about to fuss at him for his language when she noticed the looks of fright on the boys' faces. "What's the matter?"

In a voice barely audible, Frank said, "It's Ma and Pa."

*****

As the wagon came to a stop in the yard, Mary stared in disbelief at the couple. Everything about them seemed gray—from the various shades of their grimy and tattered clothes to their skin tone. The man had on an oily hat with a brim that probably used to stand out straight but now drooped on both sides. She couldn't tell if it was his receding chin that made his buckteeth look so prominent or the other way around. He had an unnaturally flat nose. There were holes in the elbows of his coat and the knees of his trousers, but she doubted it was from hard work. She guessed there were likely holes in the seat of his trousers, too, made from general laziness.

The woman was mousy-looking, with a sharp nose and close-set eyes that looked furtively about but never made any eye contact with Mary or the boys. Her hair looked as if it hadn't seen a brush in months, maybe years.

In a nasal voice that somehow found its way through his flat nose, the man pointed toward Frank and Pete and said, "There they are!" Looking at Mary, he snarled, "What are you doing with our boy and our nigger?"

She felt a hand grip her arm and looked to see Frank's panicked face.

He whispered, "Please don't let them take us!"

A hot, visceral feeling surged through Mary that made her think of the time a mother bear with cubs turned on William when he had accidentally stumbled upon the group. *I now know exactly how she felt!* She pulled Frank's hand loose and said, "Don't you worry. It'll be over my dead body that they take you."

Reaching under the wagon seat, she put her hand on the pistol and started to bring it out when John said in a low voice, "Go easy, Miss Mary. Don't do nothing foolish. You might be able to talk through this."

Somehow, his voice of reason made it through the river of anger and indignation flowing through her veins, and she paused. Releasing the pistol, she climbed down from the wagon but reached in and lifted out an ax before striding purposefully toward the couple. She was happy to discover that she stood half a head taller than the man and a full head taller than the woman. She also outweighed either of them.

The woman stepped back and hid behind her husband.

Resting the ax on her shoulder, Mary faced them squarely and said, "My name is Mary Elizabeth Thomson, what is yours?"

The man tried to step back but stepped on his wife's foot and stumbled. He ripped off his hat and slapped her with it. "Stupid woman, get out of my way! What's the matter with you?"

The woman cowered with her arms over the back of her head.

Mary now regretted taking the ax with her because it was taking every ounce of her willpower not to strike this bully of a man. With his attention on his wife, Mary tapped him hard on his head with the flat side of the ax.

He bellowed and turned around in surprise.

"If you feel like you need to beat on somebody, why don't you beat on me?"

Incredulity was in every part of his expression. He glanced at the wagon, then back at her. "Where's your man at?"

"It's not any of your business. Besides, anything you would want to say to him you can say to me."

Shifting his weight, he said, "Well, I'm not used to dealing with a woman."

"You're just not used to dealing with a woman who's not afraid of you. Now tell me what your name is and state your business, or get off my property."

He tugged on his hat, tried to gather himself, and said, "Name's Norman Nelson, and I'm here to get what belongs to me. That boy there is my son, and the other is my nigger I bought. You done stole them."

"Can you prove they're yours? Got a bill of sale and a birth certificate?"

"A birth certificate? I don't need none." He reached behind him and pulled his wife forward. "Tell her, woman. Tell her you give birth to that boy."

A smile tugged at the corner of Mary's mouth. "Which boy are we talking about, the white one or the black one?"

Even the mousy woman's eyes and mouth popped open on that one.

Norman declared, "If you wasn't a woman, I'd strike you for saying that."

Jutting her jaw forward, Mary said, "Please, don't let that stop you." She felt her face getting hot and knew it must be turning red.

The woman said, "That white boy is mine." Then she quickly stepped behind Norman.

"Listen to me, both of you," Mary replied. "We found those boys half-starved, hiding in a tree up on that hill. You abandoned them as if they were a couple of puppies you didn't want and left them to fend for themselves. What ought to be done to the both of you is tie you to a tree and horse whip you."

Norman said, "There's financial matters to consider here. We're poor people, and I need those boys to help me work my farm."

"So that's it," Mary said with disgust. "It's about money, isn't it? That's the reason you crawled out of the hole you've been wallowing in and came looking for them. Tell me how much you want for them."

A sly look came over Norman's face, and his wife leaned forward and whispered something in his ear. He offered, "Well, a person needs to think about how much they'll be worth over time. Soon they'll be strapping young men who can do a young man's work."

"That's foolishness," Mary retorted. "You don't pay for a horse based on how much it'll be worth in five years. You pay what it's worth right now. These are young boys we're talking about, who eat a lot of food, probably more food than they earn. I'd say right now they are costing me money. That's what I have to think about." Mary cringed inside at how that must be sounding to Pete and Frank, talking about them like they were property and trying to pay a low dollar for them by talking bad about them.

Norman appeared uncertain of what to do with this counter from Mary.

Suddenly, Mary had an idea. "Now that I think about it, maybe I should let you take the boys back. Me keeping them is a losing proposition. You go ahead and take them." She enjoyed the look of surprise on Norman's face. Then she added, "But you'll have to pay me for what I've put into them while I've been keeping them up."

This brought the mousy woman out from behind her husband. "You mean you want us to pay you money? You must be touched in the head if you think we're going to do that."

Mary put on an air of indifference and shrugged her shoulders. "That's up to you. Makes no difference to me. If you can't pay me for them, I guess I'll just let them hang on around here until they get older, when I can sell them for a decent price."

The woman pulled Norman's arm, and they walked away a few paces and engaged in an animated, whispered conversation.

Mary used that as an opportunity to turn around and wink at the audience on the wagon. She turned back around just as the Nelsons returned.

He said, "You've caught us in a disadvantaged position. While we love the boys and want them back, we don't have any money we can spare." The expression on his face looked like he had bitten into a green persimmon.

Knowing she had won, Mary said, "Is there more you'd like to say?"

As if he were spitting out a mouthful of distasteful food, Norman said, "So we're going to have to let you keep the boys."

"I don't know," Mary said. "The more I think about it, I

think the boys need to go with you." She turned to the wagon. "Frank, you and Pete come here." When they joined her, she turned back around and saw that the Nelsons were beating a hasty retreat to the road.

Mary could no longer contain herself. She burst into laughter while hugging the boys, one in each of her arms, raising them off the ground and turning in a circle. When she stopped and put them down, John had joined them.

"Boys," he said, "you have just witnessed the best horse trader in the South. Miss Mary, when you told them they were going to have to pay you, I thought the man was going to swallow his tongue. It was all I could do not to laugh out loud."

Mary put a hand on the boys' shoulders and looked them in the eyes. "Listen to me. There was no way in the world that I was about to let them take you. I figured out quickly that they really didn't want you anyway; it was just about money to them. What I did was show how corrupt they are and caught them in their own lies." She hugged the boys' necks. "I love you, I love you. Don't ever forget that."

Frank and Pete returned her hug as if she were a rope thrown to a drowning person.

Tears sprang up in her eyes, and she looked up at John, who was wiping tears of his own.

Chapter Thirty-Six

MARY

When they arrived at Thomas's store, Frank said excitedly to Mary and John, "We've sold nearly our whole wagonload of firewood without even trying. People were stopping us on the street to buy it. I'll bet we could sell a wagonload a week if we tried."

"Yeah," Pete agreed. "Maybe even two loads a week."

John said to Mary, "Sounds to me like these boys are planning to cut down every tree on the farm."

"Wonder what they'll do when that happens?" she replied.

"Are you kidding?" Frank said. "That one tree we worked on gave us this load, and we didn't even get finished cutting it up. I'll bet there's at least one or two more loads left in it."

Just then, the door of the store opened, and Thomas stepped out. Smiling, he walked toward them and said, "If it's not the belle of the county. Hi, Mary. Hi, John, Frank, and Pete. It's good to see you all. Did you have a good drive in?"

For Mary, Thomas's smile had become like an elixir. No matter what kinds of worries might have been on her mind, they evaporated at the sight of it.

He offered his hand to Mary as she stepped off the wagon. They kissed each other's cheek. "I'm glad you're here," he said softly.

"And I'm glad to be here."

John said, "Mr. Thomas, do you want me to pull around the back of the store and let the boys unload the rest of this wood for you?"

"Yes, that'll be great. Thank you, John. But wait. Have you all heard the news?"

"What news is that?" Mary asked.

"Lincoln won the election."

"Praise the Lord," John said.

"What do you think it will mean?" Mary asked.

"Most of the people in the city are happy about it. I'm just hoping it will mean this war will soon be over, and healing and rebuilding can begin for everyone."

John said, "The rebuilding will be easy. It's the healing that'll be the hardest." He spoke to the mules and steered the wagon toward the back of the store.

"John's right, you know," Thomas said as he and Mary turned to go into the store. "Families have been torn apart by this war. It may take a generation before some folks forgive and get over it."

"And some folks may never forgive," Mary noted.

"I suppose you're right, but if a person has had to forgive God, like I did after Anna died, forgiving people is not that hard a thing to do."

Mary stopped and turned to him. "I've never heard you talk about that."

"It's not something I'm very proud of. I got angry at God after Anna died and blamed him for it. I guess you could even say I held a grudge against him. Sounds silly, doesn't it—holding a grudge against God?"

"It doesn't sound silly to me at all. I can understand why you did. I'm still not sure how I feel about him. Don't misunderstand—I'm not blaspheming by saying I don't believe in God. I just can't figure out how things work and what his role is in things and what our role is."

"Well, if you ever do figure it out, please inform me because I don't have it figured out yet either."

As if on cue, they both turned and continued toward the front door.

This was one of the things about her relationship with Thomas that Mary enjoyed. They could fall into serious conversation about important matters at the drop of a hat, and then somehow, they both knew when the other was finished talking about it, and they could pull right out of it and be in a lighthearted moment.

The more time she spent with him, the harder she found it to come up with reasons not to marry him. He had yet to officially ask her to do so, which was just another thing she appreciated about him. No doubt he had been ready to marry her months ago, but when he had seen that she needed time, he immediately slowed his pursuit of her and hadn't brought up the topic of marriage since then.

A customer passed by them on their way out of the store. "Are you coming to the celebration tomorrow, Thomas?"

"What celebration is that?"

"We're going to celebrate Mr. Lincoln's election. It'll be an old-fashioned celebration, the kind we used to have—horse races, food, music, dancing. You need to come."

"It sounds wonderful. We'll be there."

As the woman continued walking, Thomas looked at Mary and said, "I hope I didn't speak out of turn. I should have asked you first if you'd like to go to the celebration before I boldly said we would be there."

"I'm not offended at all. It sounds like a lot of fun, sort of like our shucking bees and New Year's Eve events out in the country. I haven't been to one in what seems like forever." Looking at Frank and Pete, she added, "And I bet these two have never been to anything like it." To Thomas, she said, "We'll all go together, the whole gaggle of us."

*****

The next morning, excitement filled the kitchen as everyone in the house talked at the same time about the celebration.

Abigail said, "Everybody gets cold biscuits and leftover ham this morning. I didn't have time to fix a big breakfast and cook all the food for the celebration, too. Y'all are just going to have to fend for yourselves."

"Is it really going to be as much fun as y'all say it's going to be?" Frank asked.

"That much fun and more," Florence answered. "You never know what's going to happen at one of these because you never know who will show up. And there will be more food than you have ever seen."

Mary said, "I'm going to go finish getting ready. Any of you girls want to go with me?"

All three of them scurried to her side.

"I think that means yes," Thomas said. "I hope you don't mind, Mary, but I found some things in the store last night that the boys could wear—if that's okay with you."

Pete tugged at his shirt and asked, "What's wrong with this?"

"Not one thing," Thomas answered. "This is a special celebration, and I thought you might enjoy wearing something special." He looked at Mary.

She looked at the boys and said, "If I had known we were going to such an event, I would have tried to find you something special to wear. It's fun to wear special clothes every once in a while. You'll be surprised how it can change how you feel. I think you should give it a try, but I'll leave it up to you."

They both looked at Thomas. "We'll try it."

"Excellent! You womenfolk get on upstairs and do whatever you do to get ready while I get these two characters fixed up."

Forty minutes later, Mary and the girls came down the stairs with a rustle of cotton, linen, and wool, but they came to an abrupt halt when they spied Frank and Pete standing in front of Thomas.

Each of the boys had on a new pair of shoes, checkered pants, a white shirt with a bowtie, and a buttoned-up vest and matching jacket. Sitting on top of their heads were black felt bowler hats. Both boys looked as uncomfortable as a dog with a thorn in its paw.

Mary wanted to laugh out loud, not at how humorous they looked but at how cute they were. However, their pained expressions told her that if she laughed, they would immediately start stripping off their costumes, so she said, "If you two are not the handsomest young men in Chattanooga! You cannot go with us to the celebration dressed like that."

"Why not?" Thomas asked.

"Because everyone will be noticing them and ignoring me and the girls. That's something no woman can tolerate. Twirl around, girls, and show them how we look."

Thomas whistled. "Boys, we're going to be the most popular men at the celebration—but not because of how smartly we're dressed. It'll be because everyone is jealous of us because we'll be with the prettiest girls there. Don't you agree?"

Frank's eyes sparkled as he stared at Mary and the girls. "Yes sir, Mr. Thomas."

"Then run and open the door, Frank, and let's let this parade begin."

When they reached the courthouse square, the broad lawn on each side of the courthouse was a patchwork quilt of color, featuring all the women and girls in gaily colored dresses. The air was filled with voices and laughter and neighing and snorting horses.

Thomas said to Mary, "I'm surprised to see some of the people here who I know are Southern sympathizers. I know they aren't happy about the Lincoln election."

"Perhaps they're just excited about getting out and having fun after all the dreariness of this war."

"You must be right. There hasn't been a gathering like this since the war started. It feels like a breath of fresh air."

Suddenly, a crowd of people began surging past them.

"What's going on?" Thomas asked one man.

"The horse races are about to start!" the man answered excitedly.

Thomas scanned the faces of his crew. "Let's go watch!"

They allowed themselves to be swept along to the east side of the square, where a man was standing on a wagon seat with his pistol held aloft. In front of him, stretching across the middle of the street, were numerous horses—a black gelding, a painted pony, a dappled gray horse, two bays, and three roans. Some of the riders were robed in fine dress like Thomas, but most were dressed in work clothes.

Off to one side was a mob of men shouting loudly, holding money in their fists above their heads. Other people, lining the edge of the street, shouted the names of some of the riders and waved wildly at them.

Suddenly, the man in the wagon fired his pistol, and a wild cheer erupted from the crowd as the horses sprang forward. Young boys tried to match the pace of the horses by running along the edge of the street, while some of the crowd moved to the northeast corner of the square to see the horses when they made their final turn toward the finish line.

Mary grabbed Thomas's arm and stood on her tiptoes as she watched the horses turn to the left and race down the south side of the courthouse, heading toward the western side. "Who do you think will win?"

"My money would be on the black gelding. I've seen him race before, and no one's beat him yet," Thomas answered.

"Let's get closer to the street to see the finish," Mary said excitedly.

They worked their way forward through the packed crowd, and soon they heard a cheer from the direction of the northeast corner.

"They'll be coming into view any moment," Thomas said.

Mary leaned over and looked up the street toward the sound of the cheer just as the hammering, dirt-slinging hooves of the horses came into view. The riders were lying as flat as they could on the necks of their horses. Some were kicking the sides of their horses with their heels, while others were slapping their rears with their hats—all trying to get one last burst of speed from their horses, with the finish line in sight.

"I think the paint is in the lead," Mary said.

"I think you're right," Thomas agreed.

All of a sudden, a horse appeared on the edge of the wad of horses and began passing all of them.

"It's the black gelding!" Thomas yelled.

"Look at him run!" Mary said. "His legs look like they're six feet long."

The other riders turned their heads to look at the black horse and rider as it passed them, which triggered even more furious attempts to get their horses to run faster. But it was to no avail. The black gelding and rider flew across the finish line to the echo of the crowd's roar.

"How thrilling!" Mary said as she caught her breath. But as she turned around to see the rest of their entourage's reaction, none of them was anywhere to be seen, not even John or Abigail. Looking around frantically, she said, "Oh, my word. Where are they? Something could happen to the children."

"I'm sure they're fine," Thomas said. "They're just walking around, taking it all in. Wouldn't surprise me to find John or Abigail, or both of them, keeping an eye on them."

"I suppose you're right, but I'll still feel better when I can lay my eyes on them."

They walked slowly through the crowd while at the same time trying to turn to keep an eye out for any sign of them.

After a bit, Mary said, "There's John," and started walking purposefully toward him. When she reached him, she asked, "Where are all the children?"

Continuing to lean against a large oak tree, he pointed and said, "Right over there. The boys are showing off for the girls."

Mary looked in the direction he was pointing and saw a group of children in a semicircle yelling at two boys who were rolling on the ground, grappling with each other. "Is that—?"

"That'd be Frank," John finished her sentence for her.

Mary took a step toward the children.

"Miss Mary," John said, "why don't you let them work things out by theyselves?"

Mary turned around. "But they're fighting."

"Yes, ma'am. But that's the way with boys. They's always trying to prove theyselves, kind of like two young bulls. They have to find out how strong they are. Those boys aren't going to hurt each other. Now they might get a bloody nose or a black eye, but that's about it. Worst thing that could happen would be they lose and get their pride hurt. But they might learn that when two elephants fight, the only thing that gets trampled is the grass."

She looked at the boys, then at Thomas and then John. "You really think we should just let them fight?"

"I'm with John on this one," Thomas said. "I had my fair share of fights growing up, and I'll bet William did, too."

Though her immediate attention was on the fate of Frank, Mary couldn't help but take note of how easily Thomas talked about her late husband. He never tiptoed around the topic and didn't get upset if she brought it up.

Thomas said to John, "By the way, where are my daughters?"

"They went with Abigail to the other side of the square to set the food out."

Just as he was speaking, Abigail appeared from around the corner of the courthouse, with Florence, Emma, and Mary Beth following in her wake.

When the girls veered toward the fighting, Abigail quickly intervened and steered them toward Mary, Thomas, and John.

By the time they arrived, Frank's fight had come to an abrupt end, and all the children dispersed. Mary watched him stand up and brush the dirt off his new clothes. She took note of a hole torn in one of the elbows of his jacket and the blood on his face.

Pete handed him his hat, and they shared a few words. It only took them a couple of seconds of surveying the crowd before they spotted Mary and everyone else. Looking every bit like a bantam rooster, Frank puffed his chest out and took exaggerated strides toward them.

"What was that all about?" Mary asked him as she inspected his face.

"That boy said Pete couldn't play with the rest of us because he was a nigger and a slave. I told him Pete was my brother. That's when the boy laughed at me and said I was stupid, that Negros and whites wasn't meant to live together unless the Negros were slaves. That's when I lit into him."

Mary licked her thumb and rubbed blood from the corner of his lip.

Frank looked her in the eye. "Pete can be my brother if I say so, can't he?"

She returned his stare and said, "Frank, I think that's up to you to decide."

Emma said, "You all need to come see all the food there is to eat."

The sound of a fiddle caught Mary's ear. "Let's go this way first and see what kind of music is playing."

They all followed the sound and found a wagon with a

fiddle player and an accordion player standing on it. As they were playing, another man climbed on board and pulled an Irish whistle out of his pocket and joined in. The crowd started clapping in time to the lively tune.

Thomas tugged on the sleeve of Mary's dress. When she turned, he was bowed low before her.

He stood and said, "May I have this dance?"

Mary looked around. "But no one else is dancing."

"So?"

His broad smile and sparkling eyes were more than she could resist. She curtsied and extended her hand. "I'll be happy to."

It was immediately clear to Mary that she had never danced with someone as smooth and graceful as Thomas. He moved her in a wide arc through the edge of the crowd as everyone backed up to give the dancing couple room. He spun her at a dizzying pace, and she nearly lost her balance, but Thomas kept a firm grip on her and held her upright.

When the song ended, the audience applauded loudly.

Mary looked at the musicians and applauded, as well.

Thomas leaned in and said in her ear, "They're applauding for us."

Mary looked around and saw all eyes were on her and Thomas.

He took her hand and raised it as he bowed toward her. She curtsied toward him and then toward the crowd.

When the applause died down, the performers struck up another song, and the crowd closed in around the wagon.

Florence grabbed Mary's hand. "You were wonderful! You and Father looked like a prince and princess."

Mary kissed her cheek. "You're sweet, but it was because your father is such an amazing dancer. I was just trying to keep up with him." She noticed Pete and Frank staring at her. "What did you boys think?"

Frank swallowed and said, "I've never seen anything like it. It reminded me of fireflies."

Pete said, "I want to learn how to do that."

Mary gave a gentle laugh. "That's an idea. It would be good for both of you to learn how to dance."

After listening to a few more songs, they meandered through the crowd. Occasionally, Thomas stopped and spoke to people he knew. Some Mary had met, while others Thomas introduced to her.

A familiar sound drew her attention. "Why is someone is chopping wood?"

"Sometimes there is a wood-chopping and wood-splitting contest," Thomas said.

"Let's go see," Frank urged them. "I want to see if they're as good as me and Pete."

When they arrived at the site, two men, one big and brawny and the other tall and thin, were swinging axes at a feverish pace, trying to cut their logs in two. Wood chips flew into the air at each blow of their axes.

Mary's first thought was how foolish they were to swing at that pace, knowing they could never keep that up over the course of an entire day, but she also acknowledged that chopping wood for a contest might be a different matter. She paid attention to the technique of each man and found fault with both. Even though the large, muscular man was easily going to win the contest, he focused on using brute force to chop the log rather than letting the heft of the ax be the driving force.

When his log fell apart, those watching applauded and cheered. He shook the hand of the other man, whose log was only two-thirds of the way completed. Then he looked at the crowd and said, "Who else wants to try and beat me?"

No one stepped forward.

"I'll give any man twenty dollars if he can beat me," the man boasted.

Again, no one took his dare.

The man's arrogant attitude grated on Mary, so she impulsively said, "What about a woman?"

All eyes swung toward her.

"What do you mean?" the man asked.

Stepping forward, she said, "I mean, if a woman beats you, will you give her twenty dollars?"

A murmur ran through the crowd. She heard someone say to a neighbor, "That's the one they call the Woodcutter's Wife."

The man laughed loudly. "And which woman would that be? You, perhaps?"

A second before, Mary had some regret about being so bold, but the man's stinging laugh of derision obliterated her regret. She felt furious. Looking the man in the eye, she took a few steps toward him. "Yes, I will be the one who beats you."

The man laughed again and said, "Lady, if you beat me, I'll give you forty dollars."

The crowd's murmurs grew louder, while some hollered at those in the distance to let them know what was about to transpire.

Mary tried turning the tables and taunted him. "You probably don't even have forty dollars."

The man's eyes bulged, and his face turned red. He sputtered, "Don't you worry about that. I've got the forty dollars."

Keeping her voice calm, she said, "I don't want any worthless Confederate money."

He threw his ax to the ground and shoved his hand in his pocket. He jerked out two coins. "Here's two twenty-dollar gold pieces." He slammed them down on a stump and said, "Beat me, and they're yours."

Mary walked over to the other ax while saying, "You need to get prepared to be forty dollars poorer." She untied her bonnet and laid it on the ground.

The number in the crowd had swelled, and they edged forward to watch this David-and-Goliath contest.

Mary picked up the ax and examined the blade as two men rolled new logs in front of her and her opponent. Stepping toward the log with her left foot, she hefted the ax over her right shoulder and said, "I'm ready when you are."

"Somebody count us off," the man shouted.

One of the log rollers said, "On your mark, get set, go!"

On Mary's first swing, she realized she had forgotten about all the extra clothes she was wearing, especially the tightly bound corset. It hampered her swing and made it difficult to take a deep breath, but she redoubled her efforts, preferring to take long, measured swings rather than rapid, short ones. She felt the seam on her right shoulder split open, and she was glad of it, as she could now swing more freely. Soon she saw her left elbow tear through the sleeve of her dress. Large chunks of wood flew through the air at each blow of her ax.

She refused to sneak a look at her competitor, choosing instead to focus all her attention on what she was doing. She couldn't help but hear the crowd cheering and jeering. She thought she recognized Thomas's voice in the bedlam but couldn't be sure.

The wide, cut-out V in her log deepened until there were only a few inches left before it would be cut in two.

Seeing that she was nearly finished, Mary swung as hard as she could for three more strokes, and the log split in two.

A huge cry erupted from the crowd.

Mary turned to look at the burly man and saw him staring at her in disbelief with his ax stopped in midswing.

Silence fell on the crowd as they gazed on to see what would happen next.

The man lowered his ax to the ground and propped its handle against the log. He picked up his two gold pieces and carried them to Mary. A drop of sweat hung tenuously on the end of his nose. He pursed his bottom lip out and puffed a burst of air upward, sending the sweat drop into the air. A smile slowly spread across his face. "Ma'am, if I hadn't been right here and seen what just happened, I'd call any man who said it happened a liar. But you beat me fair and square. Meaning no disrespect, but you're one hell of a woman." He offered her the two gold pieces.

Everyone applauded approvingly.

Mary took the coins and turned them over in her hand, inspecting them. Then she held them out toward the man. "I didn't really want the money. I just wanted to prove a point."

Looking surprised, the man stared at her dumbly for a

second, then smiled again. Taking the coins from her, he said, "Thank you. My wife would have given me a thrashing if I'd come home forty dollars poorer and told her how I lost it."

Chapter Thirty-Seven

MARY

Thomas closed the door to the buggy, and Mary listened to the frozen ground crunching under his boots as he walked to the other side. In a few seconds, he opened the other door and stepped inside, causing the buggy to lean in his direction. When he sat down, she scooted as close as she could to him. He pulled the heavy horsehair blanket onto their laps. "It's a cold night, isn't it?"

"Yes, it is," Mary replied, "but it's been a perfect night. That was the most elegant meal I've ever eaten. The plates were almost too pretty to eat on. And the wine was delicious."

He took the reins in hand and spoke to the horse, which began easing forward. "I thought you'd like it. The restaurant only opened a few weeks ago, but everyone in town has been talking about it. I'm told the owner moved here from France."

She looped her arm through his and leaned her head on his shoulder. "Well, it was a nice surprise."

"It's Valentine's Day. It was supposed to be special."

As they moved slowly through the street, Thomas asked, "Do you care if we don't go straight back to the house?"

"You must have been reading my mind. I don't want to go back, either, just yet." Not caring where he took them,

Mary closed her eyes and let her head gently sway on his shoulder as the buggy leaned this way and that on the uneven and potholed street. *Surely, tonight will be the night.*

For the past two months, she'd been expecting Thomas to ask her to marry him. First she thought he would do it at Christmas, but when that date passed, she anticipated him asking on New Year's Eve. She had managed to keep her disappointment hidden and looked ahead on the calendar to see what might be the next opportune occasion. It was when she saw February 14 that she circled the date in her heart. "That's when he'll do it," she had told herself.

And her answer? When they'd first started courting, her answer to herself had been, "I have no logical reason to say no" because he embodied all the traits a woman could want in a husband. But she was still left feeling rather ho-hum about it. "No reason to say no" was an answer that held no passion—and passion was what she wanted.

However, in the past two months or so, she had felt herself finally falling in love with him, the kind of love that made her long to be with him, to miss him when they weren't together, to think about him during the day, to desire to make love with him. This last item was one that she'd not been sure would ever show itself again. Sure, she could have had sex with him and enjoyed the release it would have given her, but she wanted to be in a place where sex would be a way to say how much she loved him. The sexual part of her marriage with William was so perfect, she didn't believe it could ever be matched, so she tried to keep it pushed out of her mind, even when Thomas began courting her. Now, though, without having to force herself to feel it, she had a deep longing to have him lie between her legs and to give all of herself to him and hold all of him inside her.

And so, riding with him in the buggy, under the cloak of darkness and feeling the warmth of his body, she felt her passions rising. Fantasies filled her mind. What she felt like doing she dared not act on; instead, she squeezed her eyes shut more tightly, enjoying the fantasies, but, at the same time, unconsciously pulled his arm into her breast.

It dawned on her that the buggy was no longer moving, so she slowly opened her eyes. Through the front opening of the buggy, she saw the full moon shining off the Tennessee River. She sat up. "Where are we?"

"We're outside the edge of town, where we came for that picnic last fall. I love this spot because you can see so much of the river as it slowly bends and wends its way through this area. It looks like it moves so effortlessly and unconsciously. If something gets in its way, it just goes around. That's probably how Horseshoe Bend got created. The river doesn't fight to have its way—just so it can still have a way. I admire it for that."

Mary took in his words and held them in her mind as if she were looking at them with a spyglass, trying to be certain she didn't miss anything. She said, "I wish I was more like the river. I get caught up in always wanting things my way."

Thomas put his warm hand under chin and lifted her face toward his. "You're more like the ocean than a river— relentless, powerful, persuasive." His voice was husky. He lowered his face toward hers. "You're not like any woman I've ever met."

She thrilled at the warmth of his breath on her face.

"It's why I love you." He covered her lips with his.

Mary felt fire in every corner of her body. She pressed her lips into his and put her hand on the back of his neck.

Letting go of her face, he wrapped his arms around her, broke off their kiss, took a breath, and kissed her even harder.

She clutched a handful of his hair and gently bit his lower lip. Her other hand brushed past his thigh where she detected his arousal. She felt the pounding of her heart in her chest and in her head. Her face felt flushed, and she was breathing rapidly. Grabbing the lapels of his coat, she laid back on the seat and pulled him down on top of her. "Take me," she whispered.

"Are you certain?"

"I've never been more certain of anything in my life."

*****

Some time later, Mary kissed the top of Thomas's head as the side of his face laid on one of her breasts. His ragged breathing and exclamations of pleasure had quieted, and he appeared to have fallen asleep. She wiped away her tears of pleasure and joy that came unbidden while making love with him. Not even her fantasies could have prepared her for the pleasure and satisfaction she just experienced.

Thomas stirred and moaned. Lifting his head, he looked at her and smiled. "That was unbelievable."

"Yes, it was." She nudged him and said playfully, "Now sit up so that I can put myself back together."

After he sat up, she did the same and began rearranging her clothes. When she finished, she looked at him.

He moved out of the seat, got down on one knee, and took her hand. "I set my mind to do something today, and it wasn't what just happened, though I've dreamed about that many times. When you first gave me permission to call on you and made it clear that you wanted us to take our time, I determined that I would do just that and that I would not bring up the topic of marriage. I've been true to that commitment, as hard as it has been to do so. However, I believe it is time for us to at least talk about it. I can't promise you that I can make you as happy as William did, but I can promise you I will try. I don't have all the answers to the questions that putting our two families together will generate, but I think you and I can figure them out.

"I'm going to tell you something I've never shared with anyone because I didn't want it to influence you or cloud your thoughts and feelings. There was a time when William and I were talking about the war, and he made me make a promise. I promised him that if anything ever happened to him, I would take care of you. And while I would have fulfilled that promise to him, no matter how I felt about you, I can honestly say that I love you like I have loved none other, and what I'm about to ask you has no motivation but love. I would be honored if you would let me spend the rest of my life with you. Mary Elizabeth, will you marry me?"

Thomas's side note about the intimate conversation between him and William caught her off guard, and a lump formed in her throat. At the same time, though, tears welled up in her eyes at Thomas's tender and heartfelt proposal. She cleared her throat and said, "Thomas, I would be proud to be called your wife. I will marry you."

He moved beside her, and they kissed and embraced.

"You've made me so happy," Thomas said.

"I can't wait to tell everyone, not that any of them are going to be surprised. I think they've all just been waiting."

"You're probably right."

"You do realize," Mary said, "that before we get married, we have to build a house for all of us."

"Yes, of course. What do you think about building a big house in the space beside your house? There's plenty of room, with ample shade, too. We could even build it out of lumber from the sawmill rather than building a log house. There are men we can hire to build it, so it won't take away from any work on the farm."

Mary considered his idea. "You know I want to stay on the

farm, so thank you for that. A house built out of lumber will be awfully expensive, especially one big enough for all of us to live in."

"My store has been extremely profitable. I've been putting money aside in hopes that this might happen."

She laughed. "So you knew I would marry you?"

"I think *hoped* would be a better word than *knew*."

"We might hire someone to build it, but I can guarantee you that John and I and the boys will want to have a hand in the building."

"Certainly. And you need to come up with the design of it, too."

"Nothing fancy. Just a big room for us all to eat in, plenty of bedrooms, and a large porch. Oh, and a kitchen large enough to fix the big meals we'll be preparing. I'm getting excited just thinking about it." An idea popped in her mind. "You know, my birthday is April nineteenth. Do you think we could have the house finished by then and get married on that date?"

"What a great idea! If we have to hire extra workers, we'll make it happen."

Chapter Thirty-Eight

MARY

On a bright spring day in April, with the sweet smell of locust blossoms filling the air and blackberry vines blooming, Mary and John stood on opposite sides of a massive poplar tree, taking turns pulling the two-man crosscut saw through the trunk. Frank and Pete stood to one side with axes in hand, focusing on the top of the tree.

"It's moving," Pete said to Frank.

"Not yet," Frank replied. "Almost."

The only sound in the woods was the rhythmic *zzzzz* of the saw as Mary and John's attention was glued to the saw and trunk.

Suddenly, Frank said, "Now," before yelling at John and Mary, "There she goes!"

John and Mary stopped immediately and looked at him.

"Get out of the way!" Frank called to them.

As they pulled the saw out of the tree, there was a loud cracking sound. They moved as fast as they could and joined the boys.

All eyes were focused on the ancient mammoth of the forest. More loud popping and cracking rang out like rifle fire as the tree seemed to shudder. The erect tree slowly began to tilt, then picked up speed as gravity pulled it toward its final resting place. Ear-splitting sounds echoed through the woods as the heartwood ripped. Limbs from other large trees were torn off in the wake of the descending tree, while smaller trees were annihilated. There was a thunderous crash when it slammed into the ground.

In striking contrast to the violent display, leaves floated lazily through the air like snowflakes and gently landed on the forest floor.

"Wow," Pete said in amazement, "I've never seen a tree that big be cut down."

"Me either," Frank agreed. "I can't believe how loud it was. I wonder how old it was."

Mary said, "John, why don't you show them how to tell the age of a tree?"

The boys followed him to the left-behind tree stump, where he showed them how to count the rings.

Frank and Pete put their fingers on each ring and counted silently. After a few moments, Frank looked at Pete and said, "How many did you get?"

"I counted ninety-seven."

"I got one hundred and one."

Frank looked at Mary. "Is that possible?"

"That a tree can be that old? Certainly. This tree is going to provide some sturdy logs that'll be the foundation for the new house."

"I'm just sorry we couldn't get it built in time for your wedding in nine days," John said.

"It couldn't be helped. All those spring rains made it too muddy to do the ground work. But the house is laid out now, and once we get these logs in place, things'll move pretty quickly."

"Where are you and Mr. Thomas going to live until the house gets built?" Frank asked.

"We'll just keep doing as we have been. I'll go into town and visit, in between planting in the fields. We can't let everything else get in the way of tending to the farm. Those tobacco seedlings are ready to plant, aren't they, John?"

"Yes, ma'am. They looking good, too." He looked at the boys. "What about that plot of ground you boys been working on—how's it looking?"

Pete said, "We disked it so many times yesterday that the dirt's as fine as cornmeal."

"All that's lacking is laying out some furrows," Frank added.

"I want to be there when you plant," Mary said. "I've never seen how it's done. Raising tobacco's going to be a brand-new adventure for me." Nodding at John, she reminded him, "You're going to have to take the lead on this project."

"When you see how much money we'll make on such a small plot of land, I think you'll be glad we gave it a try. I'll admit, it does take a right smart amount of work tending to it until it's harvested, but still, I think it'll be worth it."

"Well, let's get busy getting the logs out of this tree," Mary said. "I'd like to get them snaked out of here and up to the house before dark."

Pete and Frank sprang into action, climbing along the trunk of the tree like a pair of raccoons, and finished trimming the branches off the trunk. Meanwhile, Mary and John measured a length of trunk before taking the crosscut saw to it.

Several hours later, as the sun headed toward the horizon, Mary backed the pair of mules toward the tree while John lashed two logs together with a section of chain. He hooked the other end of the chain around the single tree behind the mules.

Mary moved over to one side, out from behind the mules, in order to avoid being struck by any dirt and rocks they might throw when they started pulling. At the same time, the boys stationed themselves in front of the mules. She popped the mules with the reins. "Take us home."

The mules leaned into their horse collars, expecting to move a normal load like a wagon or a plow, but the weight of the logs stopped them in their tracks. They took a half step backward so that their harness would go slack.

When they didn't immediately try to pull again, Mary yelled at them, "Come on, you sorry excuses for a pair of mules. Time for you to earn your keep." She slapped them harder with the reins.

This time, the mules leaned forward until everything pulled tight, and then they slammed their hooves into the ground and began dragging the logs forward.

"Frank!" John called out. "You two make sure they go to the left of that outcropping of rock."

Frank and Pete each grabbed the cheekpiece of the bridles on the two mules and turned them as instructed by John, while Mary worked to do the same with the reins.

Zigzagging their way out of the woods to avoid trees and rocks, the mules snaked the logs out into the open and began plodding toward the house.

Pete yelled at Frank, "I'll race you to the barn!"

"You're on!"

As they ran toward the barn, John said, "I guess I might have had that much energy when I was that young, but I sure don't remember it."

Mary laughed.

Several minutes later, she spotted Frank running toward them, waving his arms and saying something.

Pulling back on the reins to stop the mules, Mary waited anxiously for him to reach them. Her mind had already imagined horrific things that would prompt Frank to come running for them without Pete. She tried to still her racing heart, but not very successfully.

John waited quietly beside her.

With eyes wide, Frank reached them and said, "They's some men standing outside the house. Me and Pete didn't know any of them and wasn't sure what to do, so he's staying hid in the barn and keeping an eye on them."

Mary asked, "Why didn't you just speak to them and see what they wanted? It might be some of our neighbors."

"They didn't look right. Their clothes are all ragged, and some of them are barefoot. They look mean."

Mary and John exchanged a look.

He responded to her unasked question, "I don't know. May be some deserters."

With knitted brows, Mary said, "Let's hurry and get there and find out." She restarted the mules but at a quicker pace this time.

By the time they made the turn around the barn and headed through the yard behind the house, a white froth of sweat rimmed the edges of the mules' horse collars.

Just as Frank had said, a group of four or five men stood just off the porch. They all turned to face the returning log expedition.

Pete came running out of the barn and joined Mary, John, and Frank.

Mary immediately regretted having left all the axes back in the woods. She pulled the mules to a stop and dropped the reins.

As the men approached her, she saw no malice in their eyes, only fatigue and defeat. There were also no signs they were carrying weapons. It was then she recognized they were wearing the faded clothing of Southern soldiers.

"Can I help you?" she asked.

One of them stepped forward and said, "Could you spare us a bite to eat, ma'am? We ain't ate nothing in two days. We're just trying to make it home to our people in Alabama."

"Why have you deserted from your unit?" Mary confronted them, feeling agitation.

All the men looked at her with surprise. "Oh, no, ma'am," the spokesman said. "We're not deserters. Have you not heard?"

"Heard what?"

"Lee surrendered to Grant at Appomattox courthouse yesterday. The war's over. Everybody's going home."

*****

For the next five days, an increasing number of soldiers filled the road that passed by Mary's house. Some stopped and asked for food, which she never refused to provide. Each time she saw them close up, she was shocked at how emaciated they were, but what broke her heartwas the empty, dead look in their eyes. Even though they said where they were heading, they looked as if they were lost—lost in their souls. *This is the cost of war that no one can calculate; when soldiers go home in body but their hearts are long gone.*

Mary and John stood watching four soldiers head back to the journey on the road, carrying biscuits and ham Mary shared with them, when they spotted the postman approaching the house.

"No letters for you today, Miss Mary," he said. "I'm just spreading the word about what happened last night. The president was shot and killed."

Mary staggered back a step, feeling as if she had been struck in the chest with a fist. "That can't be. Surely, you're mistaken."

"No mistake, ma'am. He and Mrs. Lincoln were watching a play when a man shot him in the back of the head and killed him." He wheeled his horse around and headed off to share the stunning news with others.

Mary slowly turned to face John and saw his cheeks were shiny with tears as he stared at her blankly.

In a choked voice, he said, "Somebody done killed Mr. Lincoln. Lord, what's this world coming to?"

"I'm so sorry, John." Taking his hand, she said, "Let's go sit in the shade."

As if he were a little child, John silently allowed her to lead him underneath the oak tree. He sat on the ground, while Mary took a seat on a nail keg.

He folded his arms on his tented knees and rested his forehead on his arms. In an agonized tone, he asked, "Why would anyone want to kill Mr. Lincoln? The war's done over. What does it matter?" He looked at Mary. "I told you that I met him one time, didn't I?"

"Yes, you did, but tell me about it again."

"He was walking in front of the White House, just like any other man, except you could see his head above everybody else's." Holding up his right hand, John continued, "He shook that hand. Talked to me like he'd knowed me all my life. Looked me in the eye, he did. And he listened to what I had to say. Didn't matter to him that I was a Negro and didn't dress fancy like all the other men trying to get his attention. He treated me like I was somebody. As long as I live, I won't never forget it."

Pete and Frank came walking up.

"What's going on?" Frank asked.

"The president's been killed."

"What president?" Pete asked innocently as he sat down beside John and looked up at him.

"Of the United States," Mary clarified.

"The president of our country?" Frank asked. "That can't happen. Nobody kills the president."

"It's true," Mary said quietly.

"Why did they kill him? I thought people didn't like him because of the war. But the war's done over. Why now?"

"I don't know the answer to that," Mary said.

Both boys looked at the still-silent John.

Mary decided to explain. "John knew the president."

They looked at her with disbelief.

"It's true. He met him, talked with him, even shook his hand."

Their heads swiveled in John's direction.

"Wow," Pete said under his breath.

"That's why John's so upset," Mary said.

They sat quietly for a few minutes until John wiped his face and said, "There is an African proverb that says, 'If there is character, ugliness becomes beauty. If there is no character, beauty becomes ugliness.' Mr. Lincoln was nothing to look at, some would even say he was ugly. But it was his character that made him a great man, a beautiful man. You boys need to never forget that. Pay attention to your character—be honest, be true, care for your fellow man—and you will always be admired."

"And you will make me proud," Mary added.

*****

The next morning, Mary was in the barn cleaning out some of the stalls before going out to join John and the boys as they planted tobacco, but her mind was on the sadness that she had seen on John's face at breakfast. Even though he wasn't one to show a lot of emotion, she was still able to detect it by his silence at the table and his lack of enthusiasm as he headed out to the field with Pete and Frank. She had tried to convince him to let her and the boys do the work today, but that suggestion only seemed to hurt his feelings and made him try harder to hide his sorrow.

As she was spreading new straw in the stalls, she detected movement in the doorway of the barn. Turning, she saw the silhouette of a man in the doorway. *Another soldier looking for food.* She propped her pitchfork against a post and walked toward him. "I'll get you a biscuit and some bacon."

As she passed the silent man, she noticed that the empty right sleeve of his shirt was pinned to his shoulder, and a patch covered his right eye. A scraggly, reddish beard covered his face. "Maybe I can spare a mug of apple cider, too," she said.

She didn't wait to see if he was following her because she didn't have time to dally, as she was eager to see to the tobacco planting. Striding into the kitchen, she grabbed a biscuit and some bacon, then poured a mug of cider out of the jug.

Walking back outside, she handed it to the man, who was standing just off the porch and looking up at the boys' room they'd added last year. Something in the way he held his head struck a chord with her but not loud enough that she pursued it.

Still in a hurry, she sat the mug on the porch and held out the food. "You can sit here and rest while you eat and drink. I've got to head out to the field. Good luck on your journey home."

When he took the food from her, she walked past him. Again, a bell of familiarity tolled, but this time, she searched for exactly what it was. *Was it his nose? Or his chin?* Suddenly, she stopped walking.

At the same time, the man spoke for the first time. "I am home, Mary."

As if in a dream, Mary turned around slowly and looked with purpose at the war-mangled man. *His eyes!*

The soldier stepped toward her. "Mary, it's me, William. I'm finally home."

Tiny specks of light darted in and out of Mary's peripheral vision as blackness closed in on her, and as she whispered, "William," she crumpled to the ground.

Chapter Thirty-Nine

MARY

Mary ran frantically through the thick fog, trying to follow the direction from which William's voice was coming.

"Mary!"

She stopped, turned in a circle, and opened her mouth to call back to him, but nothing came out.

From out of the fog a hand appeared and touched the side of her face. She flinched.

"It's me, Mary. It's William."

Gradually, the fog lifted as Mary regained consciousness. She found herself lying on the ground, with the soldier who called himself William on his knees beside her. She looked past the ravages of war that had given him the appearance of being an old man and found the young man she married. "William?"

The left side of his face smiled back at her, while the right side with the patch over his eye remained frozen. He nodded his head. "Yes, Mary. I've come home."

Splinters of questions and a mixture of emotions collided as they swirled within Mary, giving her the feeling that she had been lifted off the ground and was in the middle of a tornado.

He offered her his left hand, and she grasped it as she rose to a sitting position. She closed her eyes in an attempt to stop her head from spinning. When she opened them, she saw tears streaming from his good eye.

In a broken voice, he said, "I didn't think I would ever see you again."

She managed to grab hold of a thought out of the swirling storm and said, "I thought you were dead."

"I'm sure you did. I thought I was, too, and in a way, I was."

"Where have you been?"

"The short answer is that I've been in a prisoner-of-war camp."

Her gaze shifted to the right side of his face and dropped down to his empty sleeve. "What happened to you?"

Looking down at the ground, he said, "Our position was being overrun by the Yankees, and I was standing beside one of our cannons when it exploded. Exactly what happened after that I don't know because I was unconscious for weeks. But I'm guessing they thought I was dead and ran off and left me. Some Yankee discovered I was still breathing, and instead of shooting me in the head, he took me to a field hospital. I woke up in Hammond General Hospital in Maryland." Glancing at his empty sleeve, he said, "I still had my arm then, but it was a mess. After a couple more weeks, they cut it off and sent me down the road to Point Lookout, a prisoner camp."

As he spoke, she noticed his sunken cheeks and gray complexion. There were tiny scars radiating out from under his eye patch. All she could think to say was, "I thought you were dead."

He looked at her. "I know, and I don't blame you. I almost didn't come home."

Compassion finally overcame her shock, and she touched his arm.

He gave an almost imperceptible flinch. "To come home like this," he said, "just half a man, what good am I?"

Mary's thoughts tripped over a sudden rush of feelings about Thomas, and she bit her tongue and withdrew her hand. *My God, what am I going to do?* Standing up, she said, "Let's go inside."

William stood up and said, "Can I give you a hug?"

"I'm sorry," she replied. "It's just such a shock. I don't know what I'm doing or thinking." She put her arms around him and felt his arm around her. After all the turmoil she went through in accepting it was okay to love Thomas without feeling like she was betraying William, she now felt as if she was betraying Thomas. *Should I kiss him? What will he think if I don't? How can I explain it? Should I tell him everything?*

As they broke their embrace, they looked at each other, and William leaned in to kiss her. She closed her eyes and stood perfectly still.

He held his lips on hers for a moment, then stepped back. "What's wrong?"

"What do you mean? There's nothing wrong, except my dead husband has come home alive."

"I felt like I was kissing you, but you weren't kissing me."

She turned her face away so that he couldn't see her blushing. "Don't be silly." She headed toward the house. "Come inside and let me fix you something hot to eat and drink. You look like a skeleton."

As he followed her, she heard him ask, "What's that addition on top of the house?"

"There have been lots of changes since you were gone," she answered as she passed through the door to the kitchen.

She stoked the fire and put some coffee on to boil, then got the spider skillet out. As she fried some bacon and eggs for him, she told the story of John saving her from being raped and then told his backstory. "At first I let him stay here because I felt I owed it to him, but it wasn't long before I began to see that he was indispensable to running this farm. I just couldn't do it alone. So we came to an agreement, and I've shared the profits with him. This spring we decided to raise a plot of tobacco. He has experience doing it and said we had a good place for it. But besides being a hard worker, he's a thoughtful and wise man and has given me lots of advice along the way. When I was grieving for you, he was always willing to listen. He even saved my life a second time."

"Really?"

"Yes. I came down with typhoid. Several people around here died from it. John sat with me day and night until my fever broke."

"Sounds like I'm deeply indebted to him. But he's not your slave, is he?"

"No, not at all. He's a free man."

"Is that his room that's been built on top of the house?"

"Goodness, no. He would never agree to living in the house for fear of it bringing reproach on my reputation. No, he stayed in the barn for quite a while until he moved into the woodshed."

"I see," William said thoughtfully.

She sat his plate of hot food in front of him along with a cup of steaming coffee.

He leaned over and smelled the coffee. Closing his eyes, he said, "You have no idea how many times I have dreamed of the smell of coffee. Sometimes the dreams were so real that I would wake up expecting to see a cup in my hands."

As he lifted it to his lips, she watched his hand trembling. She saw him struggle as he awkwardly cut up his eggs. *Should I offer to help? Will it make him feel more helpless? Will he think I don't care if I don't offer to help?*

In between bites of food, he said, "So if that room is not for John, who is it for?"

Thankful to have something to focus on rather than him, she said, "That story is even more fantastical than John's arrival. He and I were on Bitter Hill last July."

"What were you two doing up there?"

Mary held her breath as she considered if she should tell him the truth. She exhaled slowly and took a tiny step forward. "I asked him to go with me. I had grieved for you so much, William, day and night, thinking of you, wondering what had become of you, hoping every day you'd return, then being disappointed at the end of each day when you didn't. Because I never heard a word from you, I came to the only logical conclusion I could find, and that was that you were dead. When I finally accepted that horrible truth, I decided I wanted to bury you beside our children."

His eyebrow went up. "Bury me?"

"I know it sounds crazy, and I don't really mean bury you, but I had to have some sense of ending. I asked John to make a grave marker for you. It was so heavy there was no way I could carry it up there by myself, so he helped me." She stopped to give him time to absorb the scene.

For several moments, he stared at his plate of half-eaten food. Finally, he nodded his head. "I understand. I never thought about that, but I can see how that would help you. Maybe me coming home was a mistake. Perhaps things would have been better, easier, if I'd stayed dead."

Though she wouldn't understand until later, it was at that exact moment that she resolved to sweep away her planned life with Thomas and devote her life to restoring the life and soul of her first love. "Don't talk like that," she said in a sharp tone. "You were the love of my life, the one I gave myself to. How can I not be thrilled to have you home again? But you have to understand that you've been looking forward to this homecoming for God knows how long, whereas I gave up on it ever happening. Be patient with me." She smiled, then said, "Now let me tell you about Frank and Pete."

Furrows appeared on William's forehead, and he cocked his head to one side.

As she launched into her story, even she was surprised at how emotional she became in the telling, and it emphasized to her just how much the boys had come to mean to her since that first meeting on Bitter Hill.

William appeared mesmerized by her story and pushed his plate to one side, merely sipping coffee every once in a while.

As she wound her story down, her voice cracked as she said, "I feel like they are the children I was never able to have."

William reached over and wiped away a tear with his thumb. "Then they are truly the luckiest boys in the world that you are the one who found them."

She looked at his plate. "Is there anything else you'd like to eat?"

"It was really good. I guess my stomach has shrunk. I'll tell you what I'd really like to do."

"What's that?"

"I'd like to take a hot bath in the scalding kettle and put on some clean clothes." Tugging at his shirt, he added, "Then I want to burn these."

"Of course," Mary replied as she stood. "Let's get to it."

They walked out of the kitchen and headed toward the ever-present kettle to begin filling it with water.

William pointed toward the hewn logs intended for the house Mary and Thomas were going to build. "What are those for?"

In another one of those fateful moments where decisions are made without forethought, Mary, a woman who prided honesty above all other virtues, chose to lie to her husband, which would result in her walking a path littered with more lies. "We're going to use those for the foundation of the tobacco barn."

"Judging by the size of them," he said, "that's going to be some barn."

"You're right. They still have to be sized and cut some more. This tree they came out of was so tall and perfectly straight, we decided just to cut these long ones in the woods, drag them here, and cut them to size later."

Arriving at the kettle, she knocked away the charred remains of the last fire she had built there when killing hogs with John and the boys. "I'll start a fire while you start hauling water over here." Her last word had not crossed her lips before she realized she'd spoken out of the depths of habit from years of marriage to William. Her mouth filled with vomitlike regret, yet she couldn't figure out how to unsay what she had said. With dread, she looked to see what her words had done to him.

William looked like a scarecrow, standing, unmoving. He looked from Mary to the well, to his empty sleeve, to his left hand.

Uncertainty filled the distance between them, and neither spoke for a moment.

Mary was about to apologize when William turned and walked to the well.

She went about gathering kindling and wood but mostly kept a watchful eye on him.

Setting the bucket on the side of the well, he tied a rope on the handle and used his teeth to pull the knot tight, then he pushed the bucket into the well.

Mary heard the echo of the splash into the water and breathed a sigh of gratitude for the high water table they were blessed with so that he wouldn't have far to pull the bucket back up.

William gripped the rope and pulled, then stood for a moment with the taut rope in his hand. He slipped the rope between two rocks and jerked it tight. He released his grip and leaned over into the well and grabbed the rope, pulled it up, and repeated the process until he had the bucket of water in his hand.

Mary couldn't help but be proud of his determination and ingenuity at problem solving. *Do I praise him and tell him how proud I am of him? Or will he feel undeserving for having to work so laboriously at something he used to do without thinking?* As she debated with herself, she noticed him having trouble untying the wet rope from the handle. She was certain he was getting frustrated, but again, she was uncertain whether to intervene.

Suddenly, his hand slipped, and his elbow knocked the bucket back into the well.

Mary was shocked as a stream of swear words spewed out of his mouth. She'd never heard that kind of vile language from him. She walked over to him and rested her hand on his arm.

He jerked away and snapped, "What?"

Backing up a step, she said, "I was just going to tell you that it's okay; don't worry about it."

"Don't worry about it when I can't even draw a bucket of water? What kind of man am I?"

"How many times have you tried to do that with one hand?"

Her paused, and after a couple of seconds, he said, in a calmer voice, "Never."

"Exactly. It's just going to take time. Why don't you go finish arranging the wood for the fire, and I'll draw the water."

William hesitated, then followed her suggestion.

A couple of hours later, steam was rising off the water in the half-filled kettle.

Mary stuck her fingers in the water. "I believe that's hot enough. You get in, and I'll go get you some soap. I'm just going to burn those clothes you are wearing. I'll bring some out of the house."

He started to unbutton his shirt but stopped. "I don't want you to see me."

A part of her was glad to hear him say it because she'd already thought about what he might look like and how she would cover her reaction without hurting him. "I understand. I'll go inside and get the things while you undress and get in."

When she stepped inside the house, she closed the door and leaned her back against it. Taking in a deep breath, she exhaled slowly. *What in the world am I going to do? Who is this person the war has returned to me? Just when my life was about to recover and move forward*—she couldn't finish her thought because she wouldn't allow herself to say it even to herself.

And what about Thomas, and Florence, and Emma, and Mary Beth? How will I ever—how will they ever . . . She closed her eyes and pressed the heel of her hand against her forehead. Eventually, she pushed herself away from the door and went to the bedroom to get some clothes out of the bureau and to pick up a bar of soap off the washstand.

She returned to the backyard and headed toward the kettle, where she saw the back of William's wet head and his shoulders. "Here's your soap," she said as she got closer.

He whirled around in the water. "That's far enough. Just throw it here, and leave the clothes on the ground there."

This time Mary decided to follow her instinct and continued walking toward him. "I'll do no such thing. You came home to me as my husband, and I'm still your wife. I don't know what you're afraid will happen when I see you. But let me tell you, since you've been gone, I've seen lots worse." She kept her eyes glued to his, refusing to satisfy her curiosity about what the stump of his arm looked like. Standing two feet from the kettle, she offered him the soap.

Slowly, his thin arm lifted out of the water, and he took the bar of soap with his bony fingers.

She smiled and asked, "You want me to scrub you up? Because it looks like you sure need it."

Half of his face gave her a weak smile. "Thank you, Mary, but I'd really like to do it myself."

"Fair enough. When you get done, I'll give you a shave."

"That'll be nice."

"I'm going back in to wash up dishes. I'll find your razor and put a good edge on it."

Inside the kitchen, she bent down to pick up the skillet off the hearth when a new thought jerked her upright and caused her to drop the iron skillet on her toe. She cried out in pain and hopped around on one foot while trying to hold the other foot in her hand. She finally sat in a chair, rocking back and forth in pain. When it began to subside, the startling thought wormed its way back to the front of her mind. *What am I going to do when John and the boys come back in from the field?*

While John might catch on quickly to what she was trying to do, the boys would start firing unfiltered questions and blurting out about the plans for the wedding to Thomas and the building of the new house. She quickly decided that she had to go out to them and tell them everything before they came back to the house.

Putting aside what she had told William she was going to do, she headed out of the house and toward the barn. "William," she said as she passed by him, "you're going to have to wait on that shave. I forgot that I had promised John and the boys that I would come out and help them plant the tobacco. When you get finished, just do whatever you'd like. We'll be in before supper."

She disappeared into the barn without waiting for a reply, then exited on the other side and broke into a run.

Chapter Forty

JOHN

With their backs bent and their heads covered with broad-brimmed straw hats, John, Frank, and Pete shuffled barefoot through the soft soil of the tobacco patch.

John paid close attention as Pete made a hole in the furrow with a wooden hand peg, made from the limb of a sassafras tree, and Frank placed a tobacco plant seedling in it, pushed dirt in the hole with his foot, creating tiny clouds of dust, then tamped the soil.

John lifted a dipper of water from the bucket he was carrying and poured it around the plant. "You boys are doing a fine job," he said. "We're just about done."

"I thought Miss Mary was going to join us," Pete said.

"Mother must have got busy," Frank explained.

John and Mary had talked about how the boys referred to her in starkly different terms. Neither of them was told to do so; it had just sort of come to be, and she and John had agreed that it was best to let the boys find their own way.

He turned his head to look and see if perhaps Mary was on her way to them at that very minute. That was when he saw her running toward them, holding her skirts up with one hand to keep from tripping over them. He stood up straight and faced her. "Hold up, boys," he said. "There she comes now, and something's not right."

"What's wrong?" Frank asked.

"Don't know," John replied, keeping his voice calm. But inside, he had a bad feeling about whatever it was that was chasing Mary toward them. "Watch your step," he told the boys, "and let's get out of the field."

The three of them walked to the end of the row just as Mary got there.

Her face glowed red, and she was out of breath. John read panic in her eyes.

"What's wrong?" Frank questioned.

"What's happened?" Pete asked.

John said, "Boys, let's let her catch her breath. She'll tell us soon enough."

"I was in the barn," Mary finally blurted out. "There was this man . . . I didn't pay any attention . . . went to get him some food . . . something about him . . . I didn't know . . . his arm—"

"Miss Mary," John interrupted her and placed his hand on her shoulder, "you're not making no sense. Slow down, and tell us what happened."

"It's William. He came home."

John stared at her in disbelief. "That can't be. He died in the war. Are you sure it's not somebody pretending to be him?"

"No, it's him. I didn't recognize him at first because he lost an arm and an eye because of an exploding cannon. He's thin and looks like he's aged ten years or more, but it's him."

Pete looked up at John. "Who's William?"

"Is that who you were married to before we came?" Frank asked Mary.

"Boys," John said, "I want you to go down to the creek and fill up the water buckets for me."

"But—" Frank began.

"No buts," John cut him off. "Do as I've asked."

When they were out of earshot, John said, "Miss Mary, what in the world are you going to do? You supposed to marry Mr. Thomas in three days. We're going to start building the new house. Mercy me, what are you going to do?"

"He's still my husband, even though in my heart I buried him. I can't tell him I'm going to marry the man he remembers as his best friend. Besides, I can't marry Thomas. William and I are still married."

"You mean you not going to tell him anything about you and Mr. Thomas?"

"No, I'm not. I believe if I told him the truth, it would kill him. He might even kill himself."

"Surely not."

"He's not the same as he used to be. He doesn't have that strong heart he used to have. And he's a lot quicker to fly off the handle. I guess it's to be expected after what he's been through. But I think I can help him heal, help him find himself."

"I see," John said slowly. "But my father used to say, 'One falsehood spoils a thousand truths.'"

Mary nodded. "I know that's true, but I've already lied to him about the logs lying in the yard that were intended for the new house, and once you start down the path of lies, there's no turning back."

"Then what are you going to tell Mr. Thomas? That man loves you more than anything on this earth."

The appearance of strength she'd been holding while she spoke to him of William suddenly fractured, and tears welled up in her eyes. "I love him, too. I don't know how I'm going to tell him." Her voice caught. "And then there's the girls . . ." She looked at the ground and closed her eyes.

"Miss Mary, you're in a position where you can't win. No matter what you do or say, somebody is going to be hurting terrible. What can I do to help?"

"First of all, I've got to explain things to Frank and Pete. I was afraid you all would come back before I could tell you about William, and the boys would spill the beans."

As she finished her sentence, the boys appeared at the edge of the field and made their way to John and Mary.

"Boys," Mary said, "I've got something to tell you. Something has happened that I never dreamed would happen."

Frank took a step back. "Mother and Father came back for us?"

"No, no, nothing like that. I don't think you need to worry about that ever happening. No, this is something else that mostly involves me but is going to affect lots more people, including you two."

Frank frowned, while Pete gave John a questioning look.

John said, "This is not my story to tell. This is Miss Mary's."

When both boys were looking at her again, Mary said, "My husband, William, the one who disappeared, the one I thought was dead, has come home."

The shock from Mary's news silenced their tongues, and they gave her unblinking stares.

Mary continued, "William is at the house right now, taking a bath in the big kettle in the yard. He is blind in his right eye and wears a patch over it. And his right arm is missing. What all this means is that I'm not going to marry Thomas. I can't marry him because I'm still married to my husband, William."

Frank's tongue finally became unfastened from the floor of his mouth, "You mean Mr. Thomas and Florence, and Emma, and Mary Beth are not going to move out here, and we're not going to build a new house?"

"Yes, that's what I mean."

John saw the disappointment on their faces. "I know you boys was looking forward to all that happening, but sometimes things happen that nobody but God expected to. It can't be helped. Even though I've never met Mr. William, I learned a lot about him by listening to Miss Mary talk about him when I first came here. I think you and me are really going to like him."

His words seemed to soothe the sting of Mary's news.

Looking at Mary, Pete said, "You're not going to send me and Frank away, are you, just because your husband came home?"

Mary threw her arms around both their necks and squeezed. "When are you two going to get that possibility out of your heads? I've told you over and over that you are mine, you are the children I always wanted, and nothing or no one is ever going to change that." She let go and looked at them. "We're family, and William is going to come to love you just as much as I do."

A little finger of doubt tapped John on the shoulder. *I hope he does.*

"There's just one more thing," Mary said. "You boys know how to keep a secret, don't you?"

They both nodded their heads.

"This may be difficult for you to understand," Mary began,

"but I don't want William to know that Thomas and I were planning on getting married and living on the farm. I'm afraid of how deeply it would hurt his feelings. He's suffered enough hurt for a lifetime. He nearly lost his life when a cannon exploded beside him, then he lost his arm and eye, was sent to a prisoner-of-war camp, and almost starved to death while there. He probably thought he would never live to see me and his beloved farm again. But somehow, he survived it all and made it back home. How do you think he would feel if he came back and learned that his wife had married his best friend?"

"Pretty mad," Pete answered.

"And very sad," Frank added.

"I think you're exactly right. And that's why we aren't going to let him find out."

They looked at her thoughtfully.

Frank asked, "Do you want us to lie about it?"

Mary glanced over at John, and he said, "You boys know we've talked before about how important it is to be honest and tell the truth, don't you?"

They nodded.

"That's still awfully important, but this right here is a special kind of situation, one like I haven't never heard of. And special situations sometimes calls for changing the rules a bit. If you tell a lie so you can cheat somebody or so you can get out of trouble, that's wrong. But the lie Miss

Mary's asking you to tell is the kind that will keep from hurting somebody. Wouldn't you agree, Miss Mary?"

"That's exactly right," she said. "It's what we call an exception to the rule. This lie will actually be helping someone."

"What about Mr. Thomas?" Frank asked. "Is he going to tell the lie, too?"

"And what about Florence, Emma, and Mary Beth?" Pete chimed in. "Are all of them going to lie?"

Chapter Forty-One

MARY

When Mary, John, and the boys got back to the house, she found William asleep in their bed and decided it would be a perfect time to go talk to Thomas.

She wheeled the buckboard to a stop in front of Thomas's store and breathed a silent prayer. Even though she'd gone through dozens of scenarios of telling him about William during the drive in, she was still unsure what she was going to say.

As soon as she entered the store, her eyes lit upon Thomas working behind the counter. In her heart, fear, pain, love, and dread piled one upon another like heavy feed sacks. Just trying to breathe became difficult.

Thomas looked up from what he was doing and saw her. His face practically glowed at the sight of her, and a broad grin creased his features. He gave his customer his change and rushed to greet Mary. He gave her a bear hug and lifted her off the floor.

All his hug did was increase Mary's heaviness. In spite of her best efforts, she was unable to hold back her tears.

Setting her back down on the floor, Thomas joked, "Is it bad luck for the bride and groom to see each other this close to the wedding day? I didn't know you were coming to town today." It was then that he stepped back to look at her. "My God, Mary, what's wrong?"

A thousand words pushed up from within her, but the tightness in her throat made it impossible for them to reach her tongue. She opened and closed her mouth several times, trying to force out any kind of sound. Her hot tears ran down her neck and disappeared beneath the neck of her dress. She found it impossible to look him in the eye.

He grabbed her hands. "Mary, you're scaring me. Say something. What's wrong?"

She finally squeaked out, "We need to talk in private."

He looked around and said, "No one's in the store," then went and locked the front door. "Let's go into the office."

Once inside, he closed the door as she sat down.

When he sat down in front of her, she took a breath and began, "What I'm going to say to you is going to be one of the hardest things I've ever done. Above all else, I want you to be certain of how much I love you, and the last thing I want to do is to hurt you. Something has happened that I never dreamed would happen. It's so unexpected that I keep hoping it's a dream, and I'll wake up, and nothing would have changed. But everything has changed. Everything." She paused, then said, "William has come back home."

The intensity in the small room sucked every drop of sound out of it and left the two of them sitting in a vacuum.

She watched his eyes fill with confusion while the blood

drained from his face.

"William?" the name rolled slowly off Thomas's tongue.

"Yes, this morning. He appeared at the barn door while I was working. I walked right past him to go get him some food, thinking he was just another returning soldier, and didn't even recognize him. He's lost an eye and an arm, and he's so thin he looks like a scarecrow. But then he spoke, and I looked more closely and realized who it was. It really is William."

In slow motion, Thomas sat back from the edge of his seat and slumped in the chair. His face went slack. "Where has he been? Why hasn't he written you?"

"I had those same questions. He told me the Yankees found him half-dead after a cannon exploded beside him and his army had retreated. They took him to a field hospital and then to a regular hospital. That's where they amputated his arm. Right after that, they put him in a prisoner camp. No one was allowed to write or receive letters; plus, William wasn't sure if he wanted to come back home. He thought I wouldn't have anything to do with him because of his injuries. But he finally decided to make the trek back here and see for certain what I would do."

Thomas rubbed his hand over his face. "This is incredible. How is he?"

"He seems changed. I can't exactly put it into words, but it feels like there's a darkness about him that wasn't there before. I supposed it's to be expected, and perhaps it's because he's just weary. Once he's refreshed, he might be himself again."

"What did he say when you told him about us?"

This was the moment Mary dreaded, and she could not look him in the eye. She said quietly, "I didn't tell him."

Thomas sat back up. "You didn't tell him? Why not?"

"I don't know. Maybe because I felt sorry for him. Maybe because I'm a coward. I just know that there was a moment when I looked at him and thought about telling him. It felt like my heart was being ripped in two."

"Do you love him?"

"I told you one time that I would always love William. He was my first love, and we spent ten years together."

"But that's all past tense," Thomas said. "I guess what I need to know is, does this change anything for you and me?"

A fresh set of tears began to wash Mary's face. "Oh, Thomas, I love you so much. I was looking forward to spending the rest of my life with you."

His eyes reddened, and tears pooled in them. "I see. You *were* looking forward—but not now."

"I can't marry you, for one because my husband is still alive. But also, what kind of person would it show me to be if I decided to desert him or divorce him? Is that what you want me to do? Divorce him?"

"Yes, I do." He fell to his knees in front of her. "I want you all to myself. I want a family that is whole. I want to grow old with you."

She brushed the tears from his cheeks with the palm of her hand. "And I want the same thing, truly I do. But I think when you see William, you will understand my feelings. Would you really want to destroy your best friend?"

Getting off his knees and sitting back down, Thomas ran his fingers through his hair. "My God, Mary, this is impossible! Am I supposed to just pretend I don't love you and that my heart doesn't ache for you every moment of every day? I don't know if I can do that." His eyes opened wider. "Oh my God, what about the children? What are we to tell them?"

"I told Frank and Pete that we are going to treat the wedding plans as a secret between us and that William must never know."

He shook his head. "It won't be that easy with Florence, Emma, and Mary Beth. They are going to be so disappointed. They were looking forward to having you as their mother."

"And I'll continue to do everything I can to be involved in their lives. They can come stay for visits, and I'll come stay with—" She broke off her thought.

"No, you won't," he said. "You can't come and stay with us, not without William. I can't promise to control my urges if you are lying in bed just down the hall from me." Suddenly, he left his chair and kissed her.

Quick as a wink, Mary's heart turned to Thomas, and lust surged within her. She threw her arms around his neck and kissed him back. More than anything, she wanted to hold him inside her and get lost in passionate lovemaking. She kissed the side of his face and thrilled at his hot breath on her neck. When she reached for the buttons on his shirt, the image of William standing in the doorway of her barn rose up. She squeezed her eyes tight, trying to push the image away, but finally had to push herself back from Thomas. Shaking her head and gasping for breath, she said, "No, no, I can't . . . we can't do this."

He tried to pull her toward him. "Yes, we can."

She saw the blood in his cheeks and the hunger in his eyes. She stepped out of his arm's reach. "We can't do this. I'm married to William, and you're his best friend. What we must do is work together to restore his spirit."

"What the hell does that mean?"

She could tell he was getting angry, so she softened her tone. "Please, Thomas, you've got to listen to me. There's more to it than just the physical changes in William. He's edgy and flies off the handle. He's just not the same. There is no telling what kinds of horrors he has seen and experienced. He needs me, and he needs you, now more than ever."

Thomas turned his back to her and shoved his hands into his pockets. It was several moments before he said, "I know what you are saying is the noble thing to do. It's just that I don't feel like being noble." He turned back around to face her. "It's just my luck that I happened to fall in love with an honorable woman. But I'll make you this promise, I will do the best I can to come around to what you are asking, and I will try to be the friend that William needs. For the time being, though, my work is cut out for me in explaining things to the girls."

Chapter Forty-Two

WILLIAM

Back at the house, William was trapped in a recurring dream of when he and a fellow prisoner had eaten a raw rat they had killed. Trying to swallow the first bite of it, while at the same time controlling his revulsion at what he was doing, had been nearly impossible. But one bite was all he had gotten because another prisoner had knocked him in the head with a rock and stolen his portion. Even in his dream, the blow was so real that it startled him awake.

He opened his eye, expecting to see the drab, muddy confines of the prison, and so it took him a few moments to recognize that he was staring at the ceiling of his bedroom in Tennessee. Like an expert card dealer shuffling a deck of cards, his mind assimilated the jumbled pieces of his memory and brought into clarity his journey back home. However, he wondered for a moment if being in his bed back home was simply another dream. It was when he couldn't detect the ever-present stench of the camp nor his own body odor that he was convinced he was indeed home.

He looked around the room and spotted a bald-headed Negro, with head bent low, sitting in a chair to one side. At first William frowned, but then he remembered Mary's story about John. When he swung his legs off the side of the bed and sat up, John stirred from his nap.

Rising from the chair, he approached William. "Mr. William, my name is John. Are you feeling more rested?"

"I suppose if I slept for a hundred years I would never feel rested from the war. Where is Mary?"

"She drove into town to tell Mr. Thomas the good news about you coming home. She asked me to sit here and keep an eye on you and make sure you was okay. Can I get you something to eat or to drink?"

"You think I can't take care of myself?" William snapped.

John backed up a step. "No sir, I don't think nothing of the kind. I was just trying to be helpful."

John's humble reaction to his harsh tongue irritated William, but at the same time, he knew there was no reason to be so harsh toward him, so he tried to smooth the edginess that he felt. "I didn't mean to speak so harshly. It's just a lot to take in, to be where I was and now to be back home again. I'm afraid I'm only dreaming and that I'm going to wake up back in that prison."

"Yes sir, I can see that. Well, you can set your mind at ease about all that. This here ain't no dream, even though it seems the same to me. We all done give up any hope that you were alive and would come back. We all decided you'd died."

"Whose 'we'?"

"Miss Mary, Mr. Thomas, and me. Everything she told me about you caused me to believe that if you was alive, you would find a way to come home, and she felt the same way, Mr. Thomas, too."

John's words pricked William's heart. "So she used to talk about me?"

"Nearly every day. There was always things happening that made her think of you, and she'd tell how you did this or that, or what you'd think about this thing or that thing. For a long time, she didn't do nothing but cry when she thought of you."

William had not realized that John's first words about Mary talking about him had been but the tip of a sharp knife. Now, though, with the image of Mary crying for him every day, that knife was shoved to the hilt into his heart. He grabbed his chest and doubled over.

"Mr. William!" John exclaimed as he rushed to his side. "Are you all right?"

William blinked the stinging tears from his eye and caught his breath. "I'm okay," he said hoarsely. "I'll be all right. Let's get outside."

He rose from the bed and, with John shadowing him, walked out into the sunshine. Familiar smells that he'd not taken the time to notice when he first arrived at home filled his nostrils: the sweet aroma of locust blooms and apple blossoms; the heavy, earthy smell of hay and manure from the barn; the tart smell of sap from the freshly cut logs lying in the yard; the thick aroma of honeysuckle. And with the smells came a thousand memories, all of which included Mary. Suddenly, a thought occurred to him. Turning to John, he asked, "Is there any of Mary's hard cider in the kitchen?"

"Yes sir, I believe there is. Want me to fetch you some?"

"Yes, please. She used to make the best apple cider."

"She still does," John said with a smile. "I'll be right back."

As he waited for John to return, two boys exited the barn door and made their way toward the house. When they got close, William said, "You must be Frank and Pete." He watched as they looked at his empty sleeve and bandaged eye. "Yes, I'm a cripple," he said.

When the boys said nothing back, he realized he'd cut them off with his comment. He tried again, "Which one of you is Pete, and which one is Frank?"

Pete pointed at his chest with his thumb and said, "I'm Pete. That's Frank."

"I understand you're living here now."

"Yes sir," Frank replied. "My folks ran off and left us, and Miss Mary found us and took us in."

"She says we're family now," Pete added.

"If that's what she says, then that's the way it is," William replied. "Because once my Mary makes up her mind about something, neither hell nor high water is going to change it."

"I'll say amen to that," John said as he handed William a cup.

"So you've seen that side of her, too?" William asked as he

drank the cider. He enjoyed the sweet taste on his tongue and the mild burn in his throat as it went down.

"Oh, my goodness, yes sir, I have," John said. "She's a force; that's what she is."

William smiled. "I'm glad that hasn't changed. As mad as it would make me at times, that inner strength of hers made me stronger, too. I always thought I was pretty strong until I got to know Mary."

"I'm not so sure she'd agree with you," John said. "To hear her tell it, you're the one who made her a stronger person. And now for you to come back here after all you've been through—well, a weak person couldn't have done it. No sir."

As quickly as a strong wind can blow a cloud over the sun, William's mood turned dark again. He gave a wave of his hand toward his missing eye and arm. "This doesn't look like a strong man to me. I'm only half a man. Why, I couldn't even draw a bucket of water to take a bath today. Mary had to do it for me." He turned his back on their staring eyes. "The only reason I came home was because I had no other place to go to. I surely couldn't find a job and start a new life." He suddenly realized he was facing Bitter Hill. Pointing to the top, he said, "John, I hear I was buried up there with my and Mary's babies. Is that so?"

"In a manner of speaking, I guess you could say so, sir. Mary wanted a marker for you, so I made one, and we put it up there. But that's only because we thought you was dead. We sure didn't mean to show you no disrespect."

William gave a derisive laugh. "How many people can say they've looked at their grave site? I think I'd like to go up there and take a look."

"It's an awful steep climb," John said. "Are you sure you're up to it?"

Turning around to face him, William growled, "Don't you think I know how steep it is? I've been up there plenty of times." In a distant tone, he added, "Too many times." The shadow of the cloud that covered his heart only moments ago suddenly lifted. "Look, I'm sorry I'm so snappy and cross. I don't know what's wrong with me."

"That's okay. Me and the boys'll go with you to the top if you want us to."

"I'd rather go alone."

"I understand, but Miss Mary told me to keep an eye on you, and if she finds out I let you go up there alone, there'll be the devil to pay."

For the first time since coming home, William chuckled. "No doubt that is true. Then come along."

Pete and Frank ran past him and John.

"Race you to the top," Pete yelled at Frank.

They quickly disappeared into the trees, scattering loose rocks as they went.

"I suppose I was that young and foolish at one time," William said.

"I guess we all were," John agreed. "But slow and steady is my pace now."

"Mine is slow, too, but not as steady as I'd like," William said as he grabbed a sapling and began pulling himself up the hill.

John said, "You need to give yourself some time to get your strength back, Mr. William. Some of Miss Mary's cooking, plus some sunshine, will go a long ways toward putting you back on your feet. Nobody that's been drug behind a wagon, so to speak, like you have been can jump right up and walk away."

William considered John's words. "I guess you been through a whole lot in your life, too, haven't you?"

"I've seen my share of trouble," John answered simply.

William concluded that John had said all he wanted to say about his past, so he quit talking to him and focused on climbing Bitter Hill.

Halfway up, he spotted the familiar rock outcrop, made his way over to it, and sat down. To no one in particular, he said, "I've spent many an hour sitting on this rock right here, thinking what a blessed man I was and what a cursed man I was."

"That so?" John said.

"When I would sit here and look at my farm and think about Mary, I would say to myself, 'You are blessed beyond measure.' But then there were four dead babies on top of this hill that made me feel cursed. And now there's this." He tugged on his empty sleeve.

John said, "There is a saying in Africa: Rain does not fall on one roof alone."

"Yeah? Well, that may be true, but it doesn't make it any easier when the rain rips your roof off and destroys everything in your house." William's thoughts tumbled into a dark well—thoughts of self-pity, self-loathing, and anger toward God. After a few minutes, he said, "I've changed my mind about going up there. I'm going back down to the house." He climbed off the rock and headed down.

*****

Later, as the day changed its gray cloak of dusk into the black cloak of night, William heard the sound of Mary approaching in the buckboard. Getting up from the chair where he'd been sitting on the porch, he waited until she pulled to a stop. "You sure have been gone a long time."

She alighted from the buckboard and turned to him. "I traveled as quickly as I could. You know how long it takes to go to and from Chattanooga. Have you rested well since I've been gone?"

Ignoring her question, he asked, "How's my friend, Thomas? What did you tell him about me?"

"He was as shocked as the rest of us at the news you had returned home. He's coming tomorrow to see you. Have you eaten supper?"

William noticed how quickly Mary seemed to brush past the subject of Thomas and also that she didn't give him steady eye contact. "What's the matter?" he asked.

"What do you mean?"

"I mean something's wrong. Is there something you're not telling me? Is Thomas okay?" She approached him and came to a stop in front of him. Though they were but inches apart, to him, it felt like ten feet.

She said, "There's nothing wrong. And Thomas is fine. He's eager to see you."

"And the girls, are they all right?"

"Yes, William, everyone's fine. Now tell me if you've had anything to eat."

"John fixed us all some supper."

"Let me go take care of the horse and buckboard, then you and I can sit on the porch together. I want to hear what you think of John and Frank and Pete."

Anger flashed through William. "You don't think I can take care of the horse?"

"I didn't say that," Mary replied.

"You don't have to. I know you're thinking it." Even as he gritted his teeth in irritation, William regretted the accusations he was throwing at Mary. He was thankful that night had buttoned up everything into darkness and he couldn't see the hurt or anger, or both, on Mary's face.

"First of all," Mary said in an icy tone, "don't tell me what I'm thinking. You never were a mind reader, and you aren't now. And secondly, since you've been gone, I've learned to do everything by myself without even thinking about it. If you want to put the horse to bed by yourself, go right ahead." By the time she finished talking, her icy tone had heated to one of anger.

William suddenly felt as if he had been dipped into a vat of shame. "I'm sorry, Mary. I don't know why I said all that. Why don't we both go to the barn?"

"And I'm sorry I snapped at you," she replied in a calmer tone. "What you have to realize is that your being gone from here was hard on me, too, not in the same way as it was for you but hard nonetheless. Now come with me, and let's take care of this tired horse."

He walked beside her toward the barn. *What's hard for me is to see how your life has moved forward while my life has gone backward.* He managed not to say what he was thinking, fearing that he would say it the wrong way and make it sound like he resented her. *Maybe that's what it is—maybe I do resent her.*

In the barn, Mary lit the lantern while he held the reins to the horse. "Tell me what you think of John," she said.

"I judge him to be a good man, even a wise man. There's a tremendous calmness in him. I'm glad he found his way here and has been such a help to you."

"I'm glad you like him. I really don't know what would have happened to the farm if he hadn't come along. This is definitely not a one-person job. And he knows how to do most anything you can imagine, even making our chairs."

William held the tongue of the buckboard steady as Mary unfastened the harness, then led the horse to an empty stall. He located the stiff brush in the same place it had always been kept and began brushing down the horse.

After Mary hung up the harness, she joined him and said, "And how do you feel about Frank and Pete?"

"They are quite likable, and they're quite spirited, too. What is your plan for them?"

"What do you mean?"

Hyperalert to any change in Mary's tone, William heard the defensiveness in her question and realized that he must move cautiously. "I mean, I understand that you had to take them in and care for them, and I'm glad you did. I was just wondering how long you intend to keep them."

"They are not a piece of livestock that you buy and sell!" she answered tersely. "Frank and Pete are my children. You hear that word? *Children.* And I'm hoping you'll come to see them as your children, too. I intend to raise them until they choose to leave home."

Before William could grab his thought, it shot out of his mouth. "So this is *your* farm now, I suppose, and I have no say-so about what goes on here." He immediately started to apologize but knew that it wouldn't erase the sting of his words. Instead, he braced himself for a deserved onslaught from Mary.

However, she surprised him with her soft tone. "William, this was and is *our* farm. We worked it side by side, in tears, sweat, and blood. From the day you disappeared, I had to start making every decision about this place—when to plant, where to plant, what to plant, when to harvest, when to cut wood, how much wood to cut, how many chairs to make, how to spend what little money there was—all of it was on my shoulders. Then these starving, frightened children fell into my lap. I did what I thought was the right thing to do: I took them in. I took them in without having any sort of plan as to how things would play out. Before I knew it, my heart was entwined with theirs like a honeysuckle vine woven into the branches of a young tree. They became *mine*, and now I want them to be *ours*."

William found himself defenseless in the face of her calm, reasoned tone. His impulse was to hug her, but he had yet to sense she was receptive to that, so he said, "If you love them, then I am certain I will come to love them, too. I just hope they know how fortunate they are that you are the one who found them."

"I think they do because they mention it often."

William's voice trembled as he said, "Please be patient with me, Mary. I feel as unbalanced as if I had lost a leg instead of an arm. All these changes are just difficult to adjust to."

"I understand." Taking his hand and pulling on it, she said, "It's been a long day for both of us. Let's go to bed. Everything will look different in the morning."

He allowed her to lead him toward the house and toward the one thing he had most looked forward to but also the thing he feared the most as he drew closer on his journey home, that is, going to bed with her. Every time he had tried to imagine himself with her, all he could see was her revulsion at the red stump of his arm just below his shoulder. He found it impossible to visualize them holding each other and pleasing each other in the familiar ways of the past. And yet, night after night, while lying on the cold ground of the prison camp, he ached to feel the warmth of her naked body against his, to feel the safety and security that being close to her always made him feel. Now, as he walked through the door of their bedroom, all he felt was trepidation and uncertainty.

Chapter Forty-Three

MARY

The next morning, Mary moved around in the kitchen as if the floor was a mud bog—the resulting effect of a night without sleep.

Things could not have gone worse last night. She had done her best to appear at ease and to prepare herself for the differences she expected there to be in William. She had figured that the best approach was to follow his lead and proceed at his pace. Unfortunately, he had interpreted her lack of initiative as her not wanting to be with him. Yet when she reached to undo his pants, he had pulled away from her.

In the past, he had always enjoyed having the lamp lit and looking at her body, but last night he made her blow it out, which she suspected was because he felt self-conscious about how he looked. When she laid down beside him, she had expected him to reach for her, so when he didn't, she reached for him but was surprised to find he still had his clothes on.

When she had kissed his lips, she felt no passion either toward him or from him, which left her feeling like it was purely perfunctory.

All of that, plus, she had found it impossible to be there with him without thinking about Thomas and feeling like she was betraying Thomas. *How strange to lie in bed with your husband and feel like you are betraying another man.*

After lying still in silent frustration, she had decided to literally take matters in hand, and so reached for his male member. What she felt there she couldn't have helped but be shocked and so jerked her hand away. Instead of the rigid member she had always been used to, she found a lifeless piece of flesh. She knew she reacted poorly, but it had been impossible to disguise her feelings. That had been the moment when William threw the covers off and stormed out of the room into the night, swearing as he went.

She had lain there trying to decide if she should go after him or let him be by himself, eventually deciding that anything she said to him would probably have made things worse. So she remained awake the rest of the night thinking about Thomas coming today and what would happen.

As the fire began crackling in the fireplace, she placed the spider skillet close to it and cut some slabs of bacon into it, then started some coffee brewing.

She'd seen Pete and Frank head toward the barn to help John with morning chores but had yet to see any sign of William. She walked out onto the porch and filled her lungs with the morning air, hoping that it would sharpen the dullness that she felt, though at the same time she scanned all around to see if she could see William. Her eyes locked onto a movement close to the bottom of Bitter Hill.

After a few moments, William walked out from the trees and stood, looking toward her.

Hoping that she was doing the right thing, Mary walked slowly toward him and was encouraged when he began moving toward her.

When they were six feet apart, they stopped and stared at each other.

Cautiously, Mary began with the truth, "Last night was a nightmare."

"Yes, it was," William agreed. "I'm sorry for behaving badly."

She took a step toward him. "There's nothing to apologize for. Neither one of us knew what to do with each other. Maybe we shouldn't have tried that so soon after you coming back."

He took two steps toward her so that their bodies were nearly touching. "I thought the same thing. Sometimes when a person tries too hard to make something happen, it just makes a mess of things."

"We certainly did that," she said with a small smile. She reached toward him, clutched a handful of his empty sleeve, and said, "This"—then she touched the bandage over his eye—"and this are not who you are, William. They are what happened to you."

In a voice filled with emotion, he said, "Then who am I? Because I'm certainly not who I used to be."

Sympathy filled her heart, and she put her hand on the side of his face. "But I think you are. Somewhere inside of you is that Scotsman I married. He just got buried during the war. Soon enough, I believe the old you will find its way back."

He brushed back the hair from the side of her face and put her earlobe between his thumb and finger. Gently rubbing, he said, "Be patient. Don't give up on me."

She leaned her head over and raised her shoulder, squeezing his hand between them. "I made that mistake one time. I'll not do it again."

*****

"Anyone want this last biscuit?" Mary asked.

Simultaneously, Pete and Frank said, "I do."

John said, "You sure don't have to worry about what to do with leftover food around here. These two eat like pigs."

Mary cut the biscuit in half and handed it to them. Laughing, she said, "Here's all you get."

The boys stuffed the half biscuits into their mouths and washed them down by finishing their milk.

That produced more laughter, even from William, Mary noted.

Looking at John, she said, "So what's your all's plan this morning?"

"I thought me and the boys would go see about plowing the cornfield. It ought to be dry enough, and it's time we get that seed in the ground."

"Why don't you take William with you and show him the tobacco patch?" Looking at William, she said, "Would you like to do that?"

"I thought Thomas was coming this morning."

"Oh, I suspect it'll be midmorning before he gets here. I'll clean up these breakfast dishes and work on patching the knees of a certain boy's pants that got a hole in them. When Thomas gets here, I'll take him to where you are." *What I really want is time for Thomas to hold me and to tell me it's going to be all right, that I can do this—that we can do this.*

John said to William, "I'd sure like to show you that patch of tobacco and to let you see what good workers these boys are."

"You talked me into it," William replied. "It'll be good to smell freshly plowed earth, earth plowed up by a plow, not by exploding shells. And I'll get a chance to see if I can work a horse and plow with one arm."

Mary and John shared a glance that lasted only a millisecond but long enough that, evidently, William saw it.

"You two don't think I can do it, do you?" he barked.

An icy chill filled the room, and Mary felt angry that Pete and Frank were being subjected to William's sudden changes in mood. "You can think what you want to," she said, "and so can I. If you want to get behind the plow, there's no one at this table that's going to get in your way. So have at it." She got up and began gathering the dishes. "All of you get out of here and head to the field. I'll be there later with Thomas." She saw confusion on the boys' faces but trusted John to help explain things to them so that they wouldn't feel they were at fault for any of the discord.

John held the door open, "Okay, you two, go get the mules ready. Me and Mr. William will be right there."

The boys walked through the door, then broke into a run toward the barn.

When Mary noticed William standing, looking at her, she stopped what she was doing and placed her hands on her hips. With her eyebrows raised, she waited to see what he had to say.

But either he had nothing to say or couldn't figure out how to say it, because he stood there mute.

After a moment, she said, "Be gone with you. I'll see you in the field later."

She watched him and John through the window until they disappeared into the barn, then she slammed her fist against the top of the table, causing the remaining dishes to jump. Collapsing into a chair, she laid her head on her folded arms and cried, "I can't do this."

When tears dripped onto the table, she jumped up, gruffly wiped her face with the back of her hand, and said aloud, "Stop your sniveling and crying because that's not going to change anything. Put one foot in front of the other and quit feeling sorry for yourself."

Chapter Forty-Four

MARY

At midmorning, Mary was sitting in the sun on the porch sewing a patch onto Frank's pants when she heard the sound of an approaching buggy. A wave of relief washed over her as she recognized Thomas. But on the heels of the relief came guilt for feeling that way about a man other than her husband. *Right or wrong, I'm glad to see him.*

She laid aside her sewing and stood up to greet him.

Alighting and walking toward the porch, Thomas turned his head this way and that. "Where is William?"

"He went to the field with John and the boys."

Thomas's face relaxed. "Then let me give you a hug."

Mary let herself melt into his warm embrace. "Oh, Thomas," she sighed as she laid the side of her face onto his chest. "This is going to be harder than I thought. Last night was a nightmare."

He slowly rubbed his hand up and down her back. "What happened?"

"William and I tried to go to bed together. But I couldn't get you out of my mind. I felt like I was betraying you by lying with him. And he was not himself, not the way he used to be. I know he felt awkward because he couldn't do anything the way he used to do it. And he's so self-conscious about how he looks, he almost wears it like a cloak of shame and draws attention to it. At the least little perceived slight, he flies off the handle, calling himself a cripple. He finally stormed out of the bedroom last night and never came back. Then this morning, I thought we had made up and things were going to be okay. But after breakfast, he got mad again, and I got mad back at him. All I wanted after that was for you to come and carry me away in your arms."

Thomas pressed her body into his. "I'm here now. Just stand here with me, and let your mind rest for a few minutes."

She closed her eyes as he gently rocked her from side to side.

Eventually, he stopped and said, "Are you having second thoughts about what to do about William and about us?"

She stepped back a bit and smoothed the front of her dress. "Thomas, when you see him, you are going to feel just like I do. There is no way I will ever intentionally wound him after everything he's been through. I just can't." With a wry smile, she added, "What I wish is that we were living in the days of Abraham in the Old Testament, except that instead of Abraham having two wives, I could have two husbands."

Thomas did not return her smile. "Have you thought about how hard it is going to be to return to being just friends and pretend nothing ever happened between us? I just don't know if I can stand the pain of it."

She gripped his arms and gave them a firm shake. "You

will do it. You'll do it for William, and you'll do it for me because I can't do it all by myself. There will be times I will be weak and want to give into the flesh. Those are the times you have to be strong. And there will be times you'll be weak, and I'll have to be the strong one. Do you understand?"

He nodded. "I understand, but God help us if we're ever both weak at the same time."

"I'll be praying that never happens. Now let's go to the field to see William."

*****

As they drew near the field, Mary could see the dark brown rows of dirt that had been turned by the plow and smelled the rich, loamy soil. Crows walked among the rows, picking out exposed worms and bugs. Pete was walking behind the plow, and John and Frank were standing at the end of the rows, but William was nowhere in sight. Mary got an uneasy feeling.

She saw Frank tugging on John's shirt and pointing in her direction.

John saw her and waved. "Good morning, Mr. Thomas," he called.

Thomas waved back. "Hello, John. Hello, Frank."

"Hey, Mr. Thomas," Frank answered.

Joining them at the end of the plowed rows, Mary asked, "Where's William?"

John's countenance fell. "It's bad, Miss Mary. He done got mad and walked off toward the creek. I don't know where he's gone to."

Mary frowned. "Tell me what happened."

"Well, me and Frank and Mr. William watched Pete plow for a while, then Mr. William said he wanted to try his hand at plowing. I didn't think it was a good idea because you got to hold on to that plow with both hands to make sure it runs straight and to keep it in the ground when you hit a root or a rock. But I didn't say none of that because it ain't my place to do so.

"He slipped the reins over his head and under his left arm. At first it seemed like he might be able to manage everything. He held on to one handle with his left arm and sort of leaned against the other handle with his right side. But sure enough, that plow struck a root, and the right handle of that plow smacked him hard in the side, causing him to lose his balance and fall down. He held on to the handle, and the mule drug him for a ways before me and the boys could run out there and stop him.

"I tried to help him up, but he swore at me and pushed me away, said he didn't need no help and to leave him be. So me and the boys stepped back and let him have his way. He got up and managed to reset the plow in the row and headed toward the end of the row. He done fine until he got there and had to pick that plow up and turn it around. He commenced to swearing and kicking at the plow. He even picked up a dirt clod and throwed it at the plow, but he missed it, and it hit the mule.

"You know what happened next—the mule spooked and took off running, bouncing that plow across the field and dragging Mr. William behind it. The boys ran the mule down and stopped him. By the time I got there, he was getting off the ground. His shirt was nearly tore off him, and his face was all scratched up. He lost his bandage off his head so that we all saw the black hole where his eye used to be. Pete didn't mean nothing by it, but he pointed and said something about the hole. That's when Mr. William stormed off and headed toward the creek."

Mary closed her eyes and shook her head. When she opened them, she looked at Thomas. "This is what I was telling you about. I'm going to go find him."

Thomas reached for her arm and stopped her. "Let me do it. You stay here with the others. Maybe I can talk to him."

"Are you sure?"

"Yes." Turning to John, he said, "Point me to where he disappeared into the woods when he headed toward the creek."

Chapter Forty-Five

THOMAS

Thomas spotted William sitting on the bank of the Chickamauga with his back toward him. As Thomas got closer to him, William said, without turning around, "I don't know who that is coming, but go away. I don't want to see anyone."

Thomas said, "That's just like a hardheaded Scot, thinking he has to do everything on his own."

William turned around, and his face lit up. Struggling to his feet, he said, "Oh, Thomas, my best friend."

Thomas suppressed his shock and revulsion at how William looked and opened his arms as they met.

William walked into his welcoming embrace and draped himself on Thomas.

When William immediately started sobbing, Thomas was uncertain what to do.

"Oh, Thomas, Thomas, I am lost, and I need your help. I don't know what I'm doing. I don't know who I am anymore."

In that instant, Thomas's heart broke for his friend, and he patted him on the back. "Listen to me, old friend, I'm here for you in whatever way you need me. You're going to get through this because you're a fighter and because you're a

Scotsman."

"I don't feel like a fighter anymore. I feel beat down." He
stepped back and wiped his face.

Thomas couldn't help but look where William's eye used
to be. He pulled his shirttail out of his pants and tore a strip
from it. He reached over and started tying it around
William's head while also covering his eye. "First thing
I'm going to do is get someone at the livery to make you a
fancy leather eyepatch, something that will make you look
dashing." He smiled at William, and William gave him a
weak smile back. "There you go. Give me a smile."

William said, "Things are all messed up between me and
Mary. We've already had more arguments in twenty-four
hours than we used to have in a year."

"You all just need time," Thomas said, trying to sound
nonchalant.

"Will you talk to her for me? Tell her I'm sorry. Tell her I
love her."

Suddenly, Thomas felt like he was holding the reins of two
horses pulling in opposite directions. His heart began
beating faster, and his mouth went dry. "You should talk to
her, William. If you keep trying, she'll listen to you."

"I can't. I just don't have the confidence that I used to. I
misinterpret everything and then say things that are hurtful.
I need your help. Will you help me?"

The plaintive plea of his friend was more than Thomas

could stand. As hard as he tried, he could not find a way around William's request. And though he was certain that agreeing to help would only make it more difficult for him and Mary to carry on their charade, he said, "I will do what I can."

*****

As Thomas and Mary walked back to the house, he related to her his conversation with William.

When he finished, Mary exclaimed, "He asked you to do what?"

"I had the exact same response inside me," Thomas said, "and I started to tell him I couldn't do it. But, just as you told me would happen, looking at him and remembering how he used to be and seeing how he is now—I couldn't refuse him. He was my best friend in the world. How could I have said no to him?"

His question hung in the air for several paces, then fell to the ground unanswered.

Taking a deep breath, he finally said, "Mary, you have to find your way back to the love you once had for William." Uttering that fateful advice caused his throat to choke with emotion, and his heart felt as if someone had grabbed it and ripped it in half.

"But how do I do that?" Mary asked. "How do you love a man who has been dead with a heart that has filled itself with the love of another man? Can a heart be big enough to love two men equally at the same time? Must I force my love for you to diminish in order to make room for William? Because if that is what I have to do, I don't think I can do it."

As she spoke, a black shadow moved across them both. When they looked up, they saw a buzzard circling overhead. It felt like an omen to Thomas; his mind tumbled down a cataclysmic hill as a dark chill struck him in the chest. He grabbed Mary's arm and rushed with her underneath the shade of the trees lining the path. "Listen to me," he said as he read the concern and confusion on her face. "I will never not love you—never. The taste of your lips and the warmth of your body underneath me will linger until my dying breath. I don't know what the shadow of the buzzard passing over us will bring, but I'm suddenly afraid."

Mary put her hands on the sides of his face and kissed him lightly on the lips. "No matter what happens with this triangle we've created, no matter how confusing what I do and say may be, trust that my love for you will never die. What we are going to do, we will be doing for—"

"William." They said the name together.

Thomas sighed. "I'm better now. I just got a little shaken. Come on, let's get to the house so that I can return home."

As they reentered the path, Mary said, "You haven't told me how things went when you told your girls about all that has happened."

"It didn't go well—not at all. I was bombarded with questions. They were hurt and angry, too, and all went to bed crying. I tried but was unable to console them. I'm not certain if Mary Beth understood everything and don't know how well she is going to keep our secret. Little kids are so honest and blunt about everything. The best plan is probably to keep her away from William, at least for a little while until she gets more used to this new situation."

"I don't know how we can manage that," Mary replied. "You know William is going to want to see the girls." She paused, then said, "Or maybe not. He's so self-conscious about how he looks that he might be reluctant for them to see him. And, just as you said about Mary Beth, she would be the one to point straight at his eye and arm and start asking questions, which would not go over very well with him."

"I hadn't thought about that side of things," Thomas replied. "Even though I think William really needs to get out and see people and get past being self-conscious about how he looks, it'll serve our purpose better if he chooses to remain secluded for a while longer."

They walked through the barn, then stopped at the well for a drink.

"You all have the sweetest-tasting water out here," Thomas said.

"I'll have to agree with you. Must be because we're so close to the Chickamauga. Can I give you something to eat on the ride back to town?"

"If you have a leftover biscuit, I certainly wouldn't turn it down," he answered with a smile. "Don't you dare tell

Abigail, but you make better biscuits than she does."

Mary laughed. "I'll take that as high praise." She disappeared into the house and came back out holding a biscuit toward him.

He took it, and they walked to his buggy. Before he climbed in, he stopped and faced her. "How long until we see each other again?"

"I don't know."

"Maybe it'll be easier for you to love William if I remain absent. So I'll try that but make no promises how well I'll maintain that approach."

"And if William takes a notion that he wants to come to town to see the girls, I'll write you so that you can prepare everyone."

Without another word, they stepped into each other's embrace. Thomas thrilled at the feel of her against him and ached at the knowledge it might be a long time, or forever, until he held her again.

They tilted their heads back and gave each other a long kiss.

Mary ended the kiss, and Thomas stepped into the buggy. Without a word, he clucked to the horse and drove away.

Unbeknownst to either of them, William had been standing in the barn for the last few minutes, staring at what transpired between them.

Chapter Forty-Six

MARY

May 27, 1865

My dearest Thomas,

Please don't be angry because of the confession I am about to make to you. I have done as I promised to myself and to you—I have focused myself on rekindling my love for William, trying at every turn to find the man I was married to. Yet, though I have not seen you in the flesh in a month, my dreams are filled with images of you and of us being together in the most intimate way. The dreams are so real that I wake from them with my gown damp with sweat and surges of pleasure running through my body. And then I cry. I cry because we will never be—not the way I want us to be.

I am writing this to you because I feel weak, having become fatigued by William's ever-changing moods and attitude. There are moments when he is his old self, joking, laughing, determined. It's then that I feel the memory of how he and I used to be. It is a memory like a forgotten quilt that has lain hidden in the bottom of a chest, full of memories of when it kept you warm in bed on cold winter nights or hugged your shoulders as you sat by the fireplace. Though it has a musty smell because of its disuse, it is its familiarity that lets you overlook those things, embrace it, and smile at discovering it.

Those moments with William quickly turn bittersweet as he descends into what I can only describe as a bottomless well of despair and melancholy. It's like he and I have switched roles from how we were before he disappeared. Back then it was I who battled melancholia, and he would try to pull me out of it. I now feel horrible for how I was back then. I must have been impossible to live with.

Now, even though I've not felt melancholy in some time, there have been times when I have found myself tumbling down the well with him as I, too, am overwhelmed with a sense of hopelessness with this whole situation. It is then that I try to remember Frank and Pete and that I must be strong for them, for I am all they have. Of course there is John, but he doesn't truly need me. And there is you, but you have your girls to live for. If not for the forces of fate that brought those boys into my life, I know not how I would survive.

Just today William was trying to wield a scythe that John had adapted especially for him. I think it must be the nature of men to measure themselves by how well they can perform. I find this extremely frustrating. If that is all that gives a person worth, that would mean that babies should be left in the woods to die. That is a harsh picture, I know, but you have to admit it is true. William was so intent on it succeeding, but it was not to be. It was but one more disappointment for him to put in his sack of disappointments that makes his fall into the abyss inevitable.

It is in those times of frustration that his temper erupts in the vilest of ways, and he becomes unrecognizable as the man I married. Out of his mouth spews a despicable stream of words, regardless of who may hear them, even the boys. That is when I feel my heart retreating from him, for I could never love such a man.

In most instances he apologizes after the storm has passed, but apologies become meaningless when the same offense occurs over and over again. A wounded heart, over time, can become calloused, and I fear that happening to me, for the only thing worse than a wounded heart is a hardened one.

Though I have never seen a porcupine, I feel like I am trying to embrace one in my efforts to draw closer to William.

I think it would be good for him to see you again and perhaps more often. Possibly an invitation from you to come visit him would encourage him to let himself be seen by the girls, for I know there's a big part of him that is eager to see them. This might be a step toward him accepting himself as he is.

And maybe acceptance is the best word to explain why William continues to struggle. He cannot accept the fact that he will never be the same as he was, at least not physically. What I can't get him to see is that his appearance doesn't matter to me. It is his heart of old that I want to find, that kind, loving, gentle man.

This brings me to a delicate matter that I probably should not mention, but it is one that is perhaps William's greatest source of frustration. I'm referring to he and I being in bed together. How shall I put this? If it is the case, as some believe, that a couple is not officially married until the marriage is consummated, then mine and William's relationship since he returned is not yet official. Nothing that I do or say seems to help that situation. I have even told him that I can live without it, though I will admit to you that it would be most difficult when I know satisfaction lies as close by as your loving embrace. I'm hopeful you can talk with William about this and help him see things in a different light.

I have laid bare my soul in this letter and am thankful beyond measure that I have a friend like you who will listen, not just with his ear, but with his heart as well. Do not feel burdened with all that I have said; instead feel thankful that we still have our friendship, even if we can't share our passion.

For the past fifteen minutes, I have stared at this page, trying to decide what words to choose in closing. If I put "forever yours," it might be interpreted that I am disingenuous in my determination to grow my relationship with William, but that would be an incorrect interpretation. "With much love" doesn't give an accurate measurement of how much I truly love you. There does not exist a scale large enough to weigh my love for you. If I sign, "Longing to see you," the word "see" does not describe the length and breadth of my longing.

So I will simply sign my name, trusting that you will understand there is no combination of words that can accurately sum up my feelings and thoughts.

~ Mary ~

Chapter Forty-Seven

WILLIAM

Falling to his knees at the foot of his premature grave at the top of Bitter Hill, William cried out, "Dear God in heaven, help me! I have no one else to turn to who can lead me out of this darkness." His words dissolved into tears as he bent over and touched his forehead to his knees. Silently, he continued his prayer. "Holy Father, you have seen how tormented I am and how I torment those around me that I love. Why do you let this go on so? Why have you deserted me in my time of need?

"Where does this anger come from that erupts so violently from me and sends everyone scurrying away from me? It comes on me so suddenly that I have no chance to put a brake on my wicked tongue. I have hurt Mary so many times with my words that I have contemplated cutting it out with a butcher knife. Even though that would be one more flaw in this crippled body of mine that she would be embarrassed by, at least I would be mute and incapable of inflicting pain by way of my mouth.

"I am soul-sick at seeing Frank and Pete look at me with fear in their eyes at the monster I have become.

"It is only by your hand of grace and mercy that I was able to return here—but to what end? What value do I have? What purpose is there for me here? What would you have me do? Show me, Father, I beg of you. Take my hand and—"

He felt a hand placed gently on his back, and a sense of peace came over him. He wanted to peek to see if he, like Moses, might get a glimpse of God, but his fear of offending him kept his eyes squeezed shut. In a whisper, he said, "Thank you, Father."

"William, it's me," Mary's voice whispered to him.

He rose back up on his knees in surprise and stared at her. "Mary, it's you?"

"Yes, William." Kneeling down beside him, she said, "I didn't mean to scare you by sneaking up on you. I thought you probably heard me coming. What are you doing up here? I've been looking everywhere for you."

He looked at his grave marker. "I guess I came to see if I could find the person who is buried here."

"Why, whatever do you mean?"

"The person whose memory you buried is not the person I am now. I know that. You know that. Even Thomas, if he spent more time with me, would know that." Pointing at the marker, he continued, "That is who you loved. It's not fair for me to expect you to love this person I have become. I'm unworthy of your love. Hardly a day has passed since my return that I have not done or said something hurtful toward you. I've apologized so many times that I'm ashamed to ask you anymore because I know my apologies have become meaningless."

Mary said firmly, "What name is on that marker?"

"My name is."

"Say it."

"Say what?"

"Say the name that is on the marker."

"William Thomson."

"Exactly. And what is your name?"

It dawned on him what she was trying to do. "But I'm not—"

She cut him off. "Answer my question." There was an edge in her voice. "What is your name?"

"William Thomson."

"Exactly." She pointed at the marker. "That William Thomson is a Scot." Poking him in the chest, she said, "You're a Scot, are you not?"

"True, I am."

"And everyone knows that Scots are hardheaded, determined, and conceited, are they not?" There was a tiny twinkle in her eye.

"We've been accused of such, but I beg to—"

She held her hand up in his face. "Don't try to deny it. Everyone knows it's true." She grasped the front of his shirt with both hands and said, "That man there and you are the same. It's just that things have happened to you that never happened to him, and they were the sort of things that he never dreamed of." Her face grew more serious. "You lost your arm, and you lost your eye, which means there are things you can't do anymore. So what?" She let go of him and placed both her hands on her abdomen. "Things have happened to me, things inside of me, so that I can never have children." Tears filled her eyes, and color rose in her cheeks. Her voice broke as she said, "But that doesn't mean I can lie down and give up, or that I can turn into an angry and bitter woman."

Like a sharpened scythe, Mary's words sliced through the stalks of William's defenses, leaving him without rebuttal. He felt as if he were choking on the emotions rising from deep within him. "Mary." His voice sounded unnatural in his ears, and he coughed to clear his throat. "When you found me here, I was in earnest prayer. I was begging God to take my hand and lead me out of this darkness. Then you touched me, and I thought it was God touching me. A feeling of peace swept through me, the kind of peace I have not felt since I was kidnapped by General Bragg's men."

She placed one of her hands on top of the other on his chest and said, "Inside there beats the heart of the man I married. I loved him, and I love you. You did not grow to love me less when I became barren, and I don't love you less because you can't do some of the things you used to do."

The dam that had held back the flood of William's emotions broke. He threw his arm around her and pulled her to him. "Oh, Mary, you are an angel from God above. No other woman on earth is like you."

She returned his embrace, and they kissed, and it felt real to him.

Suddenly, he felt a stirring deep within his loins and heat filling his member that he thought dead. He leaned forward until Mary lay on her back and he between her legs.

With a look of surprise and understanding, she reached for and squeezed his rising maleness.

Pleasure surged through him.

There was a flurry of hands and clothes, and he felt himself sliding into that pleasure place that is like no other.

Mary looked up at him, smiling. "Oh, yes, Thomas."

William stopped in midthrust. He felt like his heart had turned to ice. "What did you say?"

Confusion replaced her smile. "I said, 'Oh, yes, William.'"

He withdrew his shrinking member and said, "No, you didn't. You called me Thomas."

Her face turned as red as coals in a fire. "I couldn't have. Why would I have done that?"

"That's what I would like to know." He stood up and fastened his pants.

She reached into the folds of her dress and pulled out a small package. "It must be because of this."

"What's that?"

"It's a package from Thomas to you. It's the reason I was looking for you in the first place. As I was giving the postman a letter earlier, he gave this delivery to me. I guess my mind tripped across his name just as we were together now. I can't explain why." She reached for him. "Please, come back down here to me, and let's finish what we started."

He thought about her explanation and could see some logic in it, but the tiny seed of doubt that had been sown back when he saw Mary and Thomas embracing prevented him from accepting it. "I can't. Not now." Reaching for the package, he took it from her. He tore away the paper to reveal a small box. Inside he found a folded piece of paper. Unfolding it, he read aloud:

Dear William,

Enclosed you will find the leather eyepatch I promised you. I'm certain it will make you look as dashing as any man around.

I invite you to come see me and the girls so we can have a look at it. They have done nothing but ask questions about you since you returned and are eager to reunite with you.

Please come at your earliest convenience.

Your eternal friend,

Thomas

Mary rose from the ground and straightened her clothes. "A leather eyepatch? You never mentioned that to me."

William ignored her question and removed the black leather eyepatch. He started to remove his bandage to try it on, but paused and looked at Mary. He had yet to let her see him without it being covered.

"It's okay," she said. "It's not going to bother me. Take it off, and I'll help you tie this patch on."

As soon as he removed it, she positioned the patch centrally over his eye socket. Then she took the two leather strips attached to it, pulled them to the back of his head, and started to tie them together. "Feel okay? Too loose or tight?"

He put his hand on the patch and situated it in a more comfortable position. "Just a little tighter."

She complied and stepped around in front of him. A big smile broke upon her face. "Oh, William, it does make you look dashing! I love it! Let's go down so you can see it in a mirror."

He was uncertain if her words of praise were false or not, but nonetheless, it felt good to have her bragging on how he looked. "Perhaps we can try to lie with each other another day."

She hugged him and said, "I'd like that very much."

As they started down the hill, he said, "I think I'm ready to go into town. I need to see those girls and to let them see me."

Chapter Forty-Eight

JOHN

In mid-July, John and William walked among the chest-high tobacco plants, pulling finger-long, finger-thick hornworms off the leaves and crushing them underfoot while at the same time shooing away gnats and biting flies.

William said, "Are you sure all this work is going to be worth it? Growing tobacco is tedious work."

"Yes sir, Mr. William," John replied. "You just wait until we take our tobacco to sell. You're going to thank me then, and you'll forget all this sweating and backbreaking work. But I'll warn you that we still got lots more work facing us, especially when it comes time to stick this tobacco and hang it in the barn. That's when we'll be glad we got them two young boys to climb among the rafters. It's sure not a job for an old man." John wished he hadn't added that last line because it opened the door for William to think about himself and all the things he wasn't able to do.

"Not a job for a one-armed man either, is it?" William said.

"I can't say if that's so or not. Never saw one try it. You might be the one who can find a way to manage the job. You don't give yourself enough credit, with that sharp mind of yours. There's always a way to get a job done. Don't forget—you finally was able to cut hay with a scythe once we got the right design for you."

"That's more a tribute to you being willing to keep working on it than it was my determination to learn how to use it."

"Excuse me for saying so, Mr. William, but that's just not so. Wouldn't have mattered how many different designs I come up with if you wasn't willing to try using them. You sell yourself short too much. You spend too much time dwelling on what you can't do rather than on what you can do." He hoped he hadn't spoken too honestly and watched out of the corner of his eye to see William's reaction.

When William didn't explode in anger, John took that as a positive sign. It seemed to him that since William returned from his visit with Thomas, his mind had been more settled, and he was less prone to fly off the handle. He had even watched him spending more time with Frank and Pete and could see that it made a difference in them. Everyone needed to have a father who was proud of them, and William was finally helping fill that empty place in their lives.

Several minutes passed before William said, "I've never asked you what you think of Thomas."

"Exactly what do you mean?"

"Since the time that you've come to know him, what kind of man do you judge him to be?"

John was uncertain where William was going with this, but he felt the need to step carefully. "I don't suppose it matters what I think of him. He's the kind of man that he is, no matter what I think. He's your best friend, isn't he?"

"For over ten years he has been," William replied. "But I only know him as I see him. You're a man of wisdom, John, a man who sees things clearly and will always give an honest answer. I'm just curious about your opinion of Thomas."

"Well sir, the first thing I come to know about Mr. Thomas is that he loved you and Miss Mary. His grief over believing he'd lost you was a sad thing to behold. And he took special care to see that Miss Mary was all right. Matter of fact, I think he's the main reason she didn't die of a broken heart."

"I see," William said slowly as he nodded his head.

An alarm sounded in John's mind. There was something about how William said "I see" that caused him to rehear what he had just said to him. Once again, it was the last sentence that he should have left off.

Then it hit him. Suspicion—that's what he heard in William's tone. John felt trapped out here, alone with William in the tobacco field. There was no quick and easy excuse he could have used to go somewhere else and thereby cut short whatever William was going to say next. And he was for certain that there was more William was going to say.

He considered changing the conversation by talking about the weather but feared it would sound too deliberate, like he was trying to hide something.

Several more minutes passed. Finally, William said, "Do you judge him to be an honest man?"

This time fear leaped up in John's heart. He feigned ignorance. "Who's that, Mr. William?"

"Thomas—we're talking about Thomas."

"Well sir," John began slowly, "I can tell you that in all the times I've been to town to trade with him and talked with people who've traded with him, I never heard anyone accuse him of trying to cheat anybody, and I never felt like he tried to cheat me. That's saying a lot about a man who's in the kind of business he's in."

"I suppose that's so," William replied. "But there's more than one way for a man to cheat someone."

If he'd been standing beside an anvil when the blacksmith struck it with his hammer, William's words could not have rung any louder in John's ears. He refused to allow himself to look at him for fear his face would betray him and so pretended to give his full attention to plucking off the hornworms. As moments ticked by, he wondered if he should have given a response to his statement, if that was what he would have done if he hadn't known about Thomas and Mary's plans to wed.

When William didn't press him further, his mind turned, and he wondered if all his fears were the result of his own imagination—that because of what he knew, he was on guard against letting something slip or William finding out the truth. The longer he entertained that thought, the more relaxed he became, and he called himself foolish for getting so distraught.

Then, without warning, William said, "There's many kinds

of love, John. There's the love of a man for his parents, of a parent for a child, of that between siblings, of the kind of love between friends. And then there's the love between a man and a woman."

"Surely you speak the truth, Mr. William. Though I was never married nor had any children, I have seen all those kinds of love. And that last one you spoke of, the love between a husband and wife, that's the kind of love that has carried many a person through dark and lonely nights."

"Ah, but you misquoted me, John. I said the love between a man and a woman."

"I'm sorry, sir. You're right. I guess I was just assuming you meant between husband and wife."

"The kind of love I'm talking about can lead to marriage, for sure," William explained. "But sometimes unexpected things get in the way, and the path to marriage can't be realized. That, John, is the saddest kind of love."

Chapter Forty-Nine

MARY

One August morning, as Frank, Pete, and William settled around the table for breakfast, Mary asked, "Where's John this morning? I haven't seen him."

Pete said, "We haven't either. We figured he was already in here waiting on us to get finished with our chores."

She looked at William.

He said, "I haven't seen him either."

"Frank," she said, "go out to the woodshed just to see if he's still there for some reason. I suspect he's gone out to the field to check on something before breakfast."

Frank exited the kitchen as Mary poured William some coffee. "What's on your agenda today?" she asked him.

"I'm thinking about going into town to the livery. Some of our harnesses and reins are worn out. I'll see what he's got and then drop in on Thomas, too."

"That sounds like a good idea." She was pleased that he had become more comfortable being among people and that he and Thomas seemed to have reforged their friendship. What Mary didn't ask was why he never invited her to go with him to town anymore. If she did accompany him, it was because she had come up an excuse to invite herself. Even though she felt her love for William was returning, she had not been able to turn aside her feelings for Thomas, and it had been weeks since she'd seen him. She was just about to say she needed to go into town with William when Frank came back in with a worried look on his face. "What's the matter?" she asked.

"John's still in bed. Said he didn't think he'd be working any today. Said he wasn't hungry either."

William and Pete stopped eating and looked at him.

"Is he okay?" William asked.

"I can't tell. Something about him looks different, but I don't know what it is."

A hammer of alarm drove a stake in Mary's chest, and her mind was flooded with dreadful imaginings. Finding her voice, she said, "I noticed him coughing the last couple of days, but he said it wasn't anything. I'm going to check on him. Y'all eat your breakfast."

It was all she could do to keep from breaking into a run toward the woodshed, but she hadn't wanted the boys to see her and become panicked, at least not until she discovered what was going on.

She tapped lightly on the door, then entered.

John lay on his bed with a sheet pulled up to his neck. The sag in the bed made it appear as if there was nothing to him except his bald head, which rested on a pillow.

He turned his head slightly toward Mary and coughed. "Good morning, Miss Mary. Excuse me for not getting up, but today's not a good day for me."

Mary sat on the edge of his bed and saw bright red lines zigzagging across the whites of his eyes, though the white was more yellow than white. When he took a breath, his chest rattled like dry limbs beating against the side of the house during a wind storm. "What's wrong with you, John?"

"Well, ma'am, I think my time is up."

His simple pronouncement nearly shoved her onto the floor. "What do you mean by that?"

"My father used to say, 'Even though the old man is strong and hearty, he will not live forever.' That's me. I believe my time is up."

"Why do you say that?"

"My insides don't feel right, haven't felt right in some time. And this morning, I woke up and just didn't feel like getting out of bed. That's a feeling I ain't never had— never. I think my body's telling me it's time to move on; my time here is done."

Mary felt her face growing flushed. "Don't be silly, John. You've just got a cough. I'll fix up a remedy for you, and you'll be fine by tomorrow." Her words sounded confident, but even she could hear the tremor in her voice.

"There's nothing to be done, Miss Mary, so don't be putting yourself to all that trouble. Even if you fixed something, I wouldn't take it. All I'm doing is waiting for the angels to come get me."

Standing up, Mary said emphatically, "I won't hear of it. I'm going in to fix something, and you will take it." She rushed out of the shed without waiting for him to object.

When she reentered she kitchen, all eyes turned to her. She started to blurt out what John had told her but held her tongue long enough to formulate something less dramatic for the boys. "John's not feeling well today. I'm going to fix him something for his cough that will make him better, probably by tomorrow. Pete and Frank, why don't you all go see if the hayfield is tall enough to get another cutting off of it."

As the boys headed out of the kitchen, William said, "There's something more to what's wrong with John, isn't there? I could tell by your face you were trying to hide something."

Mary's words came in a rush. "John says he's dying, William. Just like that, he said it. Says he's not going to take any medicine, that he's just going to lie there until he dies. What are we going to do?"

William frowned and said, "What makes him think he's dying?"

"I don't know. Just something inside him tells him it's his time. I tried to talk to him about taking a remedy, but he said he wouldn't do it. I told him I would make him do it. That's when I came in here."

"You go ahead and fix what you want to, but you and I

both know that no one makes John do anything. Let me go talk to him, and I'll see if I can change his mind."

Mary stood in the kitchen watching William disappear into the woodshed. Waves of panic followed by numbness alternately washed over her. Suddenly, she rushed into her bedroom and sat down at the desk. Taking out a piece of paper, she wrote:

Thomas,

Come as quickly as you can, and bring the girls with you. John is dying.

~ Mary

She folded the paper, slipped it into an envelope and addressed it. Then she went out on the porch to wait for the postman to come by.

*****

WILLIAM

When William walked over and sat on the edge of John's bed, he knew. He knew because he'd seen it in the eyes of men before—that resignation, the giving in to the inevitable, that lack of willingness to fight anymore. But seeing it on the face of this black man for whom he had such deep respect and whom he had come to view as a friend moved him more than all those men he'd seen die in war and in the prisoner camp. "John," he said simply, "I don't want you to die."

John was quiet for a moment as he studied William's face.

"Yes sir, Mr. William, I can see that, and I'm sorry I have to leave you, but that's not for me to decide. My body's just give out on me."

"I know you're tired. It's like you've lived three lifetimes. I know I have no right to ask this of you, but please, don't die just yet. I still need you." His last four words barely fought their way through his closed-off throat.

"I'm not dying today," John said. "I'm pretty sure of that. I've gots to get my good-byes ready to say to all of you. That'll take me a day or two to think about. I expect the good Lord will give me time to do that. But once that's said and done, it'll be time to leave this old, worn-out body." He laid his hand on top of William's. "Now you all go on about the day's business, and tell Miss Mary that I don't intend to take whatever it is she's fixing up right now for me, because I know she is. Tell her to leave me be to think. I'll be fine. Y'all come check on me this evening. I might want something to drink by then. Now run along."

John's calmness about it all found its way into William's fearfulness, and acceptance took a chair. He said, "I'll do as you say."

Chapter Fifty

JOHN

It was three days later when Mary silently ushered Florence, Emma, and young Mary Beth into the dimly lit confines of the woodshed where John lay in his bed. "This is your opportunity to say good-bye to John," she said, "and for him to say the things he wants to say to you." She gave each of them a brief hug and kiss, then quietly stepped outside.

"Like pearls on a necklace, that's what you three are," John said with a smile. "The prettiest things I'll see all day, until I see the angels come to take me away."

Florence moved closer. "I want you to know I'll miss you. I didn't know what to think of you at first, but you've become one of my favorite people."

John nodded his thanks.

Florence stepped back and nudged Emma, who stepped forward. "You're the only person I've been close to who has died, except Mother, and I don't remember that very much. I don't know how I'll feel when you're gone, but I'm quite sad now, and I wish you didn't have to go."

John nodded again.

Emma stepped back and nudged Mary Beth, who didn't move.

Florence took her hand and pulled her closer to John. "Say what you want to," she told her young sister.

Mary Beth said, "Are you going to come back like William did when he died?"

A small chuckle rattled inside John's mouth. "No, child, that's not the way it'll be this time."

"I like you, and I don't want you to leave."

John looked at each of them and said, "I want to thank all three of you for those nice things you had to say. You all are some of the sweetest, kindest, most well-mannered children I ever saw, and that's in spite of the fact that your mother died. I know that's made it a hard road for you three, but you've done well. You should be proud. I'm going to leave you with an African proverb. It goes like this, 'When you learn to follow in the path of your father, you learn to walk like him.' Your father is a good man with a good heart, albeit a heavy heart. But he made a decision to do the right thing by Mr. William, and he stuck to it. Not many men would have done what he did. They'd have thought about themselves. If you all learn to have his same kind of heart, you will grow up to have a blessed life."

Florence sniffed and wiped at her nose. "Thank you."

"You're welcome. Now you all run along. I've got other people to see before this day is done."

With their heads hanging low, the girls exited into the afternoon August sunshine.

Before the door shut, Abigail walked inside. Immediately, she started crying. "Why are you going to die? What's the matter with you? Don't you know people still want you to be here? You're just being selfish—that's what you're doing."

John smiled at her. "Come sit beside me," he said.

Wiping her tears with the palms of her hands, Abigail did as he asked.

"If I was a younger man, I would stay, and I'd try to court you."

"Oh, John," ripped from her mouth, and she melted into tears. When she regained her composure, she said, "Well I'll tell you right now, I wouldn't have you. Why, I wouldn't turn my head for a tall, skinny man like you. You hear me?" Her voice betrayed her as it began breaking. "I wouldn't have you," she whispered as her tears began flowing again.

"Shush, and listen to me," John said. "You've had a hard job raising those girls and taking care of Mr. Thomas, and you've done a really good job of it. But your job's not finished. You've got to continue keeping an eye on Florence, Emma, and Mary Beth, and Mr. Thomas is going to need your help with himself."

"What do you mean?"

"His heart is still set for Miss Mary. I see it in his eyes when he looks at her. I don't know how he's finally going to settle that, but I think you're going to be able to help."

"I don't know how, but I'll do what I can."

"You'll do fine. Now get on out of here because I've got other folks coming."

Abigail leaned her tear-streaked face close, and with trembling lips, she touched John's lips. "I love you, John. I'll see you on those streets paved with gold."

Frank held the door for her as she opened it, then he stepped inside and approached John. "They say I'm supposed to tell you good-bye before you die, but I've never known anyone that died that I also loved." His voice began to tremble. "I never told you this, but you're the first man that I've ever loved. I sure didn't love my Pa, and I never knew any of my kin. When you and Miss Mary found us and brought us here, I figured you were going to be mean like my Pa was. But you wasn't. You've been more of a pa to me than he ever was." He looked down at his feet. "I don't want you to die."

"Now, Frank," John said in a kindly tone, "what you've just told me about loving me and thinking of me like a father to you, well, that's just about the kindest, most heartfelt thing any human has ever said to me. I felt it right here." He patted his chest. "Those are the kinds of words that make it easy to leave here with my heart burden-free. I know you don't want me to leave. But you are going to be fine. You've grown into such a strong young man, but you're going to have to be even stronger now. Mr. William is going to rely on you. Don't you let him down. When the time finally comes for you to leave home and find your own way in life, I want you to remember this proverb:

Don't set sail using someone else's star."

"What does that mean?"

"That means you find your own way, your own path. Don't follow somebody else's because it might not be right for you. Now shake my hand and send Pete in."

Frank took his hand and held it. With reddened eyes, he left the room.

Pete walked in and sat on the edge of the bed with a bowed head, saying nothing.

"Pete," John began, "you are going to have the most difficult path of anyone I leave behind because you are going to be a black man living in a white man's world. It will not be easy for you. People will tell you to remember your place and to quit acting uppity. What you will need is wise friends who give wise advice. The medicine man in my village in Africa once said, 'Ears that do not listen to advice accompany the head when it is chopped off.' So find those kinds of friends and listen when they give you advice. Do you understand?"

Pete nodded his head without looking up.

"Look at me, Pete."

Pete raised his gaze to John's face. When their eyes met, he said, "Thank you for showing me how to be a good man."

"You're welcome, son. Now move along. I'm getting tired, and my good-byes aren't done yet."

The longest shadows of the afternoon stretched across the yard as Thomas opened John's door and entered.

With his eyes closed, John said, "That must be you, Mr. Thomas."

"Yes, it is, John. We're coming in in the order you told Mary that you wanted us to. Can I get you something?"

Opening his eyes, John replied, "No thank you, sir. I was just resting my eyes for a moment and thinking about what you and I might talk about."

Thomas said, "John, you came out of nowhere to mean so much to all of us. In one sense, I've barely gotten to know you—you've been here such a relatively short time—but in another sense, I feel as if I've known you all my life. Your life story is one that should be recorded and shared with the world so that others can be inspired by it. I mean that sincerely."

"What you've said there is sure a mouthful, Mr. Thomas. I don't know how much of it is true, but I do thank you for those kind words. You know, when I first met you, I wasn't sure what to think about a single man raising three daughters. Most white men in your position would have gone right out after their wife died and found the first woman they could to be their new wife, mainly to have someone help raise those girls. But not you. That's because love means something to you. It's not enough to have a woman because you for sure could have any number of them, but you wouldn't love them. And then, low and behold, you fell in love with Miss Mary."

Thomas replied, "John, I didn't mean to—"

"Let me finish," John interrupted him. "I know you didn't mean to fall in love with her. But's just the way love is sometimes—it happens accidentally. There's nothing wrong with you loving her. How could a man not love someone as remarkable as her? But things got complicated when Mr. William come home. That's when you decided to do something that no other man on the face of this earth would do. You decided you would take a step backward and let your best friend take back his wife. Now here you are still in love with Miss Mary, and you don't know what to do about it. Am I right?"

Thomas replied, "If you were wielding a butcher's knife, you could not have separated the pieces of my heart and laid bare the truth any more clearly. And you're right, I *don't* know what to do."

"Let me tell you, Mr. Thomas, the path you are walking is as thin as a man's razor and just as dangerous. The direction you must follow is your friendship with Mr. William. If you'll work on growing that, you'll get to the place where you won't want to betray him, and you'll see that Miss Mary should be his."

Tears filled Thomas's eyes. "Is that possible?"

"With God's help, it is."

Thomas blinked, and tears splashed onto his shirt.

John said, "Now it's time for you and me to say good-bye. My last prayer to God this morning was that he would give you the strength to do the right thing. You are a good man, Mr. Thomas. I'm glad I got to know you."

Thomas placed his hand on John's shoulder and gave it a squeeze. With a nod and a slim smile, he rose and left.

William had been waiting just outside and entered the darkening shed. As he settled beside John, he said, "As I've watched each of these people leave this woodshed, I've come to see that you have been the wood peg that has held everyone together through this dreadful war. I don't know if I've ever adequately thanked you for helping Mary and then Frank and Pete, but I am eternally grateful. If not for you, Mary might not have even been here when I returned."

"I can say I'm glad I come here, too, 'cause it's one of the best things in my life that ever happened to me."

"And then there's everything you've done for me," William continued. "When I came home, I—" He paused for a moment. "The only way I know to say it is, I wasn't right; I wasn't me. That anyone would have anything to do with me, especially an ex-slave and me fighting for the South, was something I never expected. It was your kind and unflustered manner of dealing with things that helped me find myself. Because of that, I will think about you every day and will be thankful that our paths crossed."

"Thank you, Mr. William. You are very kind. When you first came home, I could not see what it was about you that made Miss Mary fall in love with you. You were as hard to approach as it is to approach a chestnut tree with bare feet. But in the last several weeks, I've begun to see it. I've begun to see who you were and now who you are. I think the one thing still holding you back is Miss Mary."

William's eyebrows knotted together. "Why do you say that?"

"It's her love for you that seems like it scares you, like you're afraid of it. I see it in the way you're not always easy and comfortable when you get close to her. Your hands get close to each other, but you never take her hand."

The furrows on William's forehead deepened. "I never realized it, but what you say is true. Mary's love is so encompassing and so freely given." He looked down. "But I fear I'm not the only one she loves."

"Ah, the truth finally shows its face. Of course you're not."

William's head jerked up. "Who is it?"

"We both know who it is. What you got to understand is that what happened between them was as natural as Chickamauga creek flowing into the Tennessee River. There wasn't nothing wrong with it. But you came back— the thing she had finally given up on came true, and now her heart is set on you and on being your wife. You need to welcome and embrace that like a soldier who's been fighting in the hot sun all day long with nothing to drink would a cup of cool water. Drink deep from that cup, Mr. William. Take it all in with a breath of thanksgiving that the one thing you hoped to find when you came home is right here, right now."

William's facial muscles relaxed, and a small smile pulled

up the corners of his mouth. "It's true, isn't it? She does love me."

"She does, sir."

William sat straight, took a deep breath, and let it out. "I haven't taken a breath like that since the day I was kidnapped by Bragg's army." Laying his hand on his own chest, he said, "You've calmed the uneasiness in my heart, John. If any man deserves to walk through those pearly gates, it is you. I pray that your journey there will be swift and easy. Thank you, John."

Chapter Fifty-One

MARY

Mary stood in the black doorway, silhouetted by two lanterns and a small fire in the yard behind her that the others had gathered around.

She walked carefully to John, found the table beside his bed, and lit the candle that sat on it, then returned to the door and closed it quietly.

Joining him once again at his bedside, she saw the light flickering in his eyes. "Would you like a drink of water?"

"A drink of water would be nice, if you don't mind."

She poured water from a pitcher into a tin cup and held it just below his chin.

He made a futile attempt to raise his head to drink from it. "Guess I'm going to have to have some help."

Holding the cup in her left hand, Mary used her right hand to lift his head so that he could drink. She watched his Adam's apple bob as he drank.

After a few sips, he said, "That'll be enough. Thank you."

She eased his head back onto his pillow and set the cup aside.

For nearly a minute, they sat and looked at each other. Mary's mind traveled back to the day he first appeared and saved her from being raped, then a flood of memories poured in, reminding her of all their times together on the farm. "It's hard to know where to start," she said.

"Yes, it is." John agreed.

"Let me begin with, you saved me. Not just from the man who was trying to violate me, but you saved me from my grief and sadness after William disappeared. You saved me from the typhoid. And you saved me from giving up on this farm. I've always heard of guardian angels, but I didn't know they could be black." She smiled.

John chuckled. "That would come as a surprise to lots of folks. I suspect some would even tell them to leave if one showed up. I've often pondered over why I ended up on your farm because it for sure wasn't on purpose. I can take that question all the way back to why did I get kidnapped in Ghana and get sold in America as a slave? Why did I end up on that ship in Charleston Bay? Why did I join the Union Army? Why did I walk away? I've decided the answer to all those questions is, so I could end up here with you. My mama used to say that nothing happens by accident, that there's powers and forces at work in this world that we can't see and know, and they're trying to help us find the path that will lead us to where we're supposed to be. My mother called it Nyame. Since I came here and learned to read and study the Bible, I now know that it is God. That's why I ended up here. And I have thanked God every day that he brought me here because this is a special place, ruled by a special woman. In Africa, you would be a great and powerful queen. People would name their daughters after you. It is your beauty and your heart that set you apart. If I could, I would get out of the bed and put my knees on the ground in front of you."

In spite of her discomfort at his praise of her, Mary resisted the temptation to cut him off. He had taught her to be respectful and let people have their say before saying anything back. When she was sure he was finished, she said, "And if you had never left Africa, you would be a great and powerful king, as you were destined to be. While I regret with tears the horrors you went through before you arrived on my farm, I'm so very thankful that you came. One time you and I discussed the phrase in Tennyson's poem that says, 'tis better to have loved and lost than never to have loved at all.' At that point in my life, I wasn't sure that was true, but now, as I'm about to lose you, I can say with all my heart that it is true." She looked away from him for a second and then refocused on his face. "I wish I knew what you told all the others who've come in here today."

"I told them all what I thought they needed to hear—the truth. It was different for each one. What you really want to know is what I said to Thomas and to William, and if I spoke of you to them."

She gave him a knowing smile. "As usual, you have read my mind."

"Yes, I spoke to them of you, just as I am about to speak to you of them. There was a time after William disappeared that your heart was torn between living and dying. What helped you choose living was the arrival of those two lost boys, Frank and Pete. Because you chose living, your heart opened up, and Thomas walked in. You didn't even know it when it was happening, until one day you realized you loved him in the special way of husband and wife. There was nothing wrong in that. By the time William reappeared, the portion of your heart that held the memory of your love for him had faded. You and Mr. Thomas could have run off together, but you didn't. You decided to try and do the impossible—to return to being only friends with him while you worked on awakening your love for Mr. William. I know that made you sad, but you did what you believed was the right thing to do. And I think you did, too."

As he was speaking, Mary felt her chest tightening. She said, "But have I chosen the impossible? Will I ever think of Thomas as just a friend?"

"I don't know the answer to that one, Miss Mary—I just don't know—because I can see you still love him and you want to be with him. The heart moves slowly sometimes. It has to sort of get used to a thing before it can turn in another direction. That's what I'm hoping for you. It'll help if you'll throw yourself into those things that you do love—them boys, the farm, and Mr. William. I believe that one day you'll look at Mr. Thomas and you'll be happy you're friends, and you'll be happy that you're married to Mr. William."

"Then that's what I'll do," she replied.

In a tree outside, an owl began calling.

"I believe that call's for me," John said. "Before I go, look over yonder along that wall, and lift up that piece of canvas.

Mary did as she was told and found the canvas in the shadows. She lifted it up and saw what looked like some kind of a long box. "What is it?"

"Come get the candle and see."

She retrieved the candle and illuminated her find. "It's a casket."

"It's my casket. I been working on it in my spare time. Made it out of chestnut, the longest-lasting wood there is. I'd appreciate it if you'd bury me in it."

Her vision of the casket blurred as tears filled her eyes. She had to clear her throat in order to speak. "We will."

In the distance, there was a rumble of thunder.

Mary sat back down beside him, stroked the sides of his face one at a time, then ran her hand over his smooth head. "I have lived in the presence of greatness," she whispered to him.

He closed his eyes, she kissed his forehead, and his final breath left him.

*****

With rain falling so hard that visibility was only three feet, the soaked funeral party made its way back down Bitter Hill, slipping and sliding and grabbing hold of trees to keep from falling pell-mell to the bottom.

Mary Beth was riding on Thomas's back. Her hair, and that of her sisters and Mary's, hung limp and heavy.

Pete and Frank were trying to help Thomas and the girls, while Mary was trying to make sure William was okay while being careful not to make it look like he needed her assistance.

Lightning crackled above them, and a loud clap of thunder followed.

Emma screamed.

"It's okay," Thomas said above the din of the falling rain. "The lightning is going to stay up above us on the high hills, and thunder can't hurt you."

When William was close enough for him to hear her, Mary said, "We got John and his casket up the hill and buried just in time. We'd never have gotten it up there as slick and wet as this is now."

"You're right," he agreed. "I thought we were going to get by with just the light rain that started falling after he died last night."

Mary paused to catch her breath, and he stopped with her. "Mother always said that if it rained during a funeral, it meant the angels were weeping."

Nodding, he said, "I've heard that, too."

Just then, Frank went sliding past them on his backside. Reflexively, Mary grabbed the collar of his shirt, just before he got out of arm's reach, and stopped his fall.

He scrambled to his feet, and they continued the descent.

When they all reached the bottom of the hill, Mary said, "All you men go inside the barn and shut the door while the girls and I take off our wet clothes on the porch. Then we'll go inside and find some dry things to put on. I'll gather some dry clothes for you all, plus some rain slickers, and bring them to you, and you can change before coming to the house."

The chill and misery created by the soaking rain prohibited anyone from protesting or questioning Mary's plan.

Mary, Abigail, and the girls walked to the porch, where they watched the men until the barn door closed behind them.

Mary started unfastening her dress.

Florence said, "You mean we're going to take our clothes off right out here in the open?"

"Yes," Mary said as she slipped her dress off her shoulders and let it fall to the floor. "I don't want all these drenched clothes in the house. We'll wring them out, and then I'll hang them up to dry when it stops raining."

"But what if somebody sees us?" Florence asked.

Emma, who had already taken off her dress and was helping Mary Beth take hers off, said, "Quit being so dramatic. Who's going to see us? Nobody's out in this rain."

The two sisters made faces at each other, and Florence

began undressing.

A bit later, they were all in the kitchen, where Mary and Abigail were slicing bread and ham for everyone to eat.

"This has been a bittersweet visit," Thomas said. "I dislike the reason for our coming, but I'm so glad we were able to be here to say good-bye to John."

William put his arm around Thomas's shoulder. "I'm happy you were here, too."

Thomas reciprocated the gesture, and they smiled at each other.

Mary smiled at them. "You two look like old times. As we all have many times in the past, we now turn the page and begin a new chapter in our lives. I, for one, look forward to seeing what it brings."

"As do I," Thomas agreed.

Chapter Fifty-Two

MARY

That night, Mary lay beside William in the afterglow of making love, holding his hand and listening to the rain and thunder outside. The hair on her temples was damp with tears of joy and pleasure—and something else that she searched her heart to try to identify. It felt like the warmth of the summer sun, mixed with the feeling she got when she smelled fresh-cut hay and how it felt to sit by the Chickamauga and watch it slowly drift by.

Peace and contentment, that's what it is. She smiled and sighed at the understanding.

William said, "It's been a long, long time since I've felt such a peace in me."

Rolling onto her side and looking at the profile of his face against the candlelight on the nightstand, Mary said, "What do you mean?"

"I know it doesn't make sense since we just buried our dear friend John only hours ago, but if I died tonight, I would die a happy man."

"I understand," she commented. "Since our first baby died, I have been lost—lost in grief, sadness, anger, and self-pity. I'm sorry for all the pain I have caused you in the past. I know I was hard to live with."

He rolled over and faced her. Putting his finger on her lips, he said, "Hush, don't say that. I would go through it all over again just for the privilege of lying by your side at the end of the day. Everyone who has known you, Mary, said there is not another woman like you, and that's not false praise—it's true."

Mary replied, "The rising tide of life's changes nearly drowned me, and I almost gave up, but now you and I have a chance to start over again. Not many people are given that chance. I don't know what challenges life will throw at us in the future, but if we face them together, if we bend and don't break, we will survive and be stronger because of it."

William caressed the side of her face. "I loved you yesterday, I love you today, and I'll love you tomorrow."

She turned her face and kissed his palm. "You know, all this rain has made it impossible to work in the fields. Why don't we travel to town tomorrow and get a few supplies that we need? We've talked about replacing some of our harnesses and horse collars, and I wouldn't mind having some cloth to make some dresses and shirts out of. It seems like I hardly get shirts made for Frank and Pete before they've already outgrown them."

"That's a good idea. We'll head out first thing in the morning."

*****

Driving through the quagmire that the streets of Chattanooga had become proved to be much more of a challenge than Mary had thought about it being. At times, the mules were knee-deep in the mud, and at other times, the wagon nearly went down to its axle. "If we ever stop moving," she said to William, "we may never get going again."

Suddenly, the wagon lurched to one side as a wheel dropped off into a deep rut.

The unexpected jolt sent Frank flying out of the wagon, and he landed face first in the mud.

Pete stuck his head in between Mary and William and said, "We just lost Frank. He fell out of the wagon."

His voice was so calm, Mary wasn't sure if he was being serious or if he was playing a prank on them. But when she looked over her shoulder, she saw Frank picking himself up out of the mud. He was completely covered in a blanket of mud, from the crown of his head to the soles of his shoes.

Pete immediately started laughing and pointing at him.

Mary pulled the wagon to a stop and started to get out, but William put his hand on her and said, "No, I'll go see about him. You'll end up looking like him if you try and walk through all that mud."

"Shut up your laughing!" Frank yelled at Pete.

But Pete was rolling in the bed of the wagon, holding his sides, he was laughing so hard.

As Frank began walking toward the wagon, Mary could see that he was not harmed, at least not physically. She also could see the humor in the situation and had to fight herself not to join in laughing with Pete. "Pete! Shush your laughing, and help your brother into the wagon."

When William got Frank to the wagon, he had to put his arm around him and hold him to prevent him from grabbing Pete and pulling him down into the mud with him. "Come on now, boys. Y'all stop that! The longer we sit here, the deeper this wagon is going to sink into the mud. If you don't hurry and get in, all three of us are going to be down here pushing to get it unstuck."

With that warning, Frank allowed Pete to pull him up onto the bed of the wagon.

With Mary cajoling them with every breath, it took several tries before the mules were able to get the wagon going again.

When they finally made it to Thomas's store, he and another man were up to their knees in mud, putting their shoulders to a wagon that was apparently stuck.

"Uh-oh," William said, "that's what I was afraid was going to happen to us. Come on, boys, let's see if we can help."

Without a word, Pete and Frank jumped down, and the three of them slogged their way to the wagon, while Mary sat and watched from twenty feet away.

The owner of the wagon was swearing at everything on earth and in heaven.

Thomas stopped to catch his breath and saw William and the boys, then Mary. He waved at her and said to William, "Boy am I glad somebody showed up. We've been working at this for thirty minutes."

William said, "Maybe with the three of us working with you two we'll get it moving again. I'm going to put my shoulder underneath it, just behind the front wheel, and try to lift it some while you all push."

"Whatever you say," Thomas replied.

"Okay, everyone!" William said. "On the count of three, I'll lift, you push, and give those horses the taste of the whip!" He crouched underneath the wagon and counted off. At *three*, everyone gave it their all.

For a couple of seconds, nothing happened. Then there was an almost imperceptible inching forward.

"It's moving!" William yelled. "Keep it up!"

Suddenly, there was a loud crack as the front axle broke, and the wagon fell onto one side, pinning William underneath it.

Mary screamed and practically flew off the wagon seat. Holding her skirts in one hand, she trudged through the thick mud, losing one of her shoes in the process. Her heart was in her mouth as she approached the broken wagon where Thomas and the boys were on their knees and huddled around the spot where William lay trapped. "William!" his name tore from the back of Mary's throat.

Thomas looked at her with fear in his eyes. He was as pale as a ghost.

All Mary could see of William was his arm. The rest of his

body was mashed into the mud underneath the wagon.

"What are we going to do?" Thomas asked in a weak voice.

She grabbed him and shook him. "Go find some men to help, and bring a pry pole that we can lift this wagon with." When he left to carry out her orders, Mary took hold of William's hand and called his name. But there was no reply. *Dear God, dear God, dear God—please, I'm begging you—don't take him from me again. Please don't make me walk that path.*

After what seemed like an eternity, Mary heard the voices of men approaching.

It was another eternity before the wagon was finally lifted and Mary could see William's still form. "Help me get him out," she said to Thomas.

After wiping the mud from William's face, she put her ear close to his mouth and waited. Her heart jumped when she felt the faintest of breaths coming from him. "He's alive!" she exclaimed.

"Let's get him inside the store," Thomas said, and he directed several men to help carry William.

As they rushed through the store and back to Thomas's bedroom, Mary saw all five of the children with uncertain expressions on their faces as they held each other's hands. A piece of her wanted to pause and speak to them, but she wouldn't allow herself to do so.

The men filed out of the bedroom, and she and Thomas

walked to opposite sides of the bed.

William coughed, and blood spilled out of his mouth and trailed down both sides of his face.

Mary's heart sank, and tears welled up in her eyes. She looked up at Thomas in the unrealistic hope that he could do something.

"Do you want me to go get the doctor?" he asked.

"Don't you dare." William's gargled voice said.

"Oh, William," Mary said. "Thomas and I are right here with you. Are you in pain? What do you want us to do?"

He opened his mud-smeared eyelids and looked around until his eyes lit upon her. The slightest of smiles tugged at the corners of his mouth. "My sweet Mary. There's nothing you can do. I feel like all my insides are busted up." His body emphasized his point by causing him to produce another bloody cough. "Now I understand how John knew his time was up." His eyes turned toward Thomas. "My best friend."

"Yes, yes, absolutely," Thomas said as tears rolled down his cheeks.

"Thomas, there is no man on earth I admire and love more than you. We've shared each other's burdens through the years and had many wonderful times together. I don't know of anyone who deserves to be happy more than you do. And, Mary, it's time for you to have a happy life, one with a future full of promise. I know that you two love each other, not just the love of friendship, but the kind of love that a man and a woman share when they want to marry each other."

Mary felt like her chest was going to burst it was so full of emotions—emotions that swirled like an ever-increasing whirlpool. "William—" she began, but he held up his hand and stopped her.

"Let me finish." His voice sounded weaker. "I'm not mad about what happened between you. Neither of you meant any harm in what you did. I hold nothing against either of you. Mary, I told you last night that I could now die a happy man." He convulsed with another cough. When his eyes refocused, he said, "I just didn't know it would be so soon." He paused to get a breath. "Give me your hands."

Thomas and Mary placed one of their hands in each of his. "I give you both my blessing to marry each other. Promise me you will do this."

Mary wanted to jerk her hand away from him and from the promise he asked her to make. *How many twists and turns can a heart take before it breaks forever?* She looked at Thomas, who was looking at her. She saw in his eyes his willingness to agree to William's pledge but also the uncertainty of whether she would agree. She squeezed William's hand and looked at him. When their eyes met, she knew—she knew that she would do as he asked, not today and not tomorrow, but in time, after her heart had healed from losing him a second time, it would bloom again with love for Thomas.

THE END

Epilogue

Two years after William's death, Thomas paced back and forth on the porch of the house he and Mary had built on the farm. He ran his fingers through his tousled hair.

Florence, Emma, Mary Beth, Pete, and Frank stood just off the porch, underneath the shade of the oak tree.

"What's taking so long?" Emma asked.

"Because it just does!" Florence snapped at her. "Don't you know anything?"

"I'm getting tired of waiting, too," Pete said.

Mary Beth said, "And I'm hungry."

Suddenly, through one of the open windows of the house, came the sound of a tiny baby crying.

Thomas froze, and everyone looked toward the window.

In a moment, Abigail pushed open the front door and announced, "Mr. Thomas, you've got yourself a son!"

Cheers erupted from the children.

"And Mary?" Thomas asked. "How's Mary?"

"Oh, she done fine, like she's been having babies her whole life. That ol' doctor that told her she couldn't have no more children didn't know what he was talking about."

"Can I see her?"

"Not just yet. Give me a minute, and I'll come back and get you."

Abigail disappeared back inside the house. As she did so, the children rushed to hug Thomas.

"We've got a brother!" Florence said excitedly.

"What about me and Pete?" Frank asked with a smile. "I thought we were like your brothers."

"I'm talking about a *baby* brother. Y'all are no fun."

Everyone laughed.

But their laughter was interrupted when Abigail burst through the door with a look of shock on her face.

They stared at her open mouth.

"What?" Thomas asked in alarm. "What's happened?"

"Mr. Thomas, you've got *two* new babies."

"Two?" he asked in confusion. Then it clicked with him. "You mean she had—"

"Twins!" Abigail exclaimed. "Miss Mary done had twins!"

Screams and yells of delight filled the air.

"Come on in, Mr. Thomas," Abigail said. "She want to see you now."

Thomas followed her back to their bedroom.

He found Mary lying still, looking pale, with a baby on each side of her. He sat down carefully beside her. "Oh, my Mary, look what you have done—twins. Are you okay?"

"Besides being tired, I've never been better or happier in my life. The blessing I thought I would never be given has been granted to me in double measure."

He leaned down, and they kissed. Then he looked at the babies. "You forget how tiny a newborn is. They look like little birds."

Mary said, "What do you think we should name them?"

Thomas looked at her. They locked eyes and smiled.

Simultaneously, they said, "William and John."

~~~~~ THE END ~~~~~

You can follow David Johnson on Facebook
https://www.facebook.com/DavidJohnsonbookpage/

and Twitter @DavidJohnson_

He would also like to hear from you with any questions or comments. You may contact him at davidjohnsonbooks@gmail.com.

Made in the USA
San Bernardino, CA
30 December 2017